Praise for

VENGEANCE B

"Peopled with intriguing characters, the w *engeance Born* is unique and filled with compelling mystery. I'm looking forward to seeing where Kylie Griffin takes that world next."

—Nalini Singh, *New York Times* bestselling author

"A great debut novel; Kylie Griffin has me hooked . . . Dangerous, intense, enthralling . . . Griffin has given her readers a whole gamut of emotions to feel and leaves [them] with the hope for more stories set in this compelling universe. It's not only good on the first read, it's still good on the second."

—Jean Johnson, national bestselling author of *The Shifter*

"A compelling and fascinating world that pulled me right in!"

—Joss Ware, award-winning author

"Kylie Griffin spins an intriguing story of two races who are mortal enemies, and the half-breeds that are despised by both, who must transform their cultures. The book has solid world building, sympathetic characters, and a twisty story line. I'm looking forward to the next in the Light Blade series."

—Robin D. Owens, national bestselling author of *Heart Secret*

"A breath of fresh air. In the world of paranormal romances where a lot seem to follow the same pattern, this one was unique, creative, and I just couldn't put it down . . . What a wonderful debut novel!"

—*All About Romance*

"Enter a bold new series, the Light Blade, where a long-standing war between the demon and human realms rages. Promising new talent Griffin's characters face danger and hidden secrets that threaten to change the world as they know it. A terrific debut!" —*RT Book Reviews*

Berkley Sensation titles by Kylie Griffin

The Light Blade Series

VENGEANCE BORN

ALLIANCE FORGED

ALLEGIANCE SWORN

Allegiance Sworn

KYLIE GRIFFIN

BERKLEY SENSATION, NEW YORK

THE BERKLEY PUBLISHING GROUP
Published by the Penguin Group
Penguin Group (USA) Inc.
375 Hudson Street, New York, New York 10014, USA

USA / Canada / UK / Ireland / Australia / New Zealand / India / South Africa / China

Penguin Books Ltd., Registered Offices: 80 Strand, London WC2R 0RL, England
For more information about the Penguin Group, visit penguin.com

ALLEGIANCE SWORN

This book is an original publication of The Berkley Publishing Group.

Berkley Sensation trade paperback edition ISBN: 978-0-425-25602-2

An application to register this book for cataloging has been submitted to the Library of Congress.

PUBLISHING HISTORY
Berkley Sensation trade paperback edition / April 2013

PRINTED IN THE UNITED STATES OF AMERICA

10 9 8 7 6 5 4 3 2 1

Map illustration by John Wrench.
Cover art by Gene Mollica.
Cover design by Lesley Worrell.
Interior text design by Kristin del Rosario.

To the ELE girls (& a certain henchman),
who kept me focused and on track with encouragement
and ugly sticks.
My loyalty and love to you all!

~ TWD ~

ACKNOWLEDGMENTS

In the production of any book, a team of people help the author create and bring to life their characters, the setting, and the story. I'd like to recognize the expertise of a very special group who've worked on the Light Blade series from the beginning.

My beta readers (you know who you are)—you're all amazing and I couldn't have done this without your damn good feedback! Keep it coming!

John Wrench—your IT, art, and mapping skills are awesome; thank you for bringing the Light Blade world to life in black and white.

Gene Mollica—aka the cover wizard, you envisage my characters and their world so well.

The Berkley art and editorial departments—another group of wonderful people, your time and effort has made this series the best it can be.

Elaine and Leis—again, my heartfelt thanks for your support and guidance in helping me get this book to print—we did it!

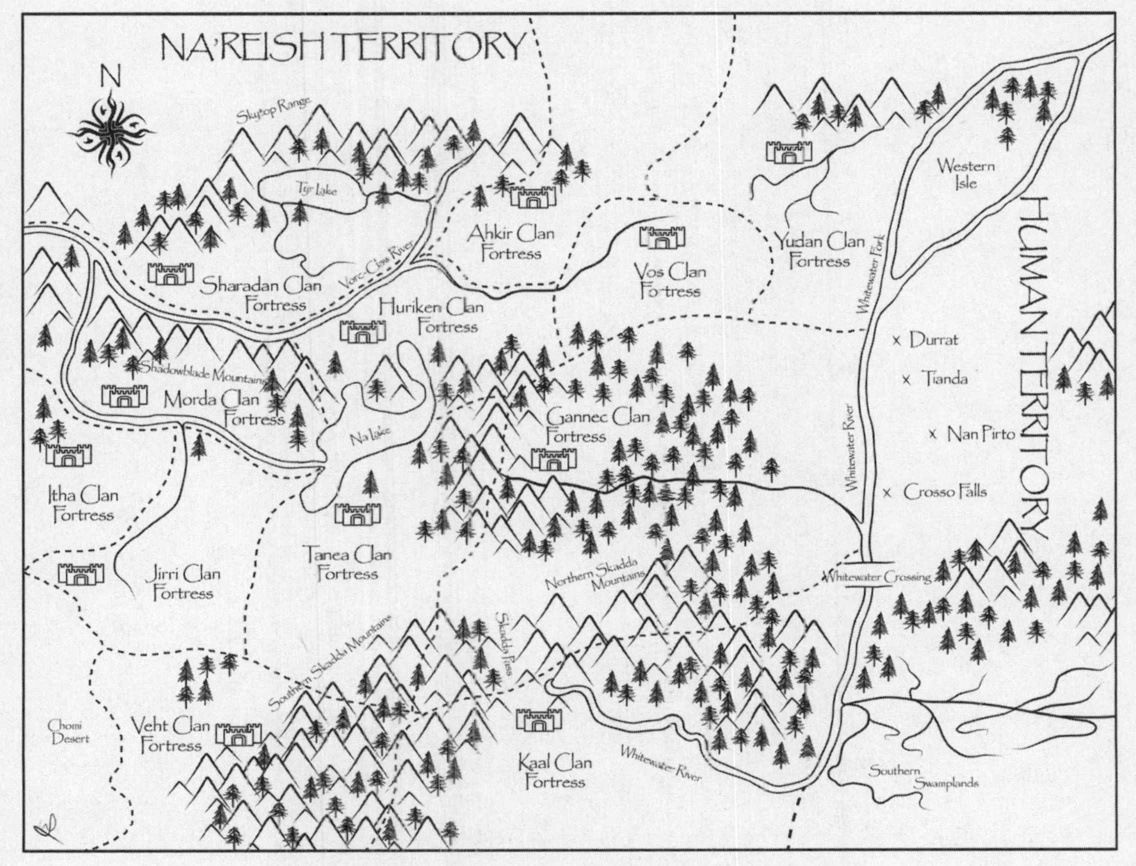
NA'REISH TERRITORY
N
Skytop Range
Tyr Lake
Vorc-Claw River
Sharadan Clan Fortress
Ahkir Clan Fortress
Vos Clan Fortress
Yudan Clan Fortress
Western Isle
Whitewater Fork
HUMAN TERRITORY
Huriken Clan Fortress
Shadowblade Mountains
Morda Clan Fortress
Na Lake
Gannec Clan Fortress
Itha Clan Fortress
Tanea Clan Fortress
Jirri Clan Fortress
x Durrat
x Tianda
x Nan Pirto
x Crosso Falls
Whitewater River
Whitewater Crossing
Northern Skadda Mountains
Skadda Pass
Southern Skadda Mountains
Chomi Desert
Veht Clan Fortress
Kaal Clan Fortress
Whitewater River
Southern Swamplands

Chapter 1

HATRED throbbed in time with Arek's heartbeat, the fierce emotion sustaining him as much as the blood pumping through his veins.

He kept his gaze downcast, fixed firmly on the stained wooden boards of the ferryboat. Imprisoned in the cargo cage, he felt the skin of his back twitch as the polished leather boots of the *Na'Reish* boat-master thudded past on his way to the foredeck. Curled and hooked on to the demon's belt was a thin-braided lash, his preferred tool of choice when disciplining his human cargo for the slightest infraction.

Looking up at the demon had proved provocation enough. Fury roiled and knotted in Arek's gut. The dozen welts marking his shoulders still stung. Each had been delivered with an expert hand, placed with enough force to cause maximum discomfort yet tempered to avoid permanent injury.

A painful lesson, one he craved to reciprocate with lethal intent, but retaliation meant using his Gift to kill the *Na'Reish* and exposing his secret. Something he couldn't do. Not yet. The *Na'Reish* killed human Light Blade warriors on sight. He'd make his death count, taking out as many demons as possible, giving them no chance to drink his blood.

"'Ware starboard!" The cry came from the *Na'Reish* watcher standing at the bow. "Dock ahead!"

The boat-master leaned against the railing, his long legs braced wide as he peered ahead. At nearly seven feet tall, he was an imposing figure, all muscle and brawn, his purple-hued stare missing nothing that went on around him.

As he turned, the late afternoon sunlight caught the mottled pattern of demon markings on his skin. They were dark, irregular in size and shape, and almost as black as his hair. They covered the sides of his broad face before curving over his jaw and down his neck to disappear beneath the collar of his shirt. His wide grin pulled back black lips, revealing a mouthful of pointed teeth sharp enough to puncture human skin.

A shiver crawled across the back of Arek's neck. How many humans had this demon fed on? Did he prefer the services of a blood-slave or did he drain them outright?

With the way he was dressed, he could probably afford to do the latter. From the dark leather of his polished boots, and the fine woven fabric of his shirt, the boat-master had to be *Na'Reishi*, one of the demon elite, perhaps a Lordlings son. Not a first get but possibly a second or third. The eldest would be at his sire's side, being groomed for Clan leadership, not trafficking human-slaves across the border.

"Prepare to dock!" The boat-master's gravelly bellow instigated a flurry of activity on deck.

Through the flat-steel bars of the cage, Arek watched a dozen *Na'Reish* warriors, all wearing leather armor and bearing weapons, emerge from the aft cabin door, then spread out to take up alert positions across the deck.

The half-dozen human-slaves on the port side of the sleek-hulled boat ceased their poling. Wiry muscles flexed as they laid the wooden poles on the deck, then crouched beside them. With no breeze and the sun still providing late season warmth, sweat shone on their near-naked bodies and their ribs heaved with exertion but none voiced a complaint. Those on the starboard side pushed the vessel sideways.

The boat's speed slowed, but with the cargo hold set low in the slave-boat, Arek saw nothing over the side railing other than open sky. After three days travelling up Whitewater River, he knew they were well within *Na'Reish* territory. Had they reached their final destination or was this just an overnight stop?

Arek glanced at the men and women crowded in around him. All were young and healthy, taken in raids from crofts and farms along the border to be used as blood-slaves in the coming war. His lip curled. They were a portable food supply for the demons.

His patrol had been investigating the increased number of raids, and one of the first to discover the bodies of their elder-kin and very young massacred in their homes. Eleven of the prisoners were from the village of Ostare; each of them recaptured after his Light Blade patrol had tried to free them in a rescue gone wrong.

Arek grimaced. A rescue where he'd seen Kalan, their leader and his best friend, nearly killed. He'd tried to give the others time to save Kalan. Had he survived? Had they managed to get away? *Lady of Light*, he hoped so.

He touched the blood-encrusted wound on his head, the one received in his gambit to give his patrol time to escape. The gash itched but at least it was healing and the motion sickness was gone. He'd been prepared for his Final Journey into the afterlife, expected it when the rescue failed, but after he'd fallen, a man named Yenass and his sister had carried him away from the fighting.

Arek's lips thinned. Yenass had swapped clothes with him when it became clear they faced recapture. And stepping into the path of the hunting *Vorc*, the vicious beast used to track them, the farmer had given his life to save theirs.

Arek closed his eyes. He could still hear the sickening sounds of the *Vorc's* teeth ripping into Yenass's flesh, his agony-filled cry cut short. A swift death, thank the *Lady*.

Mother of Mercy, *may his soul rest and find comfort in Your presence.*

Arek still didn't understand why *She* had accepted the farmer's courageous sacrifice instead of his life, but whatever *Her* plans, he now had a life-debt to repay. Helping those from Yenass's village escape this slave-trader would be a start.

The boat jolted, the hollow thump as it hit something reverberating through the entire hull. Arek blinked. Those around him remained seated. A few, like him, watched the activity on deck with wary interest. Many though wore blank-eyed stares, their shoulders slumped, seemingly resigned to their fate—serving as slaves to the *Na'Reish*.

Tension chewed his innards. There was no way he'd call *any* demon master. Flexing his wrists and hands, Arek ignored the burn as the coarse rope bit into his abraded skin, but the knots binding him were too tight.

He'd expected the diligence of the *Na'Reish* warriors to slacken off during their journey, particularly once they'd crossed the border between human and demon territory. Yet day and night, every few hours, the bonds were scrutinized, eliminating any chance of breaking free.

"Tie off!" The boat-master turned toward the cargo-cage and flicked a hand in their direction. "Get them unloaded and processed for auction."

They were being sold? Every muscle in Arek went tight. The woman nearest him gave a soft, desolate cry.

"Processed?" hissed the man beside him. "I ain't bein' auctioned like a bleater by these cursed demons!"

Several others echoed his fierce protest. Arek swallowed a savage grin. These people might be farmers and crofters, but they had heart.

He reached out and clasped the farmer's broad shoulder. Dark eyes locked with his.

"Be patient," he murmured, just loud enough for him to hear. "Wait until we disembark. Remember, their warriors go first, then us. If we can knock the gangplank into the water it will cut their number in half. Give us time to get away."

Hope flared in the man's gaze. "It could work. Iffen there's a chance some of us'll get away, I'll take it, and so'll the others."

He relayed the impromptu plan to those closest to him, and in turn they spoke to their neighbors. Talk died down as one of the *Na'Reish* deckhands moved from the foredeck to follow the boat-master's order and unlock the cage.

The hinges grated loudly. Arek's pulse raced as the door swung open. It was a relief to stand and stretch, even if it meant being herded like bleaters, single file, to the gangplank. He and the farmer joined the line last.

The riverbank beyond the wooden dock was little more than a wide, sandy clearing edged by thick forest. A stable and small set of stockyards stood on one side, while thick wooden poles with iron rings and chains rose like denuded trees on the other. Arek's gaze narrowed. He doubted the poles and chains were for tethering the shaggy war-beasts corralled in the yards.

Blackened stones ringed a dead fire pit in the center of the clearing. One of the boat-hands was setting up a makeshift table and chair out of crates beside it. He placed a thick ledger and stylus on the table. Some sort of record keeping?

Ten *Na'Reish* warriors, their boots thumping in a staccato rhythm, headed down the gangplank. They took up sentinel positions around the edge of the clearing. The nearest directed the first humans off the boat and to the left, toward the stockyards.

Arek pressed close to the farmer. "Ready?"

They stepped off the gangplank together. The man dropped to

his knee on one side and hooked his hands under the planking. Casting a swift look over his shoulder, Arek did the same on the other. A deckhand had a foot on the top of the gangplank.

"Now!" he hissed.

Even with bound hands, they managed to haul the heavy wooden structure free of the boat. It clattered against the dock and collapsed into the water with a splash. The deckhand followed with an even larger spray of water. Defiant shouts filled the air behind them.

Arek pivoted, grinning when he saw four villagers leap upon the lone *Na'Reish* warrior nearest to them. Their combined weight took him down. He sprinted to help. Roars of rage came from around the clearing.

"Run!" someone cried. Men and women scattered in all directions.

Arek slid into the struggle with the downed *Na'Reish* warrior, ignoring the burn of gravel on his bare feet. The tangle of bodies heaved as the demon struggled to free himself. The half-dozen bodies piled on top of him negated the advantage his enhanced strength usually gave him. Sunlight caught on the silver-etched hilt of a dagger on the demon's belt. Arek yanked the curved blade free of its scabbard and summoned his Gift. It surged inside him.

As the demon roared out his anger, Arek plunged the sharp tip deep into his side, and pushed his power through the blade toward the heart. The demon's cry ended on a strangled gasp. He ceased struggling. Purple eyes stared sightlessly skyward.

Dead.

Fierce satisfaction burned through Arek. Elation lit the faces of those around him. He sliced the rope binding the wrists of those closest, then his own.

"Into the forest!" he urged. "Go, now!"

Shouting behind them warned Arek the boat-master was organizing his crew. They had mere minutes before more *Na'Reish* joined them on the shore. The trees were closer than the river, and with nine enraged *Na'Reish* warriors bearing down on them, retreat seemed the sensible option. With cover, they could lose their pursuers and he stood a better chance of eliminating them.

And, by the *Lady*, kill the demons he would.

Or he'd die trying.

Chapter 2

AREK pulled up short, along with a handful of others, before he even reached the forest. From between the trees, a wall of *Na'Reish* riders on *Vorc*-back emerged. Enough to block their escape route. A cry of disbelief and terror came from the woman on his left.

The snarls and growls of the *Vorc* sent chills racing along Arek's spine. The bristle-furred beasts stood a man high. Claws as long as his fingers gripped the ground, and their powerful barrel-like bodies were hunched over, ready to launch forward and take them down if they fled. Their riders held them on a tight rein, waiting to see what the humans would do.

Arek hissed a curse and tightened his grip on the hilt of his stolen blade. The weapon would be useless against a snout full of razor-sharp teeth, let alone the dozen vicious predators facing them now.

Where had these *Na'Reish* come from? Their segmented armor was black, the design on their leather chest plates a stylized mountain peak with a crescent moon. They weren't the boat-master's warriors. They belonged to another Clan.

Behind him, footsteps pounded on the ground. Arek's lip curled. Well, he had sworn to die trying to kill these bastards, as many as possible. With them believing he was a crofter, the element of surprise was on his side.

Heat surged through his body, a yell of defiance broke from his throat as he swung round and dropped into a fighter's crouch. The first *Na'Reish* warrior took him to the ground in a bone-jarring tackle.

Arek twisted, using every shred of strength he had to avoid being pinned. He thrust upward with the dagger. The blade sank into the mottled flesh under the jaw of the demon's throat. Hot blood sprayed over his hand. The metallic stench of it assailed his nostrils. His Gift rushed through the blade. The demon convulsed. A heartbeat later he lay dead.

Pushing the body from him, Arek rolled to one knee. Something heavy hit him from behind, hard enough to knock him to the ground and the breath from his lungs. Strong fingers wrapped around his wrist, the one holding the dagger, and squeezed. Flesh crushed against bone.

Arek grunted. Once, twice, his hand was slammed against the ground. Pain shot through his fingers. His grip loosened around the hilt. A third assault knocked the dagger away. It skittered across the sand, then his arms were wrenched behind his back.

"Cease struggling, Light Blade," hissed a deep voice. "And you'll live."

Arek tried bucking his opponent off, but the *Na'Reish* was solidly built, heavy-boned and muscled. A hand grasped a fistful of his hair and pushed his face into the dirt. Grit and sand stuck to his sweaty cheek. Leather armor creaked as the demon shifted forward. The musky scent of sweat and the minty odor of crushed needle-leaves overpowered the odor of blood.

"Meelar's warriors are too busy restraining the others, they don't know what you are—" An angular face framed by jet-black hair slicked back into a ponytail appeared in the corner of Arek's vision. Pale black lips peeled back from white teeth. "But they will if you don't control your power *now*."

The sounds of fighting faded as the *Na'Reish's* warning penetrated.

Icy disbelief raked down Arek's spine. If the warrior had sensed his Gift, why wasn't he tearing his throat out? What game was the *Na'Reish* playing at?

"I'm prepared to die for my people," he panted. "Death by your hand or the boat-master's makes no matter, demon!"

His hair was released.

"It's not your death I seek, Light Blade." Rope secured his wrists once again. "My Clan needs you to live."

A cold tendril snaked and tangled in Arek's gut. He'd heard too many stories of what human-slaves were forced to endure and seen too many atrocities to back up those tales to willingly submit to enslavement.

Images of warriors and friends he'd lost during battle, their throats ripped out as the demons fed on their life-blood, filled his mind. With his identity as a Light Blade revealed, did the demon intend to keep him alive just to taunt him before finally killing him? It would be consistent with the type of behavior he'd witnessed from the *Na'Reish* in the past.

Heat whipped through Arek's veins, as scorching as a smithy's furnace. He fought to twist free, uncaring that the rope binding him stripped more skin from his wrists.

The demon's weight shifted again. "*Lady of Light*, if you won't cooperate, then I'll take that choice from you!"

Lady of Light?

Demons didn't believe in a human deity.

A sharp blow behind his ear sent him tumbling into unconsciousness.

"WHAT'S this, *Na* Meelar?" Imhara called, as she handed the reins of her *Vorc* to the mounted warrior beside her. She slid from the riding pad to the ground, ignoring the low bow directed at her by the *Na'Reishu* deckhand. Instead she walked straight toward the dock where the Meelar was only now coming ashore. "Seems like you're having trouble controlling your slaves?"

The boat-master's head snapped up, his broad-cheeked face slackening in surprise. "*Na* Kaal. You're early."

Early enough to catch the *Na'Reishi* slaver in an awkward moment, and from what she'd seen on her approach to the riverside dock, Meelar and his warriors had lost control of what should have been a manageable situation.

The red stain coloring the brawny boat-master's face wasn't sunburn, and his tight expression conveyed his desire to berate her for catching him at a disadvantage, but rank had its privileges. A small smile twitched the corners of her mouth. The slaver might belong to the same caste as her, but as Clan leader she outranked his second-birth.

Meelar ran a hand through his black hair, smoothing the dark strands back in a nervous gesture. "I wasn't expecting you for another two hours."

A move designed to keep him off balance, something she did with every visitor to her province, and more fortune to her to have witnessed his blunder. While taking advantage of his humiliation didn't sit well, it was required to survive the power plays and constantly changing politics within the ranks of the *Na'Reishi*. Any show of compassion would be deemed a flaw, one to be exploited.

"It seems some of your cargo have made it across to the other side." Imhara waved a gloved hand toward the river, where three humans were scrambling out of the water on the opposite shoreline. She swallowed her smile and arched one eyebrow high. "Can my *Na'Hord* assist you in recapturing them?"

Meelar's gaze jerked in the direction she indicated, then slashed back to her. His dark brows dipped hard and low while his lips pressed into a thin line. Did he resent her offer of help, or the style of clothing she wore?

After more than a score of forays through her province, he should have been used to her eccentricities by now, but then, in his world, *Na'Reish* women seldom wore leather breeches, shirts, or vests. Even fewer sported swords on their belts, and as far as she knew, she was the only one able to wield a blade. Or a dagger or throwing knives . . . or any other weapon her male counterparts cared to train with or brandish.

While other *Na'Reish* women depended on their males to look after them, her father had made sure she could look after herself. Thank the *Lady* he had.

His training had helped her stay alive the night their family had been attacked. Five years later, the murderer remained unpunished. Heartache burned in her chest. She pushed back the memories and sucked in a deep breath to control her emotions. Now wasn't the time or place.

Necessity was a cruel mistress, yet without her hard-learned lessons, she wouldn't wield the power or possess the reputation she did now. She didn't care if other *Na'Reish* disapproved of her style of dress, or gossiped about her lack of a mate or how she flaunted convention with her conduct. All that mattered was that they held a healthy fear or respect for her as Clan *Na*, leader of the Kaal.

"No need. My warriors are capable of tracking a few stray humans." Meelar's refusal came as no surprise. He whipped a hand at his boat-crew. "Take half the *Na'Hord* across and hunt them down!"

His underlings scrambled to obey. Imhara rested her hands on the hilt of her sword and turned to survey the terrified huddle of humanity by the stockyards. By the look of their coarse-woven clothes, they were farmers or crofters.

All in good condition, males and females in their prime. How many of them would live to see another moon? Half their number? A quarter? Her mouth flattened and she swallowed against the bitterness rising in her throat. The *Na'Reish* valued their animals more highly than they did their slaves.

Imhara smoothed her expression into something more neutral as Meelar turned in her direction. "Almost five dozen," she mused. "Impressive raid."

She glanced toward the dead Clan warrior sprawled on a blood-soaked patch of sand. Another body lay over by the stockyards. Meelar's warriors weren't known for their complacency, yet the humans had secured a weapon. How had they managed that?

Rassan, her Clan Second, crouched above one of the humans. He made short work of tying the man's ankles. Her eyebrows lifted. As scout, and first to arrive at the clearing, perhaps he'd witnessed the outbreak, but why had he felt it necessary to get involved in the melee?

With an ease that belied his brawny six-foot size, Rassan rose from his crouch. His thick biceps flexed as he dusted off his hands and readjusted his weapons belt. Standing eye-to-eye with her, yet nearly a foot shorter than most *Na'Reish* warriors, he made up for his lack of height in skill. His reputation of being one of the most lethal fighters in the twelve Clans was well earned.

To any who watched, he seemed to have dismissed the unconscious human, but his dark violet gaze locked with hers and gleamed with an intensity that prickled the hair on the back of her neck. Something about the man on the ground interested him.

Imhara flicked a quick glance downward. A shock of dirty blond hair obscured her view of the human's tanned face. Lying there, his arms bound, the man looked like a stripling youth next to the warrior, but then any human male would. Yet Imhara surmised the farmer would equal Rassan's height.

Underneath the sweat-stained shirt, broad shoulders fleshed with lean muscle tapered to a flat waist. A pair of worse-for-wear breeches covered long legs, the threadbare hems brushing midcalf.

There was strength in this man; he was no stranger to hard work, but while the skin exposed below his breeches was dirty, it was a shade lighter than the tone on his arms, neck, and face, almost as if he'd once worn boots.

"I've delivered almost four hundred slaves to the *Na'Rei* in the last three months."

Imhara turned her attention to Meelar. His tone suggested their *Na'Reish* leader would be impressed by his success. Savyr's demand for blood-slaves had risen and so had the bonuses for those who provided excellent service. There was a good chance Savyr might reward the slaver, lifting his standing among the ranks of the *Na'Reishi.*

"Have you heard why the *Na'Rei* needs so many?" she inquired.

Meelar shrugged. "Some say that Savyr is preparing for war with the humans."

"It would explain why he's called for a full Enclave."

The meeting was set for the new moon, just over a month away, as the first snows were due—an unusual time for a Clan-*Na* gathering. It was also interesting that the Enclave coincided with the rumors of an alliance between the human Blade Council and a band of *Na'Chi*, the half-breed offspring all *Na'Reish* preferred to deny existed.

"Perhaps he'll inform us of his war plans then," Meelar commented.

Imhara grunted. Did Savyr intend to invade human territory during winter? It was a hard time to wage a conflict of any sort but certainly harder for those being attacked.

If war against the humans loomed, then it would explain why he'd also increased the Clan tithes. Missives sent from neighboring provinces complained of the losses of skilled crafters, slaves, and produce.

His letter to her had asked for regular access through her province using the slave-route. Patrols using Skadda Pass and Whitewater River were offered a fast, easy route in and out of human territory. The forest on both sides of the border provided cover for them as well as Meelar's slave-raids.

Power through geography—the Kaal Province could play a major role in Savyr's plans, and she wasn't above taking advantage of her position if it meant ensuring the safety of her people. The impending Enclave would force her to adjust the time line of her plans, but she was nothing if not flexible.

Another of life's hard-learned lessons. She fisted a gloved hand, satisfaction souring fast like her mood. It was time to end this charade with the boat-master.

"I expect the usual ten percent tribute, *Na* Meelar." She stabbed a finger at him as he took a breath to protest. "Regardless of whether you recapture those escaped slaves or not."

Imhara held the boat-master's gaze until he tilted his head in submission. She nodded for Rassan to begin choosing. At least six humans would be saved this day. She wished it could be more, but demanding a further tribute would draw attention to her actions. Best play it safe. For now.

"Have your warriors finish their auction preparations swiftly." Tattooing the slave-mark on the others would take a couple of hours. A swift glance at the sun made up her mind. "Your slave-train should make it through the pass by dusk."

Meelar's purple gaze lit with surprise then more disapproval. "My *Na'Hord* have been away on this raid for almost two weeks. They're hungry and tired and would appreciate the comforts of a soft bed, food, and entertainment."

Demanding Clan hospitality was justified, but she had no wish for company, not with new humans to introduce into her fortress. They'd been frightened enough, and their transition into their new lives would be delayed if their captors stayed overnight.

Imhara pointed with her chin toward the corralled war-beasts. "I've supplied half a dozen head to make transporting your cargo across the mountains simpler. Quicker."

Meelar would be unlikely to provide the humans with blankets during their trek, so they would most probably sleep beside the docile beasts. The animals' shaggy coats would provide them with warmth at night as the caravan made its way into Gannec territory.

"Their saddlebags are well provisioned with supplies for your journey through the mountains. Consider them a gift, an alternate source of Clan hospitality." She waved a hand. "I'd advise you to be through the pass by dusk. I don't have to tell you how unpredictable the weather can be in the ranges."

A month ago, the boat-master's *Na'Hord* had been the ones to find the frozen corpses of a patrol who had left travelling through Skadda Pass until too late in the day. They'd been caught in a freak, late-summer blizzard.

Meelar's lip curl was just short of a sneer, but she suspected he'd heed her warning. He executed a shallow bow. "Until next time then, *Na* Kaal."

Imhara returned to her mount, leaving Rassan in charge of securing the small group of humans she took as payment for the slaver's access through her territory. Her mouth twisted. Meelar would write it off as part of the trade.

Vice. Exploitation. Reputation. Power. Everything she abhorred about her race but was forced to perpetuate to ensure the survival of her Clan's legacy. She shook her head. Their ancestors would turn in their tombs to see how ingrained corruption was within *Na'Reish* society now.

Imhara leaned against the side of her mount, inhaling the strong, heavy musk of its coat, a soul-deep weariness weighing her shoulders down. *Lady's Breath*, so many relied on her.

She shivered. How much longer could her Clan go on living this double lifestyle? How much longer could she? Yet discovery would condemn every one of them to death.

"*Na* Kaal."

Rassan's deep voice came from behind her. She took another deep breath and turned. Deep violet eyes flecked with the faintest yellow met hers. His head tilted to one side, silently questioning.

"We're ready to leave," he reported, his voice reflecting none of his concern for her. His worry warmed the coldness inside her, gave her the strength to focus.

"Then let's go." Her smile was strained. "Double-time."

She mounted and settled into the saddle on her *Vorc*. Meelar's warriors were already dividing into groups. One to tattoo and register the humans, another to saddle the war-beasts in preparation for their journey over the mountains. The deckhands were securing the slave-boat for the time they returned to complete another raid-and-run.

Imhara dug her heels into the sides of her mount, eager to get away from the river. She caught the gazes of two of her *Na'Hord*, and nodded sharply. They peeled off and disappeared into the forest to begin their task of following Meelar, making sure he left Kaal territory.

She glanced toward Rassan and his unconscious passenger, impatient to finish their journey now the unpleasant task of dealing with the boat-master was over. She wanted to get back to her fortress as quickly as possible and find out what her Second found so fascinating about the human draped across the saddle of his mount.

Chapter 3

"A Light Blade warrior?" Imhara stopped short of the thick wooden door of her bedroom. Her heart began to race.

Whirling on her boot heel, she stared at Rassan, all thoughts of settling the new arrivals into their quarters and the myriad tasks still awaiting her attention at her desk in the library gone from her head with his startling revelation.

She frowned. "But he was dressed as a farmer." There'd been no armor, no boots, no *Lady's* amulet around his neck. "Are you sure?"

"I felt the power of *Her* in him. He used it to kill Meelar's warriors. The way he used the blade, the moves . . . he's had training. He's no crofter or latent Gifted."

In the flickering light of the lantern hung on the wall by her door, half of Rassan's face was darkened by shadow, and the effect served to reinforce the seriousness of his claim.

"You've never doubted my Gift before." His mouth curved into a wry smile. "Why start now?"

Lady of Light, if he was right, then this human could be the key to Clan Kaal's survival, the answer to her prayers, especially given the timing and content of Savyr's last missive.

The Clan gathering wasn't the issue. She'd attended many over the years, but the subject of her status as an unmated female was now on Savyr's agenda; not that she'd revealed this to anyone yet, least of all Rassan.

After her parents' death, she'd expected pressure to mate. The why wasn't too hard to figure out. Savyr made no secret of wanting Kaal Province and sole access to the slave-route. She had her suspicions about who had murdered her family, but there was no doubt in her mind that Savyr had given the order.

After four years of fending off every *Na'Reishi* Lordling and anticipating and dreading when the *Na'Rei* would force the issue, the wait was over. One order from him to mate and a refusal would mean her life, and the lives of every man, woman, and child—human, *Na'Chi*, and *Na'Reish* alike—in her Clan.

Agreeing would elicit the same fate, as there was no way her Clan could keep their lifestyle a secret from their new *Na*. If war with the humans was imminent, mating her or killing her would give Savyr exactly what he wanted.

Imhara balled her fists. Neither scenario would happen. Not now. Not in a month. Not in this lifetime. Nothing would stop her making sure her Clan was safe.

She sucked in a slow breath, trying to calm her rapid pulse. Her attention should be on the human and the plan she'd worked so hard to bring about. It was within her grasp.

"Of course I believe you, my friend. I meant no insult," she murmured and laid a hand on Rassan's arm. "It's just that we've waited so long for the improbable to happen. Where did you put him?"

He nodded toward her room. "In there, on your bed. It's the only place secure enough to hold a Light Blade."

"Secure enough?" Her jaw dropped and she shot a startled glance at the door. "You shackled him to my bed?"

Deep laughter rumbled up from her Second's chest, but it was quickly smothered when she glared at him.

"You'd risk an enraged warrior loose in the fortress?" One dark eyebrow winged high on his forehead as he folded his brawny arms. "Because you know that's what he'll be when he wakes up."

"But to manacle him? He's not a slave, Rassan."

"I know that but he doesn't. Until you can convince him he's not, I won't risk anyone's safety, let alone yours, by leaving him unfettered." He shrugged, a grin still twitching his lips. "Besides, your bed is the only one equipped with chains strong enough to hold him. It was the most logical place to put him."

Nothing turned off males with the ambition of mating her to become the new Kaal *Na* faster than flaunting her preferences as a *Na'Reishi* whose proclivities extended to taking unwilling human lovers.

Heat rushed into her cheeks. "But the chains are only for show—" The idea of using them on anyone . . . She grimaced and shook her head. "Keeping him locked up will only reinforce the message that he's my slave."

The smile disappeared from Rassan's face. "Make no mistake, Imhara, he will try to kill you." His large hands gripped her shoulders. "Talk to him. Explain what you can."

"I can really see a Light Blade warrior taking me on my word that this Clan follows the Old Ways." Her retort was harsher than she intended it to be. "Convincing him isn't going to be easy, Rassan."

"Give him time to absorb it. Don't free him without someone else being there with you. Promise me that."

Imhara nodded, sighing heavily. Those rescued from the slave-raids were always suspicious, at least until they experienced life here. How long would it take to convince the Light Blade?

A familiar gnawing sensation roiled in her gut. "There may not be enough time between now and the Enclave for him to adjust."

While establishing her controversial reputation had been a temporary measure, Imhara wondered if her plan to elicit a Light Blade's help to save her Clan was too ambitious. She bit her lip. To him, she was his enemy. He'd spent his whole life killing her race. What if he wouldn't trust her?

Rassan placed his hand on her shoulder and squeezed. "Wait until problems arise before worrying about them, Imhara." His tone softened. "You're tired. Perhaps you should wait until morning before meeting the Light Blade."

She shook her head. "I want to be there when he wakes. He's going to need answers."

"Then I'll stay with him. You take my room. Rest. Sleep."

Warmed again by Rassan's concern and his unswerving loyalty, she met the younger man's violet gaze. "Thank you for the offer, but this is my responsibility."

The dark-haired warrior inclined his head. She turned toward her door.

"Imhara"—his hand caught her elbow—"your weapons," he murmured. "Let me take them. No need to give the Light Blade any incentive to break free."

She grunted and unbuckled her belt, the metal jingling softly in the quietness of the corridor. "More than he already has, don't you mean?"

As Rassan looped the belt over his shoulder, his grin returned. "Patience and time, Imhara. Give the human both and you'll achieve your goal. Remember that." She nodded. "And when you need a break, come wake me and I'll watch over him."

Rassan left her standing in front of her bedroom door, his boots thudding on the stone floor as he walked to his chamber at the end of the hallway. Imhara waited until he went in before placing her hand on the metal latch of her door.

Taking a deep breath, she pushed it open and entered her room.

Chapter 4

AREK fought his way back to consciousness, the need to know why he still lived stalking him like a *lira* driving its prey into an ambush. It took an eternity to shake off the fog numbing his mind, but little by little, he pieced together a series of impressions.

His muscles ached, like he'd been in one position too long, yet whatever he rested on was soft and warm. Coupled with that, he lay on his back, his arms pulled back, stretched wide to either side of his head. He flexed them and tried to move, but cold metal bit into his wrists and the sound of chains rasped against metal and wood. The same happened when he tried to move his feet.

His heavy eyelids finally opened. He stared up into a shadowy darkness that wavered and flickered. Disoriented, he blinked, wondering if he had motion sickness again. To his right, a crackling, popping sound broke the silence. A familiar sweet scent filled his nostrils.

Flames eating needle-tree wood.

Firelight created the dance of shadows and light, not motion sickness. He turned his head. A dying fire burned in a grate. To one side of the fireplace, a shuttered window gave no indication of the time of day, but the flames threw out enough light so that he could see he was in a small stone-walled room—

—chained to a bed.

Every remaining wisp of fog in his mind cleared. The softness of a pillow dipped beneath his head as he craned his head back. The bed was a thick, four-poster, with intricate metalwork across the head and, as he looked downward, along the foot rail.

He frowned. His last memory was of lying facedown in the dirt, a *Na'Reish* warrior straddling his back, then . . . nothing. Now he lay between sunlight-scented sheets, a hand-sewn cover on top of them smoothed over him, as if the occupant of the room cared for his well-being.

His breath caught. Had he been sold while unconscious? Who had bought him? The why was evident—he lay in some *Na'Reishi's* bed—and it sent chills all over him. Being bought to labor at the beck and call of a demon was sickening enough, but the idea of serving as a bed-slave . . . His skin prickled and adrenaline spiked through his veins as another, far more frightening possibility unfurled.

Was the *Na'Reishi* male or female?

Mother of Light, it didn't matter. He'd be free or dead, probably the latter, before he would be used or submit to either. But *Lady* be damned if he was going to wait around for his new owner to appear.

His muscles and joints were stiff, and more than a little sore, but that didn't stop him twisting and tugging at his bonds, keeping his movements quiet, testing for any give until the skin under the manacles throbbed and bled.

Arek hissed a soft curse. He glared at the thick metal shackles banding his wrists. They held fast. He remained tethered, arms and legs spread.

Helpless.

With a silent groan, he collapsed back onto the pillow, the air in the chamber now cool on his sweat-soaked body. He welcomed the ache in his wrists and ankles but not the futility souring the back of his throat.

Lifting his head again, his gaze swept the room, looking for something, anything that might help him escape—and froze. In the corner, where the shadows were darkest, he made out a slender figure sitting in a rocker-chair. He tensed, every muscle in his body tightening as the seconds passed.

A log in the fireplace cracked as it collapsed and sent up a flare of fresh flames. The light banished some of the shadows wreathing the lone figure. She slept, oblivious of his scrutiny, another hand-sewn blanket, twin to the one that covered him, tucked over her lap.

And female she was.

A slave tasked to keep watch over him?

The strands of a ponytail draped over her shoulder, covering the rounded curve of a breast, the locks long enough to rest on the arm of the chair. The sheen was so black it was an ebony blue and seemed to absorb the light from the fire. Unraveled, he guessed her hair would fall to the middle of her back, thick and wavy after being freed from the tie. Long enough if she was astride a man's body that just the tilt of her head would slide the strands over his hips or chest in a silky caress.

Heat shot through him, spiraling southward so fast he almost groaned. As pleasant as that image was, it was neither the time nor place to be distracted. Arek blinked in an effort to clear the picture from his mind.

In the dim light, the woman's face remained lax with sleep. Her smooth skin had a sun-kissed tan that spoke of time spent outdoors. She seemed no older than him, someone who had seen nearly three decades of life. Her features were striking rather than beautiful—a high forehead, defined cheekbones, a slender nose, and a rounded yet firm jaw. Present circumstances aside, he'd have looked twice if their paths had crossed elsewhere.

She shifted in her slumber, the light of the fire flickering across her face. Full and expressive, the color of her lips looked dark, almost black. Arek frowned. Were the shadows playing tricks on him? The woman's head turned, her cheek settling against the back of the rocker.

Goose bumps prickled over every inch of his skin. A dusting of fine, black splotches, the same ebony blue color as her hair, marked the side of her face. They extended onto her cheek and jawbone, becoming larger in shape and size before continuing down her neck and beneath the collar of her shirt.

He didn't need to see where the skin markings went beyond the collar. They covered the back of her torso, buttocks, and legs. Similar patterns marked the bodies of the demons he'd killed in battle.

She was *Na'Reish*, not a slave. Nausea rolled in his gut at his previous lustful thoughts.

Was this demon his new owner?

His lip curled as a dark heat seared its way through his veins. A gut-deep growl rumbled up from his chest.

She stirred. Black lashes lifted to reveal amethyst-colored eyes that glowed in the firelight. A couple of blinks cleared the sleep haze from them, then her gaze locked with his.

"You're awake!" The sleep-husky voice held a note of excitement.

Slender hands threw back the blanket covering her. Long, breeches-clad legs unfolded and bare feet touched the stone floor. She rose from the chair, all six feet of her. Given her willowy build, her height didn't surprise him.

Her shirt hung past her hips, untucked for comfort, but it clung to her curved form well enough for him to see the lean lines and flex of honed muscle, a body as fit and toned as any warrior. One who had trained for years.

Unexpected for a *Na'Reishi* female, particularly given that *Na'Reish* culture was strictly patriarchal. Not that he'd seen many females during his time on border patrol, just a few from a safe distance, and always as part of a well-guarded caravan.

This female was dressed as a warrior, yet those travelling with the caravans had always worn dresses and finery. He'd only ever seen males on the battleground, never a female. Her father, any brothers, or other males in her Clan would be tasked with her protection; therefore, the idea of her being a part of a patrol was doubtful.

So, why would a female of her rank feel the need to learn the warrior arts?

His musing was cut short as the *Na'Reishi* female smiled and took a step toward the bed. Firelight glinted on pointed teeth, overshadowing the innate gracefulness of her walk.

Arek's blood ran ice cold. He sucked in a hard breath and strained against his bonds. When they refused to give again, his gaze slashed to hers and he bared his teeth. "Come any closer, demon, and I'll kill you!"

Chapter 5

THE demon stopped short of the bed, swaying backward as if she'd hit some unseen barrier. Arek expected an arrogant retort, a blaze of anger, even some sort of physical abuse in response, not hesitation or the calm yet curious narrowing of her gaze as she considered him.

"How would you achieve that given your present predicament?" she asked.

Her voice, a low, sultry rasp, brushed across all his senses like a caress, sent his blood surging through his veins. His skin prickled with heat, the swift rush of desire catching him off guard.

Merciful Mother, how could he feel such a thing when he knew what she was? He twisted his wrists against the manacles, fought to control his body, hoping the fresh pain would dull the unwanted reaction.

"I didn't realize the *Lady's* warriors had the power to kill with a thought." The upward twitch of her mouth served only to stroke his anger.

"Had I such a gift, you would now lie dead on the floor," he growled. "If you think my threat idle enough to mock me, move closer, and let's see how well you trust these chains."

Arek called on his power, felt the answering spark deep inside him, and hoped she'd dare. He didn't need a blade to focus his Gift. One careless touch, just the brush of her hand against any bare skin, and he could push it through his flesh into hers. It'd hurt, and would feel like he'd touched fire-seared metal drawn from a furnace, but he would kill her.

She altered her stance, a subtle shifting of weight onto the balls of her feet as if she were preparing for his attack, a move he'd seen a thousand times on the training grounds in the Light Blade compound. Again he wondered why a *Na'Reishi* female would need to know how to defend herself.

"I'm sorry, Light Blade." Her soft apology was accompanied by a grimace. "My attempt at humor was inappropriate."

Her regret seemed almost sincere.

"I find nothing amusing about this situation."

"No, there certainly isn't." Her chin lifted. "Let's begin again. My name is Imhara Kaal. I'm the *Na* of this Clan."

He snorted. "I don't give a copper chit what your name is, demon. It doesn't change the fact I'm chained to your bed and held here against my will."

"*Na* or *Na'Reishi*, not demon."

"What?"

"There's so much I have to tell you, but this is important." Resolve deepened the huskiness of her voice. "If you are to survive in my world, you must show respect. To me. To those of my Clan. To all *Na'Reish*, even if it goes against every fiber of your being."

"If you think I'll submit to any demon, then you're a fool." Arek jerked against his bonds. Metal clashed against wood, bit into his wrists. "I'm not your slave!"

One dark eyebrow lifted slowly. "Your current circumstances imply otherwise." Arek's breath hissed from between his teeth. He curled his hands into fists. Her expression softened. "On your side of the border, you were a free man. A Light Blade warrior, no doubt highly respected by your fellow warriors and society alike. Your people value equality and personal choice.

"I understand all that, but in *Na'Reish* territory you will be seen as nothing more than a slave. We live in a caste-based system. Power assigns rank. Rank defines privilege. Privilege determines choice. Here humans reside at the very bottom. You have no privilege, or rank, or power. And that eliminates choice. Your people are vessels to serve ours. Whenever, however, and in whatever fashion suits our pleasure."

Every word out of her mouth twisted his insides tighter and tighter. His blood heated and another growl erupted from his throat. This was why he'd answered the call to be a Light Blade. No one deserved to be used or degraded like that.

Once captured, how had his mother ever endured being a slave?

Only a child of three when she'd been taken, his memories of her were few. They were more sensations or emotions rather than images, but he'd been told plenty of stories growing up, and as a warrior he'd seen evidence of how the *Na'Reish* treated their slaves.

Annika, the *Na'Chi* half sister he never knew existed until recently, was living proof of what his mother had suffered.

Rape.

Forced to conceive and bear a child of mixed blood.

Abuse of the worst kind, but then *Na'Reish* demons were renowned for such atrocities, particularly Savyr, their leader, the demon who'd taken her to his bed.

Arek ground his teeth together, sweat prickling at his temples. How many times had she been forced to submit in the months Savyr had imprisoned her? How many times had she wished for death rather than tolerate his touch? At the moment of Annika's birth and his mother's death, had she rejoiced in thwarting his plan for revenge?

Mother and child, both used as pawns, a means to an end. Arek's soul pulsed with too familiar grief while his mind rebelled at a bitter truth.

He now faced a similar fate.

His heart beat hard and his blood ran hot, demanding he give voice to his fury. The ache in his jaw grew the longer he clenched it, but he'd put up with a hundred times the pain before giving in to his temper. There was no way Imhara Kaal would get the satisfaction of seeing him lose control.

"*Na* or *Na'Reishi*—either term is the correct way to address me. I'll teach you how to identify other ranks later." The solemnity of her vow vibrated in her voice. "To call us *demon* will be seen as disrespect. You'll risk punishment or death depending on whom you offend. And the sooner you learn this, the faster you'll settle into your new life, the safer you will be."

Her amethyst gaze bore into his with an intensity that prickled his skin. Did she think dying frightened him? Every ride along the border, every patrol completed, every skirmish engaged in with the *Na'Reish*, he'd prepared himself for the Final Journey. As for a new life, he intended to escape at the first opportunity or die trying.

"I tell you this not to provoke you"—she took a step closer to the bed, halting barely an arm's length from him—"but because you're going to need to accept that outside this fortress, you'll have no power or protection other than what my name and reputation can provide."

"You say that as if you believe I'll come around to your logic." Arek made little effort to conceal his disgust and contempt. "No words, no vows, no punishment you threaten me with will ever sway me."

He flexed his fingers. Her gaze flickered to them. Satisfaction curled in his gut as wariness creased the corners of her eyes. If he ever managed to get free of the shackles, he'd wrap his hands around her slender neck and rid the world of one more demon.

Yet her behavior puzzled him. Where was the cruelty he'd been anticipating? He'd experienced the boat-master's discipline for the smallest of infractions. If disrespecting her was such a crime, then why hadn't she punished him?

"Not all *Na'Reish* advocate the caste system, Light Blade. You will see this in time." What almost looked like sincerity flickered across her face. "Here in the Kaal fortress we honor the Old Ways. The caste system doesn't exist. We live differently than the other Clans."

No caste system? No slaves? Just how gullible did she think he was? Her act to convince him was pitiful. He'd be a fool to read anything into what she said or did.

Arek's lip curled. "From where I'm lying, I see cursed-all difference, demon."

Her brow dipped low. "You stew in your anger like a stubborn child when you should be listening. Thinking."

A flash of temper, so unexpected, and the first he'd witnessed. She closed her eyes a moment, and when she opened them, the anger was gone, replaced by calmness. Her whole body relaxed. All in less than three heartbeats.

Her control impressed him. Intrigued him. Two emotions he shouldn't be feeling.

Never trust a demon. Lies and deceit dwell in their souls. It's their nature. As a child, how many times had his grandfather reminded him of this? Davyn had never forgiven Savyr for the death of his daughter.

Nothing Arek had seen in his time as a Light Blade warrior contradicted that supposition. This *Na'Reishi* female represented everything he hated. So what if she hadn't reacted as he'd expected? He needed to focus on escape, not try to make sense of her motives or actions.

“Surely you’ve been in situations where not everything was as you assumed it to be?” she asked.

She dropped into a crouch, then knelt beside the bed. It brought her down to eye level with him, giving the moment a level of intimacy that made his skin crawl.

“Isn’t it strange that I know you’re a Light Blade warrior yet you live?” She cocked her head to one side, the wry hint of a smile curving her dark lips. “Don’t you want to know why?”

Mother of Light, yes, he wanted to know, but as much as he desired that knowledge, answering would give her an advantage over him. He kept his mouth shut. What game was she playing at? Did it amuse her to taunt him like this?

IMHARA issued a soft sigh when the human’s mouth flattened into a grim line. This close, his gaze was such a rich, captivating blue, like the sky on a winter’s evening, but his eyes burned with hatred and speared her with furious intent.

If he felt intimidated by his situation, chained to a bed, his thoughts filled with the knowledge that he was helpless and subject to her whims, he gave no indication of it. She applauded his silent courage. He was going to need it in the coming days. She doubted he was the sort of human who’d reveal any sort of weakness voluntarily.

What experiences had honed such strength in him?

Her gaze traced the angry lines of his face. Beneath the dirt and grime of travel, his visage was striking—a broad forehead, thick blond brows, sharp cheekbones, and a stubble-shadowed jaw.

Not classically handsome by any means. His sun-darkened features possessed a hard, dangerous edge, but the fierceness was a familiar trait, one she recognized and respected.

In a man—*Na’Reish*, *Na’Chi*, or human male—she found those qualities appealing. Attractive. And now was no different. Yet she doubted he'd appreciate her sharing that thought with him.

Imhara issued another soft sigh. For the moment it was probably safer to focus on the task of revealing her plans.

"If our situations were reversed, I'd want to know why you hadn't killed me," she murmured. Her nostrils filled with the heavy, bitter odor of hatred, yet beneath it she detected the faintest trace of cloves.

Curiosity.

The first sign of emotion other than his desire to kill her. Thank the *Lady*. All she had to do now was fan that interest and keep it alive; establish a connection.

She wet her lips. "I know you're not likely to believe me, but I don't consider you my enemy."

"You are mine!" The words were snarled from between gritted teeth. Chains rattled as he strained against his bonds, renewing his bid for freedom.

Any other time Imhara might have admired the powerful strength in his body as his muscles flexed and twisted, but the unmistakable scent of fresh blood filled her nostrils. She glanced at his wrists. Crimson stained his skin and the edge of the shackles, some even smeared the white linen pillows.

She grimaced even as her heart beat faster. Rassan's quick thinking had saved this warrior's life. The Light Blade possessed everything she needed to see her plan to fruition—strength, tenacity, willpower, and skill—if she could convince him her intentions were genuine. But getting him to take a first step seemed impossible.

The warrior ceased struggling, the flush of anger still coloring his tanned cheeks, his breath rasping in and out of his lungs like a winded *Vorc*. Her heart ached at the futility and frustration he must be experiencing.

"I'm sorry, Light Blade. I regret that it was necessary for you to be restrained and treated like a prisoner."

"Really?" he countered, voice rough as his gaze glittered. "Then unchain me."

Rassan's warning echoed in the back of her mind.

"I can't."

"Why doesn't that come as a surprise?" A muscle leapt in his cheek. She curled her fingers into a fist, resisting the urge to reach forward and soothe the lines of tension pulling at the corners of his mouth. He'd likely bite her if she tried. "You tell me one thing, demon, but your actions betray the truth."

The validity of his accusation grated. How could she expect even the smallest sliver of trust from him if she refused to offer it first?

"We both know you'd try to kill me, and I don't want to have to hurt you to stop you."

"Hurt me? I don't think so." His mouth twisted into a fierce, feral grin. "I won't just *try* to kill you. I will."

His deep voice was so thick with menace it resonated off him in waves, the sharp odor of bitter hatred overpowering. *Merciful Mother*, his animosity for her race she could understand, but what would it take for him to see past his anger and listen to her?

Frowning, Imhara stared down at the quilt, then traced the intricate vine-leaf design portrayed with her finger, the olive green material soft, the thread raised to delineate the stem and leaves. In the forest the vine wound its way around whatever plant lived nearby, sending out multiple shoots to maximize its chances of finding sunlight.

Her breath caught as the simple tactic sparked an idea.

She lifted her gaze to meet the Light Blade's. "Slaying me would be a waste of time, warrior, especially when the opportunity to kill *Na'Rei* Savyr might hold more appeal. Wouldn't seeing him dead give you greater satisfaction?"

Shadows flickered through his gaze.

"Imagine the impact his death would have on the *Na'Reish*." The scent of cloves intensified, mixed with then overrode the heat of his anger. *Curiosity.* Again. Imhara swallowed her smile. "Think how quickly chaos would engulf the Clans as they squabbled over who would inherit his throne." She took a deep breath. "I can give you that chance. Interested, Light Blade?"

Chapter 6

IMHARA Kaal's proposition tugged at Arek like the undercurrent of a deep river. Of all the things she could have tempted him with—who was she that she could offer such an opportunity? How many times had he prayed and pleaded with the *Lady* for the chance to avenge the loss of his parents?

All Light Blades knew the *Na'Reish* executed any taken in battle, so when word of his mother's capture reached his father, it was news of her death. As far as Arek was concerned, Savyr's actions were responsible for his father's overwhelming grief and his choice to end his own life with a blade to the heart.

Every day he rode out on patrol gave him the chance to strike back at those who had taken so much from him.

"Why?" he ground out. "Why would you want Savyr dead?"

Every muscle in the female demon's face pulled tight. Her eyelids slitted. Raw heat and darkness ripped through her gaze. There was no mistaking the emotion.

Hatred.

He'd lived with it for nearly three decades.

Black lips thinned. "He ordered the death of my family."

She hesitated, shadows stirred in her gaze, morphing her tight features into something more vulnerable. Grief. He knew it well.

A thrill of energy streaked through him. The eerie similarity in their circumstances burrowed deep. He grit his teeth. The last thing he wanted to feel was empathy with the enemy.

She inhaled a steady breath, shaking off whatever memories enthralled her. "Only I survived." He stared at her, unable to doubt her sincerity this time. "He wants control of Skadda Pass and the slave-route. It runs from his province and through Kaal territory."

How much of the border between *Na'Reish* and human territory did she share? A good third by the sound of it, if it included the northern Skadda Mountain Range.

"It's the reason why my family was murdered." Her purple gaze glittered, like chips of fire-stone caught in sunlight. Nature's furious beauty—ice and heat—melded into one. The huskiness in her voice deepened. "As custom allowed, Savyr thought he'd claim Kaal territory in the absence of a suitable heir." She gave a humorless grin. "When he called an Enclave to enact this right, I took great pleasure in claiming my sire's seat alongside the other *Nas*."

"They let a female assume the title?"

"Exceptional circumstances. I was the only living heir." One dark eyebrow arched. "Besides, the Enclave and Savyr thought I'd accede to their greater wisdom and mate at the first opportunity. To carry the mantle of leadership would prove too onerous a task for a female." Her mocking tone held genuine humor. "Once mated, the title would pass to my mate."

Arek couldn't see Savyr quietly backing down on acquiring something he deemed as his. Foiling the *Na'Rei's* plan had placed a target on her back and explained why she needed to know how to defend herself. It also made him wonder how many attempts had been made on her life. And how she'd survived them.

"The corridor into our Southern Province is a significant asset," he stated. Over the years, the southern end had suffered the highest number of casualties in *Na'Reish* hit-and-run sorties for blood-slaves.

Her nod was sharp. "You can see why Savyr wants it so badly. And what he wants he usually gets." Her hand fisted in the quilt. "But I'm not going to give him Kaal territory without a fight."

The ice in her voice could cut stone. The *Na'Reish* leader was a ruthless bastard, something he'd witnessed time and again while on border patrol. He'd lost count of the number of crofters and villagers he'd helped after the *Na'Hord* had ransacked their homes and kidnapped or killed loved ones during raids.

Their helplessness and despair left him and his fellow Light Blades feeling frustrated and angry, emotions he could hear reflected in Imhara Kaal's voice. As much as he didn't want to sympathize with a demon, he could understand her determination and desire to fight against Savyr.

But he was assigning human sentiment and values to her motives. There had to be something else driving her.

He grunted. "You fight over land, then."

"No! This is about survival, Light Blade." Her gaze locked with his, the amethyst depths swirling. "Survival of my Clan. Survival of our way of life. And survival of your people." White lines etched her mouth. "I believe Savyr is preparing for war."

Arek's frown deepened.

"He's called for an Enclave in a month. All *Na* are expected to attend." The *Na'Reishi* female eased back onto her heels. "I suspect he'll reveal his plans then, but the frequent patrols using Kaal territory to cross the border, the age of the humans being brought back, the increased tithes all indicate Savyr is preparing for war with your people."

Arek's gut tightened. Her statement confirmed what the Blade Council and his own experiences on patrol had revealed—nearly five hundred humans taken and close to four times that massacred in their homes the last few months alone.

Imhara Kaal was telling the truth there—her forthrightness with such information surprised him—but with Clan feuds commonplace among the *Na'Reish*, her motives for wanting the *Na'Rei* dead were still suspect.

"You don't need me to assassinate Savyr. We both know there are scores of different ways to accomplish this." Arek lifted a brow. "What's the real reason for killing him?"

The demon pushed to her feet. She strode to the end of the bed, staring into the shadows beyond. "You mask your skepticism well, Light Blade, but I can scent it in the air between us."

"Your last four *Na'Rei's* were all murdered, in one fashion or another, for the throne. History speaks for itself."

She whirled back to him, her face slackening in shock. "You're assuming I want to take Savyr's place?"

"You're *Na'Reish*."

A muscle in her jaw leapt. She leaned forward, her hands clenching on the iron bed-end.

"Once they discover who is behind his death, his Clan will seek revenge." She flexed her fingers, easing their white-knuckled grip, her voice strong and low. "To save my Clan, I intend asking for a truce with your leaders."

A grunt of laughter exploded from him. Had she been inhaling *haze*? Most *Na'Reish* burnt the dried leaf to subdue unruly blood-slaves, but it wasn't unheard of for some to use it for their own pleasure. Fantasies and delusions were common side effects.

Lady's Breath, it would explain her insane request.

Arek shook his head. "A patrol will intercept you well before you get to Sacred Lake."

"Your presence will allay any attack." The urgency in her voice and in her expression lifted his pulse rate. "You'll have lived among us"—here she grimaced and gave a half shrug—"or will have by the time we approach your Council. You'll be able to tell them the Kaal poses no threat, that we're nothing like the other Clans."

He snorted. "No threat?"

"I know you hate me, Light Blade, and I know you don't trust me yet, but just consider the possibility that what I'm saying is true."

He was ready to shoot back a nasty response, but the waver in her voice gave him pause. She swallowed hard and her gaze swerved away from his, but not before fear darkened her eyes.

Fear of him? Of facing the Blade Council?

Or something else?

She cleared her throat and met his gaze again, determination cloaking her like a second skin. "Your *Chosen* will have an ally prepared to defend the border of human territory, from the Southern Swamplands to the tip of the northern Skadda Ranges. *Na'Reish* patrols will no longer be able to use Skadda Pass or the slave-route. If the assassination doesn't halt the war preparations, losing half their major supply line for blood-slaves will."

Her speech was sense and reason wrapped up in temptation, but the most powerful lies were half-truths cloaked in logic. He knew that from experience, having been lied to his entire life by his grandfather, the one man he'd trusted and looked up to.

Arek pushed away the ache that came with that thought and focused on the *Na'Reishi* standing at the end of the bed.

Imhara Kaal had to have some ulterior motive, something she hadn't yet revealed.

"No human will ever trust a *Na'Reish*." His voice was flat, hard. "Particularly a traitor."

IMHARA'S heart beat rapidly in her chest. Her throat tightened with the accusation. Yes, she was a traitor to her race, but they were no longer her people. By suppressing the truth of their origins, the Old Ways had been banished and forgotten. Her loyalty belonged only to her Clan now. There was nothing she wouldn't do for them.

Gathering her thoughts, she appealed once more to the Light Blade. "Consider this, there are nearly a thousand humans living in Kaal territory. Perhaps once you see and interact with some of them, your opinion of us will change."

"Then you'd better keep me chained to this bed, demon," he hissed. "That's the only way you're going to make me stay in this cursed place!"

Her blood pulsed hard in her veins. Of course he would try to escape. Given all his beliefs about the *Na'Reish*, part of her couldn't blame him, but her heart rebelled. So many years of strategic planning were being ground into nothingness with his refusal to listen.

She racked her brain to think of another way to present her proposal to him, to convince him, and came up blank. *Mother of Light*, finding a Light Blade among those captured by Meelar's raiding party had been a blessing. She'd laid out the facts as honestly and openly as possible.

Imhara squeezed the iron railing, knuckles turning white. His refusal sat like a rock in her gut. Heavy. Unmovable. To lose this warrior would end her ancestors' legacy and condemn her Clan to death.

She *couldn't* let either happen.

Her heart beat harder. There was one way to stop him escaping. A temporary measure until he understood. But the deceit involved sickened her. He would hate her more.

Yet what choice did she have? So much relied on him recognizing the potential of what she offered. And that's what was important, what she had to focus on.

Nothing else mattered.

Jaw clenching, teeth aching from the pressure, she rounded the end of the bed to sit on the edge of it, close to the Light Blade. His body went rigid. Her stomach twisted at the furious expression on his face.

"Your purpose for being here is more important than you realize." She curled her fingers around his elbow, careful to keep a layer of his shirt between his skin and hers as she exposed his inner arm. The warmth of his body, the flex of hardened muscle sent a ripple of sensation through her. This close, his earthy, musky scent intrigued her. She fought the temptation to inhale more deeply and savor it. "I can't take the risk of you escaping."

"*Get* your hand off me!"

She ignored him and clamped her other hand around the shackle. His nostrils flared and he wrenched against her hold. With the restraint and her *Na'Reish* strength, she had little trouble pinning his arm to the pillow.

"What are you doing?" he snarled.

Heart heavy in her chest, Imhara forced the words from her throat. "What I must."

Leaning forward, she bit into the flesh of his arm, careful not to sink her teeth too deep, just enough to break the skin and make it bleed. Saliva exploded in her mouth.

"*No*!" His enraged yell filled the room. Chains jangled; his body bucked and strained against his bonds as he tried to force her touch away from him.

She swallowed, his iron-rich blood coating her tongue, every taste bud demanding more, his blood as sweet and smooth as a well-aged wine. She bit back a groan of pleasure. He wouldn't understand.

The buzz of energy from the single mouthful went straight to her head. Her senses reeled, sharpened, and it took every shred of control she had to stop herself taking more than a few swallows. Had it been that long since she'd fed?

Panting softly, Imhara drew back, unsurprised to see her hands shaking. Adrenaline raced through her veins and pumped through her heart, elevating her to a blood-high in mere seconds. *Merciful Mother*, his blood was potent. She licked the last lingering taste of him from her lips as she rose from the bed.

Retreat was now the wisest option. For both of them. She needed to feed properly. The scent and flavor of him would tease her mercilessly until she sated her awakened appetite. And he needed time to recover, to reconcile his fate.

Imhara headed for the door. Hand on the latch, she turned to look at the warrior. Beneath his tan, his face was pale. He stared at his arm and the puncture marks made by her teeth.

She bit her lip, sympathizing with his horror, understanding his fear and where it came from, regretting that she'd caused it, but he had to believe the blood-bond condemned him to serving her for life. He needed to assume the cravings were a part of his addiction to feed her, and to ignore them would result in death.

At least for a little while.

Fostering that untruth didn't sit well with her. Decades of time and suppression of the Old Ways by the other Clans had bastardized the reality of the practice. Now it was used as a control measure, a parasitic way to bind a slave to their owner.

In essence, she'd done the Light Blade no harm, although she doubted he'd see it that way, even if she offered an explanation. He'd have to see the truth for himself. Later.

"*I'll kill you!*" His outrage lashed at her like a whip. "*I swear it!*"

His curses damned her to the Underworld, and she accepted them with a small nod. Unease curled in the pit of her stomach, but she pushed it aside. Her feelings didn't matter, and for the moment, neither did his.

The survival of her Clan and his race was more important. And, as always, she was willing to accept the consequences of her actions if it meant achieving that goal.

Imhara took a deep breath. "Escaping the fortress is no longer an option, Light Blade."

The look he speared her with was so vicious it was hard to disguise her flinch.

"I won't be your blood-slave!"

"In time I hope you'll come to understand why I did this." She tried to keep her voice as steady as her resolve. "I'll leave you alone now." Hesitating on the threshold, she shot a last look at him over her shoulder. "Tomorrow your new life here in Kaal Fortress begins."

With that, Imhara stepped into the darkened hallway and gently closed the door behind her, cutting off his new tirade of curses. Scrubbing a hand over her face, she fought the ache growing in her chest. *Lady* forgive her for deceiving the human, but her actions had gained them all some time. She'd done the right thing.

Glancing left, she considered waking Rassan to swap places with her, but there was no way she could sleep now. And the Light Blade probably wouldn't appreciate the company. She headed in the opposite direction, along the corridor toward the stairs and the library. Until those within the fortress awoke to begin a new day, the tasks she'd put off to greet the Light Blade would keep her occupied.

But even as she lit the candelabras and settled into the cushioned chair at her desk, her thoughts were still on the human chained to her bed. Instead of sorting through the stack of missives piled on her desk, she reached for the carved box sitting next to them.

Selecting one of the incense sticks from within, she lit then placed it in the small hole drilled into the lid. For long moments she watched the glowing tip burn and smoke twirl and drift toward the darkened ceiling, and filled her lungs with the floral scent.

Imhara placed her fingertips on the intricate moon within a sun carved into the side of the box. "*Lady*, I pray I've taken the right path with this human."

Morning would come soon enough and she'd see, because now there was no going back.

Chapter 7

"YOU look as sleep deprived as the Light Blade."

Rassan's deep voice jerked Imhara upright in her chair. Frowning, she stared at her surroundings, her thoughts still consumed by lists and numbers from the ledgers scattered across her desk—accounts for supplies, those owed and paid as well as provided, animal statistics, records of the new humans for the register, a stocktake of goods being stored for winter.

Blinking gritty eyes, she fought to focus on the books lining the shelves that covered the walls of the room before her gaze came to rest on the *Na'Chi* warrior. He stood in the library doorway dressed in conventional work breeches and shirt, not his customary leather armor. Black hair, usually tied back in a tight tail at the nape of his neck, lay in damp waves across broad shoulders.

"What were you doing visiting my room?" she asked, leaning back to stretch out the kinks in her muscles.

"Looking for you." His dry reply was softened by the hint of a smile.

He stepped past the threshold. Her mouth twitched when she spotted the ever-present dagger sheathed at his hip. He never went anywhere unarmed, and she suspected the blade lay beneath his pillow as he slept.

"When I couldn't find you there, I went looking in the lower levels and inner barracks. This time of the morning you're usually visiting our newest Clan members."

Visiting and interacting with the humans began the orientation and adjustment process. It was a ritual she took pleasure in, but this morning she hadn't been much for company.

Imhara gestured at the work on her desk. "I've been catching up on a few things."

"So I see." Rassan folded his arms. "I talked to the humans we rescued yesterday. The Light Blade's name is Arek."

"Good to know." Her smile twisted. "He didn't volunteer his name last night, and calling him Light Blade was getting tiresome."

Rassan chuckled softly as he covered the distance to the only other chair in the room, a low, spacious lounge placed halfway between the fireplace and the window, and sprawled in it.

"There was no last name and they say he was captured with several farmsteaders from the village of Ostare, but he's not one of them."

"Any of them from Ostare?" she asked, smothering a yawn.

"One. She says the *Na'Reish* patrol who raided their village was attacked by Light Blades, but the rescue was foiled by the appearance of Meelar's raiding party."

"Meelar would never have let a Light Blade live." Frowning, Imhara pushed out of her chair and strode to the window. Early-morning sunlight had yet to breach the curtain wall of the fortress and light the inner ward.

The hard-packed ground was already occupied by a small group of people, *Na'Reish*, *Na'Chi*, and human alike, all loading implements and supplies into the back of drays for work in the fields outside the walls. *Lady* willing, the last of this season's crops would be harvested by dusk.

"Do they know how the Light Blade ended up among them or why he was dressed like them?" she inquired.

"No."

She could make a few assumptions, but eventually confirmation would have to come from Arek. His cooperation was going to be considerably less forthcoming than it might have been several hours ago. Imhara fisted a hand and tapped it against the sill.

"You're too quiet." Rassan's statement made her grimace. "What happened last night after I left you?"

"Everything we expected." Turning, she gave a half shrug. "He woke. He threatened me. I explained a few things. He didn't believe me."

"And?"

"And what?"

"Imhara, the catalyst for all our plans waits in your room. Yet you're down here buried in accounts and supply lists, just like it's another day, but you fist and flex your left hand. You only do that when something's bothering you."

Cursing his perceptiveness, she resisted the urge to squirm under his implacable stare. Any other time she might have brushed aside his concern, but their futures lay tied to the human in her bedroom.

"Convincing the Light Blade seems an impossible task, Rassan." She winced. Her complaint sounded whiny.

"Arek's fought the *Na'Hord* and raiding parties all his life. He's witnessed comrades fall to their blades and atrocities visited on those he protects." Rassan's response remained calm. "We anticipated this would happen."

She shook her head. "His hatred, his anger . . . it's different. Darker. More consuming. The odor is stronger, heavier than anything I've ever scented. Nothing I said to him last night seemed to penetrate." She sighed softly. "I feared he would escape before glimpsing the proof of my words."

"Feared? You say that in the past tense." Rassan leaned forward, boots scraping on the stone floor as he shifted to the edge of the lounge. "Speak plainly, Imhara."

"I blood-bonded with him."

The warrior sucked in a sharp breath, the flecks in his eyes going from dark violet to bronze. She watched his thoughts flicker across his face, processing everything she'd said and piecing it together. "You didn't tell him about the symbiotic relationship."

"No, I didn't." While Rassan showed no censure, a sharp citrus odor exuded from him. She waved aside his protest. "His promise to escape was no idle threat."

"He'll believe you've made him your blood-slave. How is that supposed to earn his trust?" Ever direct, her friend's accusation struck deep. "Your rash action may end this venture before it even starts."

"Perhaps," she conceded. "But how many years have we waited for this opportunity to let it slip from our grasp? Besides, Arek will be told the truth."

"When?"

"After he's met you, Barrca, and Jaclan."

"You task three *Na'Chi* as guards?"

She issued a wry smile at his raised eyebrow. "When he wasn't threatening me, his comments showed an analytical mind. What if the rumors of the alliance between the humans and those other *Na'Chi* are correct? Seeing you will make him think."

"Assuming he's not still enraged by your actions from last night."

Imhara grimaced then grunted. "Offer him the hospitality of this House, but if he threatens you, then safety takes precedence over his comfort. When he's ready, bring him down here." She motioned to the tomes closest to them. "I would share the journals of our ancestors with him."

"And the truth of the blood-bond?"

"That, too."

"Then may the *Lady* bless our path this day." The warrior pushed to his feet, a grim expression on his face. "I suspect we're going to need *Her* guidance and as much patience as we can muster."

Imhara drew in a slow breath, the image of a certain furious Light Blade warrior foremost in her mind. "Indeed."

MORNING sunlight pouring in through an open window drew Arek from a fitful sleep. The broad beam streaked across the stone floor before angling across the quilt to strike his face. He winced at the brightness and turned his head aside.

It took him a groggy moment to realize that he was no longer alone in the bedroom. He jerked upright, or tried to. Chain grated against wood. The manacles bit into his abused flesh and held him down. His muscles tensed for a fight he couldn't engage in. Cursing, he welcomed the surge of anger that dulled the renewed pain and consuming bitterness of being helpless. How could he have been so careless as to have not heard someone enter?

A figure crossed in front of the window. "Our apologies for waking you, Arek, but we have much to accomplish before day's end."

The deep voice didn't belong to Imhara Kaal. A swift glance at the rocker-chair showed her absent from the room, a fact that left him feeling cheated and disappointed at the same time. He'd expected her to return, to gloat, to present him with an opportunity for retribution.

Squinting against the light, he brought the silhouetted figure into focus only to discover three *Na'Reish* males had replaced her. The vestiges of sleep fled. He eyed each of them warily.

All were of similar height, dressed in the well-worn clothes of workmen, but their powerful builds and intense gazes betrayed them as warriors. Having trained such watchfulness into many new Light Blades, the look was a familiar one.

Arek's memory stirred. "You're the scout from the riverside."

"I'm Rassan."

The warrior's dark hair was no longer pulled back into a single tail. It lay loose around his shoulders, but Arek remembered the voice and angular features.

"How do you know my name?"

"We rescued five other humans from Meelar's raid caravan yesterday. One of them told me."

Rescued? What an interesting turn of phrase.

The male gestured to the blond warrior standing by the fireplace. "That's Barrca, and the one holding the tray is Jaclan."

Jaclan possessed the more youthful, leaner stature, his rounded face lacking the shadowed stubble of the other two. He offered a nervous smile and quick nod of the head as he placed the tray on the small table beside the bed. The mouthwatering odor of cooked food drifted from beneath the cover, but Arek barely looked at it, his attention stolen by the color in the young warrior's eyes.

His jaw loosened as shock washed through him, diluting his anger and taking the edge off his hatred. *Flecks of pale turquoise dotted the youth's violet gaze.*

"You're *Na'Chi*!"

Chapter 8

"WE all are, Light Blade."

Rassan's declaration tore Arek's gaze away from the young male. A swift look confirmed the scout's declaration. Tones of green flecked each of the other two warrior's eyes, yet their darker sun-bronzed skin and black lips, their larger, more powerful builds, and genetic markings were identical to any *Na'Reish*. Only the youth bore any resemblance to the *Na'Chi* he knew from Sacred Lake.

"You'll find almost half the population of this Clan are of mixed blood." The dark-haired warrior gestured to Jaclan. "His mother is *Na'Reish* but his father is human. Barrca and myself are three-quarters *Na'Reish*."

That meant more than one generation of half-blood children had survived to adulthood. Arek's jaw loosened.

"No demon tolerates your existence." The words escaped before he could recall them.

"I see that you're familiar with our race." Rassan grunted and moved to the corner of the bed, a faint smile curving the corners of his mouth. "Then there's substance to the rumors of the alliance between humans and the other group of *Na'Chi*. This bodes well."

For what? It was on the tip of Arek's tongue to ask, but this time he succeeded in holding on to the question.

"You neither confirm or deny the rumor. Considering what you believe your situation to be, I suppose I can't blame you."

Arek snorted softly. "What would you know of my thoughts?"

"You assume you're a slave within this House. You're not."

Arek bared his teeth in a humorless grin and rattled the chains binding him to the bed. "So you treat all your guests like this?"

"You're the first Light Blade we've been able to rescue. Imhara disagreed with my decision to use restraints, but I wasn't prepared to compromise her safety."

Arek's gaze narrowed. The *Na'Chi* had ordered him chained to the bed, not the demon?

Violet eyes flecked with somber green flickered to the bite mark on his arm. The *Na'Chi's* mouth tightened. *He knew.* The knowledge was there in his expression.

"Imhara's . . . actions . . . were her way of protecting you from what lies outside these walls."

Arek stiffened. "You excuse what she's done to me?" The words exploded from him in a heated rush.

Rassan shook his head. "I don't, but I understand her fears better than you. She damaged any chance of you trusting her to give you time to understand your situation."

"My situation?" he growled. "Don't you mean my *place*?"

The flecks in the warrior's eyes changed briefly to black, his mouth pulled down at the corners, but then he continued talking as if he'd never heard Arek's comment. "The explanation of what she did to you belongs to her, and she'll address it once your needs have been seen to."

Arek's innards prickled at the promise of seeing Imhara Kaal again. All he had to be was patient. The thought helped bank the outrage seething inside him.

"My needs?" he asked.

From his breeches' pocket, Rassan produced a metal key. Gesturing with his chin to the opposite side of the room, he flipped back the quilt and inserted it in the lock of his ankle restraint. "Through that door lies a bath and clean clothes. The tray Jaclan brought holds your breakfast. The order in which you choose to eat and bathe is yours."

Arek's breath caught as the manacle snapped open. He flexed his leg, working his stiff muscles as elation surged through him.

"Be cautioned though"—the warrior's voice dropped, deepened—"should you attempt to attack or harm any of us, we won't hesitate to shackle you again."

Behind him, Barrca held up two sets of wrist and ankle chains. The metal links clinked in soft warning.

Pick your battles. Yevni's gruff voice echoed in his head. How often had the grizzled arms-master quoted that saying?

Previous experience training with the *Na'Chi* at Sacred Lake had taught Arek the difficulty of gaining the upper hand. Here it would be three to his one, against *Na'Chi*-enhanced strength and speed. Yevni's advice was sound—this wasn't a battle to be tempted by.

Arek nodded to acknowledge Rassan's warning and, in seconds, was free of his bonds. As he rose, all three *Na'Chi* took a wary step away from the bed, their gazes locked on him. He ignored them, rubbing life back into his limbs, then covered the distance to the other door in three long strides.

Peering into the small bathing room, he grunted softly when it proved to have no windows, just a privy in the corner, and a steam vent set high into the ceiling, well out of his reach. The bedroom door remained the only exit to other parts of the fortress.

The deep, rectangular pool set into the floor offered nothing but a stoppered jar of soap-sand, a few hooks on one wall, a towel, and the promised clothes hanging from the hooks. For half a second, he considered trying to rip a hook from the wall for use as a weapon, but that decision faded with the opportunity to tend his abused body and gather his strength. A better time would arise.

Leaving the door open a hand's width to let in the morning sunlight, he stripped, throwing the dirt-encrusted clothes in a shadowed corner. Privacy paled in comparison to slipping in the dark and cracking his head open, especially when he needed all his wits about him. And as much as he desired to soak away every ache and bruise, he made quick use of the facility.

Hot water. Clean clothes. Warm food. All things he'd never take for granted again.

With no desire to perch on the bed to eat, he crouched with his back pressed up against one wall and dug into the simple breakfast as fast as his stomach could tolerate. No one spoke, and the absence of conversation suited him just fine.

The revelation of there being more *Na'Chi* than those who existed at Sacred Lake had him watching his three guards as openly as they observed him. The *Na'Chi* who'd followed Annika from Savyr's fortress had claimed no knowledge of any others of their race among the *Na'Reish*. Yet here, according to Rassan's claims, half the population of Kaal Fortress possessed *Na'Chi* blood.

Generations of them.

In a *Na'Reish* stronghold.

How had they remained undiscovered for so long?

What had Imhara Kaal said last night? *We live differently than the other Clans.* Had she been speaking the truth?

Arek scraped the last of the milk-boiled grain from the bowl with a crust of bread, his gaze flitting between the three warriors. The idea that a *Na'Reish* demon tolerated half-bloods defied belief, but the presence of them here suggested it could be so.

And that raised another, more incredible situation. His perception of Imhara Kaal could be incorrect.

Yet what of making him a blood-slave?

His gut twisted, no longer able to ignore her teeth marks on his forearm. The small puncture wounds remained red, bruises decorating their edges. His fingers tightened around the bowl until his knuckles whitened.

She'd taken his blood to bind him to her, to stop him escaping. The act deliberate, calculating.

Damning.

In that, she was no different from any other *Na'Reish* he'd come across.

Arek grimaced, replaying everything that had happened to him since waking up in the bed. His gut burned every time he thought of Imhara Kaal, and every fiber of his being revolted at the idea of being her blood-slave. But now the presence of the *Na'Chi* confused the issue.

Confronting such conflicting facts proved . . . unsettling. Something he detested. Everything inside him demanded he take action, but what could he do? There was no clear path for him to take; yet another frustration to add to the growing list.

A knock at the door drew Arek from his thoughts. Jaclan looked to Rassan, only opening it when the older warrior nodded. Neither he nor Barrca moved to greet the woman, denying him the advantage of a turned back. Good training, he conceded, and shifted his attention to the visitor.

"Rassan, you asked for me?" The woman was human, her hair more gray than black. She greeted the *Na'Chi* with a smile; the warmth of it made her dark eyes sparkle. Her face was long, her tanned skin marked well with lines of age and experience. She mightn't have been wearing healer green, but the simple shift belted around her and the suede leather bag at her side labeled her as one.

Her boot sole scraped on stone as the healer took an awkward step into the room, favoring her left leg.

"Nayvia, thank you for coming." The *Na'Chi* warrior took the hand she extended, a gesture of greeting and assistance in turn. "Arek has injuries that need seeing to."

Arek placed the empty bowl aside and pushed to his feet as she turned her gaze on him.

"Welcome to the House of Kaal." She held out her hands and he placed his on top of them. She made sympathetic tsking sounds as she examined his abraded wrists. "It's an honor to meet one of the *Lady's* Light Blades. Your arrival has been much anticipated. That Rassan was able to sense your presence and save you from Meelar is a blessing."

Arek's gaze flickered behind her. "You're Gifted?"

The *Na'Chi* warrior inclined his head. "I have an affinity for detecting *Her* power in others."

Nayvia made a noise in the back of her throat. "Your skill is remarkable." Brown eyes lifted to meet his, the warmth in them genuine. "Rassan's helped discover some of our most talented students."

Students? Arek remained silent as Nayvia ferreted through her pouch. She withdrew a jar and uncorked it. The heavy mint odor of *Vaa'jahn* assailed his nostrils. She smeared it over the raw wounds on his wrists, then the healing cut on his head. For a few heartbeats it stung, then his skin went numb.

"If you have questions, Arek, ask them," Rassan said. "Our answers will be freely given."

His head snapped up, wondering how the warrior had known, then released a short huff of breath. How many times had Varian, his *Na'Chi* friend, cautioned him to contain his scent? Their senses were as acute as any *Na'Reish*. He had to be more careful from now on. "You have a school? Here?"

"I suppose it does come as a surprise to you." Nayvia's dark gaze glittered with undisguised amusement. "We have tutors and guilds like the ones you have at Sacred Lake. Potentials are identified and taught to harness their Gifts to benefit the Clan. Human and *Na'Chi* alike."

Arek search the healer's face for any sign of untruth and found none. For the first time he realized her cheek did not bear a slave-tattoo. Lifting a hand, he gently turned her head to one side then the other, looking for it elsewhere.

She cocked an eyebrow at him, then nodded in silent understanding. "You'll find no mark upon me or any other human here." She touched a thin gold band encircling her throat. "You'll see all of us wearing one of these or an armband with a moon inside a sun etched onto them. We honor the Old Ways, but outside these walls, the *Na'Reish* believe they're the mark of Kaal ownership. The absence of slave-tattoos are a deviation excused as one of Imhara's many eccentricities."

The woman spoke of the *Na'Reishi* female with affection in her voice. So had Rassan.

"Are you injured anywhere else?" Nayvia asked. Arek turned and pulled up the back of his shirt. The woman hissed, her fingertips pressing softly against his skin. "I recognize Meelar's handiwork in these lashes."

She set to work spreading *Vaa'jahn* over them.

"You're lucky to have survived his hand." Rassan's voice vibrated with cold anger. "His liking for the whip has taken many lives." Arek glanced over his shoulder and took in the chiseled tightness of the warrior's visage. "One day I shall take great pleasure in wrapping it around his throat and ending his."

Arek raised a brow. "You hold no love for the boat-master?"

The black flecks in Rassan's eyes expanded, almost blotting out the violet as his pale black lips curved into a humorless smile. "None at all."

"Done," Nayvia said.

Arek nodded his thanks.

Rassan gestured to the bedroom door. "Come, it's time you saw Kaal Fortress."

Arek's heart tripped faster as they exited the bedroom. *Watch, listen, use that knowledge to your advantage.* A wry smile twitched on his lips as Yevni's words echoed in his head. Never one to sit back and accept an unfavorable situation, he'd take the training master's advice.

Along the walls of the corridor, huge woven hangings portrayed scenes of *Na'Reish* life: fields being harvested, hunting, daily chores, and leisure sports and pastimes. The colors were faded, and contrary to what he'd expected. Not one picture depicted a battle or war.

"The weavings are some of the oldest within the fortress." Rassan brushed a careful hand over the nearest as they passed. "Keep looking around, Light Blade. Observe. I suspect by the time we reach the library, you'll have many questions." His violet gaze linked with Arek's, level, steady. "Imhara awaits us there. If you can hold on to your anger, she'll provide you with all the answers you seek."

Chapter 9

IMHARA'S pulse quickened with the sound of voices in the corridor outside the library. Her fingers tightened around the clay-fired mug in her hands as she recognized Nayvia's and Rassan's voices. Arek would be with them, although she didn't hear him conversing. From her vantage point at the window, she'd watched the small party of *Na'Chi*, healer, and Light Blade as they'd wandered the bailey, stopping to meet people along the way.

Arek spoke to some of them, but at that distance, she hadn't been able to gauge his facial expression. What had he talked to them about? More importantly, what impressions had he formed?

Would he assume the whole situation an elaborate act staged to deceive him? Heavy cynicism saturated his scent last night, so that train of thought was possible. Or had he been able to see past it and consider the whole situation more objectively?

The nerves in her stomach intensified. In a few seconds she'd find out. *Mother of Light*, she hoped he'd be more receptive to listening to her this morning than he'd been last night.

Reaching for the pot of *k'sa* sitting on the desk, she helped herself to a fresh cup, her fourth for the morning. No longer so piping hot, the creamy liquid poured a little thicker. The nutty aroma and strong flavor steadied her nerves.

As the small group appeared in the doorway to the library, Imhara placed the mug aside and propped her hip against the edge of her desk. Nayvia and Arek were the first to enter, her hand resting on his arm as she limped her way in, a warm smile of greeting on her elderly face. "Blessed morning, Imhara."

"It is, Nayvia," she replied, with an answering curve of her lips. "The *Lady* favors us with fine weather at the end of the season."

"*She* does indeed. Makes up for the blizzards we have in the dead of winter."

Arek stood silently at her side, his twilight blue gaze fixed on her, the weight of it sending a shiver down her back. The scruffy, dirt-stained man from last night was gone, and in his place stood one who'd turn heads at any slave auction. Or any other gathering, if truth be known.

Arek's height matched the *Na'Chi* standing behind him. That put him on eye level with her, too, a pleasant change, considering most humans tended to be shorter than her. While he wasn't as solidly build as Rassan or Barrca, broad shoulders and hard, striated muscle flexed beneath the rolled-up sleeves of his shirt. Dark breeches molded over long legs like a second skin, outlining powerful thighs and calves. Evidence of years of hard work, although on the auction block his physique would have been mistaken for a lifetime spent toiling on a farm, not the battlefield.

A coveted asset, and one enhanced by his striking features, particularly his hair. It was long and loose, falling in waves to just below his shoulders, and not entirely dark blond as she'd first assumed. The morning sunlight highlighted a number of colors: light yellow, red, brown, even a few strands of pale gold.

Between his body, striking features, and incredible hair, Arek was an enticing package. One she couldn't help but admire and appreciate, firstly as a female and then as her persona as *Na* Kaal.

She was doubly glad Rassan had discovered him. Had Arek gone to auction, a slave of his caliber would have been destined for the *Isha*, a private event known only to and frequented by a select number of *Na'Reishi*, those with predilections similar to her alter ego's.

With reputations to protect, private rooms within the venue provided the secrecy guests required. Bidding was done in silence, the transaction completed after the sale. Arek could very well have found himself bought by some *Na'Reishi* to serve as a personal blood-slave.

Or worse.

And having witnessed the darker tastes of those other *Na'Reishi*, Imhara rebelled at the thought of Arek suffering such a fate.

She controlled her shudder and instead tilted her head in greeting. "Arek."

He stiffened at her use of his name. She ignored the bitter odor of mixed emotions that cloaked him. Curiosity, confusion, and wariness, mixed with the deep, familiar scent of hatred.

She waved a hand toward the lounge. "Please, come in and sit. Jaclan would you fetch a fresh pot of *k'sa* and extra mugs?"

"Not for me, thanks, Imhara." Nayvia smiled her apology. "As much as I'd like to, Effina is close to her birthing time and I promised to visit." She gave Arek's arm a squeeze. "I have enjoyed our time together, Light Blade. Be well, everyone."

An awkward silence prevailed once the elderly healer and younger *Na'Chi* left to see to their respective tasks. Arek remained just inside the doorway, Barrca and Rassan flanking him.

Soundlessly, Imhara released a long breath. Arek's refusal to come any closer grated, yet she didn't fault him. Not after what she'd done to him last night. She smoothed her hand over the leather-bound tomes stacked on the desk next to her and worried the worn edge of one with her thumb.

No matter how many times she'd run over this meeting in her mind, the actual reality of facing him was no less daunting. Yet it had to be done.

"I asked Rassan to bring you here so you could read through these," she began.

Sliding the first tome off the stack, she quickly flipped through the first quarter of the book to a page she knew almost by heart. Spinning it around on the desk to face him, she retreated to the other side of the room.

As she'd hoped, Arek ventured to the desk after her withdrawal. Rassan shadowed him, ever mindful of her safety.

"The journal belongs to Rezzen Kaal, my sixth-great-grandsire, and *Na* of this Clan just before the Great War between our races." Imhara hooked her thumb in the pocket on her breeches. "The entry I'd like you to read starts at the top of the page."

For the longest moment, Arek stared at her, his mouth tight, the corners of his eyes crinkling, as if he were about to refuse her request, but then his gaze dropped to the open page. Long fingers ran down the side of the parchment as he read.

His swift intake of breath and sudden slackening expression indicated he'd reached the section she'd waited nearly five years to show the one she hoped would help her take down *Na'Rei* Savyr.

She bit her lip when Arek lifted the tome in both hands and retreated to the lounge, all his concentration focused on the words in front of him. She shared a look with Rassan. The small curve on his lips eased the tension in her body. If the *Na'Chi* warrior responded to Arek's reaction like that, then maybe, just maybe, her great grandsire's words might have broken through the Light Blade's rigid demeanor. She prayed it had.

MOTHER of Light . . .

Arek nearly gave voice to the oath as his fingers tightened on the hard leather cover. His whole body tingled as he flipped to the next page in the journal, unable to stop reading.

It was like he was back in the great library when Kalan had brought Annika to Sacred Lake and asked him to find evidence of the *Na'Chi's* existence. The breath-stealing shock was the same now as it was back then.

Uncovering the personal journal of Irat Zataan, the *Lady's Chosen* at the time of the Great War, had led to the discovery that the *Na'Reish* and human race had once coexisted peacefully side by side. The history-shaking revelation had almost destroyed the Blade Council.

If he'd never read the journal of Zataan or heard his own grandfather admit that the truth had been concealed from the Council for nearly five hundred years, he'd have dismissed what he was reading now—this *Na's* accountings—as a work of pure fiction.

His previous discovery corroborated everything contained on the parchment in front of him. Everything except the shocking snippet of information he'd read three times and still struggled to believe.

His finger shook as he traced beneath the words on the page and spoke them aloud. "'I look forward to tonight, when Leesa becomes my mate and we can celebrate the blood-bond. In time we'll see her Gift mature and grow stronger . . .'"

His mind reeled and he was glad he was sitting down. He licked his lips with a tongue that had gone dry, unsure whether to let loose the wild ripple of laughter building in his chest or roar out his angry frustration. "Was Rezzen's wife human or *Na'Chi*?"

"Human."

His head snapped up. It took several calming breaths before he could speak, and even then his voice was hoarse. "She let him feed from her?"

"She blood-bonded with him. Willingly. The ritual is not the travesty perpetuated by the *Na'Reish* today, nor is it the enthrallment your people suppose it to be."

"And what of withdrawal and the death of the human if the feeding stops?"

"All false. The enhancement weakens when the feeding stops. Death only occurs if a *Na'Reish* overfeeds, which, in this day and age, occurs frequently. Hence the misconception." She came to the edge of the desk, gaze glittering. "Everything you've read about the bonding, the strengthening of Leesa's Gift—back then it was considered a mutually beneficial relationship between our races, a blessing from the *Lady*."

Arek ran a hand through his hair, choking back the instinctive protest in his throat. His stomach churned at the thought of a human voluntarily allowing a *Na'Reish* to feed from him. For too many years, he'd seen comrades die, their lives drained from their bodies as *Na'Reish* warriors fed from them. The demons made no secret of the fact they wanted to enslave or kill every human.

He'd believed the same of Annika and the other *Na'Chi*. Yet he'd been wrong about them. And now he was faced with the possibility that Imhara Kaal wasn't the monster he feared her to be.

He reread the pages of the journal again, wanting to deny the information contained within the ancient script. Like a well-honed blade, each paragraph sliced at and severed the remaining validity of the history he'd grown up with.

Lady's Breath, he felt like a boat left adrift in a summer storm, buffeted by uncertainty, shaken with the anchor of his beliefs ripped from him, and floundering to decipher what truths would guide his course.

He placed the journal on the padded seat next to him. *If* Imhara Kaal was right about the blood-bond, then feeding from him last night would have only enhanced his Light Blade ability to kill, not enslaved him.

Which should he believe—the facts contained within the journal or the ones he'd grown up with? The path *She'd* set him on was a torturous one.

Arek curled his hands into fists. There was only one way to find out.

Chapter 10

AREK launched himself off the lounge, the quick length of his stride covering the distance between them in seconds. He reached out to grab Imhara by the throat, drawing on his Gift as his flesh connected with hers.

The familiar surge of power and intense heat ripped through him, quicker and stronger than anything he'd ever experienced before. His sharp intake of breath echoed hers.

"Don't, Arek!" Rassan's demand had him tightening his grasp.

Gritting his teeth, Arek controlled the fiery rush, more out of shock than in response to Rassan's order. Using his momentum, he drove Imhara backward toward the wall, swinging around at the last moment so his shoulders were flush to the shelf of books, her body acting as a shield against the two advancing *Na'Chi* warriors.

She didn't fight him. Instead she placed her hands on his forearm, more to keep her balance than to pry at his hold. The jolt of awareness that came with her touch ignited hot chills skittering over his body and completely blew his focus.

Or more accurately, refocused his attention on her.

Pressed up against him, Imhara's soft, lean curves and the warmth her skin radiated through two layers of clothes proved hard to ignore.

The sensation transformed into a frisson of heat that slowly wound its way through his gut.

Shock ripped through him. Just the thought of being aroused by her made him want to thrust her away from him. He may have been attracted to her before he knew she was *Na'Reish*, but now he knew better.

She *wasn't* human. Gritting his teeth, he denied the heat leave to move any lower, yet his body and mind betrayed him.

Merciful Mother, there was nowhere to go with the towering bookshelf behind him. Allowing Imhara to pull away and create some space between them would leave him open to an offensive move.

Arek filled his mind with the images of Ostare and the villagers his patrol had found just before his capture. Children and elder-kin, their expressions frozen in the familiar rictus of death, their throats or wrists torn in a savage display of violence, the life-blood drained from their bodies.

Imhara Kaal was no different than the demon warriors who'd murdered those villagers. He wore the mark of her kind on his arm. That and the memories of the dead in Ostare eased the effect but didn't banish the unwelcome reaction.

"Hold!" Imhara's voice, a welcome distraction, focused him on the two approaching warriors. Her hoarse command was reinforced with an upraised hand and pulled both *Na'Chi* up short. Rassan tensed, his shoulders bunching and hands fisting, and for a moment, Arek doubted he'd heed her.

"You can sense just how close I am to releasing my Gift, *Na'Chi*," he warned, voice low.

"You'd be a fool to kill Imhara, Light Blade." Rassan's gaze flashed black.

Arek's own temper flared, fed by self-disgust at the effect her physical presence had on him. "If I'd wanted her dead, she would be."

"Yet you threaten her now." He gestured to the abandoned tome on the seat. "You don't strike me as the sort of warrior who would ignore such compelling evidence."

"He needed proof, Rassan." Imhara Kaal's hoarse response was calm. Still she made no effort to free herself, and that surprised him, especially when she had the skills to fight him. "Has your curiosity been satisfied, Light Blade?"

"Not quite." Arek pointed with his chin. "I want both of you to leave. *Na* Kaal and I have more to discuss."

Nor did he want or need an audience sensing his . . . adverse reactions . . . to their leader. For the moment, they were distracted by their fear for her safety, and he didn't trust his ability to hide his scent from them.

"I won't leave you in here alone with her."

"Rassan." A gentle-spoken word, one layered with tone and purpose. The *Na'Chi* warrior's gaze flickered to the woman in his arms. "I owe him this."

A muscle leapt in his jaw, the black flecks faded to the palest of yellows. "Putting yourself in danger to make up for a mistake isn't worth it. Too many others rely on you."

"We need his help."

She'd risk her life to convince him?

Arek held back a grunt. He couldn't decide if her course of action was courageous or foolish given the threat he'd made last night. There was no way he'd have trusted her had the situation been reversed.

Rassan's twisted mouth reflected his thoughts. By his side, his hands flexed. "Imhara is the only thing standing between us and the other Clans, Light Blade. Every decision she's made, every action she's taken is done to protect all of us—human, *Na'Chi*, and kin." The muscle leapt in his jaw again. "No one faults you for your hatred of the *Na'Reish*, but don't let it blind you to the truths revealed today."

Arek couldn't help but feel grudging respect for the *Na'Chi's* impassioned plea.

"The *Lady* has guided us this far." Beneath his hand, Imhara Kaal's throat flexed as she swallowed. "Let this Journey take us where *She* wills it."

A *Na'Reish* demon acknowledging the *Lady*. Yet another contradiction to add to his confusion.

The *Na'Chi* warrior grimaced, still hesitating.

"Please, Rassan."

For several long heartbeats, Rassan didn't move. Clearly he feared for her safety and disliked leaving him alone with Imhara. Arek grunted silently. Not that long ago he'd been in a similar situation with Kalan and Annika, and back then he'd worried about leaving his friend in a room with a woman he'd believed a threat to his life, too. He didn't begrudge Rassan the allegiance he felt toward his leader.

With a sharp nod to Barrca, the *Na'Chi* pivoted on his boot heel. Arek released a slow breath as they left the room, closing the door behind them.

"So, where do we go from here?" The slight waver in Imhara Kaal's voice filled him with a modicum of satisfaction. "For what it's worth, I'm sorry for what I did to you last night—"

His fingers tightened around her neck. "You fed from me and let me believe in a *lie*," he hissed. He'd laid awake for hours, horrified to think she'd condemned him to live the rest of his life as a blood-slave, but worse was the fact that he'd been helpless, unable to stop her doing what she wanted, and to prevent it from happening. "Why didn't you tell me all this last night?"

"I started to but you weren't willing to listen. You were focused on your hatred and escape." She broke off, her voice husky as she forced it past his grip. "I have no excuse except to tell you I was desperate." Her chin lifted. "I regret the pain my deception caused you, but I won't apologize for doing what I thought was best for all of us."

Brave words and a classic example of the arrogance he'd come to expect of the *Na'Reish*. So terribly similar to his grandfather in that respect, imposing what she felt was right on others. His gut burned.

"That our people once lived together is no surprise to you, is it?" Her soft question jerked his angry thoughts to a halt. "You felt the enhancement in your Gift when you grabbed me. And you know more than you're willing to reveal, otherwise you'd have carried through on your threat from last night. Your scent betrays you."

Arek ground his teeth together and debated whether to answer her or not, tempted to reject her apology outright, but he couldn't ignore her astute assumption nor dismiss the information presented in the journal.

That didn't mean he had to admit to anything out loud. Yet the possibility of everything she'd divulged, everything he'd seen, and everything he already knew culminated in an opportunity as tempting as he'd ever faced.

Savry's death.

So much would be achieved if he believed what Imhara Kaal had revealed. But to trust the word of a demon . . . *Mother of Mercy!*

How would Kalan or Kymora handle this situation? What would they do? Was this a risk worth taking?

"By the *Lady*, if you're lying to me, *Na'Reish*, or if you ever feed from me without my permission again, then nothing . . . *nothing* will stop me from killing you," he vowed, voice as ragged as his uncertainty.

Wondering if he'd regret *his* actions, Arek released Imhara with a shove. She stumbled away from him, caught the edge of the desk, and leaned on it, head bowed, sucking in deep breaths.

Fool! The Na'Reish *destroyed our lives! They can never be trusted!*

With his grandfather's voice ringing in his ears, Arek strode away from Imhara toward the fireplace. Regret soured the back of his mouth as every fiber of his being twisted at giving up the advantage.

Across the distance separating them, he stared at her and she him.

Arek wondered if his face was as ashen and tense as hers. *Lady* knew his innards still quivered like her voice from a moment ago.

"Thank you." She rubbed at the red marks his fingers had left on her throat but made no complaint about them. "For my life and for listening."

"I'm not doing this for you, *Na'Reish.* I don't trust you—" She grimaced. Lips thinning, he folded his arms and kept his voice hard. "But the journal entries compel me to keep an open mind."

The only explanation he was willing to give.

She accepted with a nod, some of the tension in her expression easing. "Fair enough."

"I want to finish reading those journals."

"Of course. There are others written by my ancestors following the Great War, but I don't keep them here in the library." He raised a brow. "Other *Na'Reish* visit this fortress on occasion. I would not have them discovered by chance."

Her logic made sense.

Imhara retreated to the other side of her desk and sat in the chair, her expression turning pensive. After a moment, her head lifted. "Arek, about the role I need you to undertake . . ."

"You want me to approach the Blade Council on your behalf. I remember."

Convincing the Blade Council and his people to accept the *Na'Chi* had been hard enough. Given their turbulent history, allying with a *Na'Reish* Clan didn't seem possible. But then, he'd believed the same when Kalan had suggested an alliance with Annika and the other *Na'Chi.*

No use worrying about that yet though. There was no way he was escorting her one foot closer to human territory, not until he was absolutely sure she posed no threat to them.

"Approaching your leader is only part of what I need you to do."

She took a steadying breath and met his gaze. "I want you to come with me when I travel to the Enclave."

Head into the *Na'Rei's* stronghold? The heart of demon territory? Arek frowned. "Why?"

"No one will suspect a Light Blade warrior as a slave."

He fisted his hands at the idea of being her slave, but the tactical advantage of her suggestion wasn't lost on him.

"You're expecting me to use my Gift?"

"Only as a last resort."

From beyond the closed doors, loud voices drew their attention. An urgent knock followed. "Imhara!"

She glanced to him. "Rassan wouldn't disturb us unnecessarily." Arek nodded. She raised her voice. "Come in!"

The door swung open. The *Na'Chi* warrior entered, his expression grim. The hand gripping the edge of the door was white-knuckled. His gaze darted between them, relief flashing across his face, his gaze lingering on Imhara as if assuring himself she was unharmed.

Imhara rose from her seat. "What's wrong?"

"Urkan Yur approaches our gates." The flecks in his eyes were pure black. "He arrives in a quarter hour."

Imhara's stiffening stance indicated trouble. Her heated curse confirmed it.

Arek glanced between the two. "Who's Urkan Yur?"

"He's Savyr's Second in Command." Rassan's deep voice vibrated with tension. "A *Na'Reishi* Lordling who rose through the ranks with Savyr during the reign of the previous *Na'Rei*, and the only warrior he trusts to lead his Clan *Na'Hord*."

Imhara's gaze slashed to him, the purple pigment within flashing bright. Her lips curled back from her teeth in a silent snarl. "He's also the black-scale winder who murdered my family."

Chapter 11

"THE workers outside the wall need to be warned."

Gone was the glacial fury within Imhara's gaze, replaced in a heartbeat by concern. Arek blinked. Her control and skill in focusing her moods continued to surprise him.

"Barrca's already seeing to it." Rassan scooped up the journals from her work desk. "And I've sent the messenger to alert those within the fortress."

Arek cocked his head to one side. "Why warn the workers?"

"Some of them are *Na'Chi*." Imhara rounded the end of her desk. "There are a handful like Barrca and Rassan who can pass as *Na'Reish*, but most can't risk being discovered." Her black lips pressed flat. "Yur is a purist."

"The *Na'Rei's* Second advocates bloodline purity?" Arek snorted. "Savyr's *Na'Chi* daughter must have put a strain on their relationship."

"You know about Annika?" Imhara shared a look of surprise with Rassan.

Arek cursed his thoughtless response. Just because he'd agreed to listen to her, it was no excuse to become complacent.

"It's good to hear Annika lives. I only met her a few times, but she showed such strength and courage, considering the life she endured at the Gannec fortress." A small smile curved her lips. "Savyr claimed a Light Blade warrior killed her, an elderly healer, and two guards. At the time I thought it odd he'd admit to a prisoner escaping from his fortress, but if you know about her, then she and the Light Blade made it over the border. It also explains why Savyr tried to cover it up. Better to endure a little embarrassment than a loss of face."

The distant ringing of a bell made Arek glance at the window.

"The watchtower has spotted Yur's *Na'Hord,*" Rassan explained. "They've reached the fields. They'll be at our gates in minutes."

"Store the journals, then see Arek safely to the hidden room with the others." Imhara began closing ledgers and placing papers into the draws of her desk.

"I'd rather he stayed here with you."

She shook her head. "I won't risk his safety."

Blackness darkened Rassan's gaze. "Yet you'll compromise your own." He held up a hand as she took a breath to protest. "Yur will dismiss a slave as a threat."

"Arek's had no preparation—"

"He spent a week travelling with Meelar."

"Not good enough."

"Imhara—"

Her sharp gesture cut him off. "No, Rassan."

"You'd let pride take precedence over logic?" he challenged. "Risk the opportunity of taking Savyr down?"

"Pride?" Imhara's eyes slitted. "This has nothing to do with pride." Arek tensed as she stabbed a finger in his direction. "Exposing him to Yur is too great a risk."

She closed the distance between them in half a dozen strides, stopping close enough so that Arek could see the deep purple striations in the iris of her eyes. Near enough to feel her body heat.

Her hand pressed against his abdomen, fingers spreading wide. Arek sucked in a shocked breath at her bold move. He almost backed away when he saw the corners of her mouth twitch. Stubbornly, he held his ground.

"Lower your gaze, *slave*." The condescending tone had him clenching his jaw. She slid her hand over his ribs as she moved behind him. Every muscle locked tight at the heated slide of her hand touching him. "Unless invited, a slave never meets a *Na'Reish* eye to eye, no matter their rank. And your hesitation to comply with my order would be viewed as defiance. Both offenses invite punishment."

A hard kick to the back of his legs sent him to his knees on the floor. She fisted a handful of his hair and jerked his head back. Training took over. He reached up to lock his fingers around her wrist. Swiveling on his knee, he twisted her arm and broke her hold. Using the momentum of his turn, he pushed her away from him, then surged to his feet.

Imhara backed off and raised her hands, the gesture a cessation of aggression.

"That is why I hesitate to agree to your request, Rassan. Not pride." Her attention switched to him. "Arek, every second Yur is in the room with us, you're going to be fighting your instincts. He'll scent your hatred, your reluctance to follow orders, and he'll enjoy provoking you until you respond. Unless you're defending your master, laying your hand on me or any other *Na'Reish* could result in your death. Give Yur an excuse to demand punishment, and you put me in the position of having to follow through. I won't put you in harm's way."

Arek met Rassan's gaze, not bothering to hide his surprise at Imhara's comment, unsure if he was disappointed or pleased he'd failed her test.

Shouts came from outside the window.

"Yur's here." Her expression twisted into a grimace, like she'd tasted something unpleasant. Tension tightened her voice. "Go now, both of you."

Rassan inclined his head. "I'll arrange for refreshments to be delivered once Yur is escorted here."

Arek followed him from the library, wondering at the warrior's compliance. Had that been Kalan, he'd never have given in, no matter how sound his argument. Plans were altered or adapted, not discarded when a leader's safety was threatened.

For several minutes they walked the corridor in silence. After descending a flight of stairs, the murmurs of voices and the odors of freshly baked bread and roasting meat filled the air.

A wide archway at the end of the corridor opened into a large kitchen. A dozen people scurried around the room. Several workers looked up at their appearance; all smiled and called a greeting to Rassan that he returned.

Some were sitting on stools near large tubs of water, cleaning and peeling vegetables. Two youths stood to either side of the great fireplace, tending a spit and several huge pots with steam rising from them. One of them brought a stack of pans to a woman making dough on the benches along one wall. Two more sliced loaves of bread at the far end. They threw the pieces into giant baskets near their feet.

Organized chaos.

Rassan called a couple of the workers over. After handing over the journals to the younger of the two and asking her to deliver them to Imhara's room, he asked for a fresh pot of *k'sa*. The second woman hurried off to complete the request.

Arek asked the question he'd been holding on to since leaving the library. "Is Yur likely to make an attempt on her life?"

That earned him a sideways look. "If he saw an opportunity to kill Imhara, he'd take it." The low pitch of his voice vibrated with controlled anger. "He's tried it before, although we've never been able to link any attempt back to him. He's too careful."

Arek nodded. "And with no heir, Savyr will appoint a successor to this Clan."

"Yes." One word, so heavy laden with emotion.

The *Na'Rei* would get what he desired—Kaal territory and easy access into human territory. Even with the Sacred Lake *Na'Chi* joining the ranks of the Light Blades, they would be grossly outnumbered if all the Clan *Na'Hord's* combined.

Separate outcomes neither of them wanted. Inwardly Arek smiled wryly. Who'd have thought he'd share a common goal with a *Na'Reish* Clan leader? What an ironic twist in an already complicated situation.

"Then why did you let her dismiss you?" he asked.

"Arguing with Imhara when she's set on a decision is a waste of breath. It's better just to act."

Arek frowned, confused. "How is retreating and leaving her to meet Yur alone taking action?"

"Imhara was right. A moment ago you weren't ready to be her slave." His dark gaze pinned him where he stood. "Tradition demands that Yur be extended the courtesy of this House. A human posing as a slave will deliver refreshments to them."

Rassan's meaning became clear.

"And you want that slave to be me?" Arek grunted. "But you just said I wasn't ready."

"She needs protection and you're the only one able to do it without arousing suspicion." Rassan's regard never wavered. "Thanks to Imhara's impromptu lesson, you now know what to expect. Her name and reputation will protect you. Just don't give Yur any reason to take advantage of you."

There was one major flaw in his plan.

"I can't mask my scent."

"A certain amount of hatred or reluctance is acceptable. Expected. But you must follow the orders given to you. Imhara will guide you and dismiss any small mistakes you make as a new slave learning his role."

Considering twenty minutes ago he'd threatened to kill Imhara, the *Na'Chi* warrior was placing a huge amount of trust in him. He couldn't fathom why, but one thing was obvious. Rassan's confidence in her was absolute. But to follow her lead, to trust her . . . *Mother of Mercy.*

Arek's innards twisted. "Won't she be angry you've gone against her orders?"

"Perhaps. That's something I'll deal with later." Rassan shrugged. "But there's nothing she can do once you go into that room."

"She could order me to leave."

"Serving is a slave's task. To make another take your place would draw Yur's attention. She won't do that." Rassan reached out to grasp his shoulder. "Protecting Imhara benefits both of us, Light Blade." Had the *Na'Chi* scented his doubt? Rassan's eyes glittered in challenge. "The question is now, are you willing to do it?"

"A warrior never loses sight of his target." Yevni's instruction from his early days as a trainee Blade. Yur was just a hurdle in the overall plan. Savyr should be his focus, Imhara the means he'd use to get to the demon leader.

"So, I address Imhara as *Na* but what's Yur's title?"

Rassan's lips curled into a fierce grin. "*Na'Reishi* or Second." He stepped inside the kitchen to intercept one of the men working there. After a moment, he turned and tossed something gold and shiny toward him. Arek caught it. Cold metal filled his palm. "Take off your shirt and put it on."

"Only one?" He nodded in the direction of one of the men in the kitchen. "He wears two."

"Two indicates he's joined. Mated." Rassan gave a brief smile. "An Old Ways tradition honored by some in our Clan."

Arek grunted. A swift glance at the borrowed armband showed the same interlocking sun and moon design as the one Nayvia had worn around her neck. The Kaal used jewelry to commemorate a past way of life, but it still felt like a mark of ownership.

The reluctance churning in Arek's gut only reinforced that impression. He shoved it aside and pointed his chin at the male kitchen workers. "They get to keep their shirts on."

"They're not Imhara's newest pet." Arek squeezed the armband until the metal bit into his fingers. The *Na'Chi* warrior folded his arms. "You play a role, Arek. If you can't accept that or don't think you can follow Imhara's lead, then we end this right now."

Lady help him. He needed to adapt. Fast. Was this how Kalan felt all those months ago when he'd met Annika in the *Na'Rei's* dungeon? How had he known when to trust her? At what point had he chosen to see her as something other than as his enemy?

Arek rotated the band around his fingers. If the truth were known, he felt more comfortable trusting Rassan than Imhara, despite knowing his allegiance lay with her. As convoluted as that seemed, perhaps it could be a start.

If Kymora knew of the situation he faced now, she'd deem it *Her* divine will. As the *Temple Elect* and his friend, she'd insist he embrace it. As much as instinct rebelled at the idea, the only way to regain some control of his journey was to walk *Her* path.

Lady's Breath, it was better than stumbling blindly.

Arek took a deep breath. "I'll do it." The decision to act settled his reservations to the back of his mind.

"Your word, Light Blade." At his raised eyebrow, Rassan's gaze took on a harder glint. "You might not trust her, but you don't understand everything yet, and there's too much at stake. If you endanger her, you endanger hundreds of lives within this Clan. I'd have you swear you'll play this role without jeopardizing Imhara."

"I said I'd do it."

"And I trusted you before, yet you threatened her and took her hostage." Rassan's gaze never wavered. "Give me your promise."

He couldn't fault Rassan for the loss of trust between them. "I swear it by the *Lady*."

The warrior stared at him for several long moments, then nodded slowly. "All right then. While custom dictates Imhara refrain from certain behaviors out in *Na'Reish* society, within these walls, and regardless of the rank of her visitors, she likes to flaunt her . . . lifestyle. Don't be surprised by anything she does."

"That's not reassuring, *Na'Chi*." Arek pulled off his shirt, handed it over, then pushed the band onto his bicep. "You realize Yur won't approve."

Pressing the edges closed, he glanced up when the warrior didn't respond. Rassan's grin had turned wicked.

Arek grunted. "You want him distracted."

"Exactly."

The kitchen help returned bearing a tray with a pot and two cups. Arek took the tray from her as Rassan nodded his thanks. In the few minutes it took them to return to the corridor outside the library, Arek prepared himself for the task ahead. Muffled voices came from within. One male. One female.

Rassan caught his arm just before he reached up to knock on the closed door. "Don't give Yur your back."

"Why? Will he attack me?"

"His hatred for humans mirrors yours for the *Na'Reish*. Don't give him the chance." Violet eyes met his. "*Lady* guide and protect you both."

Arek gave a nod and knocked.

"Come in!" Imhara's voice called from within.

Taking a deep breath, Arek planted his palm on the wood and pushed, aware of the irony of the situation he now found himself in. His grandfather would keel over in a fit to see him cooperating with a *Na'Reish* demon. Those he'd trained with in the Light Blade compound would have trouble believing it, too.

He pushed the thoughts aside. If he was going to pull off this farce, then he needed to take on the challenge of being Imhara's slave. *Merciful Mother*, a *Na'Reish* slave. His gut churned.

Arek tightened his grip on the tray. He'd never backed down from a challenge and he wasn't about to start now.

Gaze fixed on the pot of *k'sa*, he stepped into the library.

Chapter 12

WHEN the door to the library opened, Imhara ignored whoever entered, preferring to keep her gaze on Urkan Yur as he made himself at home on the lounge. Reclined in a relaxed pose, he seemed far too comfortable for her liking.

From the moment she'd first laid eyes on him, she'd fought to keep her features in a suitably neutral expression. Just the way he gazed around the room, taking in the shelves, the wall hangings, the furniture, his expression assessing, too interested, made her pulse pound.

Yur wore his hair out, although two braids tied back kept the black strands from his face. The style accentuated his angular features, and with a faint smile curving his black lips, he portrayed a geniality she knew deceived many. Few looked past the broad forehead, high cheekbones, and square jaw, his dark skin markings and unscarred face.

It amazed Imhara that others could admire his handsomeness and overlook that it covered a soul so cunning and evil. Just the sight of him, dressed in his customary hard leather armor and warrior garb black as the heart that beat within his chest, aroused the familiar burn of rage and grief.

The *Na'Reishi* warrior had murdered her parents and siblings. She might not have seen him wield the curved blade sheathed at his side, but the dark, musky odor surrounding him was the same one she'd scented on the bodies of her kin that fateful night five years ago.

Seated behind her desk, she used the barrier to help control her seething anger. While an attack might satisfy her need for blood vengeance, Yur's death would accomplish nothing. Yet.

"The purpose for my visit is explained in the *Na'Rei's* missive."

His tone gravel-deep, Yur's drawled statement rasped across Imhara's nerves yet also reminded her of the folded parchment clutched in her hand. The one he'd handed over during their oh-so-polite opening greetings.

The Gannec Clan symbol was intact on the seal. She broke the wax with a flick of her thumbnail and scanned the brief message.

"The Enclave has been moved forward two weeks?" she asked, arching her eyebrows. "Why?"

"The *Na'Rei* wishes to finalize arrangements for your mating ceremony before the Enclave."

She glanced up sharply. "My what?"

Was Savyr's intention to mate her common knowledge?

"Your mating ceremony." The gleam in Yur's purple gaze brightened. "Petitions have been submitted."

A shiver prickled the skin across her back. Her worst nightmare would be made real if she were mated to a male who cared for little other than the title of Clan *Na* and the power of leadership. Her parents had shared a rare partnership. One she dreamed of finding for herself—someday—but not if she was forced to accept a mate of Savyr's choosing.

Fear spurted through her veins before she could stop the sensation. She clamped down on it before her scent betrayed her. Yur would hone in on it like a *Vorc* scenting blood and relish in the knowledge of having unsettled her.

"Without consulting me?" She only just managed to keep panic from her voice.

Who had approached Savyr? They had to have his approval, a loyal lap-*Vorc*, or the *Na'Rei* would never have accepted any petition.

"It's been five years, *Na* Kaal. More than enough time to find a worthy male." She ground her teeth together at the unsubtle reminder. "You're a desirable female with strong bloodlines, so it's not a lack of interest from suitors. Yet you've rejected every *Na'Reishi* lord who's approached you." His gaze glittered, and locked with hers. "Patience has worn thin."

His hardening tone and direct statement confirmed that the process was a mere formality. Savyr had already proven the lengths he'd go to possess Kaal territory. Ordering her compliance shouldn't come as a surprise. So what if the Enclave would serve to announce and validate her mated status? The decision didn't change her original plans.

"The earlier date also allows him to host a Clan Challenge to celebrate your upcoming mating ceremony." Yur's mouth curved upward. "He invites you to officiate the formal events with him."

A frisson of unease scraped along her spine. She hadn't anticipated something like this. Something so *public*.

Presiding over the contests with Savyr would give others the impression she welcomed the mating. Yet to refuse would draw the *Na'Rei's* wrath down upon her sooner.

"There will also be an after-games banquet, the *Na'Rei's* gift to you and your future mate." Yur waited, watching her from beneath his hooded gaze.

The image of a ground-scurrier trapped by the glinting gaze of a scale-winder flitted through her mind. Even though she knew the day would come, her skin still chilled and goose bumped. Instead of heeding the instinct to flee, just as the small animal would, it was time to stare the predator down.

Gently, Imhara placed the missive on her desk. She drew in a slow, even breath to ease the heat of temper in her veins and to calm the fingers of fear squeezing her heart. Yur's scent reeked with woodsy anticipation, and the way he propped his arm along the back of the lounge, his long fingers stroking the nap of the fabric, only reinforced that impression.

"The *Na'Rei* honors my House." The words tasted like funeral ash in her mouth.

"Indeed." The smug smile widened until she could see the tips of his pointed teeth. "Will Rassan be accompanying you to this Enclave?"

"Of course."

She almost missed the stirring deep within his gaze. The skin on the nape of her neck prickled.

"Then I look forward to seeing your Second defend his title at the games."

Was he disappointed Rassan was attending or did he want him there? And if so, why? She made a note to warn her friend of Yur's interest. Nothing good would come of it, whatever the reason.

Movement near the door and a throat being cleared interrupted them. Imhara looked over, surprised she'd forgotten about the third presence in the room. Shock washed through her at the sight of Arek standing there holding a tray, but more pertinently, his state of undress and bowed head.

"What are you doing here?" Her question came out sharper than planned.

She sensed Rassan's hand in this. What had possessed him to ignore her order, especially when Arek had proven he wasn't ready to take on the role of her slave? Yet there the Light Blade stood, gaze lowered, stance submissive.

Clean and clothed, he caught her eye. Now she couldn't look away, not even to gauge Yur's reaction to his presence. The morning sunlight angling in from the windows caught the dips and hollows of his body, outlining every smooth line and the heavy curve of muscle along his bare shoulders and chest. Her gaze followed the fine dusting of blond hair as it arrowed down his ridged abdomen then disappeared beneath the waistband of his breeches.

Merciful Mother . . . the hours . . . no, years of training that had to have gone into developing that physique . . . Imhara leaned back in her chair, resisting the urge to rise and run her hands over him, to test the strength contained in his arms, the width of his chest, the lean flex of his waist. Instead she clasped her hands in her lap, more than a little astonished at the strength of her reaction to him.

It wasn't as if she hadn't seen plenty of naked male flesh—human, *Na'Chi*, or *Na'Reish*—in her role as *Na* Kaal and on the practice field, but her observations had been more aloof than covetous. The former reaction proved impossible to claim now, especially given the intensity of the heat warming her from the inside out.

Despite her surprise she recognized the feeling prickling beneath her skin. Sexual attraction. Lust. Desire. A combination of all three. Again she had to restrain herself from smiling. Pity neither warrior in the room would appreciate her . . . interest.

"You sent for refreshments, *Na* Kaal." Arek's tone was quiet, respectful. He neither looked up nor ventured farther into the room, waiting for her permission to approach.

Calm. Composed. Compliant.

"So I did." Imhara blinked with the reminder. She hoped Arek knew what he was doing, for he'd committed them both to their roles now. "Approach and serve us."

She caught the slight tightening of his jaw as he made his way over to her desk. Ahh, not so controlled after all. She swallowed another smile. Instead she tested his scent as he drew closer. Heat, warm spice, a trace of trepidation, but he controlled his darker emotions. He placed the tray on the desk, then hesitated, his scent deepening to an acrid mixture of tension and uncertainty.

"Pour the *k'sa*." Imhara glanced to Yur. "A cup, Second?" The warrior nodded. "Take one to him."

Gold flashed on Arek's arm as he complied with her order. The sight of the armband wrapped around his bicep sent a surge of satisfaction through her. Though she knew he'd donned it to play his part, it looked good on him, but the desire to see him wear it voluntarily and truly belong to the House of Kaal was strong enough to leave an ache in her chest, one she couldn't suppress, and one she dared not examine too closely.

Arek passed in front of her desk, tray in hand, to offer the cups to Savyr's Second. Straightening in his seat, Yur's gaze raked over the Light Blade then narrowed, his lip curling. His hand dropped to his belt, forearm brushing the hilt of his weapon.

The posture and bitter scent flooding the air brought Imhara out of her chair, her own hand straying to the dagger at the side of her belt. Reassured by the cool touch of it, she came around the end of her desk, drawing Yur's attention away from Arek. His curled lip morphed into a malevolent smile, as if he'd guessed her concern for Arek's safety. He helped himself to the *k'sa*, then dismissed the human with a grunt.

Imhara placed a hand in the middle of Arek's back, stalling his retreat. He stiffened at her touch but didn't pull away.

Reaching around to take the remaining cup from the tray, she raised her cup. "To fine weather for the Clan Challenge."

Yur lifted his in agreement. "May the strength of our champions endure the length of the games."

The warrior tilted his head back to drain the cup and seal the toast. Imhara swallowed the contents of her cup, then retreated to the table, placing the cup on the edge of it.

"So, Second, will the *Na'Reishi* lords who petitioned the *Na'Rei* be presented to me, or am I to remain ignorant of their identities until the decision is made?" she asked, relieved to hear her voice remained steady, and squared her shoulders to face Yur again.

He made her wait for his answer as Arek refilled his cup. "You'll have the chance to meet them prior to the Enclave."

"No names until then?" At Yur's shake of the head, she feigned disappointment. "How many petitioned the *Na'Rei*?"

"Three. All *Na'Reishi* of standing and rank. Warriors in their prime." Again his tone indicated he took pleasure in imparting that piece of information.

Two could play at that.

"I'd expect nothing less," she retorted, and waved Arek back to her side, gesturing to her cup. Silently he filled it again. She shot him a sideways glance as the nutty odor of *k'sa* wafted through the air. "While impressive, a male's standing and rank holds little attraction if he can't fulfill his obligations as my mate."

Mother of Light, she hoped Arek was ready to play his role. She moved closer to him.

"I prefer a male with stamina and virility." She trailed her fingertips across Arek's broad shoulders. There was little give in the flesh beneath them. A pale scar stretched from his right shoulder to the middle of his back amidst fresh lash marks. A blade had created the raised ridge. During training or while on patrol? "I've grown accustomed to a certain standard. I'm afraid an older warrior might have trouble meeting my expectations."

It was gratifying to see Yur's posture stiffen. Had he forgotten she was nothing like the other *Na'Reishi* women? How typical of him to think she'd quietly accept a mating ceremony. One that would never eventuate.

"My forwardness upsets you"—she shrugged, a half-assed apology considering she had trouble containing a smile—"but my potential mate needs to know that I'm a woman of particular tastes."

She wrapped her fingers around Arek's arm, just beneath the armband, the sleek warmth of his skin as pleasing as the fine dusting of hair covering it. Brushing her cheek against his bicep, she inhaled deeply, drawing his clean, earthy scent in to her lungs. A welcome respite from Yur's heavy musk.

"Tastes I enjoy indulging in. Frequently." Imhara slid her fingers over the wide curve of Arek's chest, enjoying the latent strength contained in his hard flesh, then traced the hollow dip of his collarbone. "As this human would know. Isn't that right, slave?"

Beneath the tanned column of Arek's throat, the rhythm of his pulse was fast. Pressing her hand flat to his chest, she could feel the heavy pounding of his heart.

When Arek didn't answer immediately, she scraped her nails down the smooth slopes of his chest and ridged abdomen. His stomach sucked inward and goose bumps prickled his flesh. She hooked her fingers in the waistband of his breeches. "Answer me."

"Yes, *Na* Kaal." That came from between clenched teeth.

Perfect.

Yur issued a deep-throated sound of disgust. While the inference drawn would be based on a lie, *Lady* forgive them, she didn't care as long as he believed.

Laughing softly, she pressed her lips in an openmouthed kiss to the warm flesh of Arek's shoulder, just above the armband. Salt and heat coated her tongue. He issued a startled gasp, his whole body going rigid as her tongue swirled over the faint ridge of a vein beneath his skin.

She peered up at him, unsurprised to see his blue gaze storm-dark, his expression pulled so tight the lines around his eyes and lips were white. Yet while he clearly resented her actions, what intrigued her was the heavy, spicy odor rising from his skin.

Arousal.

She'd witnessed enough sexual encounters to recognize the scent. A small kernel of excitement tempered with caution stirred within her. She hadn't anticipated that, and gauging by the tension radiating from Arek, neither had he. Scenting anything from him other than hostility and hatred was a major breakthrough. His response might have been unexpected, but the possibility of it not being so was . . . stimulating.

A need long denied accentuated the hollow ache in her chest. This time Imhara couldn't ignore it. For far too long, she'd denied herself the simple pleasure of enjoying a lover, the demands of protecting her Clan the convenient excuse; an excuse that wore parchment thin when weariness cloaked her with its suffocating weight.

But maintaining a working relationship with a lover had proven difficult in previous liaisons, and while she'd never favored one warrior above another, it'd created tension among the ranks of her *Na'Hord*, so she'd put aside the need. Destiny didn't favor such a journey for her.

How she wished the circumstances were different so she could explore Arek's reaction though. She dismissed the thought as quickly as it formed, calling herself a fool for even imagining something could come of their mutual arousal. Arek would never welcome any sort of intimacy with her.

For the briefest moment, their gazes connected. His jaw flexed hard, then he looked away, color staining his cheeks, but he didn't move away from her touch as she expected. He held his position, every muscle quivering with the effort.

She bit her lip, regretting that she'd drawn that response from him when he'd not intended it. On her next breath, the scent vanished. She blinked. No scent could disperse so quickly, unless Arek had suppressed his reaction. She tested the air again.

Nothing. His willpower impressed her, and left her breathless. Ironically, this time she was turned on by his show of determination and control. For now though, as tempting as it was to reflect on her response to him, her attention needed to be on Yur.

The Second's expression was blacker than Arek's, and darkness glittered in the depths of his gaze. Pulling the tail of an already provoked *Vorc* ensured retaliation. Yur was twice as dangerous and she needed her wits about her.

"I intend to continue satiating my needs, whether my mate approves or not." Imhara pinned the *Na'Reishi* warrior with her gaze. Her tone hardened. "For him to assume I'll conform to his wishes will only lead to disappointment."

The *Na'Reishi* warrior surged to his feet, his fingers gripping the hilt of his sword. A heavy charred odor assaulted her nostrils. She inched her own hand closer to her weapon, astonished yet deeply satisfied that she'd managed to get such a reaction from him so quickly.

Would he draw on her?

Chapter 13

AREK cursed under his breath as the *Na'Reish* warrior rose from the lounge. As shocked and angry as he was by Imhara's little demonstration and the effect she'd had on him, her blatant exhibition of sexual preferences enraged Savyr's Second. The scowl on his broad face was a cross between disgust and fury, as if he couldn't believe what he was hearing.

Arek placed the pot and tray down on the table. If a confrontation was coming, he wanted his hands free. Yur would have been an intimidating figure had he not faced other *Na'Reish* demons on the battlefield before. Seven feet of brawn and heavy muscle, hostility oozed from his solid-boned frame. One large hand gripped his sword so tightly every knuckle flushed white.

Listening to them spar verbally, subtle barbs and threats cloaked in civility, each word uttered with veiled politeness, Arek had been reminded of the previous Blade Council, the one his grandfather had corrupted.

Sourness coated the back of his throat. Political maneuverings for power and leverage had never interested him. Yet he understood Imhara's need to take the offensive. From what he knew about the demon culture, rank gave a female certain privileges, but power was wielded by and reserved for males alone.

In such a world, a woman as strong and willful as Imhara would threaten any male used to dominating those weaker than themselves. For a *Na'Reishi* male, putting her in her place was as second nature as breathing.

The underhanded arrogance of threatening her with a mate lent credence to her claim that this warrior had murdered her family at Savyr's behest. And while Imhara's tactics sparked Arek's anger, he'd walked into the role willingly. Honor demanded he carry through on the task he'd begun. He just wished he knew Imhara's purpose for provoking Yur.

Slowly he widened his stance, inching one leg in front of hers so that his side offered her partial protection should Yur attack. Her fingers tightened around his bicep. Twice. He froze.

"I'd rethink your personal habits, *Na* Kaal." Yur's deep voice dropped another notch, his words deceptively soft. "You'll find none of the *Na'Reishi* will favor, nor tolerate, such behavior in their mate."

She took a step closer to Yur, within arm's reach of the demon. Only an idiot or someone secure in her abilities would get that close to an enraged warrior. Arek doubted she was a fool.

"Tolerate? Favor?" The words hissed from her lips. "There are plenty of *Na'Reishi* males out there who bed humans, yet I don't see them being asked to change their behavior. If these warriors don't *favor* my lifestyle, Second, then they can always withdraw their petition."

Yur's hand arced up. His palm connected with Imhara's cheek in a sharp slap that knocked her backward. Arek caught her as she stumbled. Teeth bared, Yur kicked out with his boot.

Arek jerked her out of range. The strike caught his hip and propelled him into the frame of the desk. Pain shot through his leg. It buckled and sent him to his knees.

"Stay down, slave." An order. One expected to be obeyed.

Yur seized the front of Imhara's shirt and forced her back toward the wall. Gritting his teeth, Arek climbed to his feet. Yur slammed Imhara against the bookshelf. Several tomes tumbled to the floor.

"You will learn your place!" He raised a clenched fist.

"Get your hands off me." Imhara's order was colder than an arctic blizzard. A flash of silver arced between the demon's black leather-clad legs and pressed hard up against his crotch.

The dagger from her belt.

Yur stilled.

The *Na'Reishi* warrior held her trapped against the wall. His larger, stronger physique gave him a clear advantage, yet nothing in her stance suggested she felt intimidated by him.

Arek pushed away from the table, her courage and skill impressing him. She could definitely take care of herself, but he took another step toward her anyway.

"Hold, slave." While her order was directed at him, her gaze remained on Yur.

The tip of her blade angled upward, bit into the leather of the *Na'Reishi's* breeches and the most sensitive part of his body. Breath hissed in through Yur's teeth.

"Some might regret my making you a eunuch, Yur." Her tone implied she wouldn't. "Release me. Now!"

Yur's fist lowered. "Some males like their mates spirited, but none will allow such disrespect, *Na* Kaal." His black lips peeled back in an ugly smile. "When Savyr reveals his choice of mate, I'll look forward to seeing you tamed."

He freed her then stepped away, ignoring the dagger she kept level with his groin.

"You've delivered the *Na'Rei's* message. Inform him I'll adjust my itinerary." Imhara flicked the blade in the direction of the door. "You and your *Na'Hord* are no longer welcome within my House. You can leave now."

The look Yur leveled at Imhara promised retribution. In true arrogant *Na'Reishi* fashion, he gave her his back as he strode for the door. The thud of it slamming against the wall as it was flung open was loud in the prevailing silence.

Yur's boot steps echoed along the corridor in a rapid, angry tattoo. Rassan stepped through the open doorway, hand resting close to his weapon.

His gaze swept over both of them, then lingered on the blade still clenched in Imhara's hand. "Everything all right?"

"Yur's not staying." Her curt tone drew a raised eyebrow from her Second, but he made no comment. "See that he leaves the fortress."

Rassan gave a nod and drew the door closed behind him as he left to carry out her request. Arek drew in a deep breath and dared to relax.

He glanced to her. Imhara's swift actions had diverted what could have been a disastrous confrontation. Violet eyes met his. Fury mixed with relief swirled in their depths. One heartbeat, and another, then her shaky sigh broke the silence between them.

"Are you all right?" She nodded at his leg. "His boot isn't small or soft."

"The bastard kicks like a war-beast but I'll live." Peering at her face, Arek limped across the distance between them. "What about you? He struck you, too."

"Nothing I haven't experienced during training." She shrugged off his question, so he reached for her chin and tilted her head to one side. The dark coloring on her jaw wasn't just her *Na'Reish* markings. He smoothed a thumb over the swollen flesh, his mouth tightened at the bruise already decorating her skin.

"Yur attacked you." He dropped his hand to his side. No female deserved such treatment. "Why didn't you drive that blade home when you had the chance?"

Imhara slid the dagger in question into her belt. "As tempted as I was, that wasn't my intention."

"You were goading him?" Arek shook his head, then grunted. "You *want* Yur to report your behavior to Savyr."

"He can't do that if he's dead." She gave him a grim smile. "And if he's dead, I won't get near Savyr come the Enclave."

"You're ensuring an audience with Savyr. There's no way either of them will let this incident go without calling you to task."

"Exactly." This time her smile was genuine. "And Savyr will call me into his chambers, where he can control the situation, giving me the perfect opportunity to carry through on my plan."

"Devious and good with a blade." His own mouth curved upward.

"Devious?" One dark eyebrow arched, even though her tone remained amused. "I prefer to call it determined, Light Blade." Again her gaze met his, and this time warmth and something else he couldn't identify swirled in the violet depths. "I know Rassan pushed you into playing the role of a slave. Even though you don't trust me, you did it anyway. Thank you."

Arek nodded. Imhara might have lied to him the night before, but Yur's agenda and recent behavior only reinforced her truths. The whole situation left him feeling . . . uncertain, an unwanted yet all too familiar feeling in recent months.

"So, what happens now?" he asked.

Her smile faded and a frown replaced it. "With the Enclave moved forward, we'll leave for Gannec Clan territory at the end of the week. With our caravan of wagons and beasts, it'll take us a few days to traverse the mountains and Skadda Pass. When we reach the other side, we'll be in Gannec territory. Another day, maybe two, should see us through the forest. Then we'll set up our campsite just outside Savyr's fortress alongside the other Clans." She grimaced. "Not ideal. I would have liked the extra time so you could experience life here in the fortress and to also better prepare you for your role."

She crouched to pick up the books from the floor and smoothed her hands over their covers, her expression pensive.

"Arek, you need to know this was just a fraction of what you're going to experience once we enter Savyr's fortress."

Arek nodded slowly. "I'm beginning to realize that."

"My actions . . . Touching you as I did . . . I did not deliberately set out to arouse you—"

"I know." He cut her off. "You were goading Yur."

Even now he could still feel the ghost of her lips, the heat of her tongue pressed against the skin of his arm, and the lingering warmth of arousal.

"I won't avoid touching you if the situation calls for it." Imhara's gaze remained steady. While he was sure he made no sound or action, her expression pinched tight. "Perhaps taking you into *Na'Reish* territory isn't the best decision." She shook her head. "I need to think on this."

She shoved the books she'd been holding back on the shelf.

"For the moment, let's leave it." When she turned back to him, her smile was forced. "Rassan should have seen Yur and his *Na'Hord* off by now. We've a lot to accomplish between now and the end of the week. We could use your help." Her smile became more relaxed, warmer. "Consider it a chance for you to mix with and get to know more of my Clan."

Chapter 14

"WHO'D have thought you'd be doing this two weeks ago."

"What?" Squinting against the late afternoon sunlight, Arek peered up at Rassan, who stood in the back of the box wagon. He hefted his cargo onto the tailgate. "Loading crates? I've done it a time or two."

The *Na'Chi* warrior grinned as he took the box, stacked it, then threw rope netting over the load. "I was referring to you working side by side with *Na'Reish* Clansmen."

Arek grunted. "I suppose not." He moved aside to let a young female deliver her crate.

In her teens, the girl stood eye to eye with him, her height and large-boned build well suited to lifting boxes twice the size and weight as the one she'd just deposited on the wagon. Having only ever witnessed *Na'Reish* strength on the battlefield, seeing so many engaged in the mundane chores of everyday life took some getting used to. The girl met his gaze, gave him a shy smile and a nod, then headed back to the storeroom.

"I assumed most of the chores would be done by humans," he admitted.

The last three days disproved that assumption. Even now, almost thirty people wandered in and around the dozen box-and-flatbed wagons, carting boxes, bags, baskets, and crates filled with trade goods, food, and supplies from storerooms and the fortress. Everyone capable assisted, young or old, human, *Na'Chi*, and *Na'Reish*.

The preparations reminded him of the hawkers and traders who visited the Farmers Market at Sacred Lake. Only the purpose differed.

Arek half shrugged. "It's definitely not what I was expecting."

"Good." Rassan tossed him the edge of the rope netting.

Arek began tying it off, unsurprised by the *Na'Chi's* succinct reply. At first he'd believed Rassan's task had been to guard or monitor him, and while the warrior had never said anything or enforced restrict measures, he had little doubt Imhara's Second would act if he threatened any Clansman.

Other than just spending time with him amidst mixed company, more often than not the warrior left him to his own observations and thoughts or to converse with other humans as he liked. Were their situations reverse, Arek doubted he'd have been so generous or allowed him such liberty.

As he hitched the last tail of the netting, the sound of iron-rimmed wheels rumbling over hard-packed ground and the excited chatter of children snagged his attention. Three more wagons, filled with children of varying races and ages, entered the courtyard. Drivers directed the shaggy transport beasts to pull up alongside the stables.

One after the other, children slid off or leapt over the edges of the wagons. Their actions reminded Arek of dirt-burrowers abandoning their nests. Some raced into the stables, others ambled along at their own pace. Within a minute the first group reappeared carrying sacks of grain and sheaves of hay. Another chore shared.

Arek wiped sweat from his cheek on the shoulder of his shirt. The number of wagons and quantity of supplies hinted at an extended stay. "So, how long will this Enclave last?"

Rassan leapt off the wagon, his boots thudding on the ground as he landed. "About a month, but with the Clan Challenge and associated extended festivities, it'll be closer to two." He secured the tailgate, then dusted his hands on the thighs of his breeches. "Among the *Na'Reish*, the Enclave is used to foster allegiances or establish new ones. Some forge trade alliances, others choose more permanent ties through bloodlines."

"Like Savyr's move to mate Imhara at this Enclave?" Imhara had shared Yur's message from the *Na'Rei* with her Second that morning at breakfast. "Was this something both you and Imhara expected?"

"Yes." The tall warrior's grim grin reflected his displeasure. "Although I expected Savyr to move on this much earlier." His smile turned cynical. "The Enclave can also be a time to settle old grudges."

"Through the Clan Challenge?"

"Sometimes, although most bouts in the arena are fought to enhance the reputation and social status of a Clan or individual." Arek nodded. That fit with what he knew about *Na'Reish* culture. "And any grievances settled outside it tend to be of a less honorable nature."

Arek shot him a sideways glance. "Yur made a point of asking if you were attending this year."

"He would." The dry response was at odds with the *Na'Chi's* sparkling violet eyes. "Last year I defeated him to win the Clan Champion title."

"A *Na'Chi* warrior beating Savyr's Second, a full-blood *Na'Reishi*?" Arek couldn't help but laugh. "If only they knew, eh?"

"Indeed." Rassan's grin widened. "I took great pleasure in claiming the title."

The sound of cracking and splintering wood came from the stables. A high-pitched cry—a child's scream—shattered the moment. More cries filled the air.

A chilling howl, echoed by several others, all too familiar, froze the blood in Arek's veins. *"Vorc!"*

Rassan hissed a curse and spun on his heel. "The children!"

His shout mobilized everyone in the vicinity. Arek joined the crowd rushing across the courtyard. Children, eyes wide and faces etched with terror, stumbled through the open double doors.

Rassan scooped up a young girl who'd fallen in the panic. He passed her to the nearest adult. "Get these children to safety!"

Another howl rent the air. Growls and frantic scratching sounds, claws on wood, pulled Arek up short, just outside the stables. How many of the creatures were free? He peered around the doorway, his nostrils filled with the musky scent of *Vorc* and pungent odor of droppings.

"*Shavesh ka ris!*" A hoarse, adolescent shout came from within.

Squinting against the darkened interior, he counted a dozen stalls within. Thick-boarded, high walls kept the *Vorc* contained; the beasts were unable to climb—their only weakness. Bundles of hay were abandoned on the floor. Sacks sat where they'd been dropped, some split open. Grain scattered across the ground.

Two youths, both *Na'Reish*, faced off with a *Vorc*, a full-grown male, gauging by the height and thickness of its shoulders. Beneath the bristly coat, bulging muscles rippled as it advanced, its claws churning up the hard-packed dirt floor as if it were butter.

Both youths stood close to six feet, their heavy-boned builds puny in comparison to the animal. One bite with its sharp fangs or slash with any foreclaw would kill them. Thankfully the foreleg spurs were mercifully capped. The boys wouldn't be poisoned by a strike, but they were still in danger.

"*Shavesh ka ris!*" The one on the right dared to move forward, arms raised, a courageous action given the precarious situation. "*Shavesh ka ris!*" His voice broke on the second command.

The *Vorc* lowered its pointed snout, and the upper lip curled back to reveal long fangs dripping with saliva. It stalked left, its body language anything but submissive to the boy's directive.

On the straw-covered floor, where the *Vorc* once stood, a third child lay motionless on her side, an arm's length away from the remnants of a broken stall door that hung by one hinge. An ominous dark stain pooled beneath her.

Arek sucked in a sharp breath and searched the stable for a weapon. A pitchfork leaned against the wall, a dozen steps away. He edged around the stable door.

A large hand gripped his shoulder and hauled him back. "Your scent will only provoke the beast." Rassan's deep voice was pitched low.

"It's about to attack them."

"I know. *Vorc-Masters* with me." Several *Na'Reish* clansmen and women pushed through the crowd to join the *Na'Chi* warrior. "All humans stand clear! Someone get Nayvia and the other healers."

Footsteps shuffled then pounded away to follow his order. Rumbling snarls lifted the hairs on Arek's neck. He eyed the pitchfork but held his position by the open door as Rassan nodded to his *Na'Reish* clansmen. They entered the stable together, their advance slow and steady.

"*Kula veh*—be calm—*kula veh*—" The *Na'Chi*'s voice remained low but firm. The *Vorc's* attention shifted to him, its small, slitted eyes gleaming with feral intelligence. "Don't move, Rooke."

The dark-haired youth who'd tried to confront the *Vorc* gave a jerky nod. "Yes, Second."

"You did well to stop the animal leaving the stable." Rassan's hand signal sent three of the six *Vorc-Masters* closer to the boys. "But now we're going to position ourselves between you and the male. Only then do I want you and Ori to retreat outside. Is that clear?"

"Yes." Relief made his voice shake. "It all happened so fast, Second. Leasha said that the bolt wasn't latched properly on the stall door. She went to close it and I guess the male scented her. He broke through to get her. I think she's hurt bad. I can smell blood. Lots of it."

"Nayvia's coming." Another hand signal and a line of clansmen finally stood between the boys and the *Vorc.* It surveyed each of them with a slow turn of its head, nostrils twitching. "Back off now . . . slowly."

Scuffling footsteps and soft voices came from behind Arek, but he ignored them, holding his breath, to watch as the boys retreated, relieved both had the presence of mind not to turn their backs on the animal.

"*Shavesh ka vaag!*" Rassan reinforced his order with a downward hand motion.

At the commanding order, the *Vorc's* ears drooped and the rumbling growl ceased. Rassan repeated it. The male lowered its barrel-like body to the ground. Two of the *Vorc-Masters* converged to muzzle it and clipped a chain on its collar.

"Get him locked in a stall." The warrior turned toward the entrance. "Is Nayvia here yet?"

"Yes, I'm here!" The crowd gathered by the open doorway parted to let the elderly healer through. "Bring Leasha into the light. Hurry! I can sense her strength fading."

Rassan scooped the unconscious human child into his arms and brought her to where Nayvia was waiting with three other people.

"Put her on the ground in front of me. Quickly!"

Arek stepped back to give them room to work. Nayvia tore the shirt open and exposed the claw wounds. He winced. Four vertical tears shredded the girl's abdomen. The head injury—a large, bruised swelling on her temple—was the least of their worries.

Nayvia ignored the cries of dismay that came from those watching. She placed her hands over the raw wounds and pressed hard, eyes closing. Dark red blood welled through her fingers and escaped past the sides of her hands.

Rassan backed away, coming to join him at the edge of the circle.

The flecks in his eyes were a bright yellow, and his black lips were flat with tension. His tanned face was pale, the uneven pattern of spots running down either side of it more prominent because of it. Blood stained his shirt and hands, but his gaze remained on those kneeling over the child.

Arek's gut churned with the knowledge that her chance of surviving such severe injuries was slim. He glanced around at the people gathered, wondering where the girl's parents were. Had anyone gone to inform them?

"May the *Lady* help them both," he murmured.

A sudden spike of power came from the elderly healer's direction. While he wasn't attuned to her Gift as others in her profession were, he could sense its crisp, warm resonance. Her power rivaled Candra's, the Master Healer at Sacred Lake.

The furrows on her brow deepened. "Link with me!"

Her eyes remained closed, but the other healers who accompanied her—a human man of middle years, and two female *Na'Chi*—moved closer to form a semicircle behind her. The man placed a hand over Nayvia's then clasped hands with one of the women. She copied his actions and so did the third woman.

Others came forward to join the small group, hands grasping wrists or shoulders, forming a bizarre web of linked bodies.

Arek shot Rassan a sideways glance. "What are they doing?" he whispered.

"The man to Nayvia's left is a siphon."

"A what?"

"A siphon." At his shrug, the *Na'Chi* elaborated. "He can draw energy from any Gifted and channel it to where it's needed. Jomas is one of a dozen siphons here in the keep. Nayvia may have the expertise and skill but not the time or energy required for such a complex healing. With his help, she can tap into as much as she needs."

At the edge of Arek's awareness, the buzzing resonance escalated to a powerful thrum. It reached a crescendo then held steady, the sensation rasping at his senses but not in an unpleasant way.

No one spoke. Long moments passed.

"Look!" Rassan murmured, his lips curving upward.

Blood no longer seeped through or from under Nayvia's hands. It actually darkened, congealed, and the edges of the gashes sealed together as Arek watched.

He'd witnessed serious wounds being healed before but nothing like this. Even with only a basic knowledge of treatments, he knew a wound couldn't be closed without repairing the internal injuries first. Infection was an all too virulent danger.

What usually took several sessions to heal was happening in a single treatment. Candra, nor any of other provincial healers he knew, had ever mentioned one of their Guild members having the Gift for harnessing energy like Jomas. No one had even suggested it was possible.

How long could Jomas and Nayvia utilize the skill? Were there any limitations or drawbacks to using *Her* Gifts in such a way? Was it confined to assisting healers or could it be used in other areas? How many Guilds would covet the chance to learn more about this?

Arek glanced to Rassan. "I've never seen a siphon before. What other Gifts do your people have?"

"There are some who work with animals, others are able to manipulate the elements, all to varying degrees and depending on strength and stamina . . ."

"Manipulate the elements? You mean air, fire, and water?"

"And the weather as well as the earth."

"Earth?"

"The shifting or loosening of soil, rock, sand, and snow." Here Rassan grinned. "It comes in handy during planting season when new fields need to be cleared of old tree stumps or large rocks."

The potential of such Gifts and the knowledge that could be shared . . . Arek shook his head and glanced around the circle of people with new eyes. With the destruction of so many history annals, the extent of the damage done by generations of corrupt Blade Councilors became even clearer.

What other Gifts did this Clan have that humans had lost track of thanks to people like his grandfather, Yance, and Corvas? How could his grandfather have been so blind as to conceal such incredible information? How many more lives had been lost by his duplicity and betrayal? Sour acid rose and burned in the back of Arek's throat.

"Enough." Nayvia's soft order broke the silent. The pulsing energy cut off. Her shoulders slumped and one of the female healers caught her. The older woman lifted her head. "Leasha needs to be taken to the hospice."

The youth, Rooke, hovered close by, his violet gaze dark with shadows. "Leasha will live, won't she?" His voice wavered—worry laced with fear at losing a friend.

Arek recognized the emotions, felt them as if they were his own. Disbelief, anger, utter helplessness, fear—he'd experienced it all watching Kalan fall, impaled by a *Na'Reish* dagger during the rescue mission gone wrong. The only difference in their situations, he didn't know if his friend had survived.

A weary smile curved Nayvia's lips. "With time and care, she'll be fine."

Rooke's expression brightened. The solemn tension broke as someone cheered. Chattering began as Leasha was taken away to the hospice. Blessings were called out to the healers; almost all offered praise and thanks to the *Lady*.

A *Na'Reish* clansman with the same hair coloring and facial features as Rooke pushed through the crowd to embrace the youth. A human woman joined them, hugging them both, tears trailing down her cheeks.

Relieved parents, happy to see their child unharmed.

Nayvia accepted help to rise to her feet before being embraced by several people who'd helped form the healing link. The *Na'Reish* male standing beside him and the *Na'Chi* on his left began sharing their impressions of the event.

Arek stared once more around at those gathered, listening to conversations filled with so much warmth and respect for the healers and those who'd helped save Leasha. For one bizarre moment, if he closed his eyes, he could almost imagine he was back at Sacred Lake amongst friends.

But he wasn't.

He stood in a Clan fortress in *Na'Reish* territory. No demon he'd ever seen had shown such concern or care over the life of a human. Varian, Lisella, Zaune, and the other *Na'Chi* had hidden from them, knowing their lives were forfeit if they were ever discovered. Humans hated and feared them, for centuries.

Yet here they'd worked together to save the life of a human child. Full-blooded demons shared their lives with humans and half-bloods. Old, young, *Na'Reish*, human, and *Na'Chi*, yet no one seemed to notice, except him.

A frisson of energy skittered over his skin. Arek released a shaky breath and rubbed his face with both hands.

A hand squeezed his shoulder. "Light Blade?" *Rassan*. "Are you all right?"

Arek glanced up at him and shook his head. "There's no you, me, or them, is there?"

One dark eyebrow lifted. "Pardon?"

He swept his arm out to encompass those around them. "You're not just three races. You're a people."

"Ahh—" The warrior's expression eased into a warm smile. "Arek, our differences don't define us. It's only in your world, or among the other Clans, where they do." He gestured toward Rooke's family, then the group of healers. "What you see here is the best of the Old Ways. We're united by who we all are and what we're capable of being. This is *Her* blessing to us all."

Her blessing. Was this the reason Yenass, the crofter from Ostare, had sacrificed his life for him that day in the forest? So he could experience something he never thought possible. Was this the journey *She* wanted him to take?

Arek sucked in a slow breath, his gut tightening. The sensation was eerily reminiscent of the first day he'd ridden into battle against the *Na'Reish* as a man barely out of his teens. The sight of a full *Na'Hord* bearing down on them, howling, so much taller and stronger than them, froze him to the spot.

Yevni, his patrol Commander then, had intercepted one of the demons bearing down on him. If he hadn't Arek knew he'd have fallen. Later, after the battle was over, he'd thanked Yevni, despite the burn of humiliation for his weakness eating at him.

"There's no shame in what happened, boy. That's only justified if you ignore your fear and refuse to deal with it." Words he'd taken to heart on the next patrol and in situations away from the battlefield.

He fisted his hands. The heat of shame he'd felt then was the same now, only this time he was frozen by indecision and the knowledge that accepting the improbable would change everything.

His beliefs.

His life.

Even the path his future took.

It left him feeling like he was twenty all over again.

Chapter 15

IF he didn't look too closely at the shadowy figures gathered around the bonfire in the middle of the bailey, Arek could almost imagine he stood in the Light Blade compound at Sacred Lake during the Summer's End Festival—an unsettling recurrence of what he'd felt earlier in the day.

The evening was a celebration, a Clan feast, the last the Kaal would share together before those venturing north into Gannec territory left to attend the Enclave.

Children of all ages dotted the yard. Some pursued each other in the timeless game of chase, more were engaged in other mischief, while the youths hung around in same-sex groups, eyeing each other. The bravest couples were already sitting together. It'd been a handful of years since he'd done the same thing, yet the familiar behavior brought a smile to his lips.

Voices engaged in a score of conversations blurred together, and in the background, a half-dozen musicians provided music for those interested in dancing. The appetizing odor of spit-roasted meat still wafted in the air an hour after everyone had eaten their fill of the food served up on giant platters, pots, and baskets on the trestle tables lined up along the inner courtyard wall. A few still wandered back and forth, picking through the leftovers, but most now congregated in small groups around the fire.

Arek leaned back against the outer wall, no longer in the mood to mix, still unsettled by the revelations of the afternoon, still questioning whether he could accept what he'd seen.

He shook his head. The distinct lack of any subservient behavior from those who were human and the absence of tension between the races had to be genuine. There was no way so many could maintain such an act, particularly the children.

Who'd have thought the three races could coexist peacefully? What would his grandfather say if he could see this now? What would Kalan? The Blade Council?

"Opening yourself up to the prospect that something might be possible is often easier than accepting the truth all at once, Light Blade." The gravel-deep voice came from the shadows to his right. Rassan emerged from them, his tread surprisingly quiet for a warrior his size. "Others have felt exactly as you do now."

"They weren't expected to change their beliefs or views in less than a week," Arek replied, tone dry.

The *Na'Chi* inclined his head, conceding his point. "Yet when you met Barrca, Jaclan, and myself that morning in Imhara's room, you didn't dismiss my claim that we were *Na'Chi*. You were already familiar with our race." His violet gaze never wavered. "You made that transition before you ended up here. What's stopping you from entertaining the possibility that my *Na'Reish* kin are just like me?"

It was on the tip of his tongue to tell him, but Arek bit back his response. He might feel a growing connection with the warrior, just as he had with Varian, and while the Kaal Second had been straightforward and candid sharing information, how could he be sure that his friendship with the Sacred Lake *Na'Chi* wasn't coloring his perceptions? Skewing his judgment?

"'Faith bridges the gap between the heart and mind . . .'"

The softly quoted scripture jerked his head up, and he stared at Rassan. It was something Kymora would say . . . had said on numerous occasions.

Had the *Na'Chi* scented his confusion?

Faith . . . Arek grunted softly, a shiver skittering down his spine. If there was ever a time he needed *Her* strength, now was it. Why the hesitation to embrace it?

He'd faced similar trials in the past. Fear and uncertainty shouldn't hold sway over his actions. Yevni, Kymora, and Rassan were right. Faith would bridge the gap only if he turned his feet along that path. *She* would do the rest.

Praying he was doing the right thing, he inhaled a deeper breath. "I'm still grappling with the idea of peaceful relations with the *Na'Reish*."

"But not the *Na'Chi*?"

"No." Rassan's white teeth gleamed in a grin. Arek gestured to a group on the other side of the bailey. "The crofters you rescued with me from Meelar are handling this much more easily than me."

"Understandable."

"A few have found friends from other villages they thought gone forever."

"Welcome comfort considering most have lost everything—family, loved ones, homes, livelihoods—all because of the raids." Rassan's violet gaze scanned the gathering. "Here they can make a new life for themselves. And *Lady* willing, if your Blade Council accepts Imhara's request for a truce, we can discard the dual roles we play. Finally."

"How have you stayed hidden from the other *Na'Reish*?" One of the first questions he'd wanted to ask once Imhara had explained the Kaal Clan's history. "After so many years, I find it hard to believe you've remained undiscovered."

"Some have lost their lives and there have been times we've had to resort to extreme measures to keep our secret."

Their continuous vigilance and dedication was impressive.

Rassan gestured toward the jagged outline of the mountains beyond the fortress walls. In the moonlight, the snow-tipped peaks shone with an eerie silver glow. "It helps that we're isolated from the other territories by the Skadda Ranges. But the most effective strategy has been to limit our contact with other Clans and foster the belief that we prefer seclusion."

The Kaal ancestors must have possessed incredible foresight and drive to implement such a plan.

Arek grunted. "A difficult existence. Your ancestors made some hard decisions." And they'd been backed by even harder actions to ensure the survival of the generations. "Separated from the *Na'Reish* by choice and regarded as the enemy by us."

A lonely burden for any leader to bear, race notwithstanding.

"Something Imhara hopes to change now that you're here." Rassan's gaze was level, direct. "You need to decide whether what you've seen and experienced is enough to believe our truths."

The Clan's survival depended on the execution of Imhara's plan. But trusting her was the key. And there lay his dilemma.

Should he trust Imhara Kaal?

More importantly, could he?

Arek glanced over at the small group seated beside the far trestle table, the place he'd last seen her talking to Nayvia earlier in the evening. The elderly healer wore a contented smile as she sat nursing a small child who lay curled up in her lap. The seat beside her was empty.

"This time of night you'll often find Imhara up there, looking out over the fields." The *Na'Chi* pointed to the wall on the eastern side of the courtyard. "There's a stairway leading up to the ramparts to the left of the main gates."

A wry smile twitched Arek's lips. Rassan's conversation and timing couldn't be coincidence. "Why are you pushing this?"

"Because she won't." In the firelight, his gaze narrowed. "And because she's having second thoughts. Excluding you from our plans narrows our chances for success. Your introduction to our Clan wasn't ideal. The blame lies as much on my shoulders as Imhara's." His jaw tightened. "As I said to you the day we met on the river shore, my Clan needs you. I still believe that."

For a moment Rassan looked like he might say more, but then he gave a sharp nod and walked away. He joined a group of youths standing by the fire and struck up a conversation with them.

Arek watched the *Na'Chi* warrior for long moments. The Second's candid manner was one he could appreciate. Given the choice of blunt honesty, prevarication, or diplomacy, he preferred the former anytime. Favoring a direct approach was why he'd never make a good Blade Councilor.

No longer in the mood to socialize, Arek shoved his hands in his breeches' pockets and headed into the darkness away from everyone. The music faded and conversation became a background noise. Loose pebbles crunched beneath his boots as he made his way to the fortress gates.

Rassan was right. He did have a decision to make and time was against them. Arek's pace slowed as he neared the entrance. Above it, in the towers on either side, a pair of guards manned the watch. One glanced his way but then turned his attention to whatever lay outside the walls.

The action drew another wry smile from him. Since Yur's departure, other than spending time in Rassan's company, he hadn't detected any sign of being watched.

Who had rescinded the order, dismissing his guards? Rassan or Imhara? He suspected the latter. The cynic in him wanted to believe her actions were an elaborate trick to earn his trust, but his accusation lacked the fire of certainty. Barring a single incident, everything he'd experienced so far backed up all the evidence supporting her claim.

He ran a hand through his hair, tempted to yank at it rather than ruffle it. A year ago the idea of allying himself with the *Na'Reish* would never have entered his mind. Killing them had been his only agenda; one reinforced by his past, his grandfather, and circumstance.

A familiar hollowness ached in his gut. To think of all the years Davyn had lied to him and everyone else about the history between humans and demons. The secrets and deceit had almost destroyed the Blade Council. And what burned him the most was that not once had he suspected or sensed such intrigue.

Lady's Breath, the righteous fury he'd experienced, the approval and encouragement received from his grandfather as he'd avenged his parents' death every time he'd killed in battle felt so empty now.

Davyn's actions tainted a lifetime of memories, and while Arek understood a man was responsible for his own behavior, shame for what his grandfather had done still gnawed away at his innards. If he couldn't detect falsehoods told by family members, what qualified him to make judgments and decisions concerning Imhara and her Clan?

Arek took a deep breath and stopped in the middle of the roadway to peer up at the huge wooden double gates. The thick beams were reinforced with metal braces, and two crossbars lay in horizontal brackets, securing the fortress from intrusion. Nothing short of a battering ram would breach the entrance.

A single door had been built into one side for convenient access to the outside world. He reached out to touch the slide bolt, fingers trailing over the cool metal. How hard would it be to throw back the bolt, slip through the door, and leave?

It'd crossed his mind more than once over the last few days to take advantage of his guard-free situation. It was what he should do;

what he would have done the first day he'd woken up in Imhara's bed had he been given the chance.

His grandfather would call him an idiot to ignore the opportunity. But again, what confidence could he place in the teachings of a man who'd broken the *Lady's* tenets? No Light Blade true to his faith would even consider corrupting his honor, nor encourage others to follow suit as his grandfather had done.

His grandfather's betrayal aside, the Light Blades needed his experience. With Kalan gravely wounded and rebels attacking the *Na'Chi* and threatening civil war, didn't he owe it to them to escape and return to lead them?

Arek pressed his hand flat to the wood. His fingernails dug into the grain. Beyond lay the fields. They stretched out on either side of the hard-packed roadway and took a traveller in the direction of Whitewater River. Using the waterway as a guide, he could be back in human territory in less than a week, a few more days and he'd reach Sacred Lake.

His chest tightened at the thought of returning home. Had Varian escaped to safety with the patrol after their mission to rescue the villagers of Ostare had failed? Had Kalan survived being wounded? What if he'd died? Arek shuddered at the thought.

What of Jole? Zaune? The others in the patrol? And back at Sacred Lake, Kymora and Lisella? Also Annika, the half sister he hadn't really taken the time to get to know. Was the Blade Council coping? And what of Davyn's rebels?

There were too many uncertainties and countless unknowns. The answers lay beyond the fortress door. His fingers tightened around the bolt. Temptation gnawed at his gut like a scurrier, yet the sensation was curbed by the weight of possibilities and responsibility.

Killing Savyr would be an incredible coup.

Throwing the *Na'Reish* Clans into a power struggle would stall the war and ease the pressure facing them. A temporary measure, but one the Blade Council desperately needed.

And if . . . *if* . . . Imhara's proposed truce was agreed upon, the geographical gain of adding her Clan territory to the border would tip the balance of power to a more even scale.

The greater good would be served by helping Imhara. And that was what he'd sworn allegiance to as a Light Blade warrior.

Yet the issue of trust burned like a live coal in his chest. Every instinct screamed in protest at allying himself with a demon. There was no denying his hatred for the *Na'Reish* festered within him like an open wound, its origins sown by Savyr and obsessively fertilized by his grandfather, and then kept alive by the deaths and atrocities he'd witnessed over too many years.

Blaming Davyn didn't help. But the problem remained. How could he trust Imhara when he'd doubted her every action and then his own?

Mother of Light, it'd taken him nearly six months to adjust to living with the *Na'Chi* in their village near Sacred Lake. Now he had less than a week to reconcile with the past. What he wouldn't give to be able to talk to Kalan or Kymora about this, seek his friends' advice, their guidance.

He didn't like the idea of uncertainty paralyzing him.

Nor was hoping for the best an option.

Yet indecision knotted in his gut like a nest of tunnel vipers.

Arek hit the gate with his fist. *Lady's Mercy*, he was a Light Blade warrior sworn to protect his people, regardless of his personal feelings.

"When no clear path presents itself we must walk on faith alone. *She'll test the limits of your strength but never push you beyond them*, *Arek. If you stumble or waver She'll walk beside you until you find your footing again."*

Wisdom Kymora had often quoted. The *Lady's* words never seemed so relevant as they did now, but for the first time, he doubted his ability to honor *Her* principles.

His jaw tightened.

Failure wasn't something that sat well with him. It never had.

"If I'm to take this path, *Blessed Mother*, I'll need *Your* help and strength. I can't do it by myself."

With his whispered plea, the tangle of emotions inside him shifted, and a gentle warmth spread from the inside out, taking the edge off them. Had *She* heard his prayer?

With a soft sigh, he dropped his hand from the slide bolt. He pushed thoughts of leaving to the back of his mind and turned in the direction of the stairway. For now he'd walk the journey *She'd* set him on.

If that meant dealing with his prejudices—prejudices built on the foundation of his grandfather's lies—then so be it.

Fool! The bitter echo of Davyn's voice rose from the darkness around him.

Ignoring it he took the stairs two at a time, expecting the cold fingers of regret to scrape across his neck and slow his pace. Instead the warmth inside him grew. Once at the top, he searched the walkway for Imhara and discovered a slender shadow leaning against the parapet halfway along.

Arek drew in another deep breath. His heart thumped harder. Learning to trust a *Na'Reish* demon by becoming her willing slave would certainly be something for the history journals.

Assuming, of course, they survived their venture in the heart of demon territory.

Chapter 16

EVEN if she hadn't heard his boot heels striking the stone walkway, Imhara knew that the strong scent of spice tinged with an earthy mix of tension and determination belonged to Arek. It carried on the gentle evening breeze, strengthening the nearer he came.

She inhaled again, letting his scent settle at the back of her throat, then deep in her lungs, savoring it like she had the view of the valley spread out before her moments before. Adrenaline flooded her limbs, every nerve came alive, and the peace she'd found staring out over the land changed to eager anticipation as her attention zeroed in on him.

A twinge of excitement curled in the pit of her stomach and spread southward. She'd experienced sexual attraction before, but nothing like this, so quick, so unexpected, and certainly not based on something as singular and simple as a scent. But while she now had the time to explore her reaction, curiosity overrode it. What had compelled Arek to seek her out?

With a last glance at the moonlit valley, the silver-tinted crops and gray-shadowed hills, she turned to face him, propping a hip against the outer wall. She'd expected any visitor to be Rassan, since she'd walked away from him after an argument just before the feast about her desire to keep Arek safe.

The Light Blade's scent still titillated her nostrils, but the metallic odor of tension was stronger now and reflected in his wide stance and somber expression.

"Your Second is as driven as you to see this plan of yours succeed." A statement of fact, not a question, and no hint of resentment, just calm observation. "He seems to think you've changed your mind about my part in it. Have you?"

No prevarication, straight to the point. So like Rassan.

Imhara almost grinned.

"His frankness can sometimes be confronting." She tilted her head in apology, but since he'd raised the issue, she wasn't going to back away from it. "We've counted on you being a part of our strategy for so long, but I'm considering other options. He disagrees with any change."

"I understand his point of view." Arek shot a glance out over the valley in the general direction of the border. "He wouldn't be much of a Second to you if he didn't speak his mind."

Imhara's gaze narrowed. The timbre of his voice deepened and vibrated with heavy emotion as he imparted that tidbit of information. It sounded like he spoke from experience.

"While we might not agree on every point, I respect his opinions and suggestions." More times than she cared to count, Rassan had kept her focused on their goal. "But with this plan, there's more to consider than just what gives us the best advantage."

Facts, variables, tactics. Her father had often quoted those words in his lectures as he'd taught planning and strategy to not only his offspring and Commanders, but his *Na'Hord*, too. He'd wanted every warrior equipped to make wise decisions and capable of stepping up to issue orders, not just follow them, if the situation called for it. His teachings had served her well during the last five years.

"The most beneficial course of action isn't always the best to take." Arek ran his hand through his hair. "Logic doesn't consider emotions, and sometimes it should."

Her breath caught and goose bumps skittered over her skin. "No, it doesn't. That's why I want to give you a choice. Assuming or demanding that you take part in the venture isn't going to help."

Again his gaze flickered out over the valley to stare toward the border, and Imhara wondered what he was thinking. Was it of family? Friends? Or those he'd fought beside while on patrol?

Arek gave little away when he controlled his emotions, like he was doing now. An intriguing quality, and a challenge to her curious nature. Dealing with it could wait. She wanted to know the purpose of his visit. It was the first time he'd voluntarily sought her out, and she wouldn't rush him. The silence stretched out until all she could hear was her own heartbeat, yet she waited.

Finally he turned his head, and once more his gaze sought hers. The blue around his irises had darkened to a deeper shade of twilight. The tension radiating from him felt different. Still uncertain. Still wary, but more . . . resolved.

"I don't trust you, *Na'Reish*." His low-pitched voice was rough and his blunt statement lashed at her like a whip. She nodded though, knowing some of the fault for that lay with her. "But I'm willing to try and make this plan of yours work."

He was? A frisson of shock left Imhara feeling light-headed and flushed. "Why?"

Arek's brows inched downward. "Why what?"

"Hatred isn't an easy emotion to overcome. Some never manage to separate themselves from it." A burden she wondered if she'd ever be able to shed, particularly where Savyr and Yur were concerned. "The contingency plan will suffice. Why offer to participate when you don't have to?"

Another long silence as his frown deepened, then, "I wouldn't be much of a Light Blade if I ran from what I didn't like, *Na* Kaal."

He thought she was accusing him of cowardice? She took a breath to refute him, but he held up a hand, cutting her off.

"I can't ignore the advantage your plan would give the Blade Council." A logical reason. "But there's also faith." His lips twisted in a grim smile as he answered slowly, every word heavy with obvious reluctance. "Certain . . . events in the past few months have shaped and changed my life. I suspect this is all part of *Her* journey for me. It's not one I would have chosen, far from it, but a friend of mine would assure me it's necessary."

What events? How had they influenced him? What had happened in his past? Arek's lips pressed shut then flattened—her expression must have betrayed her curiosity—and she had little doubt he'd refuse to respond if she pushed. For now she'd be patient.

The thought of Arek joining her in their venture excited her, yet she couldn't forget the ripe odor of his distaste for all things *Na'Reish* in their first encounter in her bedroom and since.

"You're certain you want to do this?" Too much was at stake to risk being wrong. "Once you commit and we leave this fortress tomorrow, there'll be no turning back."

His nod was sharp. Imhara pushed off the wall and took a step toward him, one eyebrow arching. She understood her responsibilities and what was required of her. No matter how much she wanted to, putting her desires before the safety of her people wasn't an option.

"Then say it. Tell me out loud what you're committing to."

AREK fisted his hands. Imhara's voice had taken on that arrogant tone, the one she'd used in the library when she'd tested him. Moonlight struck her face only from the side, and it was hard to discern her true expression. With half of her face wreathed by shadows, he couldn't tell if she was pleased or ambivalent about his agreeing to help.

Couldn't she scent his resolve? Did she doubt his allegiance? Or was this her being petty making him verbalize their agreement?

His jaw clenched.

So be it.

"I'll be your slave." Saying the words out loud sent a shiver through him.

Imhara closed the distance between them, stopping with only inches to spare, so close he could feel the warmth of her body even through his shirt. With it came the light aroma of sweet-shade. The same scent present in the soap-sand he'd used in Imhara's bathing room that first day. His pulse kicked up a notch, and he dismissed it as a reaction to her deliberate move of invading his personal space.

"You did well enough to fool Yur." Her tone had softened slightly. "But once we cross over Skadda Pass, we'll be in *Na'Reish* territory and you're going to have to be my slave every hour of every day. You'll be expected to follow orders, serve, watch other humans mistreated, punished, perhaps even killed. You won't be able to intervene or use your Gift to save them. Can you do that?"

As tempted as he was to blurt out an affirmative, he couldn't.

"I'm able to control my Gift. I've done it during training and battle." His boot scuffed on stone as he shifted his weight from one foot to the other. "As for my behavior, I'm going to make mistakes." Admitting it grated but his course was set. He'd made an oath to help her, and lying would endanger them all. "I can only give you my word I'll learn as quickly as I can."

She gave a small nod. "I can accept that."

Her head tilted slightly to one side, his only warning before she laid her hands on his chest. His muscles clenched before he could control his reaction. Her warmth and scent assaulted his senses.

"And how do you feel about sleeping with me?"

"What?"

This time he backed away, extricating himself from her hold, a single step, then the cold wall of a parapet halted his retreat. Before he could move sideways, Imhara slapped her hands against the wall either side of his head, blocking him in.

One dark eyebrow arched. "You're my bed-slave."

Her gaze lowered and surveyed him with a hunger that reminded him of a *lira* stalking its prey. To his consternation, his body tightened and desire pulsed through him, as if responding to a physical caress rather than a visual one.

Adrenaline shot through him.

Lady's Breath! He'd never anticipated having sex with her.

Shocked by his body's betrayal, he fought it, struggling to wrest control and deny the heat permission to move any lower.

Everything Rassan and others had told him about her alter ego flickered through his mind, and he focused on that. While it didn't erase what he was feeling, it helped rein it in. He sucked in a relieved breath.

Was this another one of her tests? Did she think if she pressed him hard enough, he'd retract his offer?

Her tactics, if that's what they were, were exactly what he'd do if their positions were reversed. She was determined, he'd give her that. Did he dare presume she was bluffing?

"Once we leave this fortress, we'll be sharing a bed." Her quiet declaration twisted his gut. "There'll be times I'm going to touch you, and you're going to touch me . . . in front of others, Arek."

"No." The prickling sensation inside him wasn't exactly fear; it was too hot, too intense for that. He shook his head in silent protest, unwilling to examine what it was more closely, but he couldn't ignore the way the heat raced through his veins, pounding in time to the beat of his heart.

Imhara's gaze narrowed. She grasped his wrist, pushed up the sleeve of his shirt, then turned his arm over. In the silver moonlight, the teeth marks were small, dark shadows on his skin.

"You're my blood-slave." Her finger traced each one, the light touch leaving a searing trail on his skin. "You know what that means."

Blood-slave . . .

How many times had he heard utter revulsion as the words were spat from speakers' mouths during conversation?

Blood-addiction was well documented in the history annals of the Temple library. The *Na'Reish* used *haze* to sedate their chosen blood-slaves, the drug calming the human enough to allow their master to feed from them without a struggle. Used frequently, it helped ensure the addiction took hold.

Once dependent, the drug didn't have to be used to ensure compliance. The cravings and forced loyalty to their master dictated every action of the new blood-slave, and the *Na'Reish* took advantage of this weakness.

Every journal and document claimed those cursed to serve in this way could no longer be trusted, and were considered lost to the demons forever.

Tragic casualties of blood-slavery.

Or so everyone believed. A belief he still had trouble shaking despite Imhara's revelations.

He cursed under his breath. "You want me to be your whore for my next blood-high?"

"Yes." Imhara's hard tone matched her expression. "Driven by that need, the *Na'Reish* expect slavish behavior from their blood-slaves. Depravity is an accepted part of our culture now. We exploit the blood-bond." Her gaze never wavered. "As *Na* Kaal, I use blood and sex to control you. I'll give no quarter in this, Arek."

Her words struck home with the force of a smithy's hammer. Illusion or not, she'd created a reputation—the key to her success so far. It didn't matter that every action she'd taken had been calculated to move her a step closer to her goal.

The skin between his shoulder blades crawled. He'd have to play on her terms or break his oath. Something he'd never done since taking the *Lady's* vows to serve *Her* and his people. He still balked at her request.

Imhara pressed closer. Her soft curves and lean muscle were a perfect fit against him. Before he could do more than tense, she tangled her fingers in his hair, holding him so he couldn't look away, her *Na'Reish* strength mocking the intimacy of her action.

"I'm not willing to compromise on this just because you find the idea of us as sexual partners repugnant." The fist in his hair tightened and the heat roiling in his gut flared. "I have done . . . and I'm ready to do . . . whatever I need to bring Savyr down." Her purple-hued gaze pierced him, the reminder timely. "Are you?"

Chapter 17

CAUTIOUS hope filled Imhara even though Arek's expression vacillated between confusion and anger, uncertainty and frustration. She'd goaded him with what had to be his greatest fear—sleeping with the enemy—and he faced it head-on when she'd half expected him to lash out using his Gift.

Emotions darkened his gaze, and the scents radiating from him lasted no longer than the fraction of a heartbeat before changing, each fighting for dominance as he struggled with her demand.

A few days ago he'd have tried to kill her; now the restraint he showed was progress, and she sent a prayer of thanks heavenward for it. Yet just how far she could push him remained to be seen.

Instinct told her he disliked backing down, but she had to know just how committed he truly was, for both their sakes. Once in Gannec territory, and exposed to the scrutiny of Savyr and scores of other *Na'Reishi*, acting out of character or refusing to commit to this role one hundred percent would endanger everyone who came with them to the Enclave.

Arek's throat worked as he swallowed, the pulse there beating a rapid tattoo beneath his skin. "You're bluffing." Tension roughened his voice.

The challenge skated across her nerves, like a flame licking fuel.

His nostrils flared and his chest rose and fell on a sharp breath. That, combined with the heat of his hard body, reminded her that although he seemed furious and besieged by doubt, there was a familiar, spicy heat mixed in the scents surrounding him.

Sexual heat. Lust or desire, it didn't matter; a reaction to something she'd said or done. It was there.

Earlier that week, during their confrontation with Yur, she'd dismissed his response as accidental, unwanted. This time instinct told her there was more to it. Exhilaration stroked heated fingers from her scalp to her breasts, then settled low in her abdomen.

"Am I?" A small smile tugged at her lips. That he wasn't as repulsed by her presence as she believed him to be sparked wicked thoughts. Her heart began to race. "Then call me on it."

Her husky tone caught her by surprise as much as it did Arek. Provoking him probably wasn't fair, but just how he would respond filled her with anticipation, the sort she hadn't felt in a very, very long time.

He blinked, a muscle in his jaw twitching even as his eyes locked with hers. Deep blue heat simmered in their depths—like the hottest flames of a blacksmith's forge—a heartbeat before his lips slanted across hers.

His mouth smothered her gasp. She gripped his upper arms, muscular biceps taut and steel hard, intending to push him away. A gut reaction. His hands sank into her hair, his fingers mimicking the hold she had on him—tangling, tightening, taking control; something she detested in other males but accepted from Arek. This time.

His fingers applied steady pressure, angling her head so that her lips parted. His tongue speared into her mouth.

Once.

Twice.

The thrusting motion heated her faster than she thought possible, combusting her from the inside out. She caught his tongue with her lips, sucked at it, stroked it with her own, needing . . . no, *craving* it more than her next breath. He tasted of the same earthy spice that filled her nostrils.

Exotic. Exquisite.

Arek's deep-throated groan turned up the temperature until her blood boiled in her veins. She arched against him, hissing her pleasure into his mouth, her breasts and nipples so sensitive from the friction the sensation shot straight to her core.

Yet beneath all that, her heart soared. His actions restored hope in her plan and confirmed what instinct had been telling her about this warrior. With his help, her parents' legacy stood a chance of surviving.

Shoving all that aside, Imhara pushed her fingers deeper into his hair. She wanted to enjoy their kiss.

ALL of Arek's intentions to make the kiss last no more than a heartbeat or two disappeared the moment his lips touched Imhara's. One taste of her mouth, and heavy sweetness exploded against his taste buds, and the voice of logic faded away like smoke dissipating in a strong breeze.

The incredible, rich flavor had his lips parting wider, the need for another taste ripping through him in a heated surge that started in his gut and spread outward fast, shredding any coherent thought, leaving only raw desire in its wake.

The feel of her, all curves and softness, heat and strength, the warmth of her body adding to the fire in his. A throaty little moan vibrated from her. The sound of it went straight to the fireball in his gut, making him hard in seconds.

Hard and hungry.

Imhara met his tongue with her own, dancing around it before her lips closed on him, nibbling, sucking, stroking, her sweetness a heady, intoxicating drug as potent as *haze*. He wanted to consume as much of it as he could. It was all that mattered. His world narrowed to the fiery rush singing through his veins.

His senses reeled. It felt like standing in the middle of a tempest, the thunder deafening, the lightning blinding, the wind howling. All white-hot sensation and raw pleasure.

Wild, ferocious, uncontrollable.

Dangerous.

That single coherent thought shattered the moment.

He tore his mouth away from hers.

"*Mother of Light!*" Breath sawing in and out of his lungs, he gripped Imhara's shoulders and created some distance between them but found he couldn't release her. He sucked in a hard breath—several—as he stared at her. Her face was flushed, her lips shining wet in the moonlight, swollen and full from their kiss.

What had he done?

He shuddered, too aware that every nerve and cell remained charged, the heat threatening to combust again in an instant. Where he held her, the skin on the palms of his hands felt blistered.

Blood pounded through his veins. The insane hunger for another taste of her mouth tempted him as nothing else ever had. He grit his teeth and battled it, every muscle aching at the enforced command to do nothing until he had mastered his body. He concentrated on quelling that desire, determined to regain control of himself. But his thoughts kept returning to the defining moment.

Merciful Mother, he'd kissed her. *A demon*.

He hadn't been sure he could, but he had, unwilling to let her challenge go unanswered, and—here he balked at the thought—he'd found *pleasure* in the kiss.

He'd experienced desire for a *Na'Reish* demon. So hot and intense reason had gone south, just like the blood in his veins. He was semi-hard just from kissing her, aching with every beat of his heart.

And he craved more.

That fact drained the blood from his face. He sucked in another breath. How could he feel all that for her? Her goading couldn't be used as an excuse. He was an adult, not some juvenile pressed into a silly dare.

Why had his body betrayed him?

But what shocked him more was the realization that she'd enjoyed their kiss, too. He'd kissed enough women to discern when one reacted out of obligation or passion. Her fervent response equaled his.

Even now the touch of her fingers where she gripped his arms through his shirt burned. *Merciful Mother* help him if her intent ever changed and she decided to do more than hold on to him.

Arck shook his head. He wasn't ready to deal with any of this. Not now.

Lifting his gaze, he found Imhara watching him, her purple-hued gaze glittering, intent, thoughtful. Slowly she stepped back, putting more space between them, and he let her go. It was the sensible thing to do. His hands shook. He shoved them deep into his pockets.

"Well, this certainly changes things." The sultry note in her voice reawakened the need he thought he had under control. Heat surged into his cheeks. Ruthlessly, he suppressed it.

"What do you mean?" His voice rasped out the words. She wasn't going to dissect the incident, was she?

Imhara raised an eyebrow, her expression bright with awareness, as if she knew exactly what he was thinking, and she probably did, given that he had trouble controlling the scents his body gave off.

"I was prepared to use the contingency plan." Her admission wasn't the answer he expected. "But you've just proved Rassan was right and I was wrong."

"About what?"

A satisfied smile curved her lips. "You're ready to be my slave." Her eyes glittered with hope and excitement, and something else he couldn't identify. "There's a lot to cover, but we have a few days while we cross over Skadda Pass. Time enough for you to learn the basics of being a slave, and if you commit to the role, we might just stand a chance."

Arek blinked then frowned. Their kiss had convinced her?

The sense of rightness he'd felt while ascending the stairway to the wall returned, a reassuring feeling he grabbed onto with everything he had.

He let out a short, sharp breath. This had to be the path *She* wanted him to tread. He might not like it, but it would help keep him focused.

"Just to put your mind at ease, Light Blade"—Imhara's voice held a thread of amusement—"for perception's sake, we'll share a bed, but I'm not willing to take on all of *Na* Kaal's proclivities." Her smile twisted to something more bitter, tinged with a shadow of sadness. "I've done quite a few distasteful things to maintain that reputation, but forcing you to be my bed-slave is a line I won't cross. On this you have my *Lady*-sworn oath."

Strangely enough, something in her voice convinced him. Why she hadn't pursued what had happened between them, he had no idea. That she hadn't was a relief, and he felt a grudging respect for her judgment call.

It still felt odd hearing a demon invoke the *Lady's* name, yet Arek nodded. "And you have mine to see this plan through, whatever it takes."

Chapter 18

"WEATHER'S coming in!"

The call carried over the crunch and grind of iron-rimmed wheels on stones. Arek glanced up as one of the transport beasts he walked beside snorted and huffed, its harness rattling as it worked to pull the loaded cart behind it.

Skadda Pass was no longer visible, instead dark gray clouds billowed around the summit, obscuring the snowcapped peaks. The eastern slope across the glacial valley remained bathed in midafternoon sunlight, but the caravan was headed northwest, toward the ominous clouds.

"Move closer together!" Half a dozen wagons ahead, Rassan sat astride his *Vorc*, leading them along the mountain trail. As the order was called down the line, he flipped up the hood of his cloak to shield himself from the headwind he'd be turning back into once he set out along the trail again. "We'll make camp at The Overhang."

Arek hoped the site would provide some shelter from the elements. For the better part of the day, it'd been a sunlit, steady trek through the undulating foothills heading north along the steeper slopes of the Skadda Mountain Range. With the higher altitude came a drop in temperature, and everyone had donned warmer clothes or cloaks.

The thicker, more densely wooded forests of the foothills were absent and had been for half a day. Instead stunted alpine trees grew in haphazard patches on the gray, rocky ridges, most on the leeward side of spurs instead of the windswept slopes. Scraggly bushes clumped together where they could, their gnarled roots forcing their way into every crack and fissure on the rocky ground.

The trail though was wide and well worn, safe enough for wagons, but little protection against a snowstorm if they were caught out in the open, and the heaviness of the clouds ahead and the icy scent in the air foretold snow.

"Let's pick up the pace, Second!"

The hail came from farther down the line. Rassan raised a gloved fist in acknowledgment.

The sound of claws grating on stone had the transport beast letting out a snort. Arek reached out to pat its shaggy head as the heavy odor of *Vorc* musk filled his nostrils on the next gust of wind. The transport beast issued a low-pitched rumble.

"It's all right, girl," he murmured, empathizing, none too comfortable with the predator's presence, either, even though he'd seen all the riders muzzle them before the trip started.

The *Vorc-Rider* drew level with them.

Imhara.

No, she was *Na* Kaal.

Rassan's parting instruction when they'd left the Kaal fortress had been to practice using the titles assigned to every *Na'Reish* so that when they began their role-playing it would be second nature.

The black-clad figure seated on her mount certainly looked like a Clan *Na*. The leather armor buckled around her torso bore the Kaal emblem—a mountain peak with a crescent moon—the green and silver colors hand painted into the design. Her sword hung in its scabbard strapped to the pack on the back of the saddle pad, but a dagger lay sheathed on her belt and another protruded from the top of her knee-high leather boots.

Arek ran his gaze over her profile, free to study her unobserved. With her hair pulled back into a tight plait, it fell halfway down her back. The style accentuated the proud line of her jaw and neck, her demon markings clearly visible until they disappeared beneath the collar of her undershirt.

The unconscious but graceful way she moved and adjusted to her mount's gait spoke of a lifetime in the saddle. Her *Na'Hord* responded to her commands with easy acceptance, something he hadn't had the chance to see back at the fortress. She was a leader well respected, and it explained, too, the aura of self-confidence he'd seen when they'd first met.

Black breeches molded to her long legs as she rose in her stirrups and peered ahead. Dark brows veed downward and her black lips flattened. Unlike most *Na'Reishi* Lordlings who preferred the comfort of travelling in a warm wagon, she'd remained on duty with her *Na'Hord*.

Arek wondered just how many other Clan *Na's* patrolled their caravan aware of everything that was happening rather than relying on periodic reports from their Second. Very few, if he went by what he'd observed while on border patrol in the past.

"A snowstorm, *Na* Kaal?"

One eyebrow rose at his use of her title, but she made no comment. "Within the hour." She resettled in the saddle, and with an easy twitch of the reins, guided her *Vorc* closer.

"Will it delay us long?"

She gave a half shrug. "It depends. If this wind keeps up, it'll blow over and move southward through the valley in a matter of hours. Even if it holds us here overnight, being one of the first storms of the season, it should start to thaw once the sun rises." Deep violet eyes flickered in his direction. "You don't come from a mountainous province?"

A casual question asked in a cautious tone, as if she were unsure how he'd take a personal inquiry.

Arek couldn't see the harm in answering. "My duties took me to places in the mountains, but I grew up on the plains."

Her gaze returned to the jagged landscape. "It can be wild and extreme, particularly in the worst of seasons, but you should see it in late spring–early summer, when all the wildflowers and new growth appear on the slopes. So different to the barrenness you see now. Like any place, it's not so bad once you learn how to read the weather." Genuine warmth infused her voice. A gloved hand pointed to the clouds ahead. "See how the vapor rises and rolls forward along the leading edge of the storm? That tells me a warm wind pushes it from the Gannec side of the range, probably originating from the Chomi Desert. With the cooler weather here, the clouds are drawn over the mountains."

It wasn't dissimilar to the rainstorms he was more familiar with. Heat from the plains built the thunderclouds while the cooler tree-lined hills and water in Sacred Lake directed its path.

"Does the cold season stop Meelar and his slave-raiders?" he asked.

"In the dead of winter, Skadda Pass can be closed for several weeks. At other times, there have been those of his ilk who've ignored my warnings about leaving a crossing too late in the day or season. Out-of-season snowstorms do occur. It's usually the next party who discovers their bodies on the trail and learns from their mistake."

A hail from the head of the caravan drew their attention. Arek stepped farther out on the trail to see what was going on.

Ahead the road curved east, taking advantage of a natural cut in the side of the mountain, and formed a shelf wide enough for wagons to turn around in. The overhanging rock face towered above them, while the slopes above and below were peppered with trees, the thickest groves he'd seen since the foothills.

"We'll be well protected here tonight. I'll be glad to get out of this wind." A satisfied grin stretched Imhara's lips, one he couldn't help but share. The heat of a fire would be welcome indeed. “If you look along the rock wall, you’ll see iron rings hammered into it.”

For beasts or humans? Although he didn’t ask that question aloud, not really wanting to know the answer. Instead, “So, this is a regular stop?”

“It’s the only place to camp once you begin the trek over the pass, coming or going. Ahead there’s more open ground; most of it’s bare rock or screes. No place for a caravan to halt even in the best of weather. The winds up here can be dangerous. After this the valley narrows. It’ll take another few hours to reach Skadda Pass, and then we’ll be riding single file, after that we start the descent into Gannec territory.”

Wagons were beginning to position themselves in a circle on the wide shelf.

Imhara kneed her mount forward. “When we finish setting up camp, meet with me, and we’ll go over what you know about the *Na’Reish* and fill in any gaps you may have.”

The gaps most likely referred to slave etiquette. Arek nodded and turned, intending to help the driver position his wagon, when he heard a high-pitch whine pass overhead.

Imhara’s *Vorc* howled. Arek swung around, adrenaline surging through him, expecting to see the predator in attack mode. It lunged away from him, shaking its head, fighting to tear the reins from Imhara’s grasp. When it couldn’t, it tried to turn toward its back leg. She fought to control him.

“Ambush!” Rassan’s warning cry echoed around the campsite.

Arek dropped into a crouch as something hit the rocky trail and ricocheted off to the side of the road. A feathered shaft buried itself into the dirt barely an arm’s length from him.

Arrows!

More struck the campsite, some piercing the wagon’s canvas

covers, others the supplies strapped to the sides. People leapt from the seats and scrambled under the bases for cover. Arek ducked behind the wheel of the wagon. He joined the driver who was already crouched there, then peered up at the tree line, searching for the archers and a way to reach them.

How many were there? The trees offered them perfect cover and concealment. A quick look around showed the enemy's fire had concentrated on the lead wagons. Arek's gaze narrowed. Not so many as he first thought. Maybe three or four archers.

Imhara's *Vorc* howled again. Keeping below the height of the wagon, Arek swiveled on his heel. Two arrows protruded from the thick muscle of the *Vorc's* hindquarters. In swift succession another pierced its throat then its chest. Its howl turned into a strangled gurgle. Imhara jerked in the saddle then clutched at her thigh. A feathered shaft poked through the fingers of her glove.

Another arrow struck her chest armor and deflected off. A third impaled her upper arm and knocked her to one side. Grimacing, she fought one-handed to remain in the saddle, but her feet had come free of the stirrups.

Her mount stumbled backward with her shifting weight, perilously close to the edge of the trail and the steep wooded hillside. Its wounded leg buckled. One back claw slipped, grating the lip. It scrabbled for purchase.

"Imhara!" Rassan's shout came as she and the animal disappeared over the edge in a spray of pebbles and stones.

Chapter 19

AREK'S stomach knotted at the look on Imhara's face—horrified disbelief—the moment before the *Vorc* slipped and they both tumbled over the edge of the roadway. It was the same emotion he'd experienced the day he'd watched Kalan take a *Na'Reish* blade in the gut. He'd seen it coming but been unable to stop it happening.

Just like now.

A swift glance at Rassan revealed he was too involved with the ambush to be in any position to help. Who knew how long it would take to fight the enemy off or if they would succeed.

Heart pounding in his chest, Arek turned to the wagon driver. "Quick! Your gloves!"

"What?" The sandy-haired human stared at him as if he'd gone mad.

"Give me your gloves!"

The man stripped them off. "Why?"

With no time to answer, Arek pulled them on. He sprinted to the spot where Imhara had gone over. Boots skidding on loose gravel, he dropped to his stomach and peered over the lip of the trail. A vulnerable position with the archers, but he ignored the crawling sensation between his shoulder blades.

Merciful Mother! A sickening scar of missing rock and chunks of soil marred the slope before something heavy had smashed through the tree line over a hundred feet below. A few stray rocks and pebbles still rattled down the hillside.

Could Imhara have survived the fall? The hillside wasn't a sheer drop, but it was steep enough, studded with trees and bushes, perhaps enough to slow her momentum, if she'd been thrown clear of her mount.

If not . . . *Lady of Light*, he'd seen the injuries a fallen war-beast could inflict on a rider. Most had been fatal. *Vorc* were as heavy and solid an animal as them. A shiver worked its way down his spine.

Sucking in a deep breath, Arek launched himself over the edge. He dug his gloved fingers and heels of his boots into the earth to control the slide. Already loosened, more clods of dirt dislodged with his descent. He watched them skip and bounce ahead of him. Some shattered into clouds of dust as they struck once too often, some vanished into the tree line.

Enough debris had built up at the end of the scar to create a mound. He flung himself sideways and hit hard enough to drive the wind from his lungs. Better that than broken legs. Rocks and dirt cascaded over him. Gasping and coughing for breath, he covered his head until the worst of it was over.

Slowly, Arek looked up. The heavy scent of fresh earth filled his nostrils as his breathing steadied. A quick glance back upslope reassured him nothing else would tumble down on top of him. Faint war cries drifted on the cold breeze.

With a swift pray to the *Lady* for Rassan and the others, Arek rolled to his feet and headed into the stunted alpine forest. The *Vorc* lay ten feet in. It rested against the trunks of several trees, neck snapped by the fall. The coldness curling in his gut intensified.

"Imhara?"

Arek worked his way around its tail end, using the tree trunks to combat the slope of the ground. One more step and he stared at where he'd anticipated finding her broken body, and blinked when it wasn't there.

Pulse beating hard, he scoured the ground for signs of her. "Imhara!"

Only the sound of the wind whistled through the forest. How in the *Lady's* name had she walked away from a hundred-and-fifty-foot tumble with two arrows in her? Built stronger than humans, the *Na'Reish* could take more punishment to their bodies—broken limbs were rare, their bones heavier, denser; he'd seen that time and again on the battlefield—but injured internal organs bled and incapacitated them just as easily as humans.

Arek shook his head and peered around the forest. With the overcast conditions, shadows of gray obscured everything. Precious moments slipped away as he untied Imhara's pack from the dead *Vorc*. If she were alive, he'd need some of the items contained within. He slung it and her sword belt over his shoulder, then began searching for her trail.

At the base of a nearby tree, he discovered drag marks and chips of tree bark scattered on the moss, as if someone had used the trunk to pull themselves upright. And there—he stretched out his fingers to trace the clear outline—the heel of a boot. Farther on, a rock stained with a bloody handprint.

Lady's Breath—Arek released a slow breath—Imhara had walked from the fall. A wave of relief made him pause by a tree trunk. He frowned. Why such an intense reaction? He shook his head. That could wait until later.

Injured and losing blood, he doubted she could move particularly fast. Her tracks headed downhill toward a gentler incline where the spur leveled out.

He would find her. Eventually.

But now his greatest concern came from two other sources.

The first—the imminent snowstorm. If he couldn't locate her

before it hit, they'd both be at the mercy of the elements. Not a death he particularly relished.

The second—the boot prints marking the earth next to Imhara's bloody handprint. Although tall, Imhara's feet weren't that wide. Nor were there two of her.

Someone else was hunting her.

"HER tracks lead into the gully!" A deep-voiced hail jerked Imhara out of a doze. "The scent of her blood is fresh!"

While the wind carried the words to her, she knew her pursuers were close, perhaps at the edge of the tree line where the slope flattened out. Where she'd tripped when her boot had caught on a rock, then fallen. She'd left a trail even a blind ground-burrower could follow.

Fleeing on instinct hadn't helped, but it'd been the only option open to her when she'd heard them searching for her after the fall. She'd meant to stop only a moment to gather her strength and her breath, and plan her next move. But the pounding in her head made thinking impossible, so she'd closed her eyes, hoping it would help.

She grimaced, recognizing the symptoms. Head injury, exhaustion, or blood loss—any or all were probable. She couldn't afford to be incapacitated by any of them right now.

Huddled against the side of a boulder, she pressed her cheek and shoulder against its gritty surface.

"They'll kill you when they find you, Imhara," she panted. "Do you want that?" With a grunt she straightened. "No. The *Lady* helps those who help themselves."

But she couldn't ignore the warm stickiness soaking her right breeches' leg all the way down into her boot. Her arm didn't feel much better. The heavy iron odor of fresh blood filled her nostrils.

The sleeve of her shirt stuck to her skin from wound to wrist, and the back of her hand bore a bizarre pattern of drying blood.

She grimaced. The tumble down the valley wall had snapped the shafts of the arrows off and driven the heads deeper into her flesh. They had to come out.

Blood and dirt caked her clothes, so using them as bandages was out, and cauterizing the wounds to stop the bleeding required a fire. How much time did she have before her trackers found her? Probably not enough to complete that procedure.

"If she gets away, the *Na'Reishi* will have our heads."

"She's wounded. How far can she get?" The second voice rose and fell in volume as the wind shifted. Two males pursued her. Both unfamiliar. "We'll find her unconscious somewhere."

Imhara's lip curled. Such arrogance, holding a conversation while tracking someone they presumed was helpless.

Which Clan did they belong to? Who had sent them? She issued a soft grunt. Any number of names could top that list, for myriad reasons. She'd made plenty of enemies over the years. Why had they chosen to attack now?

And what had happened to the others? The caravan? Had they survived the ambush? Had anyone seen her fall?

So many questions, and no answers.

No idea if help was coming or if her Clan lay slaughtered up on the roadway. Was she the lone survivor, just like the time she'd lost her family? A shiver worked its way through her.

Imhara issued a breathless laugh. An iciness tangled with the nausea in her gut. Her laughter became ragged gasps.

Don't lose it now! The thought was a vicious command.

Gritting her teeth, she pressed her injured arm hard against the rough surface of the boulder. Searing agony shot from her shoulder to her wrist.

"*Lady's Breath!*" The hoarse curse ripped from her throat.

She panted, waiting for the pain to abate. Shivers racked her body. At least the panic had subsided.

"Come on, Kaal! Too many depend on you to give up now. You've felt like *Vorc* crap after training. You've been wounded before."

Not this badly.

The small voice at the back of her mind was hard to ignore when it was right. She crooked cold, stiff fingers over the edge of the boulder and glanced up at the overcast sky. It was still bitingly cold but the wind had dropped. Snowfall was imminent. Could her day get any worse?

"This blood is fresh!" Stones clattered on her back trail, too close. "She's headed that way."

When Imhara glanced behind her, she saw two *Na'Hord* warriors round the bend in the gully. With a grunt, she pushed to her feet, uncertain if pure Kaal stubbornness or desperation fueled her.

"Whatever works, Imhara," she muttered. Head swimming, she clung to the boulder and waited for the world to steady. "You breathe. Your heart beats. Move!"

Inhaling hard, she scanned the ground ahead. Her options were limited. Traverse the slope and go up. That required too much energy and a body not handicapped by her injuries. Returning the way she'd come meant meeting her pursuers more quickly.

So, that left continuing on into the narrow head of the gully.

A dead end.

She snorted quietly. Quite appropriate, given the confrontation to come.

Shrubs and a few boulders littered the ground ahead, chunky sentinels that would provide her with interim way stations as she headed for her end destination—a ridgeline of rock—the most defensible piece of ground she could reach in the time she had left.

Gritting her teeth, she took a halting step, then another, and another.

"See, there she is!" Imhara didn't bother turning at the triumphant announcement. She lurched from one boulder to the next, her legs shaking. "What did I tell you, Garsh?"

"Where are you going, *Na* Kaal?"

She ignored the hail and low-pitched laughter of the two males but welcomed the hot rush of adrenaline as her temper sparked. It helped her cover the last several feet. Breath coming in ragged gasps, she leaned against the cold, hard wall.

Behind her, gravel crunched underfoot. Her nostrils filled with a heavy acidic odor.

Predatory excitement.

Any further sign of weakness would increase their confidence. She turned, her armor scraping against the rock face. Every vibration shot straight through her wounded arm like slivers of glass. Biting back a moan, she drew her dagger from her belt and pushed away from the wall.

"Looks like there's some fight left in her yet, Garsh." Satisfaction oozed from the *Na'Hord* warrior on the left. His dark purple gaze gleamed as it flickered to the weapon she held. "A futile effort, *Na* Kaal. I'll grant you a swift death, if you drop your blade now."

"My life is worth more than that." Anger cut through her weariness and pain. "You'll have to work for it."

"Will we now?" He grunted and folded his arms. "You're looking a little pale and unsteady on your feet."

"And that isn't dirt staining your breeches." His companion chuckled. "She'll be lucky to scratch us with that dagger in her hand, Jedir."

"Bold words, *Na'Reishu*." She widened her stance, teeth clenched hard to hide the pain of placing weight on her wounded leg. "Come closer and let's see if I can stick a few holes in you to let out all that hot air."

Garsh's mouth tightened and a gloved fist clenched, as if he wasn't used to being spoken to by a female in such a manner. Imhara's mouth twitched. He probably wasn't.

"You boast loud for a warrior"—she injected all the contempt she could muster into her tone—"but you lack the courage to follow through."

The *Na'Reisha's* face flushed a dull red and he took a step toward her. Jedir threw out an arm to stop him. The look he shot Garsh was scathing.

"Clever." His chuckle wasn't pleasant. "We were warned you had a mouth." His glare turned on her and narrowed. "Rest assured we'll teach you the proper use of it before we're through with you."

"You can try." Imhara eased into an offensive stance. "And fail, like all the others."

Garsh's gaze widened then flickered to Jedir. Had no one told him she knew how to fight? What arrogance. And a mistake.

The two *Na'Hord* warriors took their time closing in on her. Jedir stood over seven feet tall, all brawn and muscle, more than capable of wielding the heavy sword sheathed at his waist. No inexperienced youth, not with the gray streaking his temples and the dark hair pulled back into a single ponytail at the base of his neck.

His segmented armor ranked him as Garsh's superior, perhaps a Commander. She frowned, looking between the two warriors. Neither chest plate bore a Clan symbol or distinguishing colors. Given the nature of the ambush, it didn't surprise her that they'd want to keep their identity a secret.

Several inches shorter, Garsh was the leaner warrior of the two. His sharper, more rugged features and paler mottled skin pattern definitely relegated him to the lesser ranks. Jedir's lackey, used to blindly following orders. His gaze kept darting back and forth between her and his superior the closer they came, his hand resting close to the hilt of his sword.

She kept most of her attention on the taller warrior. Jedir would make the first move.

"I'm going to enjoy this." As if his words were a signal, both warriors drew their swords and Garsh rushed her, a war cry erupted from his throat. Temper, ignorance, or nerves, she didn't care, he'd betrayed his intent.

He swung his sword. She ducked, lip curling. It cut through the air overhead. She rolled to his right, blade slashing low. It sliced deep into the back of his unprotected knee. Cloth, flesh, and tendons. His cry turned into a howl.

Pain shot through her thigh as she staggered to her feet, the move lacking her usual grace. His blood warmed her hand, the metallic scent of it rich and thick.

Garsh lay on the ground, clutching his leg. Hamstrung and handicapped. To get anywhere near her, he'd have to crawl. Whoever these *Na'Reish* gutter dwellers were, they were learning that a wounded female *Vorc* had nothing on her. Her mouth kicked upward.

"Fool!" Jedir's disdainful tone matched his expression. "I told you not to underestimate her."

His purple gaze locked on her. Promised retribution burned there. Her heart pounded harder.

In one fluid motion, he leapt straight at her. She hurled herself over the nearest boulder. The metal of his blade screeched on stone. She landed in a heap on the other side. The jolt awoke every bruise and ache. Her head swam. The burst of adrenaline hadn't lasted long.

"Get her good, Jedir!" Garsh's hoarse shout vibrated with excitement.

Footsteps crunched on gravel. From the corner of her eye, Jedir's sword glinted. She rolled away. His blade bit the ground beside her.

She rolled back, throwing all her weight onto it. The studs on her chest armor caught it. The blade bent but didn't break.

Mother of Light! She drove her dagger at his leg.

His boot lashed out, connected with her wrist. Her weapon clattered away among the rocks. His hands fisted in her hair and the edge of her armor, then jerked her upright before slamming her onto her back. The impact stole her breath. She reached for the dagger in her boot.

Jedir stepped on her wounded arm. She screamed. Her vision grayed.

"Don't faint on me, female." The agonizing pressure on her arm eased. An openhanded slap stung her cheek. "I want you conscious. Garsh will want to hear your cries when I take you."

Imhara blinked up at him, processing his words. She couldn't let this happen. She wouldn't let it happen.

"Then, when I'm finished with you, you'll taste the sting of my blade." His gaze gleamed. "You're going to bleed, one slice at a time, and feel your life drain from you." The warrior crouched, placing his sword to one side. It was within reach. "I wonder what will give me greater pleasure? Your body? Or your death?"

Imhara willed her numbed arm to move. No matter how much she wanted them to though, her muscles refused to work.

Fingers of ice speared her heart. "No!"

An insidious heaviness weighed all her limbs. She had no strength left to fight. Jedir's lips peeled back from his pointed teeth in a cruel grin. Coldness edged his mocking laughter.

"Oh, yes." He smoothed a blunt nail down the side of her cheek, then his fingers gripped her jaw hard enough to bruise. His other hand closed around her throat. "Now, let's teach you your place."

A charge of energy buzzed Imhara's senses.

Lady's Breath, this was it.

A shadow loomed behind Jedir. "I think not, demon!"

Chapter 20

USING a two-handed grip, Arek plunged Imhara's sword deep into the heavily muscled shoulder of the *Na'Reish*, where the edge of the armor exposed the skin of his neck and proved most vulnerable. With it went the whole force of his Gift, the power burning through the blade hotter and faster than he'd ever felt before.

The *Na'Reish* warrior jerked upright, his black lips stretched wide in a soundless scream. His body convulsed.

He wouldn't touch Imhara again. There was no honor in the way the arrogant bastard had taunted her as she lay helpless on the ground, threatening her with rape and a slow death.

Too many others had suffered the same fate. Arek's fingers tightened on the hilt of the sword as the faces of his mother, Light Blade sisters and brothers, farmers, crofters, traders, and others, flitted through his mind in vivid, agonizing detail. Every outraged cry, every scream of terror, every plea for mercy with none given, the realization of their deaths etched in their faces in their final moments—echoes of the past reflected in Imhara's stunned expression as she'd stared up at her opponent.

But then the *Na'Reish* saw battle only in the terms of winning and losing. Conquering or enslaving. The strong dominating the weak.

Jedir's intention had been to demonstrate his power in the basest way possible. Because he could.

A behavior Arek had witnessed too many times to count. Cold gratification filled him as the demon's gaze glazed over. Planting his boot against the leather-plated armor, he yanked the sword free. The demon toppled over. His body hit the ground with a satisfying thud.

"There's another. . . ." Imhara's warning held barely a thread of sound. Small, white flakes of snow drifted down as he knelt beside her.

"He's dead." Arek cast a glance to where the second demon lay flat on his back, staring up at the overcast sky. His Gift had poured into Garsh just as fiercely as it had with Jedir. "I just wish all *Na'Hord* were as easy to kill as him."

Her brow furrowed, her gaze clouded with pain and confusion, and it dawned on him then what he'd just said. Technically Imhara was also *Na'Hord*, but for the first time since he'd met her, he hadn't viewed her as such. How . . . *When* had that happened?

Arek cleared his throat, put aside the sword, and began unbuckling her armor. She'd be more comfortable without it. Dints and scrapes decorated it, and one buckle strap had already torn free, testament to the torturous tumble she'd taken.

"If he hadn't been so focused on the fight between you and Jedir, he might have seen me approaching." He motioned to the foliage on the valley wall. "I only had that thin line of shrubs for cover." Tossing her armor aside, he unslung the pack on his shoulder. Pulling out a shirt, he began tearing it into strips. "You did well to take him down as fast as you did."

A smile ghosted her lips. "Thank you . . ."

"He underestimated you."

"Many do."

Arek made a noncommittal sound. He'd listened to her threaten Garsh yet never thought she'd take him on. But then she hadn't known he was nearby. She'd acted and taken the offensive, believing herself to be alone.

Just like a warrior.

Just as he would have.

How she'd ever found the strength to avoid Garsh's killing blow—he shook his head—no human would have been able to move like she had with those wounds.

What would it be like to meet her on the training ground? He suspected he'd enjoy the challenge of facing her, warrior to warrior.

"Underestimating you seems to be a habit of most males"—and here he met her gaze—"myself included."

His wry tone coaxed a smile from her. "Like those two, some learn too late." Her mouth quirked. "Although I believe there might be hope for you yet, Light Blade." His own lips twitched as her expression grew somber. "Thank you for saving my life."

Her gratitude reignited his awareness that he'd just killed two demons to save one. Something he thought he'd never do.

He grunted. "Seems like we both had a hand in that." He wadded a strip of material into a pad. A snowflake touched down on the back of his hand. "The weather's closing in. Let's get you tended to."

The uneven spots of her skin markings stood out in stark relief against the paleness of her skin. Her lips actually looked more gray than black. How much blood had she lost? He pressed the pad to the wound on her thigh.

"Arek, the arrowheads have to come out."

His gaze lifted to hers. Her eyes were glassy but level. Snow peppered her hair and face. He brushed it from her cheeks and forehead, careful to avoid the dark bruise and bump on her temple. Her skin was cold to the touch.

"I'm no healer, Imhara. I could do you more harm than good." He placed his fingers against the pulse in her throat. Rapid and shallow. "We need to get you back to the caravan."

He put another pad against the wound on her arm.

"The snow's getting heavier. We'd never make it back in time."

A thin layer already coated the ground and the surface of every boulder. Gray clouds obscured the top of the valley. The premature arrival of evening would inhibit travelling even if the snow wasn't present. With both, the temperature would drop fast.

She was right. Getting back to the caravan wouldn't be possible. He muttered a curse.

"Please, Arek." Imhara's hand lifted; her fingers caught the sleeve of his arm before dropping to her stomach when he stiffened. "Leave them in and I die."

Na'Reish were tough. He'd witnessed it on the battlefield and Imhara had proven it, surviving a fall that should have killed her, and two assassins.

He still hesitated though. In his time on patrol, he might have sewn up a cut or two, but her wounds were a lot more serious. Could she withstand his rough field surgery? Yet what choice did either of them have?

"Having second thoughts?" she asked, her question drawing his gaze back down to her.

He frowned. "About what?"

"You made it clear you wanted me dead." Her lips twisted into a pained smile. "If this was your plan all along, then why did you stop Jedir?"

"You believe I want to kill you?" Shock stiffened his spine.

"What am I to think when you hesitate?"

"*Lady of Light*, regardless of how I feel about you, up on that fortress wall I gave you my oath to help you." Despite his anger, he peeled the wadded pad from her arm with care. "I hesitate because I don't know how strong you are, how much blood you've lost, or what other injuries you have that I can't see. I worry about cutting into you with a knife because of the pain I'll cause you and whether you'll survive."

He reached across her body to yank the dagger from the *Na'Reish* demon's belt. Snow was falling faster. In better circumstances he'd use flame to clean the blade before using it on anyone, but there was no time to build a fire.

"I'll take out the arrowheads." He squeezed the hilt of the dagger. "But only because I have no other option."

Two quick cuts and he peeled her sleeve away from the wound. Blood oozed from around the stump of the arrow shaft. Gently he probed the underside of her arm. No broken skin. The head hadn't gone through. He'd have to dig it out. He grimaced.

"This isn't going to be pretty. You ready?" There was no reply. Arek glanced up, wondering if the silence meant Imhara had lost consciousness, only to discover her dark violet gaze fixed on him, her frown now thoughtful. "What?"

"I'm sorry for misunderstanding your intentions. It's a comfort to know I have nothing to be scared of when you remove these arrows." Her fingers flexed as if she wanted to reach out and touch him, but she held back. "Thank you for your concern."

A solemn reply, her admission of fear the last thing he'd expected and not a particularly comfortable thought, especially when she'd always projected such confidence and strength.

Sure, he'd imagined retribution for the time she'd fed from him that first night in her room, and he'd probably alarmed her with his recent *Na'Hord* comment, but much had altered since then.

"Do whatever needs to be done, Arek. The outcome is in the *Lady's* hands." Imhara inhaled a deep breath. "I'm ready."

Such trust loaded into two simple words. He doubted he'd have put his life in her hands in a similar situation. Her courage shamed him.

Stripping off the driver's gloves, and before he changed his mind, he clasped her hand. "May *She* give us both the strength to see this through."

Her fingers tightened on his, trembling. Exhaustion or fear? Her lips parted, as if she was going to speak, but instead she offered him a wan smile and a nod.

Arek bent to the task of removing the first arrowhead. He worked as quickly as he could, aware that Imhara made no sound other than an initial intake of breath when he first probed the wound.

Her courage steadied his hand. He could offer her no less. The metal barb came out with relative ease after a minute or two, but the one in her thigh took much more effort.

By the time he tossed the second arrowhead into the snow beside them, Imhara had passed out. As swiftly as he could, he bandaged her leg and bundled her in the cloak he pulled from the pack.

After washing his hands in the snow, he pulled the driver's gloves back on, needing their warmth. Every breath exhaled became a frosted cloud. They needed shelter and a fire. Fuel wasn't a problem; he could backtrack to the tree line at the end of the gully. Debris lay aplenty at the base of the trees, protected from the wet snow by the branches overhead. But where could he leave Imhara?

He searched the landscape. A quick walk to examine the dead end brought a smile to his face. The ridge of rock and two boulders formed an enclosed area on three sides. The outward slope of the wall deflected the snow away from the shelter.

If he worked fast, he could make a lean-to roof and block the fourth side with a woven wall of branches. Once snow covered the roof, it would provide more insulation against the cold. They'd have a dry, warm place to spend the night.

With a prayer of thanks to the *Lady*, Arek relocated Imhara and their meager supplies to the sheltered area. As an afterthought, he stripped both demons of their armor and clothes. The extra layers would prove useful as the temperature dropped. Then he dragged the bodies to the other end of the gully. Predators roamed the mountains. While the snowstorm might deter some from venturing out, there was no need to tempt fate by leaving the bodies close to where they sheltered.

Dumping the armor and weapons near the shelter, Arek hung on to the belts. They'd help with carting the wood. Aware that the afternoon light and visibility was dimming fast, he broke into a jog and headed out of the gully.

"COME on, Imhara, wake up!"

The distant voice intruded on her sleep.

"Imhara, open your eyes. . . . Look at me."

A warm hand touched her cheek. She stirred and leaned toward it.

"That's it. I saw your eyelids flutter. You can do it. Come on, wake up!"

Coaxed by the voice, Imhara struggled to consciousness, but it was like wading through swamp mud. Her eyelids felt glued shut and everything felt heavy.

The first look at her surroundings ended up being a blurred image of light and darkness. Quite disorienting. She blinked, a deliberate lid-to-lid meeting, and the world jumped into focus.

She stared at a thick canopy of tree branches. A forest? Couldn't be, even though she could hear the wind beyond the limbs. The limbs lay at right angles to one another, crisscrossed over and under. No forest grew like that.

"I see that you're admiring my handiwork." The soft voice was familiar.

"Arek?" The husky croak came from her throat.

The Light Blade warrior leaned over her. "I'm here." Flickering light played hide-and-seek with shadows on his face, but she could see lines of weariness and tension bracketing his eyes and mouth. “How do you feel?”

“Thirsty.” She swallowed against a dry throat. “Tired.”

A grunt, then, “The thirst I can help you with but you can’t go back to sleep.”

A hand slipped beneath her head, his solid support a stark contrast to how weak she felt. A canteen pressed against her lips. Cool water filled her mouth, just a sip. *Mother of Mercy*, it tasted good.

“More?” She nodded at the question, wincing as her head began to throb. “Headache?” This time she whispered an affirmative. “I’m not surprised. You have a dark bruise and bump the size of a *jamet’s* egg on your left temple. It’s why I woke you.” Dark blue eyes peered into hers, checking. “Your eyes look all right.”

He lifted the canteen to her lips again and let her drink. Her stomach cramped and an intense wave of hunger washed through her. Recognizing it for what it was wiped away the last traces of her lethargy.

Blood-need.

Imhara gulped another few mouthfuls of water but craved something much richer, hotter, and thicker in texture. Several hard swallows and she kept the water down. Licking her lips, she tasted the salt of her own sweat. A poor substitute. Only feeding to replace what she’d lost would help her heal. And there was only one way to satiate it.

With a turn of her head, her cheek brushed the sleeve of Arek’s shirt. She closed her eyes and inhaled, letting his scent fill her. An earthy blend of heated male and the outdoors mixed with the faintest trace of human blood.

Her nostrils flared and saliva flooded her mouth. Only a single layer of cloth separated his skin from her mouth, her teeth. It wouldn’t take much to tear and shred it. She could feed.

Imhara shuddered and fisted the blanket, fighting the primal response.

"You're cold." Arek shifted, letting her head rest against something soft as he moved away from her. She opened her eyes to see him placing wood on a small fire.

The rock walls around them provided a much-needed distraction. "Is this a cave?"

"We're still in the dead end gully, in a shelter, part natural, part built."

The space was small, barely big enough for both of them. Kneeling by the fire, Arek's blond hair almost touched the roof. Within a foot of her blanketed feet was another wall, this one also made of woven branches. The base had two armor chest plates tied to anchor it into the ground. The thick leather would keep snow and draughts out, while a small hole near the top drew out the smoke of the fire. Dead needle-leaves strewn across the floor kept the damp of the ground from them.

Despite the warmth coming from the flames of the fire, Imhara shivered again. This time she was truly cold.

The colder she became, the more intense her hunger would be. *Light*, not a good combination.

Closing her eyes, she released a slow breath and added concern to her list. Not for herself, but for Arek.

"Imhara, stay awake, don't go back to sleep." His tone was light, cajoling, but the acrid odor coming from him betrayed his concern. His compassion made for a welcome change from bitter hatred.

"It'd probably be better if I did."

"Why say that?" She hadn't realized she'd spoken aloud until he responded. "I might not be able to wake you next time."

Grimacing, she opened her eyes to stare at the fire, listening to the flames crackle and snap as they consumed the wood, and wished she could crawl among the embers. The cold racking her body was bone deep.

"I'm just so tired." The truth, enough for the moment. Beneath the cloak, she flexed her good hand, trying to get warm. Perhaps the hunger pangs would ease if she could do that.

Arek placed more fuel on the fire, then returned to sit beside her. He nodded in the direction of the woven wall. "The armor worn by those *Na'Reish* don't have Clan markings on them. Nor could I find any on their weapons. Did you recognize them?"

"No. And we can assume none of the archers will be wearing anything identifiable, either." She shifted to look up at him. "Arek, what happened to the caravan? The others?"

"I don't know." The flickering shadows darkened his twilight eyes to ebony. A small frown creased his brow. "The first few wagons were pinned down. Rassan was calling orders to your *Na'Hord* when we saw you go over the edge of the roadway. I was the closest, so I went after you."

Only a few had fallen under attack? That hinted the ambush had been sprung too early. While steep, the hillside above The Overhang was accessible. Any wagons near the bend that hadn't reached the campsite were in a position to take advantage of that. Her *Na'Hord* could climb the slopes and work their way around to the forest from there. Rassan would have that knowledge.

"There were three, maybe four archers." His firm lips thinned. "Your *Vorc* took half a dozen arrows. You took two and your armor deflected a third. They were determined to kill you." Darkness stirred in his gaze, and a bitter heat crept into his scent. "The taller one, Jedir, mentioned they'd been warned about you. That means someone else ordered this ambush."

"Assassins for hire."

"You say that so calmly."

"It comes with the territory, Arek."

"I suppose it would." He blew out a short breath. "Will Rassan kill or capture the archers?"

"I doubt any will let him take them alive." Another uncontrollable shudder ripped through her. *Merciful Mother*, would she never feel warm again? She tried to snuggle deeper into her cloak.

Arek's hand smoothed over her forehead, his palm furnace-hot. A quick tug and his hand delved beneath the edge of the cloak and found hers. "You're wearing two extra layers of clothing, the air is warm from the fire, and you're still a block of ice." His frown deepened. "You could have cold-sickness."

Unlikely.

Should she reveal the true reason?

Imhara chewed her lip. No. Not unless she had no other choice. Arek had enough to worry about without an added complication.

"I've seen healers give hot drinks to those affected by it. We have water and fire but nothing to heat it in."

"It's all right." Her chattering teeth distorted the words almost beyond recognition. "You've done as much as you can."

"No, I haven't." He grimaced, then his expression hardened and blanked, all except his eyes. The deep blue within blazed, heated, and the pupils dilated.

A familiar odor of spice filled her nostrils. Arousal. There was no mistaking it in such close quarters. Her pulse beat harder and a shiver raced down her spine.

What was he thinking?

With a sharp inhalation, he pulled the cloak from around her and helped her to rise into a sitting position. "Not everything."

"What are you doing?"

"Warming you up." He shifted, moving behind her to lean against the wall. Her eyebrows lifted, but his answer made more sense when he slid his long legs either side of her and cradled her back in against his chest. One arm curled around her waist to steady her as he tucked the cloak back in around them both. A muscle in his jaw flexed and his scent dissipated, as if it had never existed.

Lady's Breath, even with three layers of clothing between them, Arek's body heat reminded her of being next to a smithy's forge. It was almost painful on any exposed skin. She shuddered and smothered a groan, soaking it in.

He covered her hands with his. Calloused fingers began to massage hers, surprisingly gentle, stimulating the skin until blood rushed into them, making them tingle and hurt. Her arms were next, his hands stroking then moving in slow, circular motions up each limb, avoiding her wound, working on the muscles he could reach across each of her shoulders without leaning her forward.

Imhara relaxed into his touch. It felt good. This close to him, she couldn't escape his scent. Tangy wood smoke blended with the subtle odor of spice. Not as strong as before yet present once more.

She took a slow breath in through her nose, letting it fill her lungs, savoring it, mulling over what it meant, and found she had to bite the inside of her cheek to contain a smile. Ever since that unexpected kiss between them, she'd been wondering what it would be like to feel his hands on her again. Now she knew.

The ache building inside her wasn't just a reaction of her cold limbs responding to his warmth, and she took a moment to enjoy the sensation. She should feel perturbed finding pleasure in his touch, and for wanting more, but couldn't resist being selfish just this once.

And no matter how much Arek wanted to deny it, he was far from immune to her. An attraction between them existed. Willing or not. She understood his dislike for her, his need to resist, she even respected his struggle, but couldn't help wonder what would happen if he dared to accept what was growing between them. She expected it would be explosive, much like their kiss had been.

Flint to tinder.

Oil on flame.

The raw promise of passion; the provocative images that flashed into her head almost took her mind off her hunger.

Almost.

"You've stopped shivering." Arek's breath hit her forehead in warm puffs, his voice husky. "Warmer?"

"Yes. Thank you."

The hunger had subsided to a tolerable level, but more concerning was the insidious lethargy swamping her senses. Sudden and swift, it was hard to resist. Her head dropped back onto his chest and her eyes closed of their own accord.

"Don't let me sleep." *Lady* help her, her body would shut down if she did. She blinked hard. "I have to stay awake. Talk to me."

Her plea sounded slurred.

"When we arrive at the Gannec fortress, how do I tell all you *Na'Reish* apart?" Beneath her ear, Arek's voice rumbled in his chest. "Each Clan has a crest, but how do I differentiate between the castes?"

Her sleep-fuzzed mind took her a moment to process his question.

"Look at the way we dress." She pointed her chin at the armor opposite them. "Garsh's clothes, his weapons and armor. Simple styles. Worn. Basic designs. He was probably once *Na'Reisha*, the working class, and then joined his Clan's *Na'Hord*. A male's status improves once he becomes a fully trained warrior. He becomes *Na'Reishu*, and any mate or blood-kin are elevated with him."

"Jedir was also *Na'Reishu*?"

"I assume so, although he definitely held some sort of rank, maybe a Commander." She wet her lips. "You'll have no trouble discerning which of us are *Na'Reishi*. Males wear Clan markings and colors on their armor or their finery. Any females with them will be kin or of the same status. You're either born into the rank or take it by force."

"And *Na'Reisha* are the working class?"

"Menial labor and grunt work are left to human-slaves, but *Na'Reisha* are tradesmen, merchants, other skilled workers such as tutors. Some remain in that caste all their lives, some are demoted to the rank because of age, lack of connections, disgrace, or disfigurement. Most try and improve their status by joining the *Na'Hord* or earning the favor of others in a better class than them."

The hypnotic flickering and dancing of the flames drew Imhara's gaze. Her eyelids grew heavy again.

"How do *Na'Reisha* earn favors?"

A gentle squeeze of her hand and the question centered her. She forced herself to focus and answer. Arek asked question after question and, while she knew he was doing it to keep her awake, the queries weren't random. He was methodical in the topics he chose, seeking clarification and details when needed, then going back over the information to check his understanding.

Twice the fire burnt down to embers before he stoked it up again. It was the only measure of time they had for their conversation.

"Would you mind going back over the names of the Clan *Na* again . . . ?"

Cramps twisted her gut, fast and hard. Imhara gasped, her inhalation a guttural cry. Arek's voice faded to the background. Every muscle spasmed, then a ferocious heat blasted through her, head to toe, adrenaline chasing in its wake.

Pulse hammering, she sucked in a breath as every nerve fed her an overwhelming cacophony of sensation and sound. The hard thud of Arek's heart became the pounding of a drum. His scent in her nose an overpowering reek that made her gasp. The coarse rasp of her cloak against her skin an unbearable irritant. Everything so grossly amplified or perverted it hurt.

She shuddered and would have doubled over if Arek's arms hadn't tightened around her.

"Imhara? Are you all right?"

She tried to speak but groaned instead as another wave of nausea ripped through her.

"Imhara?"

"Don't. Move." She winced at the gravelly sound of her voice.

He stiffened, every muscle in his body hardening like steel. She pushed at the cloak covering her, unable to stand it against her skin any longer. Another surge had her writhing in his arms.

His hand pressed against her forehead. "Now you're burning up. What's wrong?"

With a sinking heart, she couldn't ignore what was happening.

"I need . . ." She broke off, cursing, wishing anyone but Arek had tracked her down.

"Water?" He reached for the canteen sitting beside them. "Is that what you want?"

"No."

"Then what?"

Would he let her explain before reacting?

"Blood." She had to feed or risk slipping into unconsciousness. She had to convince him. "I need . . . your blood."

Chapter 21

"*MOTHER of Light!*" None too gently Arek jerked away from Imhara, ignoring her cry of pain as he scrambled back from her.

Keeping the fire between them, he snatched up a weapon from the pile stacked near the wall and whipped around, expecting to find her ready to launch herself at him. She still lay on the ground, her arms wrapped around her middle, panting. He blinked.

Curled up into a tight ball on the pallet of needle-leaves, she didn't look capable of moving an inch let alone the few feet separating them.

"I won't attack you." Her voice was hardly louder than a whisper. The dark smudges ringing her eyes only emphasized the sickly, gray pallor of her face.

"I thought you had cold-sickness!" His gut burned and twisted with his stupidity. "You could be lying now!"

She flinched. "As the *Lady* is my witness, I'm not."

They toy. They torment and then they strike. His grandfather's voice echoed in his head. *Demons don't change their spots! More fool the warrior who believes otherwise!*

He should have listened to his instincts when he'd seen Imhara shivering—the hard facts had been there from the time he'd taken the arrowheads out of her, but like an idiot, he'd let down his guard and trusted her.

"Arek, please, listen to me. . . ."

Tendrils of cold slithered and curled around his heart and squeezed. He'd heard a voice like hers only once before—Annika's; gravelly, thick with need—not something he could forget. He and Kalan had found her locked in Davyn's apartment, consumed by blood-rage, driven over the edge by her hunger. She'd attacked those who'd come to help. It'd taken Varian and Kalan to control her, to stop her from killing Rissa.

Annika hadn't been able to control herself.

Nor had the *Na'Reish* he'd seen on patrol.

Why would Imhara be any different?

"I've seen your kind with blood-rage," he hissed. Breath rasping in through his mouth, his pulse thundering in his ears, he stared across the small distance between them. "You feed, then discard the victim like an empty water pouch. Your hunger for blood is all consuming until you heal." His grip tightened on the dagger. "What's to stop you attacking me?"

"Not all of us are affected by it, Arek. Only a rare few." Her purple-hued eyes locked with his. "Yes, I'm starving, but I'm not a danger to you."

His lips twisted. To think he'd believed she'd been about to die from cold-sickness. Her plight had brought back memories of the failed rescue mission and the uncertainty of not knowing whether his best friend had lived or died because of his actions.

With Imhara, sharing his body heat had been the only thing he could think to do, and doing something was better than nothing. While helping her had felt good, and should have been his only purpose, as he'd slid behind her, his thoughts hadn't been on the healing benefits of their position.

In truth, all he could think about was the way her body fit against his. How her torso molded to his chest, the curved softness of her buttocks nestled into his lap, and her long legs resting between his. The sensation of cradling her against him went from pleasure to desire in less than a heartbeat, and it'd taken every ounce of will to control that need.

The heavy tension seething low in his gut made it impossible to pretend it wasn't happening. He'd been tempted to draw away, but his conscience hadn't let him, not when he knew his actions could save her life.

But it turned out she hadn't needed that kind of help.

Goose bumps prickled his skin. She was just like his grandfather, twisting situations to further her own agenda and keeping him in the dark unless given no other choice.

What was the truth? Was Imhara like the blood-crazed demons he witnessed after skirmishes, the ones who drain captured warriors or human-slaves of blood in order to heal? Or could she control her blood-need?

"You had the chance to tell me about your hunger. You didn't." His voice shook. "You speak of wanting me to trust you, yet you withhold information when it suits you."

"I was trying to protect you, not hide anything from you!" He snorted. Her mouth pulled flat, her gaze flared hot. "One moment I scent your desire, the next a loathing so intense it chokes me. I don't understand. Why do you cling to your hatred like a child clutches his mother's leg?"

Heat surged into his cheeks. "Because you give me plenty of reason to, *demon*!"

Closing the distance between them, Arek called on his Gift and pushed her flat, his hand pressed to her chest. Her soft gasp and pinched expression warned him the energy seared her senses. She shuddered.

He reined it in, detesting that she'd made him lose control, despising the extreme emotions that were shredding him raw.

"Why didn't you tell me what was wrong with you?" he ground out from behind gritted teeth.

She glared at him, the fire in her gaze bright. "Are you telling me you'd have reacted differently if I had?"

"You never gave me the chance!"

Guilt and regret flickered across her ashen face. "I'm sorry—"

Beneath his hand, her body jerked as another convulsion cut off whatever she was going to say next. Her face contorted as a muscle-twisting shudder tore through her. The seizure lasted several heartbeats, agonizing to watch in its intensity. Her body bowed upward. She bit her lip so hard blood welled from it. Sweat beaded on her cheeks like tears.

His gut contracted as she suffered in silence. One heartbeat. Two. Another half dozen. Then her body went limp.

While there was nothing weak about Imhara, there was a definite vulnerability in the way she lay there after the seizure subsided, her dry, cracked lips parted, sucking in ragged breaths. Beneath his palm, he could feel the rapid thump of her heart in her chest and the clammy dampness of her skin.

Deep inside him, something stirred. As the feeling persisted and gnawed at him, he fought it. He didn't want to feel sympathy for anyone who lied to him. She was strong, tough. She was *Na'Reish* and more than capable of deceit when it suited her.

But still, if she was as hungry as she claimed to be, or consumed by blood-rage, why hadn't she tried to bite him? His arm had been close enough.

She wasn't behaving like he'd expected her to.

"It seems your desire to see me dead means more to you than your oath to help kill Savyr." The thick slur to Imhara's voice brought his attention back to her. "So much for Light Blade honor."

Her goading pricked like a healer's needle.

Hissing a curse, he released his hold on her. "You'd use that to manipulate me?"

"Whatever it takes," she refuted. Exhaustion rode her hard yet her gaze remained fierce. "I shouldn't have to remind you, but your hatred blinds you. You haven't listened to a word I've said."

Didn't she ever give up?

His jaw clenched. "My hatred for the *Na'Reish* is shared by every other Light Blade."

"Scents don't lie, Arek. Yours is much deeper, darker. Why?"

"That's none of your business."

"It is if it endangers our plan!"

No way he was telling her anything about himself, or his family.

Yet his promise committed him, his honor bound him to seeing this through. Once given, to break with either breached the sacred trust he'd been given by the *Lady* the day he'd sworn allegiance to serve *Her*.

Nor could he dismiss the fact that Savyr's death would satisfy their common need for vengeance.

His lip curled. "What endangers it is you not telling me the truth about your illness . . . you letting me believe the cause of it was something else. If you want it to succeed, then you tell me everything I need to know. Regardless." He stabbed a finger at her. "Don't withhold the facts. Don't lie to me. Don't honey coat anything because you're worried about how I'll react. I've given you my oath. Trust me to deal with my hatred. Trust me to make the right decision. But give me the information I need to do both. It's the only way this will work."

In the name of the *Lady*, why was he giving her another chance when logic warned him against believing her? Arek scraped a hand over his jaw, the rasp of skin on stubble harsh in the heartbeat of silence. He had no explanation, none whatsoever.

"All right. You've made your point." Imhara nodded and drew in an unsteady breath. "It wasn't a lie when I said I wasn't a danger to you. If you wanted to, you could kill me right now using your Gift or the dagger." Her chin lifted, then her head tilted to expose her throat. "I'm too weak to stop you."

Beneath her skin he could see the rapid beat of her pulse. One swift flick of his wrist and the blade would slice through her artery.

Vulnerability and submission.

Something he'd never seen any *Na'Reish* offer voluntarily.

Yet she was a fighter, a warrior, to the core.

"Twice now you've given me the opportunity to take your life." He shook his head. "You aren't like any *Na'Reish* I've known."

After several long heartbeats, Imhara brought her chin down. Wary hope flickered across her face.

Her tongue swept out to moisten dry lips. "So, does this mean you'll let me feed from you?"

Chapter 22

WITH Imhara's question, the memory of her feeding from him the first time they'd met had Arek fisting her shirt again. The crawling sensation between his shoulder blades intensified and more goose bumps prickled his skin.

"*Light* save me . . ." The curse ripped from him. He grimaced at the hoarse tone. "There's no other way, is there?"

Her pinched expression answered his question. He bit off another curse.

It wasn't that long ago he'd sworn to die before letting any demon make him their blood-slave, yet her ancestors' journals backed up the information he'd found in the library at Sacred Lake and negated everything he'd been raised to believe.

Honor demanded he set his fear and dislike aside.

He ground his teeth together. "All right." Both their peoples depended on them seeing this through. "Feed from me."

Part of him couldn't believe he'd agreed.

His lips thinned. It *would* be worth it.

He expected to hear the voice of his grandfather berate him for losing his mind, and for the first time, there was silence.

"Thank you." A shaky exhalation accompanied her soft reply.

Arek rolled his shoulders. Her feeding from him still troubled him, but if he were honest, keeping him ignorant of certain facts disturbed him just as much. Trusting her wouldn't be easy but he'd try. Whether she lived up to her promise of keeping him informed remained to be seen.

If only Kymora could see him now. She'd definitely label this as *Her* divine will. But he had asked the goddess for help and the strength to change. *She* had to be helping him take this next step in his journey. There was no way he could have done it by himself.

Arek slid the dagger into his belt. "Let's get it over with before I change my mind."

Hooking an arm around her shoulders he helped her into a sitting position, leaning her side onto him so that his arm remained free. The one she would feed from. He pulled up his sleeve. The marks of her first feeding were just pale pink scars.

More would adorn his skin shortly.

Imhara's hand shook as she grasped his wrist. "*Lady*, bless Arek and his gift of blood. I receive it with thanks and a grateful heart. May the cycle of life—restoration, rejuvenation, and renewal—continue."

Her prayer held all the similarities of a ritual invocation of gratitude used by the *Lady's* Servants in the weekly services in the temple, and reminded him again of their common past. Soft voiced, her words were filled with sincere gratitude and as humble as any devotee.

But when Imhara lowered her mouth toward his arm, lips parted, he couldn't stop himself from tensing.

She hesitated, her breath hot and moist as it caressed his flesh. "Would you feel more comfortable if I used the dagger rather than my teeth to slice open your skin?"

"Just do it, before I change my mind."

She bit down, her teeth piercing his flesh, the pain sharp and swift. Her groan vibrated against his skin. He hissed—the stark memories of other, less pleasant feedings he'd witnessed in the past while on patrol flashed through his mind—and resisted the urge to pull away. Instead he stared at the flames of the fire, unable to go so far as to watch her.

Feeling and hearing it was bad enough. The heat of her mouth against the skin of his arm, the steady suck and hot laving of her tongue against his flesh, her quiet, drawn-out groan of pleasure as she swallowed, the hard pump of his heart as it raced in reaction. Every sensation sent waves of heat and cold rippling through him, a warring combination of pleasure and revulsion. Something he couldn't even attempt to explain.

A minute passed.

Another.

Then Imhara drew away, far sooner than he'd expected. Her breaths came in short, shallow pants as she wiped her lips with the sleeve of her shirt. Color flushed her cheeks.

"You're done?" he asked.

"I've taken as much as I need to last the night."

"Was it enough?"

"I'll heal eventually."

"I've seen *Na'Reish* warriors heal almost instantly. They fed for much longer though." Even as he commented, he wondered why he was encouraging her to feed from him for a third time, but then he'd given his oath to help her, hadn't he?

Her eyes met his, her gaze direct. "I can scent your discomfort, Arek. I won't prolong the feeding with a full session. I want you to see that I can control my need, that you don't have to fear me slipping into a blood-rage."

Again, her behavior startled him.

Her fingers tightened around his wrist. "You've saved my life twice now. Thank you." The strength in her grip had already improved. "By tomorrow morning I'll be strong enough to climb. We can find out then what happened to the caravan."

Arek shifted, cupping her shoulders to ease her back onto the pallet of needle-leaves so she could rest. He pulled his sleeve back down over his arm, ignoring the blood seeping from the fresh puncture marks. The wounds would clot soon enough.

The image of Imhara, her head bent over his arm, replayed through his thoughts. He could almost feel her tongue stroking his skin, licking away the rivulets, her lips brushing over the wounds in the softest of caresses.

Heat curled in his gut.

Anticipation. Not revulsion.

Mouth tightening, Arek tugged at the sleeve. His shook his head and strangled the reaction into submission.

"I have no objection to sharing this cloak." Imhara's soft comment drew him from his thoughts. "It's the only one we have."

He grunted. Practicality was certainly the reason for the offer. As the supply of wood dwindled, it would get only colder, and there were still many hours to go before dawn broke.

Yet his decision to accept wouldn't be driven by logic alone. Just the idea of curling up with her, of being that close to her again, was enough to send his blood surging through his veins and reignite the heavy heat in his gut.

Even knowing she'd just fed from him, he couldn't stop wanting her. "I'll tend the fire."

Imhara watched him. The speculative look, the hint of a smile on her lips, told him she knew exactly why he'd refused her invitation.

Lady of Light, controlling his scent around her was something he just couldn't seem to accomplish. Shaking his head, he retreated to the other side of the fire and stretched out his hands toward the flames. The heat was as solid and real as the one burning in his gut. Another reaction he couldn't seem to suppress, regardless of his intent.

"You know, Light Blade, there's usually a reason for the events we're led to experience in our lives. Sometimes the *Lady* reveals them to us, more often than not *She* makes us work it out ourselves." Imhara gave him a wry smile and snuggled deeper into the cloak. "If it's any comfort, like you, I'm still trying to figure out the purpose of this attraction and why we share the same path."

With that, she closed her eyes.

Arek stared at her. Had she just admitted to being attracted to him? He'd assumed the problem all one-sided—his—and any reaction from her, part of the role she played as *Na* Kaal.

Did she welcome the attraction or consider it a distraction? Her last comment didn't indicate either way. And asking her to clarify didn't seem prudent.

Whatever the result, her admission proved . . . disquieting.

Arek let his gaze drop to the flames of the fire. Those thoughts, and others, kept him awake well into the night.

THE morning sunlight did little to dispel the cold, the beams so weak they barely filtered through wispy fog to melt the layer of fresh snow crunching underfoot. Balling his hands into fists and blowing on them, Arek tried to ignore the chill seeping through three layers of clothing and numbing the exposed skin of his cheeks.

Walking behind him, Imhara wore the only cloak. Her face remained pale, and although her wounds had healed over, her gait as they headed uphill was careful and slow, as if the muscles in her thigh were still tender. While she'd said nothing before setting out, he suspected she was still recovering.

The air smelled clean and sweet, yet he almost preferred the thick, smoky odor of the shelter. At least there they'd been warm, but with the coming of dawn, Imhara's need to return to the caravan had grown, as had his.

How had her kin fared? Had Rassan and her *Na'Hord* managed

to rout the would-be assassins? Brow furrowing, he skirted a loose pebbled scree and glanced back to make sure Imhara negotiated it without trouble. Ahead, through the misty gloom, uneven shadows took shape—the small forest just below the caravan. They were nearly there.

A few feet in, and as his eyes adjusted to the dimmer light, uneven markings in the needle-strewn debris brought him to a halt. He crouched by the trunk of a stunted tree to study the ground. Brow furrowing, he touched the deep marks, measuring them against his hand.

"Tracks," he murmured. Imhara came alongside him. He gestured to one impression. It was wide and large. "They're fresh."

"Friend or foe?" She scanned their surroundings.

"I'd assume the latter and suggest we don't linger."

"Agre—" Her reply cut off and her head lifted sharply.

The softest whisper of sound carried through the fog. They both looked to the left where the forest thickened.

"Someone's out there." She inhaled a deep breath, nostrils flaring. "I can smell them and it's no one I know."

He tried to peer through the thick mist. "I can't see farther than ten feet in front of me."

The soft crunch of leaves and sticks underfoot carried in the stillness, but there was no way of telling just how far away they were as the fog distorted the sounds. Yet whoever it was, was coming closer.

With a shrug, Arek slid the pack off his shoulder and pulled her sword from the scabbard attached to the straps. "They're not even concealing their approach."

The odds of there being more than one rose significantly. He pressed the sword into her hands, then reached for the dagger in his belt.

"Retreat. Use all the cover you can. Move."

Imhara raised an eyebrow at his orders, but she at least had the sense not to question him. A shadow emerged from between two trees, no more than fifteen feet away.

A familiar rush of adrenaline surged through Arek.

"Too late," she murmured.

He abandoned the pack and stepped between the strange *Na'Reishi* and her, dropping into a defensive crouch. A pinch in the small of his back reminded him he had a role to play and he eased his stance into something less provocative.

The *Na'Reish* male was well over six feet tall, with wide muscled shoulders, and biceps as thick as Imhara's thighs. Tawny hair framed a broad face, one hardened by years of experience, if the lines creasing his face were any indication. The uneven spots running down the sides of his jaw and neck were almost black, darkened by countless seasons spent outside in the sun.

The stylized armor, molded leather breeches, and knee-high boots heralded him as a warrior of rank, definitely *Na'Reishi*. While he hadn't yet drawn the sword sheathed at his side, his gloved hand rested on the pommel, in clear readiness.

Thick salt-and-pepper eyebrows descended into a deep V. "You dare threaten me with a weapon, slave?"

Arek uttered a soft curse under his breath but held his position. Had he made a mistake in facing off with the demon?

"He defends me." Imhara's tone was as cold as the air around them. "Identify yourself."

There was just the right amount of haughty arrogance reflected in her demand. Again, her swift switch in personas impressed him. The warrior's deep violet eyes remained locked on him for several seconds, then flickered over his shoulder.

"*Na* Kaal." Black lips stretched in a cool smile. "It's good to see you safe and well. I'd been told you were wounded." The smile faded when she neither confirmed nor denied his statement. "Order your slave to put the weapon down."

"Why should I?" she challenged. "I don't know you, *Na'Reishi*. Now answer me."

He inclined his head. "My name is Ehran Veht, second son *Na* Veht and Commander of his *Na'Hord*."

His rank almost equaled that of Imhara's. What was the second son of a *Na* doing in Kaal territory?

"A bold move identifying yourself, considering your assassins failed in their attempt on my life."

"Those warriors were not mine." The *Na'Reishi* took a step closer, large hands lifting, fingers spreading wide. "You misunderstand my intentions."

"And I'm in no mood to bandy words. Get to the point."

Her curt impatience had Veht flexing his gloved hands.

"I'm here to help you." His attempt to placate was spoiled by the edge in his tone. "Your Second and others search with me."

"Really?"

Arek almost grinned at Imhara's dry response. Veht's black lips thinned and his jaw tightened.

His chest armor did have frond leaves etched into it, as opposed to the unmarked plates of the assassins. The thin strands belonged to the only tree to survive and thrive in the Chomi Desert. The demon's allegiance probably lay with the desert-dwelling Clan, but until Imhara ordered him otherwise, Arek wasn't lowering his weapon.

"Where are the Kaal *Na'Hord* you claim accompany you?" Arek gestured to the surrounding forest with his chin. There had to be more *Na'Reish* searching for Imhara. Could the demon be stalling? "You're out here alone."

Imhara's hand clamped tightly on his shoulder as the *Na'Reishi's* weathered face darkened. "You dare to question me?"

The sharp snapping of debris came from their left. Arek pivoted, crowding Imhara backward, toward the nearest tree. How many others converged on their location? Could she scent them?

While it had thinned, fog still shrouded the forest. Their position was vulnerable enough as it was without leaving all sides undefended. Another shadow appeared through the trees, this one a foot shorter than Veht.

"*Na* Kaal?"

The familiar deep voice eased the pounding of Arek's heart. Behind him, Imhara uttered a soft invocation of thanks.

"Rassan!"

Arek released a slow breath. The *Na'Chi* was a welcome sight. Relief flickered across Rassan's broad face as he drew closer. His violet eyes swept over them both, as if to assure himself they were all right, then flickered to Veht. He made no move to draw his weapon, just nodded an acknowledgment to the other warrior.

"Commander Veht has been of great assistance, *Na* Kaal. His *Na'Hord* helped us during the ambush, then they stayed to assist in the search for you." His gaze pinned Arek where he stood. "Stand down, slave." Imhara gently squeezed his shoulder. Arek lowered his dagger but didn't release it. "Are you well, *Na*?"

"I've fed." The flecks in Rassan's eyes flashed bronze. Imhara shifted against his hold, and Arek let her go. It was enough to draw Veht's gaze away from the *Na'Chi* and disaster. "Were any of the assassins captured alive?"

Rassan regained his stoic composure and shook his head. "Unfortunately, no."

Veht's upper lip curled. "The *Vorc*-scat scum took their own lives when they realized your Second had help."

"Then it seems I owe you an apology and a debt of gratitude, Commander."

"Part of which I'll collect right now."

Attention split between both *Na'Reishi*, Arek only saw a blur of motion, then a sharp crack of pain against his cheek. His vision exploded in a flare of white and red. Another blow sent him to the ground.

A knee landed on his back, pinning him there. His wrist was seized and long fingers dug into his flesh. Nerves screamed in protest. The dagger fell from them as a hand tangled in his hair.

"You deserve death for your insolent behavior, human!" Veht growled.

With a hard shove Arek found his face ground into the needle-debris. He fought to twist free, reining in the urge to use his Gift on Veht.

"Were you mine"—the fingers gripping his neck dug in hard—"I'd have your tongue cut out for daring to question me and your hand removed for ignoring a direct order."

"*Na* Veht." Imhara's reprimand was sharp. Arek stilled. The gritty taste of crushed needle-leaves mixed with the iron tang of blood in his mouth. "He was within his rights to defend me—as you well know."

"And that's why he lies beneath my knee eating dirt instead of with a blade buried in his chest."

With a final push and another mouthful of dry needles, the weight lifted from Arek's back. He rolled away, every instinct screaming at him to finish the fight. He remained on his hands and knees, his gaze lowered and fixed on Veht's boots. Not out of intimidation or submission, although it would seem that way to the warrior, but because he half expected another assault despite Imhara's intervention.

Veht shifted closer. "Disrespect me again and you will pay for it dearly." The threat vibrated in the air between them. Heat flared in Arek's gut but he held his ground. "Remember that, human."

"Commander, any further disciplining of my slave will be done by either myself or Rassan." Imhara's tone projected a combination of steely insistence and blatant caution. After a long moment, the black boots turned away and disappeared from his field of vision.

The skin between Arek's shoulders crawled. Instinct warned him Veht still watched him. It took everything he had to keep his head bowed. Last time he'd looked up, it'd earned him a dozen lashes across his shoulders. To do so now would invite retaliation and undo Imhara's intervention.

"Sometimes humans aren't worth the trouble, *Na* Kaal." Veht spat, the gob of spittle landing on Arek's sleeve. He curled his fingers in the debris. "You'd be wasting your time with this one."

"Oh, I don't know about that." Imhara's husky chuckling filled the forest. "I've found him a quick learner given the right motivation. My time spent training this one has been rather enjoyable."

Veht made a sound of disgust. "No disrespect intended, *Na* Kaal, but I've never seen a use for them other than as prey or breeders."

"Each to their own tastes, Commander." Her response turned hard and cold again, a clear reminder of who ranked whom. "Come, I'm eager to get back to the caravan. While we make our way there, you need to explain why you're in my territory. I received no message heralding your arrival."

A grunt came from the Clan Commander. "No messenger? *Na* Veht dispatched one over a week ago."

Arek frowned. How many patrols attempted to sneak through Skadda Pass and into Kaal territory without Imhara knowing? Their vigilance couldn't be faulted. He suspected very few made it through unnoticed, given the Kaal Clan's need for anonymity. Nor could he see *Na* Kaal letting such a practice slide without retribution, given her reputation.

Imhara made a noncommittal sound. "I wonder if he fell prey to the same band of brigands as we did?"

Had the ambushers waited that long for the caravan to come through? It smacked of advanced planning and organization. Surely it also couldn't be coincidence that a week ago, both Meelar and Yur had used the route through Skadda Pass.

Had one of them left warriors behind? He wouldn't put it past either *Na'Reishi* to do such a thing.

Veht and Imhara's voices drifted off as she drew the *Na'Reishi* away. Arek dared to look up.

"Are you all right?" Rassan's murmured query was barely a whisper.

Arek wiped blood and dirt from his mouth. Gentle probing with his tongue found a laceration on the inside of his lip. "Other than wanting to shove a dagger into the arrogant bastard's back, I'm fine."

"Don't even go there, Arek." Rassan shook his head. "Your scent will betray you. Next time, neither Imhara nor I could be there to stop them, and believe me when I say a missing tongue or hand is merciful compared to some of the things I've seen the *Na'Reish* deem as punishment."

Arek nodded. That message had come through loud and clear. Veht's vicious tactics were exactly what he expected of demons. The contrast between him and Imhara couldn't be more clear. Veht was soured wine to her honey-cider.

Rassan scooped up the pack. "Are Imhara's injuries truly healed?"

"Mostly."

"You let her feed from you?"

"Shocked?" Arek gave a wry smile. "Me, too."

The *Na'Chi's* gaze pierced him. "What's happened since I saw you go over the edge of the road after her? Tell me, then I'll fill you in on Veht's part in all this."

By the time Arek had finished explaining his side of the tale, including his suspicions regarding the identity of who might have set up the attack, they'd reached the fall site.

"Do you think Veht had anything to do with the ambush?" he asked as they halted at the edge of the tree line, near the dead *Vorc.*

"No. Once again we can't prove it, but this ambush is something Yur would attempt." Black flashed through the *Na'Chi's* gaze. "To kill a *Na* takes someone of rank or approval from someone of rank.

Yur would have both, while Meelar knows he wouldn't have the backing of his sire if he was caught or found out."

Arek glanced up the valley wall. A thin layer of snow crusted the barren incline. The weak beams of sunlight were gaining strength and the fog was finally starting to lift. Halfway up the slope, Veht assisted Imhara's climb. People waiting up on the roadway called out salutations to them both.

With distance and other noise to cover their conversation, Arek spoke freely. "Killing Imhara before she reaches the Enclave or forcing her to accept a mate achieves the same outcome—Savyr gets a free route into human territory."

"Exactly."

"She's going to need constant protection."

Rassan nodded once, lips thinning. "And your role just became more difficult. I'd give you a weapon if I could, Arek."

"I already have one." At his puzzled frown, Arek inhaled a slow, deep breath before meeting his gaze. "Not all Light Blades use a weapon to kill. Sometimes a bare hand on skin is all that's needed."

Rassan cocked his head to one side. "In the library, I was more worried you were going to snap Imhara's neck. I never realized you could kill with a touch. I thought that a rumor. So, you have this skill?"

Arek nodded. "It took years of training." His smile twisted. "Let's just say I had a need to learn and leave it at that."

"I sense a tale behind that statement. Perhaps one day you'll share it with me?"

"Perhaps." Arek gestured to the climb. Veht and Imhara had reached the roadway. "So, he'll accompany us to Gannec Fortress."

"Yes. His intervention tipped the balance of battle in our favor. We have wounded, and while the healers will use their Gifts to help them, they'll do it judiciously. We don't need the scrutiny of Veht's warriors turned on us if they were suddenly well again a day after the attack."

"And we now owe him a debt, one he'll forfeit the potential profit of a slave-raid to claim when we reach Gannec Fortress." Rassan's tone was dry. "And then there's the bragging rights. It's not every day a Commander can boast he helped save a *Na's* life."

Arek lifted an eyebrow. "His status will rise?"

"Significantly."

"And how will Imhara repay the debt?"

"Most likely during the Enclave she'll acknowledge his actions and favor unlimited access to the slave-route for any future ventures he may embark on. It will increase his wealth. Not that he'll be able to collect on it if all goes according to plan." Rassan's expression remained solemn. "Your role as Imhara's slave begins earlier than anticipated, Light Blade. Are you up to it?"

Arek shared a grim smile with the other warrior. "Do I really have a choice?" Rassan's steady look drew a grunt from him. "I didn't think so."

Chapter 23

AREK'S first view of Gannec Fortress came as the wagon he was riding in rounded a bend in the road. The thick forest they'd been travelling through most of the day thinned, giving him an almost clear view of the massive citadel and behind it the southern arm of the Shadowblade Mountains, their peaks covered in snow.

"*Mother of Light!*" The curse ripped from him.

While the mountains were majestic, the fortress claimed all of his attention. The crenulated walls stood nearly eighty feet high, manned by watchtowers with walkways in between. At this distance, only a handful of stone-slatted roofs could be seen peeking over them.

Everything—the walls, the towers, the buildings beyond—was constructed out of black, volcanic rock, as daunting as it was hard.

Only the arched barbican differed, its two sets of double gates made of iron-studded wood, its purpose just as imposing. Weighing as much as they did, each would require an independent mechanical system to operate them. Right now, they were wide open and traffic moved through in both directions, overlooked by four well-manned towers and a patrol stationed on the ground.

How many demons lived within the citadel? Sacred Lake was populated by nearly ten thousand, the largest city in human territory. This placed looked big enough to hold twice that. It made the Kaal fortress look like a crofter's settlement.

A shiver crept down the length of Arek's spine. Its design, its defenses, its size all shouted *impenetrable*. Intimidate your enemies *and* remind your allies just how powerful you were. Quite an effective psychological tactic, especially given the dominating nature of the *Na'Reish*.

The trait personified Savyr. And he was venturing into the heart of his territory?

Arek could hear his grandfather questioning his judgment, and if he were honest, all good intentions and vengeance aside, a small part of him agreed. Walking into a nest of shadow-winders voluntarily portrayed a degree of insanity. One couldn't expect to come away unscathed.

Yet, by the *Lady's Grace*, another Light Blade had survived Savyr's fortress.

Kalan.

Captured, tortured, and believing himself without allies, he'd prepared himself for the Final Journey. Annika's appearance and offer of a bargain too good to refuse had seemed like divine intervention.

Arek's lips ghosted with a grin. The *Lady* had certainly blessed both of them that day, though neither knew it at the time. Faith and hope had prevailed.

He inhaled a slow, deep breath. He could only pray for the same. While his circumstances for entering Savyr's fortress differed from Kalan's, unlike his friend, he wasn't walking alone into the sidewinders' nest.

The challenge—and that's what he had to view it as, albeit the most demanding one of his life—was not just his. Every person who'd volunteered to accompany Imhara were all committed to whatever journey *She'd* set them. And like any warrior heading out on patrol, the more information he could glean about his task, the better.

Arek glanced to his travelling companion, the same man he'd borrowed gloves from during the ambush. "Jawn, what are all those tents outside the fortress?"

"It's where the visiting Clans camp while the Enclave and Games are on. Most of the events are held inside the fortress, but there just isn't enough room to house us all."

He nodded. "I know the names of the Clans and their emblems, but how do I know which one is camped where?"

"See the colored flags flying above the pavilions?" The sandy-haired man gestured with his chin. "The two shades of brown belong to the plains-dwelling Tanea. The gold is the Vos from the north, the red with the blue is Huriken. . . ."

As Jawn identified each one, Arek committed them to memory. A minicity in itself, the sea of canvas extended the length of the fortress wall and toward the western side, and straddled both sides of a river that emerged from beneath the wall of the fortress and meandered its way into the forest.

"We'll be one of the smallest campsites here." Jawn flicked the reins against the transport beast's back, clucking his tongue to urge it to keep up with the wagon in front. "Necessity, given what we're attempting to do this time."

While the driver kept his voice low, Arek still glanced around, checking on the position of Veht's *Na'Hord*. The nearest *Vorc-Rider* was two wagons back, and four *Na'Reishu* warriors walking beside the wagon ahead were too deep in their own conversation to take any notice of two humans talking.

Near the head of the caravan, Commander Veht rode alongside *Na* Kaal, Rassan a respectful *Vorc* length behind them. Other than sharing the same tent at night, Arek had seen little of Imhara during the day, kept busy with tasks, mentored mostly by Jawn.

Not that he minded. Serving at the last three meals, he'd overheard snippets of the demon regaling Imhara and her kin with tales of his exploits. Veht reminded him too much of some Blade Councilors. How Imhara or Rassan found the patience to endure the arrogant bastard over the last few days was beyond him.

When they reached the outskirts of the city of tents, Veht and his *Na'Hord* took their leave.

"Thank the *Lady* he's gone." Jawn's sentiments were reflected in the way Imhara rolled her shoulders, as if to relieve them of tension. "Some days it's good to be a slave."

"So, given the choice then, you wouldn't be a man of rank, Jawn?"

The man snorted. "I'll stick to farming. Good honest work."

"Indeed it is. The only diplomacy involved is making sure the dirt-hogs get their fair share of mush."

Jawn chuckled, his weathered face creasing. "Sounds like you've had experience."

"My father's parents lived on a croft." Arek's mouth curved upward. "As a child, I used to spend each summer with them and help them with the harvest. Hard work but there's something to be said for seeing the fruits of your labor at the end of the day."

Simple but satisfying times. Compared to Davyn, his paternal grandparents had been so laid-back and relaxed. The only expectations placed on him had been to complete the never-ending daily chores of farm life. Looking back, those weeks had provided respite from Davyn's high expectations and ever-present bitterness, and were some of the fondest memories of his childhood.

"Killing for a living, even in the service of the *Lady* to protect others, wears on a body," Jawn commented. "Nothing says you couldn't change the way you live. Perhaps farming might be something to consider for the future if you liked it so much."

Arek grunted with the suggestion. He'd spent so long knowing exactly the path his future would take that he'd never entertained any other. Couldn't. For the moment, his destiny remained set.

Jawn pointed with his whiskered chin at a clearing at the end of the curving roadway. "Looks like our campsite ahead."

As they continued to travel along the edge of the mass campsite, daily activity stopped, demon and human alike. The *Na'Reish*—mostly male warriors—watched openly. As Imhara drew level with them, all offered her clenched-fists-to-chest salutes and bowed heads. Humans went to their hands and knees and stayed there even after she'd ridden by.

Arek caught his mentor's gaze and raised an eyebrow.

"They show respect to the whole Clan, not just *Na* Kaal." The older man kept his voice to a murmur. "It's better to show too much than not enough. Once the last Kaal has passed, they'll resume their chores."

A good fifteen minutes later, and three more similar displays of behavior, the caravan rolled to halt in an area recently cleared. Forest bordered one side, the imposing fortress wall another, while the third consisted of a line of Clan Sharadan tents.

The Kaal caravan circled the very edges of the cleared land, and Rassan called everyone to a halt.

Jawn pulled on the brake and tied off the reins. "Unpack everything and pile it beside the wagon, then we'll head over and help set up *Na* Kaal's pavilion."

Arek gave a nod, but before leaping off the wagon to help, he glanced out over the place he'd call home over the next few weeks. Everywhere he looked there were demons—eating around campfires, emerging from tents, engaging in conversation, exercising in small groups—it was hard to spot a human.

Arek inhaled a slow breath, hoping to ease the knot in his innards. Was this how Annika had felt the first time among them after arriving at Sacred Lake? Had the other *Na'Chi* experienced the same frisson of anxiety skating the length of his spine?

The humans he did see had their heads down, going about whatever task they were assigned, bodies hunched as if they were trying to avoid notice or make themselves as small a target as possible. He frowned.

"If you keep glaring over at the Sharadan camp like that, Arek, you'll make yourself a target." Jawn's soft comment drew his attention downward. "Just concentrate on the task at hand."

Arek joined the man on the ground. "Is it how you cope with this?" He waved a hand at the hubbub beyond their camp, then steadied one of the barrels being untied. "Doesn't seeing other humans scuttling about like they're afraid of their own shadow, scraping and bowing out of fear for their lives bother you?"

Jawn shot a brief look over his shoulder toward the Sharadan camp, then met his gaze, his steady, level. "Of course it does. But what purpose would it serve to protest? And you can guess what would happen if I tried to intervene."

Arek had no trouble imagining it, yet frustration still twisted in his gut. "Then how do you ignore it?"

"I play my part in Imhara's plan. By doing that, I protect my family and friends, the ones I left behind and those who are here with me." Compassion swirled in the depths of his gaze. "Focus on that, do whatever it takes, no matter the cost."

"I have done . . . and I'm ready to do . . . whatever I need to bring Savyr down." Imhara's words that night of the Clan feast, her sentiment now echoed by Jawn.

"I know you're used to helping others, but this isn't the time or place. Not here, not now." The statement brought him back to the present. "Little comfort, but what I said, does it help?"

"Yes." A wry smile twisted Arek's mouth. "I don't like it, but I understand."

He set to work emptying crates from the back of the wagon.

A commotion loud enough to penetrate the heavy canvas walls of her pavilion halted Imhara's discussion with Rassan. Voices raised in volume, although not in anger, drew her to the entrance.

Emerging from the tent, she peered around the campsite. Everything seemed normal. Her Clan were engaged in a variety of activities. Some, including Arek and Jawn, were by the central campfire cooking the evening meal, others were in small groups scattered around the wagons.

Most had stopped what they were doing to peer toward the Sharadan camp to where the noise seemed to be coming from. The steady hum of voices was drawing closer.

She shot a glance at the warrior stationed outside her tent. "Barrca, what's going on?"

The blond-haired *Na'Chi* shrugged. "Your guess is as good as mine, *Na* Kaal."

A crowd emerged from between a row of tents, a writhing mass of *Na'Reish*, warriors and civilians alike, but what caught Imhara's attention was the moving flag hoisted above them.

All black, the fluttering pennant sported a shield with two crossed daggers threaded in gold.

Adrenaline surged through her. "It's Savyr!"

Beside her Rassan uttered a curse. "What's he doing here?"

Wandering the camps on foot wasn't the *Na'Rei's* usual habit. A missive or a personal visit from Yur with a summons to attend a meeting was more his style. Ignoring the request was done at your own peril. What had prompted him to make a personal appearance?

"Looks like we're about to find out," she murmured.

A cohort of black-armored *Na'Hord* pushed the crowd back with long staves. The first figure to appear on the cleared pathway was Urkan Yur. He wasn't dressed in full leather armor like the warriors, yet the cut and style of the finery he wore projected an image just as impressive.

But the Second was nowhere as intimidating as the *Na'Reishi* striding behind him. Savyr Gannec was huge, just over seven feet tall, towering over many of the *Na'Hord* gathered around them. The latent power in his wide shoulders and thick, bulging biceps couldn't be concealed by the long-sleeved shirt or loose-laced vest. There was little evidence of him entering his fifth decade. He carried himself with the ease and confidence of a warrior half his age.

Hair the color of obsidian had been pulled back into a tight cue, the severe style emphasizing the strong lines and natural markings running down the sides of his face. Dark brows framed a predatory gaze that missed nothing. A gaze that searched the crowd and settled on her.

The surety and superiority in his slow smile was as lethal as the dagger sheathed in his belt. His look sent shivers skittering down Imhara's neck.

"*Na* Kaal." His deep voice carried, like the rumble of distant thunder. "Welcome to Gannec Fortress. We received word only this morning that your caravan was attacked by brigands. It's good to see you made it here safely."

Who had informed him of the attack? Veht? He hadn't sent a messenger on ahead of the caravan, so he couldn't have arranged for an audience with the *Na'Rei* so soon. Scouts though could have easily spotted their approach once they'd crossed into Gannec territory and reported to Savyr. What details had he been given of the attack?

Imhara kept her expression impassive. Polite. His public show of concern seemed sincere, but the crawling sensation across the middle of her back indicated otherwise. More likely he wanted to see if she'd survived the assassination attempt unscathed.

Deception and perception.

Politics and power.

The deadly game she'd been forced into playing five years ago.

Burying her dislike deep, Imhara stepped forward to meet Savyr.

By the *Lady's Grace*, this would be the last time she had to participate, and despite the danger, she intended to prevail and create a new life.

For herself and her Clan.

Chapter 24

"*NA'REI,* you honor us with your visit." Imhara sank to one knee, head bowed, and watched from the corners of her vision as the others joined her in the traditional greeting of respect. After an appropriate amount of time, she rose, but everyone else remained on their knees. "Your concern for my welfare is humbling."

Savyr's smile never changed but his gaze narrowed as it swept over her. "You are unhurt?"

"I'm fine." No way she was going to tell him about her injuries, and unless he wanted to reveal exactly what he knew and how he'd sourced the information, she doubted he'd pursue the subject. "A few of my kin were wounded, but thanks to the timely appearance of Commander Veht and his *Na'Hord*, my Second was able to dispatch the brigands quickly."

"It's fortunate Commander Veht came along when he did, then." Savyr's gaze narrowed farther, yet no flicker of emotion or odor betrayed his true thoughts on the subject. "I'd like to hear the details of his involvement, but there's another matter I must discuss with you."

A smooth change of topic.

Imhara gestured to her pavilion. "Shall we go inside where we can be more comfortable?" There were too many interested observers milling around. Was this tactic deliberately engineered? She wouldn't put it past him. "If you'd sent advanced notice of your arrival I could have had a meal prepared specially."

Savyr waved a hand. "This won't take long."

"Then accept my Clan's hospitality, such as it is."

So, whatever he had to say, he didn't want an audience. Interesting. Was it the discussion or her reaction he wanted to remain confidential? He preceded her into the pavilion while Yur ordered his *Na'Hord* to take up positions around the camp. The Second followed a moment later.

She caught Jawn's attention. "Break open a barrel of our best wine. Accompany it with fruit, bread, and cheese."

During the initial planning sessions, she and Rassan had discussed the unlikely odds of Savyr putting in a personal appearance in camp. Nevertheless a contingency plan had been designed, but she'd never anticipated having to use it.

Yet, while all her people had volunteered to fulfill certain roles, Imhara still hesitated.

"Is there anything else, *Na* Kaal?" Jawn's soft inquiry reminded her time was ticking away.

As much as she disliked extending Clan hospitality to the men who'd killed her family, refusing to would be seen as an insult, a complication she couldn't afford. Yur would never accept her gesture of generosity, but Savyr might.

She met the man's gaze, her decision tasting like ashes even as she gave the order. "Inform Yrenna her services will be needed."

The man bowed his head. "Yes, *Na* Kaal."

Her people scrambled to their feet to follow her orders. Imhara shared a look with Rassan as they ducked through the flap held open for them by Barrca.

The table, where she'd expected Savyr to sit, remained unoccupied. Instead the *Na'Reishi* leader had made himself comfortable on the cushions in the open living area. Yur settled down beside him, leaving the pillow to Savyr's right for her.

Her Second remained standing just inside the interior wall, and for a moment she envied him. His task, to supervise the service provided by Jawn and his team, while mundane, held much more appeal than joining the two warriors.

Yrenna and two other humans entered carrying bowls and towels draped over their arms. All three women were dressed in the simple thigh-length tunic of servers. One halted at her side while the other two attended to Yur and Savyr.

Imhara dipped her hands in the water. "The Kaal Clan welcomes you both to our home." Both warriors inclined their heads and copied her actions. The final words stuck in her throat, yet she forced them out. "Our hospitality is yours to enjoy."

Taking the towel, she wiped her hands dry, then unable to delay any longer, she joined them on the cushions.

The blond woman at Savyr's feet pressed her forehead to the floor. "If it pleases you, *Na'Rei*, this slave would be honored to serve you during your visit."

"I don't recall seeing her with your caravan before, *Na* Kaal." He relaxed backward onto his cushion. "Is she new?"

"A recent acquisition from one of *Na* Meelar's forays into the southern provinces." A half-lie. Yrenna had been taken from her village and brought across the border over a decade ago. When the slaver had revealed she'd been destined for an *Isha*, a bed-slave auction, her father had rescued the thirteen-year-old girl.

"The quality of Meelar's goods has been exceptional of late." Savyr's appetite for young, human women was hardly a secret. At barely half his age, Yrenna catered to that taste. "Remove your tunic."

Yrenna rose. In one graceful movement, the young woman caught the hem of her garment and pulled it up and over her head.

Imhara forced herself not to react. No matter how many times she'd witnessed another person being ordered to perform for another, the cavalier attitude turned her stomach.

Savyr sat up, his black lips curving upward, blatant interest flaring in his deep purple gaze as he examined her curvaceous form. "Your taste in humans is impeccable."

Tendrils of cold curled around Imhara's innards as the warrior reached out and smoothed his hand along the length of Yrenna's leg, hip to ankle, as a farmer would when inspecting stock.

How had the *Na'Reish* strayed so far from the *Lady's* path that they would treat another intelligent being in this way?

"She has excellent muscling. Defined, strong." Imhara's respect for Yrenna rose considerably as she stood there tolerating his touch. No way she could have done it and not kicked his arrogant jaw. "She's breeder material."

Imhara forced a small smile. Savyr would think she reacted to his compliment. Let him believe. Training with her *Na'Hord*, Yrenna was one of Rassan's best scouts.

"A tempting morsel." Satisfaction oozed in Savyr's tone. "Your hospitality is appreciated, *Na* Kaal."

She inclined her head.

Beside him Yur grimaced in clear disagreement, then his expression transformed into something more neutral. "*Na'Rei*, pardon my interruption, but you do have an evening engagement to attend."

His Second's quiet reminder drew a grunt from Savyr. "I suppose we should move on to the purpose of my visit."

He patted the cushion beside him. Yrenna seated herself at his side, her slight hesitation the perfect portrayal of nervous caution. He plucked the tunic from her grasp and threw it away.

"There's nothing to say we can't mix business with pleasure, Urkan." His large hand came to rest on Yrenna's bare thigh. The young woman bit back a gasp as his fingers slid to cup then fondle her sex.

Imhara curled her fingers in the cushion beneath her, a protest forming, then froze.

She froze because of the scent teasing her nostrils, an earthy combination of heat and spice mixed with an underlying odor of bitterness that was instantly familiar. A scent that served as a much-needed reminder of her role and a welcome distraction.

From the corner of her eye, Arek approached, in his hands a platter with an array of food. She glanced his way, drawing his scent into her lungs, needing it like a breath of fresh air, surprised at how quickly his presence calmed her.

For the briefest moment, his head lifted as he drew near. His gaze honed in on Savyr, the blue of his eyes glittering. So cold and dark. Yrenna's soft cry at whatever Savyr was doing with her intensified the bitterness of his scent.

Imhara straightened, willing Arek to meet her gaze. If he weren't careful, Savyr would notice and call him on it. His attention flickered to her.

She pointed to the floor at her feet. "Kneel."

His mouth flattened and his grip on the serving platter tightened, but he obeyed. His indrawn breath was deliberate, steady, and within a few heartbeats, his scent had dissipated to an acceptable level. Settling beside her, he bowed his head, mimicking the other servers.

Loose locks of hair fell to his shoulders, brushing the sleeveless tunic, displaying just how physically pleasing he was. From the fit of the fabric stretched across the width of his shoulders to the taut tanned skin of his bare arms.

Her fingertips itched to reach out to touch the fine dusting of blond hairs on his forearms. She tried to resist, the action proving too similar to Savyr's assessment of Yrenna, yet she needed the excuse to avoid watching Savyr grope the young woman.

No, that wasn't the truth. *Lady* forgive her, she lacked the courage to confront the consequences of her own decision. Yrenna may have volunteered for the role of Savyr's slave, but it didn't relieve the guilt of putting the woman in a situation that required her to suffer his attention.

Merciful Mother, there were times she hated being Clan leader.

Imhara wrapped her fingers around Arek's wrist, needing to feel the warmth of his skin, the strong beat of his pulse, aware of the moment he tensed, his muscles transforming into heated steel.

She kept her hold but let her gaze follow the roadwork of veins that ran beneath Arek's skin. The pale blue vessels wound around and across each defined muscle, under the gold band wrapped tight around his muscular bicep until they disappeared beneath the tunic's edge.

"Your betrothal meetings have been arranged. The first will be tomorrow, the second the night after, and the final one the next."

The meaning of Savyr's words took a moment to penetrate. Imhara focused on the demon as she let Arek go. Yrenna lay curled along his side, his large hand resting over the flare of her naked hip.

A small smile curved Savyr's lips and regret twisted within her at him witnessing her interest in Arek, but she shrugged it off. Such behavior from *Na* Kaal would be expected.

"And the name of the first *Na'Reishi*?" She kept her tone level.

"Commander Sere Jirri, second son of *Na* Jirri." Savyr plucked a goblet from the tray of the nearest server. "The first meeting is tomorrow. I've arranged for him to visit you here. Whether you share a meal, attend the Clan Gathering feast together, or make some other arrangement is up to you, but I expect you to make the time to get to know him."

She took her own goblet and sipped the contents. The Jirri possessed one of the smallest territories. Their only asset came from the gold panned from the Na River that ran across their land.

Of late, rumor had it that the precious metal deposits were depleted. Who had proposed a mated alliance with her Clan? The Jirri? Or Savyr? Either way, a second son mating a *Na* would give them access to her lands and resources, renewed wealth for a Clan on the verge of ruin, and in return the Jirri would swear their undying loyalty to the *Na'Rei.*

She frowned. "He's nearly thirty years my senior, *Na'Rei.*"

The server poured more wine into Savyr's goblet.

"His experience and maturity in Clan matters will benefit your people. Something you've no doubt missed with the passing of your father."

Bartered resources for loyalty crushed any hope for a partnership based on love and mutual respect. A bleak hollowness opened up deep inside Imhara. It wasn't like she'd expected anything different from Savyr, yet her father would never have settled for such a politically driven gambit.

Neither would she. She grit her teeth and let her silence answer for her.

Savyr glanced at her then, his gaze penetrating. "Keep an open mind and give considerable thought to your future mate, Imhara. Your verdict requires due deliberation."

"You're giving me a choice?"

"Of course." Any benevolence in his tone was offset by the hard edge in his tone. "Although if you haven't reached a decision by the time the Enclave begins, I will choose for you."

A burst of burning cold ripped through her.

A decision *before* the Enclave began?

That meant her future mate would have all Clan rights and power transferred to him. He'd usurp her place at the meeting and make decisions on her Clan's behalf with little to no knowledge of any matters affecting them.

Imhara took a deeper sip of wine. Being mated before the Enclave meant that unless her new mate kept her informed, an unlikely consideration, she also wouldn't discover the extent of Savyr's war plans concerning the humans.

If killing Savyr failed, she'd need that information when she faced the Blade Council. Given the circumstances, she couldn't go to a truce negotiation empty-handed.

The wine in her stomach soured. She swallowed hard.

Mother of Light, she hadn't anticipated this.

Chapter 25

AREK stared hard at the spot where the heel of Imhara's boot rested on the floor rug, yet with each passing heartbeat, the present situation seemed more and more surreal.

The conversation around him faded. *Mother of Light, Na'Rei* Savyr Gannec sat less than six feet away from him. The pounding of his pulse equaled the force he applied to every muscle in his body in the effort to remain still.

Keep calm! Concentrate on your task.

He gripped the serving tray tighter, his nails digging into the wooden edges, and snuck another look sideways. Couldn't resist. The faceless image of his dreams finally had form and detail.

The power and strength in the broad angles of Savyr's face and hard jawline hit first. Decades of experience marked the lines creasing his tanned skin, projecting an equal share of confidence and arrogance. Jet-black hair, the same color as the uneven spots trailing down either side of his dark brows, framed a wide forehead, yet the air of menace he exuded didn't come from just his physical looks but also the predatory gleam in his deep purple gaze.

Arek sucked in a deep breath. How many years had he imagined this scenario? Of being in the same room as the monster who'd kidnapped and raped his mother. Of facing the bastard responsible for her death. The one he blamed for driving his father to suicide.

A familiar aching hollowness squeezed his heart. Too young to recall either of them, ethereal sensations were all he had to remember them by, and time had blurred or relegated many to indistinct impressions, some so insubstantial he could no longer recall the where or why of them.

Never had he felt the absence of a weapon at his side more keenly. The urge to drive a blade deep into that wide-barrel chest and let loose the full force of his Gift burned.

Arek ground his back teeth together, knowing the action would be suicide, but the seething mass of heat and cold roiling in his gut threatened to shred his control. He closed his eyes.

Focus.

He needed to focus.

He sucked in several, slow breaths.

Second Arek Barial, Light Blade warrior, had no place here.

He was a *slave*. *Na* Kaal's server.

Nothing more.

Yrenna's soft, uneven gasp snapped his eyes open. Imhara leaned back on one elbow, giving him a clear line of vision to Savyr. The demon's large hand passed over the tips of Yrenna's bare breasts, a teasing brush, before his fingers closed around one, his grip tight enough to illicit a pained cry.

Her distress scraped across already raw nerves.

"Get your hands off her."

The raspy voice didn't even sound like his, and for a moment, Arek wondered if someone else had issued the order. But heads turned in his direction, all with varying expressions of surprise and displeasure.

"*What* did you just say?" Imhara caught his jaw and twisted his face toward her, forcing his gaze away from Savyr and Yrenna. Violet eyes, wide with shock, locked with his. "You forget your place, slave."

Her voice shook, and if he hadn't seen the nervous sweep of her tongue over her bottom lip, he'd have mistaken it for anger instead of concern.

She was worried about him, and not Yrenna?

Frustration surged through him. How could she just sit there and watch the young woman being abused? How many others over the years had Savyr tormented, subjecting them to his brand of suffering, stripping them of their dignity and destroying their souls as he had his mother?

"He's hurting her." A harsh whisper.

Bleakness swirled through her gaze, then her mouth flattened even as her expression hardened. He grunted as she shoved him hard enough to send him sprawling on the floor. He flung out his arms to break his fall. The platter slipped from his grasp and shattered as it struck the ground.

"What the *Na'Rei* does is none of your concern, slave! Rassan, get him out of here!" She dismissed him with a flick of her hand before glancing over her shoulder toward the two *Na'Reishi*. "Your pardon, *Na'Rei*, Second Yur. This one is new and still learning."

Arek climbed to his feet, an iciness slicing through him as keenly as the knowledge that Imhara intended to let this farce continue.

"Shall I put him in the stocks?" Rassan's hard-edged query came as a fist caught the collar of his tunic.

"The stocks?" Yur's snort was accompanied by a narrow-eyed glare. "What will he learn from that? Slice the tongue from his head." He rolled to his feet, his fingers stroking the hilt of his dagger. "With your permission, *Na'Rei*, I'd be more than happy to teach him the folly of speaking out of turn."

Arek saw red.

Like *Light* he would! Widening his stance, he prepared to defend himself. A thick-muscled arm wrapped around his throat. He was jerked back against a hard body.

"Let go of me!"

Rassan pinned his arms to his sides using brute force. "You're only making the situation worse, human." His hissed warning was accompanied by a tightening of the choke hold. "Your orders, *Na* Kaal?"

Out of the corner of his eye, Arek saw Yur's black lips curve upward in a wicked grin. Imhara rose from the cushions. The markings on either side of her face stood out in stark relief against her colorless skin. Nothing in her expression gave away her thoughts, but traces of anger and fear glittered in her eyes.

The silence stretched out. Savyr's keen interest and intense anticipation in her response took the edge off Arek's rage.

He quit struggling against Rassan.

Lady's Breath, what had he done?

His careless actions had placed her in a precarious situation. How precarious he wasn't sure, but he knew she couldn't afford to look weak in front of either warrior.

"Release him." Savyr's quiet order pinched the lines around her mouth tight. The stiff nod she gave Rassan betrayed her apprehension. The *Na'Chi* released him and stepped back.

Arek shifted from one foot to the other. Guilt raked him with razor-sharp talons.

"I see you begin to realize the gravity of the situation, human." The gleam in Savyr's eyes sharpened. "Sit down, Urkan. Your threat means nothing to this slave. Let me show you how to teach him a lesson he won't forget." He stroked Yrenna's cheek with his thumb. "Kneel and beg forgiveness."

His arrogance grated, like jagged fingernails over skin. Arek's lip curled.

In one smooth motion, the demon drew his dagger from his belt and sliced open Yrenna's cheek. The young woman screamed, clutching her face. Arek sucked in a shocked breath. His world narrowed to the blood oozing from between her fingers. Behind him, Rassan cursed softly.

The nightmare images of his mother with Savyr swirled in his mind. How had she coped with such a monster? All his imagined scenarios could never match what she'd truly experienced.

Savyr jerked Yrenna closer to him, one arm banded around her torso, cutting her struggling to nothing. With the flick of his wrist he laid the blade against her other cheek. Her whimper cut as deep as the blade that wounded her.

"Kneel and beg forgiveness." Steel edged every word.

Arek stepped toward him, his hatred for the demon raw and bone deep. Every instinct urged him to use his Gift. Surprise would be on his side. Yet the icy finger of logic cooled his temper. He'd never close the gap between them fast enough. An inch and a heartbeat were all the distance and time Savyr required to slice Yrenna's throat instead of her cheek.

"Use the blade on me!" he hissed. "She's done nothing to you."

"You're a slow learner, human." The blade tip pierced Yrenna's skin.

Her frightened cry squeezed his heart.

"The slave's worth diminishes the more scars she bears, *Na'Rei*." Imhara's low-voiced comment vibrated with anger. "This female is one of my best."

"You show such concern for something that can be so easily replaced." The measured look Savyr gave her lifted Arek's heart rate. "A leader must sometimes be willing to make sacrifices in order to maintain control, *Na* Kaal. Surely you know that?"

Imhara stiffened. The dark glittering of her gaze caught Arek by surprise. Her hand crept close to the hilt of her dagger. She looked ready to challenge the *Na'Rei*. To save Yrenna, and protect him?

If she turned, Savyr would see her threatening gesture. An unplanned attack held little chance of success. The situation was too volatile. Too dangerous.

The razor-sharp talons dug deeper into Arek's innards. His hatred and temper had created this mess.

Lady's Breath, it was his pride or all their lives.

The choice was his. And it wasn't a comfortable one. Not at all.

Slowly, Arek dropped to his knees.

It's better to show too much respect than not enough. Jawn's advice echoed in his head.

He bent over and placed his hands and his forehead on the ground, just like the other slaves had when the Kaal Clan rode past their campsites.

"*Na'Rei* . . ." His throat closed over, his jaw clamped shut on the words needed to salvage the situation, refusing to utter them to a demon he hated more than life itself.

His pride railed but he shoved it down.

Merciful Mother, this wasn't about him. Yrenna's quiet sobbing was a stark reminder of the suffering he'd caused.

"*Na'Rei*, please forgive this slave's shameful behavior." Arek swallowed twice. He could still see Imhara's pale face in his mind's eye. He forced the words out. "You were right to teach me this lesson. . . . Please, I beg you not to hurt Yrenna any more."

WITH Arek's hoarse words, Imhara felt her whole body loosen, every muscle weakening to the point where she had to lock her legs to stop herself from sagging back down on the cushions. Her pulse pounded so hard she could hear it in her head.

She flicked a glance at Savyr. He stared at Arek from beneath a half-hooded gaze, assessing, measuring, evaluating his sincerity. The utter coldness of his expression frightened her. Too often she'd seen that look during the Enclave, usually just before he executed someone. She held her breath.

Beneath the iron-rich odor of Yrenna's blood, the familiar heavy bitterness of Arek's anger and hatred still lingered, but an acidic mix of guilt and shame diluted its potency.

She felt sick knowing Yrenna and Arek's lives balanced on Savyr's mood. Would Arek's abasement satisfy him?

"You see, Urkan?" Savyr drawled. His arctic demeanor thawed into cruel satisfaction, feeding on Yrenna's fear and Arek's humiliation. "You just have to find the right incentive to motivate these humans."

He removed the point of his blade from Yrenna's cheek. He tasted the blood on the edge of the blade, cleaning both sides with a slow lick of his tongue. Imhara wrenched her gaze away, the knot in her stomach tightening with his sadistic enjoyment.

"While I know it's a hard task for any female, I'll leave any further disciplinary action for this slave to you, *Na* Kaal."

Imhara let the slur slide and bent her head in mute thanks. Did Arek realize just how close he'd come to death? To watching Yrenna die? Why had Savyr stopped Yur and ceded control of Arek's fate to her?

She pursed her lips. Whatever his reason for restraint, his benevolence worried her. Arek had just pushed her ass-first into a position of vulnerability.

"It's a good thing you'll be mated before the end of this season." Savyr's comment drew her gaze back to him. "Then the responsibility of dealing with slaves need no longer fall to you."

Imhara sucked in a short breath. Was that his motive? Use his generosity to pressure her into mating?

Savyr released Yrenna as he pushed to his feet. Yur followed suit.

The young woman curled up among the cushions, her head buried in her arms, her sobbing silent. A healer could staunch the bleeding of her wounds, but would they be able to repair the scarring?

"You'll pardon me if I reserve judgment on that, *Na'Rei*." Holding on to her temper, she stood. "At least until I see how well my potential mate handles any sort of responsibility."

For the longest heartbeat, Savyr stared at her with his piercing gaze. "Ambition and attitude has served you well the last few years, *Na* Kaal, but don't forget who you're addressing. You're being given the choice of mate, but this arrangement can be altered."

An icy finger scraped between her shoulder blades. She let her gaze drop in a gesture of submission and acknowledgment.

"But I do admire your sass." His chuckle was low and deep. A complete surprise. "Many don't, Imhara, but I do. Perhaps because I see so much of me when I was younger in you."

Imhara hid her grimace. That wasn't a particularly comforting comparison.

"Commander Jirri is looking forward to meeting with you." Savyr sheathed his dagger. "Make yourself available to receive his visit tomorrow." A clear warning. "Your hospitality has been"—here his gaze flickered to Arek and his lips tugged upward—"entertaining."

Imhara bowed her head. "Your presence is most welcome at our hearth again, *Na'Rei*."

Rassan saw both *Na'Reishi* out. As the small group left the tent, her gaze dropped to Arek. He remained on his knees, head pressed to the rug. Fresh anger spurted through her.

Merciful Mother, what had possessed him?

Goose bumps prickled her skin as the last ten minutes replayed through her mind. She rubbed her arms. How close had she come to defying Savyr? To drawing her blade, fearing he would murder someone she cared for.

She stared at Arek. *Lady* knew she felt a connection with him, but not once had she ever put her personal needs over the safety of her Clan, yet this time she had.

The thought left her shaking even as her anger ratcheted back up. She paced to the table, needing to work off her agitation.

"Sayla, Miry!" The two servers scrambled to their feet. "Get Yrenna to a healer."

Rassan returned as the two women left the tent, the young scout cradled between them. Her Second held the flap open, then let it close behind them and strode into the room.

"They've gone." A gruff, clipped statement. His black-flecked gaze reflected her own tumultuous emotions.

His boots thudded hard on the ground as he crossed to Arek. Fisting his hands in the Light Blade's tunic, he hauled him to his feet. Arek offered no resistance.

"You put every person in this camp in danger with your stupidity." He released the human with a hissed curse, his expression as thunderous as his low-pitched voice. "By the *Light*, I'm tempted to drag you to the stocks and leave you there for the duration of our time here!"

A flush darkened Arek's cheeks. His mouth pulled down at the corners. "I'm sorry. . . ."

"Sorry?" Imhara gripped the edge of her desk until her fingers went numb. It was either that or manhandle him as Rassan had. "Yrenna deserves more than an apology."

Eyes closing, Arek scraped his hands over his face then fisted them. The heavy acidic odor surrounding him intensified.

"*Lady* forgive me, I know." His hoarse voice wavered, and shadows darkened his gaze. "I truly am sorry."

At least his regret was genuine. That was something.

Imhara reined in her temper but censored none of her contempt. "Your apology had better be accompanied by a good explanation, or I'll be the one carrying through on Rassan's threat."

His brow dipped and a spark of anger glittered in his eyes. "What happened is my fault, I know, but I told you I'd make mistakes." His voice thickened. "I just wasn't expecting him to hurt her to get to me."

His gaze turned inward, and his hands clenched and unclenched. A tart muskiness stained his scent.

Grief.

Imhara frowned. It was much stronger than expected, considering he didn't know Yrenna all that well. What carved such lines of pain on his face? She seesawed between not wanting to intrude on his memories and figuring out what had provoked him.

The safety of her Clan had already been jeopardized once for him. His doing but she'd compounded the error. They were both to blame. She had to know if he was a liability.

"Start talking, Light Blade."

His expression morphed from shell-shocked to reticence with a flex of his jaw. Imhara folded her arms, steeling herself for . . . what? She had no idea, but they couldn't afford another catastrophe like this evening.

"In order to bring Savyr down, you demanded I be open and honest." She grimaced. "Ten minutes ago I'd have killed Savyr to save you, risking everyone I love to do it. *Lady* knows why I care as deeply as I do for you; I shouldn't, but I do."

From the corner of her eye, Rassan's brows rose high on his forehead. Imhara kept her gaze fixed on Arek. Despite her admission, Arek's expression remained closed, and any explanation remained locked behind flat-pressed lips.

"You swore allegiance to our cause, Arek." She stabbed a finger at him. "You lost control. I want to know why."

Chapter 26

"I want the truth, nothing held back, or your part in this ends now."

Imhara's ultimatum sent a rush of adrenaline surging through Arek. Need and fear clawed within him with equal fervor. *Mother of Light*, there was no doubt he owed them all an explanation for his behavior, especially Yrenna, but the idea of sharing his personal history twisted his innards. Yet he couldn't lose the opportunity of avenging his parents' deaths.

His whole body heated, scalp to toes, and his world narrowed to the heavy beat of his heart against the inside of his chest. He sucked in a deep breath, trying to ease the sensation.

Strangely enough it wasn't so much the revealing that bothered him but the pain that would come with it. Like a live brand, it burned a hole in his soul, imagining the nightmarish scenarios of his mother's life as a captive, of the desolation his father had experienced, the depths he'd descended to before he let it claim his life, leaving him behind with an embittered grandfather.

The what ifs of the difference they'd have made if they'd both been in his life haunted him since he'd been old enough to realize their absence and mourn their loss. Not that he'd any choice with Davyn reminding him almost daily.

Lady knew what scents were pouring off him. They had to be awash with conflicting impressions if the roiling in his stomach was any indication.

He flicked another look at Imhara and grimaced. Even if she hadn't risked her cover by protecting him, she was right, his oath bound him. Her threat—and there was no doubt it was one—was reinforced by a glittering gaze, and the stubborn tilt of her chin warned him she wouldn't back down.

"My patience is gone." Her arms folded. "Rassan take him to Jawn's quarters. Your part in this is over, Arek."

The *Na'Chi* started toward him.

"Wait."

Rassan halted, his gaze swirling with just as much impatience as Imhara's.

Arek licked his lips twice before he could find enough moisture to wet them. "I was three years old when Savyr Gannec killed my mother. My father never reconciled her death and took his own life not long afterward."

How many times had he uttered those words only to have the hollow maw inside him opened wide until the pain, so familiar and raw, oozed out like an infected wound to poison him, like it was now?

While Imhara's expression softened momentarily, she shrugged. "So? During his reign as *Na'Rei*, Savyr's hurt countless others in a thousand ways. My life, my clan's lives included. What makes your loss any more tragic than ours or theirs?"

Arek scraped a hand over his face. Where did he start an explanation? Most people within Sacred Lake knew of his past and had never needed to be informed of the entire story.

"Although he didn't know it at the time, my grandfather killed Savyr's eldest son in a border skirmish some thirty years ago. Savyr discovered the identity of the Light Blade warrior, then found out he had a daughter. Rather than kill Davyn, to avenge his son's death he decided to kidnap the warrior's daughter with the intent of siring a child on her. Once the child was born, he was going to send her home with it."

"The stigma of a half-demon child." Rassan shook his head. "A twisted plan but one suited to Savyr."

Arek nodded. "Indeed."

He'd never known Davyn to be anything but consumed by the loss of his daughter. Although Savyr would never know it, he'd succeeded in his goal. The shame and humiliation of having a half-blood grandchild had driven Davyn insane, proven when he'd tried to kill her.

"Savyr kept my mother prisoner for a year. She died giving birth, almost thwarted his revenge. Without her alive, no one would ever be able to prove the child's bloodline." His mouth twisted in a wry parody of a grin. "But the *Lady* works in peculiar ways. It took twenty-five years for Savyr's plan to reach fruition."

Imhara's brow creased at his cryptic remark. "What do you mean twenty-five years? How do you know all this if your mother died?"

"Because, just recently, the child she gave birth to escaped to human territory." Here Arek took another deep breath, fighting to remain calm, but the steady *thump, thump* of his heart in his chest grew more pronounced. "My grandfather had a picture weaving likeness of my mother. Annika Gannec is the spitting image of her. She revealed the details of this story."

There. He'd said it.

He hadn't been able to acknowledge Annika as blood-kin that fateful day in the apartment when Davyn had tried to kill her. Nor had he uttered the words the day of the failed rescue mission when he'd asked Kalan to apologize to her for not getting to know her sooner.

Now he had, out loud. Finally.

Rassan uttered a hoarse curse and Imhara's expression morphed as they both made the connection. Although he doubted either felt the horror he'd experienced being related to a demon. Or the anger of being betrayed by a man he'd loved like a father all of his life, despite his flaws and their numerous disagreements.

They were worlds apart in that respect.

"Annika is your half sister?" Imhara's eyebrows shot up. *"Merciful Mother!"* She shared an astonished look with Rassan. For several heartbeats no one said anything, then, "Why didn't you tell me this earlier?"

Before he could answer, Rassan spoke up.

"Imhara, he's never experienced the Old Ways until now. See this from his point of view."

Her frown deepened and her gaze turned inward. She nodded slowly. "You're ashamed of having a half-blood sister."

While her tone remained neutral, said aloud the words heated his cheeks.

"There is that, but I'm trying to deal with it or was before I was captured."

He wasn't going to hide from the truth. Not this time. He'd done that by ignoring Annika, denying their familial relationship just as Davyn had, allowing blind hatred to cloud his judgment. He was the poorer one for it.

He grunted silently. Kalan and Kymora had tried to counsel him. He'd never really listened. The *Lady* hadn't given up on him, *Her* patience and guidance endless, although he hadn't realized that until now. Kalan had always claimed he was bullheaded. It'd taken the failed rescue mission, a crofter's death, being claimed by Imhara, and seeing Savyr in person to teach him that lesson.

And, if he searched deep within, he was grateful. He didn't want to end up like his grandfather, bitter and intractable, consumed in his hatred like an addict on *haze*—a poisonous attitude that would possess him all his remaining years.

"You're talking about the other *Na'Chi* living at Sacred Lake."

Rassan's soft comment drew him from his thoughts. "Your connection with them."

"They helped me adjust to the revelations that came with Annika's appearance in our lives." *Lady*, how he missed Varian and the company of some of the other scouts he'd trained with. "Their leader is much like you, Rassan. He's a friend." This time his smile was genuine. "You're both men I admire and respect."

Bronze flashed in the flecks of Rassan's eyes. The warrior's dark lips curved into a slow grin and he gave a nod of acknowledgment. "And your friend's name?"

"Varian."

Rassan grunted. "One day I would very much like to meet him, and the other *Na'Chi*. We owe them a debt of gratitude for opening your eyes."

Imhara strode away from the table to the other side of the tent, her head bowed in thought. When she turned around, the resolute expression was back. His smile faded.

"As startling as your information is, your inability to control yourself around Savyr threatened every plan we put in place."

Her accusation stung but he accepted it. "What happened caught me as much by surprise as you. But it's a mistake I won't repeat again."

"I can't take that chance, Arek."

"You and I share a common goal." Her flat-out denial shot a frisson of uncertainty down his spine. "You *know* what this means to me."

His voice was on the rough side of hoarse. He closed his eyes, regretting that his statement came across more as an allegation than a reasonable accounting of facts. *Lady's Breath*, he hadn't displayed this lack of self-control since he'd first started Light Blade training.

"What about the next time you're in Savyr's company?" The scorn in her tone snapped his eyes open and triggered a furious rush of heat inside him.

"I'm not some green scout out on the training field," he retorted. "Give me some credit for being able to adapt."

"Slaves mean very little to any *Na'Reish*." Her mouth flattened. "Particularly Savyr. To him you only serve two purposes—to be used for food or for his pleasure. You amused him this time. Give him the smallest reason, and he'll end your life with the snap of his fingers." Creases appeared in the skin around her eyes. "Another slave will replace you before your body turns cold."

Her concern was strangely comforting, yet her doubt niggled and prodded his guilt. Yrenna had suffered because of his lack of control. Still he pushed on.

"You can't do this without me."

Her raised eyebrow said otherwise.

She was intractable as Kalan when her mind was set. He'd worked with his friend too many years to know that pushing her wouldn't be a smart move.

Reining in his frustration, Arek gave a rough sigh and adopted a more neutral tone. "What can I do to convince you?" He spread his hands wide. "I'll do anything."

"Anything?"

The inflection in her tone gave him pause yet he nodded. Her gaze turned thoughtful. He held his breath, hope rising. After a moment, a small smile curved her lips. He frowned.

What was she thinking?

"All right." She made her way toward him. "You have tonight to persuade me."

Her gaze raked over him, head to toe, the transformation into *Na* Kaal so flawless he blinked. Her blatant perusal and the touch of her hand against the bare skin of his arm set his pulse racing.

"If you truly want a second chance, let me tell you what I expect." She circled him like a *lira* stalking her prey. "Tonight you show me you can be the perfect slave. You'll serve my every need, every command, every desire. No avoiding my questions. No protesting my orders. No hiding your scent."

Holy Mother of Light. What did she plan on doing?

"I don't want a Light Blade warrior. I don't want a man who plays at being a slave when it suits him. I want someone I can trust. Someone who can perform the role required of him regardless of his personal desires."

Her pointed look brought another flush of heat to his cheeks.

"I can't be second-guessing or worrying about your actions every time we mix with other *Na'Reish*. By tomorrow morning we have to be a team, but I don't think you're capable of doing what I want." Imhara placed her hands on his shoulders and leaned in against his back. Warm, moist breath brushed against his neck, prickled his flesh. "You still don't trust me."

Her accusation lashed at him, stirred his guilt.

"It's all or nothing, Arek." A challenge, and while softly spoken, the warning was also clear. "You refuse an order or lie to me, your chance ends."

Her hand trailed over his jaw, her touch searing across his skin as she completed her circuit and came to a halt in front of him. Her fingers came to rest on his neck, just beneath his jaw, and he had little doubt she could feel the rapid beat of his pulse in the vein there.

"Care to prove me wrong? Do you have the self-control you claim to possess?"

Inside, Arek shuddered.

She wanted everything.

Trust.

Restraint.

Submission.

She'd use his attraction against him. His imagination all too readily conjured the scenarios and sensations. Arek shoved them all to the back of his mind, then dared to glance at her.

Her small, smug smile confirmed his suspicions.

And, he admitted grudgingly, her strategy was clever.

Just standing there, feeling the heat of her body so close to him, her fingers stroking the side of his throat, created a roiling tension that centered low inside him and made it hard to focus on her words. He shifted to relieve the ache between his thighs.

What was it about her that made his gut clench in unease, even as desire surged through him, rising so fast he was already half hard?

Did he really want the connection between them tested? Did he want her knowing just how much she affected him?

Did he want to reveal everything to her?

To himself?

He balked, not wanting to delve that deeply into the what ifs but the truth remained. Imhara Kaal had the power to wreak havoc with his emotions, and he'd be giving her permission to uncover them whether he wanted them exposed or not.

Find your enemy's weakness and exploit it. Advice drilled into recruits by their instructors from the first day of training.

Arek lifted his chin, jaw tightening. Imhara's mistake lay in admitting to a reciprocal attraction. Two could play her game. All he had to do was remain focused. Just like any training session. No matter what she did, or how he responded, he had to keep his mind on the end goal.

The stakes were worth the risk.

"Anything else?" he asked.

His response drew a husky laugh from her, and she twined her fingers in the thin leather laces crisscrossing his vest.

"Tonight, you serve *Na* Kaal." A gesture directed his attention to the curtained-off room they shared. "Once you go in there"—she tugged the lace on his vest until it unraveled and loosened—"this all comes off. I want you naked."

A jolt of sizzling panic sliced through him, so quick he had no chance of controlling it. Breath hissed in through his teeth.

She wanted him stripped bare.

Literally and figuratively.

"You'll kneel on the floor at the foot of my bed, head bowed, and wait like that until I enter the room. When I do, you won't look up or address me unless I speak to you." She cocked her eyebrow at him. "Are you willing to do whatever I want to earn back my trust?"

Arek took a breath to voice his refusal, his response more reactive than logical, then froze. He clenched his teeth so tight his jaw ached.

What *did* he want more? To lay the past to rest, or to succumb to his fear of exploring what lay between them?

Arek hid his grimace. It was difficult, but he tempered his fear and focused on the end result.

Savyr Gannec's death.

He mightn't be able to control his physical reactions to her—it was certainly no secret now—but, by the *Light*, he'd make her work for everything else.

"Imhara . . ." Beside him Rassan's boots scraped on the ground as he shifted closer. "You go too far."

Words edged with sharp disapproval.

"My Second believes I'm forcing you into something you don't want to do. Is that true?" Her gaze glittered in challenge. The air between them grew still and warm. "Have I overstepped the mark, Arek?"

Chapter 27

AREK'S sharp inhalation made Imhara wonder if she'd pushed him beyond his limit, but the spice in his scent spiked to a new intensity, untainted by any acrid odor, and despite the slight widening of his eyelids, his stare never wavered. A dull flush crept into his cheeks, and his lips parted so he could inhale a steadying breath.

Now *that* was interesting. Where was the protest she'd expected? Back in the makeshift shelter, he'd rejected the attraction growing between them. Playing on that should have elicited an outright refusal, which would have resolved her problem and allowed her to put her secondary plan into place.

Was he actually considering her proposal?

The heat in Arek's gaze was definitely a mixture of defiance and arousal. He may not have verbally acknowledged the bond growing between them, but whatever his decision, she just hoped that what came next would strengthen it, not destroy it.

"Arek?" Rassan's soft query reminded her that he was willing to intercede on his behalf.

Imhara held her breath, half hoping, half dreading Arek's response.

"I don't blame Imhara for challenging me after my error in judgment." His admission when it came was low pitched, rough. "She's not forcing me into doing anything I'm not willing to take on. You have my *Lady*-sworn oath on that, Rassan."

Steel and resolve burned in the dark blue depths of his gaze. Imhara's stomach fluttered and she placed her hand on her abdomen. Arek's gaze flickered to her, caught the movement.

Relief slackened his tight expression, as if he'd been waiting for some reaction from her, then his mouth curved into a small smile. There one moment, gone the next; recognition of her attraction to him. Her heart rate lifted.

Insolent warrior.

Arek might be battling personal demons and his physical reactions to her—his scent had altered enough to hint at a maelstrom of emotions seething inside him—but underlying it all he possessed a core of strength.

He didn't run from fear. He faced it, regardless of the situation. In that they were very much alike.

Admiration curved her lips upward. Nothing appealed to her more than a strong man, so it came as no surprise to feel the moist heat of arousal between her thighs.

"Satisfied, Second?" she asked, her question a little breathless.

"You tread a fine line, Imhara." The deep-pitched warning vibrated with concern. She glanced at him. The palest green colored the flecks in his eyes. "Be careful you don't cross it. You'll never forgive yourself."

Ever her moral compass and valued friend.

She gave him a somber nod. "Please arrange for a meal to be sent, then make sure no one disturbs us. This pavilion and my room are not to be entered for any reason other than an emergency."

"I'll make sure the sentries are briefed." After a final glance at Arek, Rassan took his leave.

His absence only emphasized the fact that they were now alone.

"Facing Savyr the first time after the death of my family wasn't easy. Had it not been for Rassan at my side then, I'd most likely have reacted just as you did." More than aware of how pride could shackle logic and reason, Imhara made sure her tone remained neutral even though her pulse was hammering in her throat. "I won't think any less of you if you change your mind."

For the longest minute, Arek stared at her, watching her watch him, then, "My answer remains the same." His smile returned. Quick. Teeth bared. Feral. "Perhaps *you're* the one having second thoughts?"

Very much a challenge. And one that fired her blood.

So be it.

Imhara responded with a grin of her own, a frisson of pleasure rippling through her at the thought of testing his resolve. In fact, she looked forward to it, probably more than she should, given the uncertainty of the outcome.

She snorted softly. Why deny it? She relished it all the more *because* of it.

She gestured with her chin in the direction of the partitioned-off room. "In five minutes I'll walk through that curtain. You know what I expect. Don't disappoint me."

Arek's eyelids narrowed. Pivoting on his bare heel, he pushed aside the curtain and disappeared into her room. The canvas rasped softly as it settled back into place, the only sound in the silence that followed.

Lady's Breath, she was going to need every minute of the time stipulated to compose herself. Her hands shook as she held them up to eye level. She knew why they trembled.

She wanted whatever pleasure could be found from the encounter; hungered for it with a ferocity too long denied. Perhaps, just perhaps, if she handled this as carefully as instinct warned her to, a deep-buried dream might resurface.

Imhara shook her head. It was too soon, too dangerous to let that yearning arise. Let the *Lady* guide her and *Her* will determine the result. Hoping for anything else was a fool's path to disappointment.

Unable to remain stationary, she paced the length of the outer room, counting down the seconds, then added on more.

Na Kaal's prerogative.

Keeping an opponent off balance was something she did well, and making Arek wait a little longer gave him time to contemplate his decision, the possibilities of what he'd agreed to, the consequences. It also might take the edge off his cockiness, giving her the advantage. She'd take whatever she could.

Imhara glanced at the partition.

It was time.

With a slow release of breath, she settled into her role, her course set. Heart pounding in her chest, she pushed through the curtain and into the room.

Arek knelt at the foot of her bed, gloriously naked. Imhara's heart slammed into her throat at the sight of him waiting there, head bowed, all long limbs and tawny skin. She halted, and bit back a groan.

Merciful Mother, he was beautiful.

She couldn't really describe all of the sensations flooding her senses in those first few heartbeats. Some she easily identified—pleasure, awe, lust, desire—but those she couldn't—the deep warmth that encircled her heart, the breath-stealing pressure in her chest, the overwhelming need choking her throat—they left her unsettled.

Confused.

She inhaled a steadying breath acknowledging the effect he had on her, even if she couldn't fathom the intensity surrounding her reactions. They just reinforced her original notion of him that day in the library.

He was masculine beauty personified.

And on the auction block, he'd have impressed even the most jaded of buyers. *Na* Kaal included.

Imhara took in the curve of his feet tucked beneath lean flanks, the taut folded length of his legs, and powerful muscles of his thighs. With his knees spaced evenly apart for balance, jutting hipbones and the diagonal lines of his groin muscles and a fine dusting of blond hair arrowed down, drawing her gaze to his shaft and the shadowed sac behind it.

She forced her gaze higher, not allowing herself the temptation of examining him too closely other than to note he was nicely proportioned. Up over his ridged abdomen to the wide expanse of his chest, muscular shoulders and arms, the strong column of his neck. A few pale scars marked his skin—one across his ribs, another on his side, while the longest stretched from hip to knee on his right thigh—yet they only added to his appeal.

He'd left his hair unbound, and with his head bowed, the blond-streaked locks obscured his face from view. If it hadn't been for the gentle rise and fall of his chest, Arek could have passed as a master-crafter's statue placed on display for any viewer's pleasure.

Every muscle, every limb, every ridged angle and curved line displayed stone-carved perfection. More than worthy of admiration, although—and here, her mouth twisted wryly—she doubted any artist would approve of the carnal nature of her appreciation.

Imhara let the curtain drop behind her. The canvas flapped against itself, then dragged in a soft rasp over the rug as it settled on the floor. Arek never moved, yet his whole demeanor, his rigid, straight-backed position, the tightness of the muscles across his shoulders, even the way his hands lay on his thighs, fingers stretched out along the muscles, told her he was focused and more than aware of her presence.

A warrior to the core.

She had little doubt he would use that training in the coming hours.

But tonight she wanted to learn about the man.

Yet how to begin? What would he least expect, given he anticipated the worst from *Na* Kaal?

A few heartbeats later a slow smile curved her lips.

AREK kept his head lowered as the soft slide of canvas announced Imhara's entrance. Every muscle in him went tight. He issued a silent grunt, and almost shook his head. No, every muscle pulled *tighter*, given he'd stripped to bare skin, then spent an eternity kneeling at the foot of her bed anticipating her appearance.

Her strategy of making him wait left his legs and feet aching from sitting on them for so long. He'd kept his position, determined to allay her doubts. He could feel her gaze on him, the intensity of it licking his skin like fire. Her silent regard heated his blood until goose bumps prickled his entire body, left him hyperaware of the cool air caressing every inch of him.

"You've followed my orders. Well done."

It was hard controlling the urge to look up, particularly when he heard the slight waver in her voice. Had she not expected him to follow through on their agreement? Was it nerves or the effect of seeing him naked that caused it? Distraction or admiration? The expression on her face would tell but he couldn't check.

Even though he'd chosen to subject himself to her scrutiny, he'd come so close to covering himself when she'd entered the room. He hated to start a battle from a position of vulnerability, but her response soothed some of the tension gnawing at his innards.

One strike for him.

This engagement would be a different sort than the one he was used to but he could adapt. He drew in a steadying breath.

"This is a promising start to the night. More than I anticipated." Her tone, husky yet warm, indicated she was pleased. With his actions or him? Either would aid his cause. "Where did you put your clothes?"

The scuff of her boots against the hard ground indicated her progress across the floor, not toward him and the bed, but the cushion-strewn area opposite him. While he couldn't see her, her shadow crossed the rug in front of him and the faint chafe of fabric on fabric indicated she'd made herself comfortable on them.

"I put them on the chest beside the bed, *Na* Kaal." Leaving them on the floor hadn't seemed appropriate. "I can move them to another location, if that doesn't please you."

"No need." A soft, wooden knocking almost made him look up. Was she tapping her fingers on the low table nestled among the cushions? "Approach and remove my boots."

He blinked at the order. "Remove your boots?" Had he heard her right? Belatedly adding, "*Na* Kaal."

"You hesitate to comply. Surely, you haven't forgotten the conditions of this evening?"

As if he needed reminding.

"Your request surprised me." Keeping his head down, he covered the distance between them and knelt again, this time at her feet.

Removing boots he could do.

"Your scent just changed." Imhara's long legs uncrossed and she extended one toward him. "Why?"

Taking hold of her calf and the heel of her boot, he tugged it free. He removed the other before answering. "I expected . . . something more demanding."

That didn't cover half the images he'd conjured while waiting for her to enter the room.

"Testing me already?" Pitched low, her voice was cold and hard and made him aware that he'd given her a less than satisfactory answer. His jaw tightened. "By coming in here, you showed your desire to trust, or at least to try and trust. Was I wrong in that assumption?" She made a sound of disgust. "Or maybe you just couldn't back down from a challenge." Scorn laced her tone. "You waste my time."

Her bare heels scraped on the rug and her legs folded under her. She pushed to her feet.

"I am trying!" Unable to help himself, he wrapped his fingers around her calf to stop her leaving. His pulse tripped faster through his veins. "Whenever I'm at a disadvantage . . . I don't like giving away information. . . ." The words stuck in his throat. He swallowed hard. "Not when I know it'll be used against me."

For the longest minute, she said nothing, then he heard a soft sigh. She crouched and her cool fingers wrapped around his wrist to remove his hold on her.

"Now that's what I'm looking for. An honest answer at last." Her voice softened. "Arek, look at me."

He lifted his head.

Shadows darkened her gaze. "Do you truly still see me as the enemy?"

Did he? That was the question, wasn't it? The one he'd been putting off answering.

Once he'd have replied with a resounding yes. Now his certainty flailed like a bleater caught in a quagmire.

He gave the only answer he could.

"I've seen and experienced things I never thought I would. You're nothing like Savyr or Yur." He grimaced, knowing that wouldn't be enough. "You've made me question everything I've been brought up to believe."

"Learning what you thought was the truth was actually a lie would be quite unsettling." Her head canted to one side. "Change is frightening."

A shiver rippled through him. That was a *Lady*-told truth.

"The morning after my family was murdered, I found myself

standing on the wall looking over the fields, almost at the same spot where you found me the night of the feast. I stared out at the horizon praying for the strength to be my Clan's new *Na*."

How had she dealt with that, given she had to have been overwhelmed by grief?

"I couldn't see myself filling my father's boots. My older brother was supposed to have taken on that mantle. And while I helped my mother with some of her projects, I was so afraid of failing because her support and guidance were no longer there." Her gaze turned inward and her mouth pulled down at the corners. "I can't count the number of times I stood on that wall lamenting about how unfair it was, wanting to ignore my new responsibilities, hoping they'd all just vanish, and wishing that everything would go back to the way it had been."

Arek's heart thudded. How many times had he and Kalan skipped training sessions or the tutor's history lessons to spend time hanging out at the dock with the street children because he couldn't stand one more moment of living up to his parents' reputations as Light Blade warriors? Or because he wanted to avoid another lecture from his grandfather, usually about the responsibility of avenging their deaths?

"I wasted far too much time avoiding the fact that I was the only one who could decide my fate, no matter how helpful friends were." Imhara gave a sad smile. "While the *Lady's* plan for me wasn't clear, choice gave me some control over the path I took."

Her journey, so like his own, hadn't broken her as she'd been so afraid it would. Nor had the adversity thrust upon her by her own culture or the pressure of expectation. She'd found the fortitude to forge her own brand of leadership to continue her parents' legacy.

In contrast, since the death of his parents, the path he'd followed hadn't been truly his.

Arek's chest tightened as shock tingled from head to toe.

No.

As a warrior he'd made choices. No one else had influenced him.

His Gift had always been his. His memories of being discovered during a search were clear even twenty years later. His grandfather had smiled with genuine warmth the day he'd been assigned to the Light Blade compound for training.

A long-ago memory of a tutoring session surfaced. Gifts manifested in different ways. He'd asked about his and how the searcher had known he was most suited to Light Blade training. She'd told him his ability and its strength depended on his personality and outside influences, and that it was different for every individual.

His circumstances had hardly been normal though, had they? How many friends' childhood years had been disrupted by the machinations of a demon bent on vengeance? How many of them had grown up eating their breakfast with an equal serving of duty and descriptions of the horrors from the battlefield in the form of early-morning conversation?

Very few.

Arek frowned. What if his whole life had been twisted by that then molded to fit everyone else's expectations?

His grandfather's.

His instructors'.

Even his parents', or at least their reputations, and their friends' memories of them.

What if his parents hadn't died? Would he have become a Light Blade warrior just like them? Or would he have followed another calling?

The longer he thought about it, and no matter how much he wanted to claim he was his own man, a warrior of his own making, Imhara's story showed him that wasn't quite true.

Had he followed the wrong path? Had he allowed others' expectations to shape his life?

With Imhara's boot still clutched in his hands, Arek sat back on his heels, his fingernails digging into the leather. His pulse thumped so hard he could hear the rush of blood in his head.

If he had let others dictate his life, where did that leave him now?

He wasn't a coward but the answer emerging from the dark shadows in his mind terrified Arek more than anything else ever had.

A shudder racked him, inside and out.

He honestly didn't know.

Chapter 28

IMHARA drew in another deep breath. The scents pouring off Arek were so intense and they fluctuated so wildly she could barely identify them. The base odor held a sharp bitterness, a strong combination of grief and resentment. In a second inhalation she detected the heavy piquant odor of anger overlaid with confusion. A third filled her nostrils with the pungent odor of something rotten.

Despair.

Something was very wrong.

"Arek, are you all right?" She leaned forward and laid a hand on his forearm. The muscle contracted so hard it felt like she was touching stone. She slid a finger to the underside of his wrist. Beneath her fingertip his pulse tripped shallow and thready.

His head lifted slowly, and she watched him blink, as if emerging from deep thought. The skin across his cheeks had pulled tight, and beneath his tan, his face was pale. His pupils were twice their normal size.

He looked shocked.

Lost.

"Arek?" She tightened her grip on his wrist.

He blinked again, glancing down at her hand then up. His expression twisted into a grimace. The cocktail of scents intensified;

a sharp citrus odor spiked. His mouth pressed flat and he shook his head.

Imhara frowned. Was that a refusal to answer or an instinctive reaction to some thought in his head? When his gaze locked with hers, his eyes widening, shadowed by guilt, she knew.

Arek's gaze veered away to search the room, like a man about to flee. Panic, not defiance, spurred his refusal. Whatever thoughts tormented him, he was a heartbeat away from losing control.

"Eyes down." She wasn't surprised when he jerked at her sharp order. "Do it. Now."

His gaze slashed back to her, piercing, glittering.

"What happened to no second chances, *Na* Kaal?" he snarled. "Why not dismiss me as you threatened to do?"

He was fighting, not giving up. Relief pushed the breath from her lungs.

"Because I don't understand what's happened, that's why. And until I do, all the provocation in the world won't result in me releasing you from your oath." She knocked the boot from his grip and placed her foot in his hands. "So don't even think of getting out of this that way."

His fingers tightened around her ankle and arch of her foot, tight enough to be uncomfortable yet she kept her expression cool and indifferent.

"I believe I gave you an order. Comply. Now."

Wildness darkened his gaze. Hot metal and raw fury tainted his scent. He stared at her, five charged heartbeats. She knew he'd test her, expected it, considering his emotional turmoil.

So she waited, the stillness between them palpable. Hoping. Holding his gaze, daring him with her own, the only sound Arek's uneven breathing as he struggled with whatever was going on inside him.

Then, finally, he lowered his gaze.

Imhara let out a silent breath. She didn't care that he hadn't bowed his head or that every line of his body radiated resistance. He'd done what she'd asked. It was all that mattered.

"I hope your fingers are nimble, slave." She wiggled her toes. "It's time to put those strong hands to good use."

She lay back on the cushions, hands propped behind her head. Probably not the wisest position, given it left her vulnerable if Arek attacked, but it gave her a good angle from which to observe him.

The way his jaw flexed and tensed, his mind seemed more focused on his thoughts than the massage. His technique was jerky, uneven, not even remotely soothing. Anger still rode him, but it wasn't tainted with quite the same darkness she'd encountered that first time in her bedroom, nor did it seem directed entirely at her.

"Whether you believe me or not, any question you answer will help keep you safe," she commented.

Arek's expression tightened and his gaze lifted, as she thought it would given the statement she'd made.

"Keep me safe?" he snorted. "From what?"

Their eyes met briefly, then his shifted away and down in grudging submission.

"Mostly from me. Relying only on scent to know what you're feeling, especially when I'm likely to be distracted, would be a mistake." It was probably better to keep his attention on something other than his own thoughts. "I don't want to hurt you."

The foot rubbing faltered and his lips twisted. The heat in his scent escalated sharply.

"You already have."

"What?" Imhara jerked herself upright. "How?"

Color flushed beneath his tan from his neck up. His expression shuttered. The curse he uttered was aimed at himself.

Imhara pulled her foot from his hands and scrambled to her knees. She caught his chin between her thumb and forefinger, issuing her own curse when he resisted her attempt to lift his head.

"Arek, you don't get to shut me out. Your oath, remember." She searched her memory of their recent conversation for anything that might have provoked his claim, and drew a blank. "How have I hurt you?"

"You just showed me a few unpleasant truths, *Na* Kaal." His tone was brittle, mocking. A strangled laugh came from deep in his chest, harsh and ugly. "I underestimated you. Again."

The raw scent of his pain was overwhelming. Imhara frowned, gentling her grip on his chin, letting him go so she could stroke the side of his face with the palm of her hand. He leaned into her touch, seeking comfort, the movement so subtle she doubted he was even aware that he'd done it.

His obvious need tugged at her and released the band of tension knotting her shoulders. This she could work with.

"What truths?" she asked, in her quietest, firmest tone. She stroked his temple, the lines at the corner of his eye with her fingers. "Help me understand."

Beneath her hand his jaw flexed again; fire flashed in his twilight gaze.

So defiant. So defensive.

Imhara leaned closer to him, until their faces were only inches apart. "You'd prefer I guess?"

Burying her fingers in his hair, she ran them across his scalp to the back of his head. His hair was soft and she liked the silky feel of it sliding against her skin. Arek shifted his head, twisting to move away from her touch, yet he didn't break contact. His body liked what she was doing even if his mind protested.

Good.

Twining a sun-bleached lock around her finger, she tugged, a gentle reminder to answer her, and watched his pupils dilate farther.

"I'd prefer not to talk about it at all." A gruff reply.

Effort she rewarded with another run of her fingers through his hair, this time all the way to the back of his neck, where she kneaded muscles tight with tension. His warm breath brushed past her cheek on a sigh.

"You've made that very clear," she murmured. "Guessing it is, then."

No surprise her response made him tense up again. She smoothed her hand from his neck, over the thick muscle of his shoulder, and along the curved length of his pectoral, enjoying the smooth heat and steely strength of his flesh.

"I know you expected me to behave much like Savyr when I entered the room." She reversed direction, taking her time to savor every contour and hollow, liking how his skin rippled as she skated her fingers across the broad expanse of his chest. "You thought I'd inspect you . . . touch you . . . like he did with Yrenna. I was tempted."

Arek's swift inhalation gave her a small sense of victory. Not because he responded to her touch but because he was focused on her words instead of the darkness inside his head.

"You have a beautiful chest," she murmured, and spread her fingers wide, the heel of her hand brushing over his nipple. His flesh grew taut. "You train hard, but you're lean. You do more than just practice with a blade."

She moved her hand to the center of his chest, felt the heavy beat of his heart and bent her head close enough so she could feel the heat of his body against her cheek.

"Savyr and I are nothing alike." She inhaled—the smallest hint of spice tickled her nostrils—and made a sound of deep appreciation in her throat. "Unlike him, I won't treat you like an object. When I touch you, I want you to feel pleasure."

She started when his hands seized her upper arms. He pushed her away and held her at arm's length. The fierce expression on his face and hard grip couldn't hide the way he trembled.

"Yrenna felt no pleasure with Savyr." Arek's voice vibrated with suppressed anger. "He hurt her."

Not quite the comment she was expecting but certainly a chance to clear something up.

She nodded slowly. "Yes, he did, but you're wrong about Yrenna." He took a breath to protest. She held up a hand. "Hear me out. She volunteered for that role, Arek. She knew what she was getting into."

"You handed her over to him without a second thought!"

His accusation stung. Surely he didn't think her that callous and coldhearted?

"I knew there was the possibility that Savyr would hurt her. Bed her," she acknowledged. "But Yrenna was prepared to handle whatever happened with him."

"Handle?"

"Pain and rough sex are something she likes."

"She was scared. She cried out." That came from between clenched teeth and his frown deepened, as if he were questioning his memories. "She was . . . pretending?"

"Yrenna's good at what she does. One of the best."

His breath caught and she placed a hand on his arm.

"Arek, don't judge her because you find her sexual preferences distasteful. Given we all know what Savyr is capable of, I disliked placing her in that situation, yet without her our roles would be a lot harder."

Imhara watched him work through that. She could almost guess his thoughts as emotions flickered across his face.

Realization. Relief.

Horror. Guilt.

"*Mother of Light!*" The curse exploded from his mouth.

She squeezed his arm.

"Don't." She placed a finger over his lips. "You didn't know about

Yrenna. I didn't tell you. With what happened, we both share some of the blame. Second-guessing what you might have done if you had known is fruitless. She's alive. She'll heal."

Shadows flickered through his gaze.

Smoothing her fingers over the lines bracketing his mouth, she tried to ease the tension away. She dragged her thumb over his mouth. She didn't have to coax his lips apart.

"I know what you're doing." His fingers closed around her wrist as his teeth nipped the pad of her thumb, just hard enough to sting.

A warning and an enticement that sent a tingle through her body.

"Good," she replied. "Then you may as well give in to the inevitable and stop resisting me."

She stared pointedly at the hand shackling her. He released her, one finger at a time.

Defiant and unrepentant.

She hid her smile. "Are you ready to share your truths yet?"

His jaw clamped tight.

Apparently not.

Placing her hands against his chest, Imhara shoved hard and sent him backward onto the cushions, grinning at his startled curse. She straddled his hips, hooking her feet under the taut curves of his buttocks at the same time she leaned over him and placed her hands on the cushion on either side of his head, forestalling his attempt to rise.

"Imhara . . ."

She clucked her tongue at him. "*Na* Kaal."

His eyes narrowed with the reminder. His whole body tensed and she shifted her weight lower, preparing for any movement to dislodge her. So it came as a complete surprise to feel him relax beneath her.

No, not relax.

He'd stilled, every muscle was still hard, coiled in readiness. His gaze was fixed on her, the light in his eyes watchful, almost predatory.

Anticipating her next move?

"I like your lips." Her own twitched as the air around them filled with his spicy scent. "I already know you kiss well. But I want to know what else you like." She leaned closer, watching the gleam in his eyes heat up. "Or will you let me discover that for myself?"

Chapter 29

IMHARA'S husky question set Arek's pulse skipping faster through his veins and a surge of blood rushing south. Just the thought of her exploring him, in whatever way she pleased, had his body humming with awareness. Sweat prickled his skin and he knew it wasn't because of the heat in the room.

Imhara Kaal disturbed him; the things she said, the actions she took, the way she made him feel. She challenged him. She confused him. She shook him to the core.

She'd taken his world, made him question everything about it, and continued to strip him bare inside and out, bit by bit. And to add madness to the mix, he found himself wanting her more, with no idea why.

Take Yrenna. She'd absolved him of blame, shifted some of it to herself, and reassured him, all in one breath. And, with a reference to one kiss, reignited the hunger he'd felt that night for her.

Distract. Deflect. Adapt. Engage.

She'd used each strategy on him so far. With devastating effect. It didn't matter if he resisted. She just found another way to breach his defenses.

"Why spoil your fun?" A wry response, probably more sullen in tone than he'd intended, yet her chuckle grazed his ears.

"Ahh, an invitation." Her violet eyes sparkled. Her lips were only a breath from his. "I bet I can find a better use for that clever mouth before the night is over."

It didn't take much to conjure up a dozen ways he could use his mouth, either, all involving her. With her hips locked over his, he couldn't hide the instant reaction her suggestion had on him.

"You like that idea." Imhara canted her hips against him, sliding slowly along his length. The surge of heat generated by the rough caress of the fabric hardened him in less than a heartbeat. He bit back a groan. A wicked smile curved her lips. "A lot."

Another gentle rock stole his breath.

"I like it, too." Her breathless admission set his heart pounding. High spots of color flushed her cheeks. "More?"

He couldn't help the shudder that rippled through him. Reaching up, he gripped her arms but couldn't push her away.

"I'll take that as a yes." She leaned forward and put her lips to his ear. "Do you like your pleasure soft and slow? Or hard and fast?"

The image in his mind, of her body working him over the edge, charged every nerve, tightened every muscle, and made him tremble like he'd spent three hours in a grueling training session.

Distract, deflect, engage.

She was good.

"Neither!" he growled.

He couldn't believe how quickly she'd stripped away his control. Nor could he decide whether he admired or resented her tactics.

"Liar. Desiring a demon terrifies you." Each whispered word escalated the beat of his heart. "You're just afraid you might enjoy it too much."

The raw truth in her words was too hot. Too real.

"No!" He surged upward, intending to push her off him.

Her hands slammed against his chest, pinned him to the cushions. *Na'Reish* strength.

"What are you afraid of, Arek? Besides it being so good between us?" Her demand was hard, but the way she undulated against him was gentle. Like waves licking at the shores of a lake, but with heat of a fire. "You want me."

He shuddered. "I don't want this."

"You don't want to lose control. There's a difference."

A slight shift of her weight accompanied her words. Another slide, this one harder, faster, had his body bowing, arching up against her, every muscle straining.

Lady's Breath, she was killing him.

"Imhara . . ." A plea and curse all in one.

"Your body tells me you want this. Your scent tells me you want this."

And *Light* help him, he wanted more.

Much, much more.

Imhara stilled on top of him, the most exquisite of pained expressions frozen on her face. He shuddered at the cessation of movement and knew the awful combination of agony and need she was feeling.

"Trust me or hate me, Arek. Which will it be? Only then can this pleasure truly be ours." The heat in her violet gaze was as fierce as the one consuming him. "The choice is yours." Her fingers trembled as they traced his brow, the side of his face, his lips. "It always has been."

Her words made him freeze along with everything else. He dragged in a breath, fighting the bands squeezing his chest, listened to the air rasp into his lungs then rush out.

The choice is yours. It always has been.

Time stretched out as he stared up at her. Resisting what lay between them wasn't working, but giving in to it felt like jumping from a cliff blindfolded. Yet running from his fear wouldn't solve a thing.

The heart will know what the mind and soul desires. Scripture etched into the prayer room at the Light Blade compound.

His faith and his heart. The only two things he had left to rely upon . . . could rely upon . . . with any certainty.

To follow his heart would require a leap of faith.

Arek swallowed hard. “You.” The hoarse declaration didn’t sound like his voice. Hot and cold chills rippled through him. He met her gaze. “I choose you.”

Imhara’s eyes widened and her mouth parted in shock. Her fingers dug into his chest, a sweet pinch of pain. The wide smile she gave him helped him breathe again.

He waited for the rush of panic and doubt to accompany his decision, but a sense of acceptance washed over him instead.

Imhara’s mouth brushed against his, the softest press of her lips on his. Holding his gaze, she moved forward then back, sliding against him with the lightest touch. His nerves still fired, building his need for release.

“Your pleasure is mine, Arek.” Her husky voice ran shivers up his spine.

Bracing her weight on one hand, she reached down between them. Her fingers found him, ran the length of his shaft, then pressed him hard against her swollen center. The lightning shock of her touch wrenched another groan from deep in his throat. Seed leaked from him. She pushed upward again, a slow torturous slide, the searing sensation so extreme it had him teetering on the edge of orgasm.

“I can smell your need. It makes my mouth water.” Imhara’s voice was as strained and tight as he felt. “I wager you’d taste as rich as grazer-cream.”

The thought of her going down on him, her lips wrapped around his length, cheeks hollowed, her clever tongue teasing him, her expression taut with pleasure squeezed the last coherent thought from his head.

Arek bucked against her. Her fingers tightened around him and he surged up again, the heat of her scorching him on one side, her fingers a slick pressure anchoring him there on the other. The rhythm she set, the heavy scent of their pleasure, her small cries descended into sensory overload.

"*Mother of Light . . .*" He gripped her hips, his fingers flexing then digging as fire licked then ignited every nerve.

"Don't fight it. I want to see your pleasure."

Her breathless plea, the vibrant ache of need in her voice, sent him over the edge. His whole body surrendered, imploding in a furious rush of light and heat, and sensation.

Lady's Breath, how he wished he could feel her raw heat against him instead of moist fabric, but it was too late.

Fire burned through his bloodstream. His lungs seized, breathing ceased. Every muscle locked tight. His seed jetted forth. Each spasm wrenched a cry from him, blinding him with a rush so incredible, so intense it bordered on pain.

He hadn't spent this quickly since his earlier years when he'd first begun experimenting with willing partners, but then the encounters had never matched what he was experiencing now.

When his orgasm finally subsided and his muscles weakened, he collapsed back onto the cushions, utterly spent, his breathing uneven and choppy. Imhara's touch became featherlight, still stroking, still drawing out the last of his pleasure. He shuddered and caught her hand, twining her slick fingers with his.

Merciful Mother, he'd leapt from the cliff, but instead of experiencing the sudden, sickening rush to the ground below, he'd soared like a wind-drifter. A euphoric detonation of pleasure like nothing he'd ever felt before.

Blinking the blurriness from his sight, he found Imhara watching him with a very satisfied smile, yet the heat of high arousal still burned in her cheeks and her gaze. Her hand still trembled in his.

Arek swallowed twice to get his voice to work. "You denied yourself? Why?"

Her soft laughter was strained but warm. "I was distracted." Her knuckles grazed one side of his face. "I couldn't look away or focus on anything but you. Didn't want to."

Her admission caught him off guard. He mightn't understand everything she did, but the more he thought about it, her selflessness embodied the Imhara Kaal he'd come to know. She hadn't found physical pleasure, but contentment and satisfaction radiated from her anyway. It was there reflected in her expression and smile.

Unable to resist, he cupped her cheek in the palm of his hand and trailed his thumb over her skin to the corner of her mouth. Her eyes widened. When he traced her bottom lip, her breath hitched. Her astonishment turned to anticipation.

A little awed, Arek shook his head. "You keep surprising me."

In one smooth movement, he rolled until Imhara lay on her back, and pinned her there with one leg thrown over hers. Her eyebrows rose but she made no attempt to free herself even though she could have easily done so.

Instead her hands smoothed over his chest then curled around his ribs to slide down the length of his back, following the line of his spine, stopping at the swell of his buttocks.

Such a simple caress yet one that woke the nerves beneath his skin and hardened him within a heartbeat, again a reaction he couldn't hide from her. Her fingers lingered, kneading his muscles, her gaze turning smoky and dark.

He smoothed a thumb over her brow. "What are you thinking?"

"I'm not sure either of us are ready to go there." Her husky tone stroked him as deftly as her hand had moments ago. Her lips twitched. "Yet."

Threading his fingers in her hair, Arek lowered his head and pressed his mouth against hers, teasing her, tempted to show her how quickly that slow burn inside him could escalate to an inferno but resisted.

He kissed her in soft increments, working his way from one side of her mouth to the other, then on the backward trek flicked his tongue against her lips, in slow, tiny strokes.

Their first kiss had been an impulsive act, driven by a whole gamut of emotions, explosive, an assault on all their senses. This one he was determined not to rush.

"Arek . . ." His name, barely audible, at the tail end of a breathy moan.

What would it be like to hear her cry out in unrestrained passion? Sliding his hand to her waist, he tugged her shirt free of her breeches, undid the top button, then the next two. Her body undulated, an unconscious shift that made him grin.

Her hand clasped then pressed his flat to the bare skin of her abdomen. "I don't expect you to do this. There's no obligation, Arek."

"There's none felt. My decision. My choice, Imhara," he replied, and nudged his hard length against her thigh. He watched her pupils dilate, then leaned closer, his lips next to her ear. "Do you like your pleasure soft and slow? Or hard and fast?"

Her nails dug into the back of his hand as he taunted her with her own words.

"Don't know that I'll last long either way," she admitted with a half chuckle, half groan.

Arek kissed her again, pleased when her mouth opened under his. Her lips fused to his with a pressure that betrayed her hunger. He worked his hand beneath the waistband, his fingertips grazing the swell of flesh above her pubic bone before veeing over her bare folds in a teasing caress.

Drawing back, he watched her eyelids flutter shut. He curled his fingers into her soft flesh, sliding then pressing against her moist inner folds with enough pressure to elicit a gasp from her.

"You're as hot as molten steel." His voice grated out the words. "And wet. Very wet."

He eased a finger into her, a slow caress dictated by her sudden clenching around him, then drew it back, making sure he pressed against her core. Her whole body spasmed.

"*Mother*, that's so good . . . a little faster." She bit her bottom lip. "Don't stop."

Her plea vibrated with raw need that fed his own. *Light*, if he had the time, he'd strip her bare and replace his fingers with his mouth to give her the pleasure she craved, to taste and savor it as she came. This time though, with a twist of his wrist, several rapid strokes took her over the edge.

Imhara cried out, an uninhibited, guttural sound of pleasure and shock. He smothered it, fitting his mouth over hers, sealing the sound in, feeling it vibrate against his tongue as he tasted her. A short foray and retreat as her whole body trembled.

She rocked against him, her muscles tensing and releasing in rolling waves. One arm flung out and her fingers clawed into a cushion, as if to anchor herself against the powerful explosion of pleasure. Pleasure he knew well. Her lips parted but there was no hard inhalation of breath, just another startled, deep throated cry. She convulsed once, twice, and a third time.

Every gasp, every spasm, every dig of her fingernails into his skin prolonged his enjoyment of the moment, her passionate response just as unrestrained as his own a few minutes ago, an astonishing gift of trust and vulnerability.

Considering the challenge she'd issued earlier, he'd expected only one victor in their battle, but somehow, sometime in the last hour, the stakes had changed. Their shared desire proved more fulfilling and satisfying than any competition.

"So beautiful," he whispered, although he doubted she heard him. She still writhed, consumed by the receding waves.

He gentled his strokes, letting her movements guide the pressure and strength of his touch, prolonging her pleasure for as long as she could tolerate.

Another kiss, and a nip of her bottom lip with his teeth. She gasped again, and another flood of moist heat coated his fingers. He soothed the bite with his tongue. Her flavor was unique, sweet and light, rich and addictive. He savored it and her uncontrollable shuddering.

Slowly, Arek drew back, memorizing the way their lips clung together until the last moment before parting, the wet heat a slick reminder of the pleasure they'd shared.

Imhara placed her head into the curve of his shoulder, her breath fast and ragged against his skin. Her arms slid from his waist to link loosely around his neck. He was tempted to pull her in against him, to cradle her closer still, but was reluctant to break the moment.

Long minutes passed before she lifted her head and opened her eyes. Her cheeks remained flushed a deep rosy hue.

"You like to tease." Her tongue darted out to lick the taste of him from her lips.

"So do you," he replied. With a last, lingering caress, he withdrew his hand, earning a soft moan of protest, one that brought a smile to his lips. "Greedy, too."

"Guilty as charged." She issued a contented sigh, her violet gaze sparkling. "It's been awhile since I've sought such pleasure."

Her honest admission left him speechless and wondering why. Surely she hadn't been lacking for lovers. With another sigh, this one more resigned, she rolled away from him, then pushed to her feet.

He propped himself on an elbow. "Where are you going?"

"As much as I'm enjoying our time together, I think Rassan has waited long enough."

Arek shot a glance at the curtained exit. "He's out there?" A dull flush colored his cheeks. *Na'Chi* hearing was almost as acute as the

Na'Reish. The thought extinguished any lingering desire. "All this time?"

"No." Her head shake accompanied low laughter. "Just the last few minutes."

"How do you know?"

"I can smell the food I ordered earlier." She headed for the chest next to her bed. After tossing his clothes on the bed, she lifted the lid and dug around inside it, pulling out some of her own. "He'd ensure our privacy by delivering it himself rather than allow anyone else access to the pavilion."

A swift yank and she'd stripped out of her shirt. Arek stared at the lean lines of her back. The spotted markings trailing down either side of her spine were a stark reminder of her heritage. Until that moment, he'd forgotten she was *Na'Reish.*

As she shimmied out of her breeches, he saw the trails continued along the backs of her legs, fading in color by the time they reached her ankles. His body warmed with awareness, more ensnared than repulsed.

Imhara tugged on a new pair of breeches.

Why was she changing?

Realization dawned.

"Is Rassan eating in here with you?"

She paused tucking her shirt in and peered over her shoulder at him, one dark eyebrow lifting, her gaze intent. "And if I said he was?"

A soft question underlaced with steel.

Also a timely reminder that he'd agreed to play a role—had *chosen* to play—and she did what she had to protect her people and expected nothing less of those around her.

Arek glanced at the curtained exit again, more than a little uncomfortable with Rassan being present in the room with them. While the *Na'Chi* might be aware of their mutual attraction—he'd certainly have no trouble scenting it in the air—was there any need for him to witness the evidence smeared over his body?

He fisted a hand. As uneasy as he felt, and as distasteful as the role might be, Rassan's presence was neither life threatening or dangerous.

He'd chosen to place his trust in his heart.

And in Imhara.

Pride shouldn't get in the way of his goal. Nor did he want to disappoint her. Again.

With a steadying breath, Arek rolled to his feet and returned to kneel at the foot of her bed, head down, hands resting on his thighs.

The silence stretched out; an eerie repeat of earlier this evening.

A bare foot appeared in his side vision, then Imhara crouched in front of him. Her fingers threaded through his hair, gently tugging his head up. Her gaze gleamed.

"Your faith in us is humbling, Arek." Her fingers grazed his temple, then his cheek and jaw in a caress. "Rassan stays only long enough to deliver the food." A softly delivered promise. Her slow smile tightened his chest, left him soaring high like a wind-drifter again. "Then the rest of the night is ours."

IMHARA cast one last glance over her shoulder, a small smile curving her lips at the sight of Arek sprawled in her bed. While they'd started out side by side, sometime during the night he'd shifted in his sleep until he lay on his stomach, one arm stretched out to the side, the other over his head to curl under the pillow. She liked the way the cover had slipped to wrap around his waist, leaving his bare shoulders exposed.

Sighing, she regretted even a minute's absence from his side and hoped whatever Rassan disturbed her sleep for wouldn't keep her away from him too long. She wanted to be with him when he woke.

To explore their new relationship. And to confront the fear that would come with that awareness. His, and her own.

After his astounding choice earlier in the evening, they'd shared a meal, but one where he'd insisted on carrying out his role as *Na* Kaal's slave, a companionable period of time, yet she hadn't pushed him for the reason for his transformation, content to watch him perform the most menial of tasks. While he didn't seem entirely comfortable, his demeanor reflected a more purposeful intent, a dogged commitment that hadn't been evident before.

A victory of sorts but she was under no illusion that when Arek woke he'd see his decision and actions in a new light, possibly one of capitulation. How would he react toward her? Would he reject what had happened? Would it be one pace forward, three back?

She hoped not because she'd thoroughly enjoyed every minute. A stolen moment in time and one she anticipated revisiting now that Arek had finally acted on their attraction. If they could share such incredible pleasure with just a few kisses and touching, what would it be like if they went further?

A soft throat clearing reminded Imhara that Rassan awaited her. Snatching up a cloak to ward off the cool night air, she stepped through the curtain her Second held open and headed for the far side of the pavilion, where any conversation wouldn't disturb Arek's sleep.

The pungent scent of burning oil hung in the air. The single night lamp set on her worktable cast long shadows across the rug, but the lack of light couldn't hide Rassan's tired expression as he made his way toward her.

He was still dressed in warrior leathers, the same ones from yesterday's trek. Had he even been to bed yet?

"Apologies for waking you so late in the night." His expression was more somber than usual, the flecks in his eyes glowing almost a silver gray. "But I didn't think this could wait."

Smothering a yawn, Imhara scrubbed her hands over face. "You wouldn't do it if it wasn't something important."

"This is unconfirmed and I intend on investigating this personally, tomorrow, when the *Na'Hord* enter the fortress to train in the arena . . . discreetly, of course. . . ."

She frowned. What had Rassan so disturbed that he'd open with such a long-winded explanation? He was usually much more direct. "Go on."

"Jawn and some of the others were collecting water from the river. They spent some time there, catching up with other slaves from the Clans."

Not so unusual. The Enclave was a chance for humans to mix while attending their daily chores. It was as close to free time and socializing as a slave could get.

"He overheard some troubling information." His dark lips thinned and the flecks in his eyes expanded. "One of the other slaves mentioned that a larger-than-usual number of *Na'Hord* accompanied their Clan this year. He complained about the increased workloads, supplies needed, and such."

"The Games attract many would-be champions."

Rassan shook his head. "Not this many, if the slave's account is to be believed. There's no way the Games could cater for this number."

"How many are you talking about, then?"

"The slave came from the Morda Clan." Rassan's large hand rested on the hilt of the dagger at his waist. "He told Jawn that *Na* Morda brought almost two thousand *Na'Hord* with him this year."

"Two thousand?"

"It gets worse. He thinks there's another thousand from the northern Vos, and the Itha have nearly three thousand."

"That's six thousand *Na'Hord*. All here at the fortress?"

His hard nod warned her there was more. "Jawn says it's rumored that every Clan was ordered to mobilize their full *Na'Hord*."

She grunted. "Every Clan but ours."

"It seems so."

"Where are they camped?"

"Outside the western wall of the fortress. I tried to confirm this tonight once Jawn made his report." Here Rassan's knuckles whitened around the pommel of his dagger. "The watch on the fortress wall denied me egress at either of the western towers. The same occurred when I took my *Vorc* out for a hunt in that direction. There's an extensive perimeter set out in the forest."

"If all Clan *Na'Hord* are being called in and sequestered here at the fortress, then it lends credence to Meelar's claim that Savyr *is* planning an imminent attack on human territory." Imhara chewed on her bottom lip. "But why has he excluded us from this missive, these preparations?"

"We are one of the smallest Clans."

"Technically we've sworn fealty to the *Na'Rei*. Our *Na'Hord* is his to call on in times of war."

Commander Veht had never mentioned his father's plans for Enclave other than in general terms. While he'd been on a slave raid, travelling through her lands to human territory, he couldn't claim that as an excuse for not knowing. Not when it took time to organize and mobilize a Clan *Na'Hord*. Even a second son would be privy to such information, particularly when he'd likely be leading his own warriors into battle once he returned.

She'd also spoken briefly to *Na* Sharadan just that afternoon. About the Enclave. The Games. Trade. Familial alliances. Slave caravans. Bandits. The weather. All topics touched on, but again, nothing about a war missive or a request to activate and assemble his *Na'Hord*.

"We've been kept ignorant of these plans for a reason. Savyr had the perfect opportunity to talk to me about this today. He didn't," she murmured. "Something as newsworthy as war would spread through the ranks like wildfire. Yet all we have are a few snippets of conversation from a slave or two." She shook her head. "I don't like this at all. We need to find out more."

"Agreed." The flecks in Rassan's eyes were a solid green. "I'll inform everyone tomorrow morning and warn those going into the fortress to listen for information."

"Caution them not to query directly." Foreboding scraped a cold claw across the back of Imhara's neck. "If word hasn't trickled down through the ranks about this, then it's because Savyr's threatened others to keep quiet. We're lucky to have even heard of this through one of Jawn's contacts."

Why would Savyr exclude her *Na'Hord* from this marshaling of his army? A question Imhara racked her brain to find an answer for and came up blank.

She frowned. "I want to know as much as I can about this gathering of the *Na'Hord* before the Enclave. Send someone to the Traders Market. Make up some excuse about looking for a slave with bookkeeping skills. It's the closest building on the western side of the fortress, and the only one tall enough to overlook the keep wall."

"I'll arrange for Barrca to visit tomorrow," Rassan said. "He can take Cavaan with him. Sometimes a slave can venture where a Clan member cannot." He snorted softly. "You know, you could always confront Savyr and ask."

Imhara gave a short laugh. "I think we've already used our quota of luck with him. There's also Sere Jirri's visit tomorrow." She made a sound at the back of her throat. "I wasn't looking forward to it at all, but perhaps meeting with him may prove beneficial after all."

Chapter 30

AREK woke, rousing straight from sleep to hyperalertness, wondering what had disturbed him. Propping himself up on an elbow, a quick scan of the dimly lit room revealed nothing.

The sound of voices and laughter beyond the canvas wall of the pavilion caught his hearing. Although muffled he thought he recognized at least one.

Barrca. Sentries completing a patrol. If the *Na'Chi* scout was on duty, then it was just after dawn. Their voices faded away toward the front of the tent. With the puzzle solved, Arek dropped his gaze to the figure curled up under the covers beside him.

Imhara.

She lay on her back, her head turned toward him on her pillow, one arm tucked under the covers, the other resting on the top over her stomach. The neckline of her shirt lay unlaced. Sometime during sleep it'd pulled to the side, exposing the spotted expanse of her neck and one shoulder and the upper curve of a breast.

She'd left her dark hair bound, yet several strands had worked their way loose during the night. His fingers twitched to reach out and smooth them back from her cheek, but he resisted, unwilling to wake her, not yet ready to face her scrutiny, knowing she'd want to address what had happened between them last night.

Last night.

He fisted a hand in the covers, unable to stop the sequence of events from playing through his mind, from the gut-wrenching confrontation with Savyr through to the surreal moments of passion.

His and hers.

What had he done?

His heart thudded faster, and he tensed, expecting the customary rush of guilt and doubt. He could feel it, hovering like a scavenger in the shadows, but something else held it at bay. Something he hadn't felt in a very long time.

From his past emerged the memory of the day he and Kalan had taken the Light Blade oath in the *Lady's* Temple. After nearly a dozen years of tutoring, training, and testing, he'd approached and knelt at the altar where the *Temple Elect* waited to hear him swear allegiance to the *Lady*.

His voice might have broken once or twice as he'd uttered the oath. At the conclusion of the ceremony, when the *Chosen* had placed the sun amulet around his neck, he'd looked out over the faces of the congregation, to those he'd sworn to serve, and felt such a lightness of spirit yet also anxious anticipation for what the future would bring. Adrenaline had only intensified those sensations.

Those same emotions filled him now. He didn't understand why Imhara Kaal had been able to provoke them, but his decision to trust her instead of second-guessing or doubting himself felt right. It had last night and it still did now.

"Such a serious expression . . . one much too somber for a dawn awakening." Imhara's sleep-husky voice drew him from his thoughts. Violet eyes watched him through half-closed lids. "Regretting last night?"

"Doesn't my scent betray me?"

She reached out to smooth her fingers across his jaw. The nerves beneath his skin tingled at her light touch. "I'd rather you tell me."

If he hadn't been watching her, he'd have missed the flicker of nervousness that darted through her gaze. His response concerned her that much? Or was she having second thoughts?

There was only one way to find out.

"Regret, no. Instinct says I should." He gave a wry smile. "But how much of a fool would I be to let lies rule my behavior?"

Imhara tilted her head a little, a frown creasing her brow. She shifted onto her side, sliding an arm beneath her pillow to plump it, to use as a prop for her chin. "What lies, Arek?"

Grimacing, he sat up and scrubbed a hand over his face. In the silence, the rasp of his hand over his stubbled jaw was loud. He'd already committed to sharing some of his past with her last night. While his world might have been turned upside down, one thing hadn't changed.

He still hated Savyr Gannec and he still wanted the demon dead.

"Something you said last night made me realize my whole life has been based around a lie." Unsurprisingly his voice sounded rough.

"This something was what hurt you?" He gave a quick nod and heard her sudden intake of breath. "I'm sorry."

Sincerity rang through in her apology. He hesitated, waiting for more questions, expecting her to push. But she didn't and it made it easier to keep going.

"You shared with me the story of how you coped with the death of your family and the choices you made stepping up into your father's role." So many thoughts, and images, and memories filled his head. He grunted softly. "Vengeance twists a torturous path."

"Do you mean Savyr?"

"Savyr. My grandfather. Me." To understand him, to put together the puzzle that was his life, he was going to have to give Imhara all the pieces. His breath left his lungs in one long, drawn-out expulsion. "Up until Annika's appearance at Sacred Lake, the *Na'Chi* were considered a myth. I uncovered a historical journal that revealed the *Na'Reish* and humans once lived together, and that any union between our two races produced Gifted children. The revelation was shocking."

Imhara nodded. "As it would be, considering the length of time of we've all been at war. I'd wondered at your response after you read my ancestor's journal. While you questioned the blood-bond, you didn't seem at all surprised with the idea of our races mixing."

"What disturbed the Blade Council more was discovering that some of the Councilors already knew about this, some from the present and the past, and that they'd withheld this information from everyone for generations. My grandfather was one of those Councilors."

"Oh, Arek!"

"Davyn was good at keeping secrets."

Derision soured his tone, but it was aimed more at himself than his grandfather, for his inability to suspect anything was amiss.

"Annika and I never found out we were all related until Davyn tried to kill her in his apartment. A picture weaving of my mother hung on the wall in a room he'd forbidden me to ever enter. Once we saw the hanging we discovered just how alike she and Annika were. Prior to then, I had no memory of her face and he never showed the weaving to me.

"I believed my mother's death justified his desire for revenge. Growing up I never questioned why he was so embittered." He dropped his voice to mimic the man who'd raised him. "'*Train hard, listen to your instructors, be the best! Avenge injustice with the blade of your sword!*'"

Arek swallowed against a tight throat. How many times had he heard that lecture at breakfast before he headed off to the training grounds?

"I always thought Davyn wanted me to live up to my parents' reputation as Light Blade warriors. I suppose that was part of it, but after the Councilors' duplicity was exposed, I questioned his motives." The memories came fast, so vivid it was like they'd happened yesterday instead of months ago. "When I saw my mother's image hanging on the wall in his apartment, there was no doubt why he wanted Annika dead. The shame of having a half-blood grandchild was too much for him. Another secret he had to conceal."

Davyn's humiliation had been his for weeks afterward, the emotion mocking, eating away at his innards as his family's reputation faced the scrutiny of others. Despite that, Arek attended every day of his grandfather's trial. Before the new Blade Council, Davyn's actions to conceal the past were revealed through his own testimony and the statements of others.

Arek rubbed the center of his chest. Every secret uncovered had felt like a dagger thrust into his heart. "There was no honor in what he did."

Nor could he reconcile the man he'd grown up loving and respecting as the one standing defiantly silent as judgment had been passed. No remorse, no sign of regret, no attempt at an apology for anything he'd done, just contempt and bitter disgust burning in his gaze as he was led away to be imprisoned.

Arek stiffened as Imhara's arms slid around him from behind, one hand coming to rest over his heart, her chin on his shoulder, her breasts pressing against his spine.

He tried to shrug her off but she held on. "I don't want your sympathy."

"I'm not offering any." A soft retort, close to his ear. "Don't you think I know what betrayal and deceit feels like? Treachery has shaped both our lives."

Her reminder vibrated with old pain. He pressed his palm over her hand on his chest in mute apology.

"Yet you chose hope, while I embraced hatred." He forced the words out. "All my life I've let it consume me, and I've allowed others to encourage it. Then to learn it was all based around lies . . . How do I reconcile a life wasted serving the *Lady* for the wrong reasons?"

He shuddered and her arms tightened around him.

"Now I begin to understand." Her lips pressed against the top of his shoulder. "A life serving the *Lady* is never wasted, Arek. You may think you strayed from *Her* tenets, but *She* knows your heart. *She'd* have guided you on your journey, regardless of the influences in your life."

Imhara shifted, sliding around to sit beside him, her hands reaching for him, her fingers twining through his. Her violet gaze linked with his, steady, somber yet strong.

"When our paths twist or turn and we lose sight of the ground ahead, I like to think *She* walks beside us, nudging us in the right direction." A small, warm smile shaped her lips. "I also believe sometimes *She* places people in our way to help us on that journey. Think about who you've met on yours—Annika, the other *Na'Chi*, your friend Varian, my Clan. . . ."

Her words reminded him of the conversations he'd had with Kymora, particularly in the months following Davyn's betrayal. He hadn't listened to his friend then, too consumed by anger and confusion.

"Our journeys intersected because *She* knew we needed one another." Imhara's smile reached her gaze. "And I'm awed and thankful your courage to trust me last night was stronger than your desire to hate. A weaker person would have taken the easier path."

Like so many of the other Blade Councilors, past and present.

Like his grandfather.

A shiver slithered down Arek's spine. He'd come so close to choosing that path.

"I don't want to end up like Davyn."

"You won't." She pressed her lips against his knuckles. "You value honor and integrity. You serve and protect others. You've made mistakes, but you've chosen to learn from them."

So direct.

A trait he'd always appreciated and respected, even in the enemy; although he didn't know what Imhara was to him now, he couldn't class her as an adversary anymore.

"*Lady* willing, we'll bring Savyr down, Arek." Her fingers tightened around his, her touch warm and welcome, a sensation that settled around his heart. "Together."

"LOT seven! Five fine slaves, three male, two female!"

The deep-chested voice of the auctioneer carried clearly over the hum of the crowd to where Imhara sat with other *Na'Reishi.* The raised wooden stands allowed those of rank to escape the crush and odor of the sweaty bodies standing in the packed cobblestoned square.

"These humans have been brought all the way from the High-Ranges Province in the far north. Strong, young, and some of the best breeders brought across the border in years!"

Imhara hid her grimace at the livestock reference, but the slaves, presented in simple tunics, groomed and oiled, provided a much-needed diversion.

For Sere Jirri. Not her.

The brawny warrior's voice cut off midsentence as his attention shifted to the auction platform. Every time a new lot came onto the stage, his distraction gave her a reprieve from their conversation, although the word could hardly be used to describe what they'd been doing for the last hour.

A discussion required interaction, a two-way dialogue on a variety of topics. But in typical male *Na'Reishi* fashion, the older warrior assumed his command, numerous military campaigns, and stable of

Na'Hord challengers for the Games were of more importance than expecting any deep and meaningful commentary from her.

Beginning her own conversation or making comments about the increased number of *Na'Hord* warriors present for the Games, hoping it might lead to information about Savyr's hidden army, resulted in a change of subject. Questions were completely ignored or deflected. If this was his strategy for impressing a potential mate, it was no wonder he remained unattached.

"I'll take any bid!" The auctioneer swept his staff in an arc as wide as his smile, inviting not only the *Na'Reishi* to participate but the lower classes, mostly all Clan *Na'Hord*, standing in front of him.

A rattle of stones on wood came from Imhara's left. The *Na'Reishi* male, a trader by the fine cut of his clothes, sat on the edge of his seat, close to the stand railing. Several small azure gems sparkled in the sunlight in a shallow wooden bowl attached to the railing.

"A generous opening offer!"

Another bid, this time from farther left of the first patron. More came as the auctioneer singled out each human with a prod of his staff, then proceeded to outline their attributes. Within minutes the number of stones sitting in bowls had multiplied. The higher the price, the more excited and vocal the crowd became.

"First call, good *Na'Reish*! As it stands the lot belongs to *Na* Eayl. . . ."

Imhara fingered the pouch at her belt, feeling its weight, and wished she possessed ten times as much so she could buy every lot on offer and avert the fate she knew awaited those on the block and chained to the posts behind. Watching so many lives bartered for a handful of precious stones, seeing their frightened expressions, made her heart ache.

Looking away from the dais, she scanned the crowd. As the first auction of the Gathering and one of the more reputable, it had attracted quite an audience. The majority of the stands reserved for Clan *Na's* and their blood-kin were full.

Urkan Yur occupied the Gannec platform, surrounded by a smattering of Gannec *Na'Reishi* females. Those closest to him weren't paying any attention to the auction. Instead they fawned and leaned toward him, trying to engage him in conversation. Imhara shook her head. What they saw in the conniving side-winder was beyond her.

They weren't the only females in attendance. The brightly colored dresses of others stood out in the crowd. The more stylish, the higher ranked the female.

The gossamer fabric draped on the overhead frame provided relief from the midday sun, as did the gentle breeze, but not enough, if the flushed faces of the *Na'Reishi* females were any indication.

Shifting on the padded bench, Imhara plucked at the ties on the neckline of her shirt, glad she'd chosen to wear her customary breeches and shirt. Her choice might have earned Sere Jirri's silent disapproval, but she'd rather endure that than the discomforting layers of material and rising temperature of the arena.

Rassan and a half dozen of her *Na'Hord* as well as several Jirri warriors—their escort this morning—stood at the foot of their platform. Her Second nodded, one dark eyebrow lifting as she caught his gaze. She rolled her eyes in an exaggerated movement, conveying her opinion to his unspoken question of how her meeting was going. His lips twitched upward.

"Second and last call!" The auctioneer's call drew her attention back to the dais. Lifting up the staff, he brought the end of it down hard, closing the bidding. "Bought and sold to *Na* Eayl of the Vos Clan!"

The five humans were herded off the block, the handlers exchanging them for another lot. All children, and none over the age of ten. They huddled together in the center of the stage, wide-eyed, shying away from the approaching, seven-foot auctioneer.

"Now for a real treat. A mixed dozen. Young enough to train without too much trouble!"

He grasped the smallest child by the back of her tunic and lifted her high in the air. The girl kicked and squirmed. Her efforts to free herself drew a smattering of laughter. Her chin trembled but she held on to her tears, a brave front given her circumstances.

"Perhaps you're looking for that special Gathering feast gift. All are sweet enough to satisfy the most discerning palate!" The burly auctioneer placed the child back on her feet, and she ducked behind an older boy. They looked similar enough to be siblings. "Opening bids?"

They came quickly. Imhara's gaze narrowed, recognizing two of the opening bidders. Both well-known traders who preferred purchasing children to train as blood-slaves as they proved more cost and time efficient than purchasing who knows how much *haze* to sedate an older slave. An added expense most traders tried to avoid, given the price of the drug.

"A drink, *Na* Kaal?" A tap against her leg accompanied Arek's soft inquiry. Head bowed, he held up a cup.

Imhara realized then just where her hand rested and took a slow, deep breath. Loosening each finger, she moved her hand away from her dagger and took the cup Arek offered.

A timely interruption.

"Water." At least her voice remained steadier than her temper.

From where he knelt at her feet, Arek shifted to grasp one of the stoppered jugs beneath the small table between her and her host, then poured water into her cup. He placed a second one within reach of the Commander.

The model slave. Circumspect and attentive, particularly given he'd noticed her slip in character. *Light*, she was getting tired of hiding behind a personality and a lie, and this time around, enduring seemed a lot harder.

Imhara drained the cup, almost tempted to ask for something stronger as a refill, but then set it aside. A quick feel through the gems in her pouch, she extracted the largest stone she could find and held it up high, making sure it caught light and auctioneer's eye.

"Ahh, someone with a keen eye for quality." The auctioneer pointed his staff in her direction. His smile revealed both rows of pointed teeth. "*Na* Kaal holds the highest bid."

Heads turned her way, and she made sure everyone saw the gem before she placed it in the dish in front of her. The exorbitant bid might seem like overkill, but she'd had enough.

Of the auction and of Sere Jirri.

Damn Savyr's instructions to get to know her potential mates.

"You could have taken the bid with a gem half that size, *Na* Kaal," her host murmured, tone disapproving. "Why so determined to purchase this lot?"

She slanted him a sideways look. "How often does a slave-raider bother to bring such young humans back across the border? A rare occurrence, given they're high maintenance and a nuisance to transport." The barest of smiles curved her lips. "They'd certainly make a unique betrothal gift to my future mate."

The lie slipped easily from her tongue. Immediate interest sparkled in his gaze.

"First call!" came the cry. Imhara rose from her seat, satisfied when no one bid against her. "Second and last? Sold!"

She gestured Arek to leave the platform. Below, Rassan murmured to their *Na'Hord*, and she knew they'd be ready to accompany her once she descended. She signaled Barrca to make arrangements for delivery of the children to their campsite. The *Na'Chi* nodded, collected the gem from the dish, and threaded his way through the crowd to the registrar. He'd also see the children safely to the campsite.

"Where are you going, *Na* Kaal?" Sere Jirri's imperious question grated. As much as she didn't want to, she paused at the stairway to the stand. "Surely you can't be leaving so soon?"

"This meeting is over." Projecting a bored expression, she faced the older warrior. "My *Na'Hord* have training to attend in preparation for the Games, and I have other business needing my attention. Thank you for your hospitality, Commander."

Confirming the presence of the amassing *Na'Hord* on the western side of the fortress was more important than wasting time with a pompous warrior old enough to be her father. Clasping the hand Rassan held out to her, she took the half-dozen steps to the ground.

"*Na* Kaal, this is a betrothal meeting!" Jirri's voice rose a notch, loud enough to draw the attention of those in the nearest stands and the back of the crowd. "Your behavior is most inappropriate."

Muffled chuckles narrowed Imhara's gaze. Her mood soured further. The next stand over, *Na* Tanea watched their interaction with keen interest. He'd long opposed her holding a position of leadership.

Did the second son of the Jirri Clan think by scolding her like an errant child he could embarrass her into sitting down again? Even if she were willing to ignore his rudeness, backing down equaled submission. Something *Na* Kaal would never do.

"How much longer would you suggest we continue this farce, then?" A calm response accompanied by a pointed look. "We've met and I've seen and heard enough to know our mating would end in disaster."

The warrior glared. "I beg your pardon?"

"No need to do that." She met his furious gaze. "I find your self-absorbed arrogance unacceptable. I like a good conversation and would have been quite happy to engage you in any topic you spoke about today, but you've shown no interest in acknowledging my opinion on anything."

"Your opinion?" His surprise said a lot about his attitude toward the females in his family and didn't bode well for any potential mate. The warrior's gaze flickered to Rassan. "Matters of war and military campaigns are best discussed by those with knowledge and experience."

She'd spent the last five years butting heads with stubborn *Na'Reishi* males who assumed her Second actually made all the important decisions while she remained a figurehead, one with the undeniable bloodline.

"That's an unfortunate error in judgment." Imhara pinned her host with a stare. "I hope this isn't how you'd treat *Na* Tanea if he were your guest instead of me. Would you allow another to ignore your rank, Arras?"

The thin-faced warrior straightened in his seat, his amused smile freezing as she included him in their conversation. Imhara held back a satisfied grin as she watched him weigh the implications of his answer from the corner of her eye. He wasn't laughing now.

The way his mouth pursed betrayed his displeasure with having to answer. "Of course not."

"So, as a *Na* I'd be within my rights to issue a challenge for the insult?" she inquired, voice flat and hard.

All talk in both stands ceased. Jirri's gaze widened while Tanea's narrowed. Imhara waited, letting the interested spectators and their expectations pressure the Clan leader into answering.

He shifted in his seat. "You'd be within your rights, *Na* Kaal."

Forcing his support would likely give him another reason to hate her, but Imhara didn't care. Not when his answer was the one she wanted.

She cocked her head to one side. "Perhaps you might be interested in what I have to say now, Commander Jirri?"

Her unspoken threat hung in the air between them. Listen to her or risk a challenge.

Which would he choose, given she had the option of facing him in combat or appointing another, and that someone would likely be Rassan?

Humiliation or death?

Personally, either outcome suited her mood.

Jirri looked to Tanea. Expecting help or advice? But the other male could do nothing, not without contradicting himself in front of two stands full of witnesses. Maintaining his reputation worked in her favor.

"Commander Jirri?"

The older warrior's gaze snapped back to her, his nostrils flaring. Very slowly he dropped his head in a nod.

Submission.

He'd listen.

"If you're looking for a trophy mate who'll sit quietly by your side while you scold and browbeat her when she does something you don't like, I'm not it. I speak my mind, quite often." She gave a half shrug. "You're just not suitable mate material in my ledger, and if my honesty insults you, then just add that to the list of reasons why our mating wouldn't work."

Her comment drew some snickering, quickly muffled but audible all the same. This time it wasn't aimed at her. Jirri's mottled skin flushed a deep red. He rose from his seat, one large hand fisting.

Rassan shifted beside her to take up a defensive stance. She laid a hand on his arm.

"Commander Jirri, I'm clearly not the *Nu'Reishi* female you were expecting as a mate. Perhaps you'd best withdraw your petition. I am who I am and any mate of mine must accept that."

"Accept you as you are?" The warrior issued a sound of disgust. "No male of worth would put up with your attitude. A lesson you'd learn swiftly with the help of a strong arm and a good thick belt."

Imhara didn't bother wasting breath replying. She jerked her dagger from its sheath and sent it flying.

A dull *thunk* accompanied Sere Jirri's yelp as he leapt up from his seat. He glanced down at the blade buried in the wooden panel between his legs, just beneath the seat cushion he'd vacated.

A move no *Na'Reishi* could or would protest despite any dislike of her or her behavior. Her rank demanded respect, regardless of her gender, and Jirri had stepped over that line.

"Is that your temper speaking, second son?" She waited a heartbeat for the deliberate reminder of who outranked whom and the consequences of his actions to sink in. A sudden indrawn breath betrayed him. She tsked him. "I didn't think you'd be careless enough to try and bully me a second time."

A familiar scowl transformed his face.

Imhara dropped her hand to the hilt of her sword. "That *attitude* might work with your kin, but any warrior who lays a hand on me can expect to lose it." She gave him a cold smile. "Keep the dagger. Consider it a parting gift. Enjoy the rest of the auction."

Imhara nodded, and her *Na'Hord* led the way, clearing a path through the crowd. She left a seething yet silent Sere Jirri behind. Two dozen strides later, Rassan drew level with her.

"Well, you certainly left an impression on him," he murmured, then shot a swift glance over his shoulder. "He's headed straight for Urkan Yur. No doubt to complain about your rude behavior."

Imhara refused to look back. "You expected me to placate him?"

"I didn't know that word was in your vocabulary."

She jerked her head around, a heated retort on her lips, then saw the corner of Rassan's mouth curve upward. Her temper fizzled and she shook her head.

His deep chuckle grazed her ears. "Some canny moves there, Imhara. Nicely done."

"It felt good." She grinned. "I won't deny it."

"Remind me never to play Battle Squares with you," Arek murmured.

His quiet reference to the widely popular *Na'Hord* leisure-time game widened her grin.

"Nothing like providing the highborn with some light entertainment," Rassan murmured. "I wager the Clan Challengers will be debating the contest-that-almost-was by the time I reach the training grounds this morning. Care to join me today, Imhara?"

"Full combat?"

He nodded. "Real weapons. No holds barred."

The idea appealed. With preparations for the Enclave manic over the last few weeks, she'd been restricted to shorter, less intense sessions with Rassan. But his reason for sparring was hardly exercise related.

"You have a devious mind, Second."

His grin widened. "No harm in reminding everyone just how good you are with a blade."

She chuckled and nodded. "All right."

"Good."

"*Na* Kaal!" The hail came from behind them. A young *Na'Reishu* male pushed his way through the edges of the auction crowd toward them. "A moment of your time, please!"

Dressed in the tailored garb of a trader, the youth wore a cloak pin on his collar. One etched with an emblem she recognized.

Imhara shared a look with her Second and stopped in the shade of the nearest building. Arek took his customary place two paces behind her.

"*Na* Kaal, thank you for waiting." The youth gave a nervous tug of his tunic and bowed from the waist. "Trader Ilahn extends his warmest greetings." He pulled a folded parchment from his vest pocket. "He hopes you'll find the time to honor his House with a visit this Gathering."

Imhara took the missive, cracked the wax seal, and scanned the sheet. "Tell Trader Ilahn I accept, and that I look forward to his hospitality."

"Yes, *Na* Kaal." The youth bowed again, this time with a relieved grin. "I shall!"

Tucking the parchment into her vest pocket, she watched him disappear into the crowd.

"The House of Ilahn sends an *Isha* invitation?" Rassan inquired.

She nodded. "Set for tomorrow evening."

"Isn't that when you're expected for your second betrothal meeting?"

"Really? Would you mind going in my stead, then?"

His snort made her grin. "I doubt I'm your intended's type." His tone grew more serious. "You do realize that missing it could incur Savyr's censure?"

"I'm counting on it, Rassan," she murmured. "I'm tired of waiting. It's time to force his hand and end this once and for all."

Chapter 31

AREK tried to clear his lungs with deep breaths of fresh air. The sickly, sweet odor of *haze* still lingered in his shirt, and he could taste it in the back of his throat. He already felt light-headed, and a fine sheen of sweat coated him, both side effects of inhaling the smoke.

While he'd kept his breathing shallow during the hour-long tour with Trader Ilahn, a personalized service offered to his guests by the middle-aged *Na'Reishu*, it'd been thickest in the slave quarters in the underground levels of the pleasure house.

Escorted from one small room to the next, Imhara took her time as she questioned Ilahn about each slave—where they'd come from, their age, the slaver who'd transported them, any training they'd already received; she even made an offer for three, each one politely declined. It was the perfect performance of carnal interest with the controlled demeanor of a seasoned buyer.

Arek struggled to control his anger and shock as the handlers stripped, then sexually aroused the slaves. Chained to the wall hand and foot, the *haze* heightened their sensitivity and left them unable to control their responses.

Although he'd seen plenty of atrocities in his time on patrol, their blatant abuse and disregard for human dignity sickened him, and by the time the pleasure house owner escorted them to the buying floor, his jaw ached.

Had he not recalled Yrenna's healing face and reminded himself of the potential disaster of interfering, he might never have made it through the tour. He envied Imhara's flawless portrayal of her persona, yet it offered insight into the depths of her fortitude.

The dark-haired trader stopped in front of a closed door, the last in a long corridor. A young *Na'Reisha* boy stood nearby. Just like all the staff within the pleasure house, he dressed in black, the emblem of the House sewn into the collar of his shirt.

"Freydan will be stationed just outside your stall, *Na* Kaal." Ilahn pushed open the door. "As you know, for the duration of the *Isha*, I request that you remain within to safeguard your privacy but also my other clients. Freydan will take care of any requests or arrange for any service you require during the proceedings."

The boy bowed low. "It's an honor to serve you, *Na* Kaal."

Imhara acknowledged the young *Na'Reisha* with a nod.

"At the *Isha's* conclusion, he'll escort you to the reception room upstairs if you'd like to socialize, or if you wish to leave, to the private street exit." A genial smile accompanied Ilahn's words. "I do hope you'll take advantage of our hospitality."

Another bow from the trader, then he retreated along the landing. Arek wondered if he was off to greet another client or supervise some aspect of the evening's event.

"The *Isha* will begin in fifteen minutes, *Na* Kaal." Freydan motioned them into the room and closed the door quietly behind them.

Arek paced the length of the room, needing to work off some of his frustrated anger from the last hour. While small, the room reflected the luxurious decor he'd seen throughout the rest of the house: a padded recliner filled with cushions, a small table set with dishes and bowls of fruit and other appetizers to tempt the palate, jugs and flasks of a variety of liquid refreshments, even spigots and a basin with drying towels on the opposite wall.

"No expense spared," he murmured dryly, and tested each spigot. Hot and cold water ran into the basin.

"The House of Ilahn caters to the specific needs of a select few and is paid handsomely for doing so." Imhara took a seat on the recliner. "The family runs a legitimate trading business, but their true wealth comes from the darker side of commerce."

Aware of her scrutiny, he turned and walked the length of the room, taking in the widening walls that gave the room its unusual dimensions. The stone on the fourth wall only went to waist height, then a huge panel of glass stretched to the ceiling. It was curtained from the other side. Built into the center of the stone façade was a small wooden hatch.

He smoothed a hand over the huge glass window. "What's beyond the curtain?"

"A small chamber where Ilahn presents the slaves. A bidding dish, similar to the one used yesterday at the slave auction, sits behind the hatch."

Arek frowned. "I thought Ilahn's clients demanded privacy. If the curtains are opened, won't we be able to see into other rooms?"

"They only line this side of the chamber."

Walking the corridor, he'd counted the doors. "Ten buyers. Two dozen slaves. Will he sell them all?"

Tension edged his voice, but he couldn't help it. Imhara remained quiet for a few heartbeats, then drew in an audible breath.

"Arek, you demanded I be honest with you. Are you sure you want to hear this?"

"I need to know what's coming. Give me the variables and I can plan my moves."

"This isn't a training scenario, Arek."

"I understand that," he retorted, and faced her square on. He ran a hand through his hair. "But I analyze information, I consider scenarios, I plot strategies. It's what I know and how I'm going to get through this."

"All right," she assented. "Most of Ilahn's clients are male, so the females will sell. They're all young, attractive, none over the age of twenty-five, and in excellent health. Those qualities are highly sought after in a bed-slave." His gut still tightened as she listed their attributes so matter-of-factly. "Ilahn allows each slave two auctions to sell before he assigns them a room upstairs to earn off the cost of his purchase."

"This goes on in the reception area Ilahn mentioned?"

"On the same floor."

"What happens in those rooms?"

"Whatever's demanded and paid for." Her flat tone sent a shiver crawling along his spine. "If they earn him a tidy profit, he keeps them. If they don't, he sells them to another pleasure house somewhere else, or a regular auction house."

"Ilahn offered you the chance to socialize later. Have you done that in the past?"

"Of course. *Na* Kaal's reputation has been built using such exposure." Imhara rose and wandered to the table of refreshments. "I socialize but I've never engaged the services of any of Ilahn's bed-slaves. I've always brought someone with me."

Someone like him. Although Imhara didn't say it, her look inferred it.

She poured two drinks and offered one to him. When he glanced to the door, she shook her head. "Don't worry, the nature of the business conducted here ensures no one intrudes into any room without an invitation."

He took the goblet. Imhara retreated to the recliner, but instead of drinking, she stared into her cup, a frown pinching her brow, the first hint of anxiety she'd displayed since entering the house. When she took a sip, she did so with a grimace.

"I can't read your scent, but I'm pretty good with body language," he commented. "Your discomfort has nothing to do with the quality of the wine."

"I was trying to imagine this place through your eyes, thinking back to the first time I set foot here." Her gaze lifted to meet his as she leaned against the raised back of the seat. "Hiding how appalled I felt was . . . difficult, and I've been exposed to this all my life. Considering you've had only a few days, you've managed to mask your scent quite well."

"While it hasn't been painless, I told you I could adapt." He shook his head. "Watching you slip into your persona . . . You do it with such skill. . . ." She flinched. "I didn't mean that as a criticism, Imhara."

"Neither is it something to be proud of or known for." She took another sip of her drink, then offered him a wry smile. "You can't live a double life without some of what you do staining your soul."

Her somber response made Arek wish he'd held his tongue. Before he could say anything though, the curtain over the window was jerked aside and light spilled into the room. One of Ilahn's black uniformed helpers unlatched the wooden hatch, then moved out of sight.

"*Merciful Mother!*" The tableau revealed made Arek step back from the window. Shock tingled through him.

Chains hung from the ceiling throughout the chamber, all evenly spaced apart. The slaves, each stripped naked, dangled like seedpods on a *cheva*-bush, one to every anchor point. Their handlers lined the wall behind them.

Imhara moved up beside him. "The *Isha* will start shortly." Her shoulder brushed his. "You might not want to watch, Arek. The proceedings get rather . . . graphic."

"Graphic?" Even as he queried, the images of what he'd seen in the cells below played through his mind, and his innards grew colder. He glanced at her. "What happens?"

Her eyes closed briefly, then her chin lifted and pointed at the scene. "Look at them. Their relaxed faces, unfocused gazes, the small tremors in their muscles and bodies.

"Ilahn drugs them with another burn of *haze* before auction. It makes them more compliant, but given the right amount, it also heightens the senses." The skin around her eyes tightened, the markings around her temples creased. "You saw earlier how easily they were aroused. Buyers like to know the slaves they're purchasing are able to perform."

"Perform as in they molest them . . . until they peak?"

"Some of Ilahn's staff prefer to couple."

Rape.

She was talking rape.

Ice rushed through Arek's veins. It thawed with a rush of anger. "You have to stop this!"

Her jaw flexed. "How?"

He stared out through the window at the twenty-four men and women. They were conscious yet helpless, stripped of all control.

Mother of Light . . . to have your own body betray you, to be forced to endure an assault . . . Arek could imagine nothing more horrifying. . . . And to witness their humiliation . . .

"No!" He shook his head. "You can't stand by and do nothing!"

"I'm not!" Fire filled her gaze. Her nostrils flared. "I did do something, I am doing something!"

She snatched her leather pouch from her belt and shook it. The gems inside rattled together.

"Weren't you listening earlier when I tried to buy some of them from Ilahn before the auction? He refused to sell them." Her fist clenched around the pouch. "Tonight, I'll purchase as many of them as I can, and when they're delivered to our campsite, the healers will take over." Her voice broke. "*Lady* forgive me, I do the best I can with what I have!"

The furious agony twisting Imhara's expression impacted his stomach like a fist. She pivoted on her heel, strode away from him, and slammed her goblet onto the small table. Liquid splashed over the metal rim and spread in a dark red stain across the polished wooden surface, eerily reminiscent of a pool of blood.

Her shoulders hunched and the defensive posture struck another blow. Arek shoved his hands through his hair. *Light*, how many times had Yevni warned him about letting his anger control him?

Imhara had attempted to purchase three slaves prior to the auction. One woman and two youths barely out of their teens. At the time he'd assumed it part of her act, an idiosyncrasy of *Na* Kaal.

"Rest assured, Arek, if it makes you feel any better, the choices I've made, the actions I've taken, they all weigh on me."

He grimaced at the hoarseness in her voice. She straightened and turned, but her shoulders stayed rigid and tight.

"But any judgment owed will come from the *Lady*, not you." Her gaze remained shadowed as she returned to stand at the window, ignoring him to focus on the auction. "I've told you before, I do what I have to."

She had, several times.

In his time spent living with the Kaal Clan, every significant memory involved actions she'd taken for her people. To save their lives. To protect them. To give them a future. The only time he'd seen her do something for herself—and even then it held a dual purpose—was the night he'd spent serving her as a slave.

The *Na'Reish* on the other side of the glass deserved his anger, not her.

From the corner of his vision, Ilahn's first handler had already freed the female slave in his charge from her shackles, the woman

Imhara had attempted to buy. The blur of jerky movements, the woman's cries, a mixture of pain and pleasure, drifted through the small hatch and confirmed exactly what sort of activity the handler was engaged in with her.

The perverted production might serve as proof for buyers of a slave's potential, yet the darker implications weren't lost on Arek. With every slave raped or molested, watching the prolonged display would build the carnal appetites of those who chose to stay and engage additional services, their hunger a vice Ilahn profited from.

"Bidding will begin once she's forced to peak," Imhara said, her voice flat and expressionless.

Nausea rolled in Arek's gut, for the situation beyond the glass, and for the pain he'd caused Imhara. Deflecting others was a tactic he'd resorted to often enough in the months before he'd been captured.

He grimaced. Neither of them could leave the room with this unresolved, not when their survival depended on them being a team.

Taking a deep breath, Arek placed a hand on the small of her back, the need to slide his arms around her and comfort her stronger than he anticipated. She stiffened.

Could she scent his intentions? Even if she did, her posture, the silence, the tension radiating off her stopped him from completing the move.

Instead he found the leather pouch at her waist and tugged it free.

"Which gem is appropriate for a bid?" Fumbling one-handed with the drawstring, he shook it open, spilling the gems onto the windowsill. Some were as large as his fingernail, others as little as a grain, and they came in all shades of mesmerizing colors. They sparkled in the light.

"What are you doing?" Ice coated her question, thick enough to make him flinch.

"Which gem, Imhara?" His heart beat hard as her silence drew out beyond what was comfortable. "Please."

"Any of the smaller blue or green ones."

He plucked a green one from the collection. "Tell me when to put it into the dish."

"Arek . . ."

"When my temper rises, my reasoning weakens. I react and end up hurting others." He spread his fingers wide on her back, a single, careful caress. "Letting my frustration speak for me was stupid. You didn't deserve my anger."

"No, I didn't." The ice was still there. "You acted like a *jamet's* ass, Arek."

He took her quiet censure without protest. "What you do here takes incredible fortitude. . . . Your strength shames me." He swallowed against a dry mouth. "I'm sorry, Imhara."

Her rigid posture relaxed, just a fraction.

"You truly mean that." Her tone thawed a little, enough to ease some of his anxiety.

"I do."

"If you ever treat me like that again, you will feel the brunt of *my* temper." A thread of steel in her tone assured him she would follow through.

"Of that, I have no doubt," he murmured.

Another long silence.

"Then apology accepted." She plucked the gem from his hand. "I'll do this on my own."

"No, you won't." More tension bled from him, roughened his voice. "Watching this pains you as much as it does me. But if we do this together, it might make it more bearable."

Her fingers tightened around the gem, and she released an uneven breath. This time her silence proved more tolerable.

"Hold out your hand." Imhara placed the jewel on his palm, then closed his fingers around it. She brought them to her mouth, and her lips brushed his knuckles. "Don't underestimate your own strength, Arek. Especially the sort you lend others." She leaned into him, finally relaxing. "And you're right, it does help to share the load."

Chapter 32

FIVE lives.

Four men and one woman for a pouch full of gems.

Imhara pushed aside her disappointment—five was better than none—and signed the bottom of the parchment in front of her, then handed the stylus to Ilahn.

The dark-haired trader bent over the desk and added his florid signature to the document. "You have an eye for fine flesh, *Na* Kaal."

He blew on the ink, then pressed his House seal to the softened wax in one corner. The stylized *I* surrounded by the interlocking rings made the transfer of ownership official. He handed the document to her with a bow.

"So did a number of other buyers." Imhara carefully folded the paper and tucked it into her pouch. "No doubt the impeccable quality of your slaves accounted for the intensity of the bidding."

Voices and soft laughter came from the other side of the privacy screen used to divide the reception area into two sections: this small foyer where Ilahn finalized all transactions and business arrangements, and the lavishly decorated main area where he entertained.

Imhara cocked her head to one side and identified several *Na'Reishi* highborn voices, all regular clients to the House. The numerous odors circulating in the air indicated they hadn't wasted any time taking advantage of Ilahn's services.

Beneath the lighter scent of food, it wasn't hard to detect the rich-iron tang of blood and the heavier, spiced heat of arousal.

"*Na'Reishi* Evec's mate has already expressed disappointment on missing out on the slave of her choice. He was one of your purchases, *Na* Kaal. The strapping breeder taken from Tianda." Ilahn's smile widened. "She's keen to track down his new owner and negotiate a new deal."

Imhara just bet Miana was. The highborn female's bedroom reputation extended to feeding during sex, her appetite for both acts so insatiable that many of her slaves died.

She shook her head. "I'm not interested in a private sale."

More laughter accompanied a feminine drawn-out groan of pain. It wasn't hard to guess what was going on, not with the scent of fresh blood saturating the air. Ilahn's slave would be covered in bite marks by the time the group in the reception room finished with her. Imhara hoped the trader had an exceptional healer working for his House.

"Now that our business is concluded, my hospitality is yours to enjoy, *Na* Kaal." Ilahn rose from behind the table and one of the ever-present house staff took his place.

"Imhara Kaal, I thought I heard your voice! It's so good to see you!"

The sultry greeting tightened every muscle in Imhara's body, and it took every ounce of self-control to hide her instant dislike.

"Miana." She pasted a polite smile on her face and turned.

Tall, elegant, and beautiful, the *Na'Reishi* female's long, black hair was tied back from her face by an intricate style of plaits interwoven with deep, bloodred gems. They matched the exact color she'd painted on her lips and fingernails. The formfitting dress had a plunging neckline that exposed her markings and accentuated her curves. The burgundy material was so rich and dark it looked almost black.

The colors complemented her nature perfectly.

"I didn't expect to see you this Enclave, not with a mating to organize." Her violet gaze flickered over her, taking in her appearance. "You can't attract a male in breeches and a sword belt, Imhara. You might want to exchange them for a dress at some stage. Don't underestimate the power of making yourself presentable for your mate."

"Presentable? I'm comfortable dressed as I am." Imhara chuckled softly. "I'm afraid our opinions must differ, Miana."

Miana's eyebrows arched and she gave a half shrug. "So it seems." Her gaze drifted left and her lips curled in a too satisfied smirk as she spotted Arek. "Well now, who might this slave be?"

Imhara resisted snorting out loud at the unsurprising change of subject.

"Ilahn, please tell me this male belongs to your stable, and if so, then why wasn't he presented to me earlier?" The *Na'Reishi* woman moved straight to Arek, her strides graceful, sensual, her expression predatory.

And far too covetous.

Imhara held perfectly still, keeping her expression quite neutral despite the rush of something hot and dark tearing through her veins. Instinct urged her to step between Arek and the advancing woman, not wanting her anywhere near him.

She'd been afraid he'd attract this sort of attention. Yet while she believed he could control his reactions, she didn't trust Evec's mate.

Miana circled behind Arek, deliberate in her invasion of his personal space, then reached up to stroke and tangle her fingers in his hair. Imhara's gaze narrowed, the heated darkness inside her surged.

The thought of breaking Miana's fingers came from nowhere. A swift twist and jerk would do it.

Arek stiffened, his gaze remaining downcast, but it flickered in her direction. She flattened her hand against her thigh, the smallest gesture of restraint, and he held his place.

"He's gorgeous," Miana purred, and leaned in to inhale his scent. Her tongue darted out to wet her lips. "And I bet he tastes just as good as he smells, too."

The image of her sinking her teeth into him spiked another dark rush of adrenaline. Miana's fingers traced the width of his shoulders. Arek's hands fisted then flexed as his chest rose and fell on a deep breath. Imhara inhaled but couldn't detect any betraying scent coming from him.

Such control. A marked improvement in a small amount of time.

The trader cleared his throat. "*Na'Reishi* Miana, I apologize but . . ."

"If Imhara's contracted his services, then I'll double your asking price."

"Price isn't the issue, *Na'Reishi*."

The woman pouted. "Then what is the problem?"

"He's mine, Miana." Imhara chuckled, the sound soft, almost mocking. "I own him."

Closing the distance, she flicked a fingernail against the gold band on Arek's bicep. The faint ting drew Miana's violet gaze and a squint of annoyance. She couldn't have missed seeing it, or the Kaal emblem etched into the metal, just chosen to ignore it.

"Well, that's a disappointment." A heavy, feigned sigh, then a sly smile. "You must come and join our celebration. Evec has his little female to amuse him and his friends. We can have our own private celebration. Your slave can be our entertainment. I can't wait to taste him."

Imhara stepped in between them, her smile anything but friendly. "I have no intention of sharing him, Miana, and to assume otherwise would be ill-advised."

Wanting to protect Arek, or any human male, from the dangerous female came as no surprise, but what she felt for Arek went a lot deeper than ensuring his physical well-being. Her heart was definitely involved—a startling revelation—although just how much he'd claimed of it she wasn't sure.

Now though wasn't the time or place to work it out.

"Pass on my greetings and apologies to your group, but I have other plans. Good evening, Miana." Imhara then turned her attention to Ilahn. Socializing held little appeal now. "I'd like a private room, *Na'Reishu* Ilahn."

No way was she going to risk exposing Arek any further. The public venue gave those visiting some leeway to touch another's slave, but the highborn female enjoyed pushing the limits.

"Of course, *Na* Kaal." Ilahn inclined his head.

Annoyance flashed through Miana's gaze at being so promptly dismissed. Her cheeks flushed, but before she could say anything, one of the House staff moved to escort her back to the main reception area. Imhara gave a small, satisfied nod as they disappeared around the edge of the screen.

"Just for a limited time or overnight?" the trader asked.

"Overnight."

Word of her absence from the second betrothal meeting should have reached Savyr by now. After humiliating Jirri and now skipping a meeting, she couldn't see the *Na'Rei* waiting until tomorrow to discipline her.

Yet no one in camp, except Rassan, knew her whereabouts, and while he wouldn't withhold the information, he'd take his time revealing it. As any good Second would when his *Na* didn't wish to be found.

"Do you want one of your new slaves to join you this evening?" Ilahn's query drew her back from her thoughts. "The blond male you purchased would make for an excellent pairing with the one you brought. The stamina of youth coupled with a slave already familiar with your preferences. The perfect training session."

The *Na'Reishu* was a smooth talker, as depraved as his business, but like the fancy surroundings of his establishment, well practiced in using the trappings of congeniality to hide his darker side.

Beside her Arek shifted, the soft scuff of his boot on stone accompanied the sharp odor of anger, there one moment then gone the next. Imhara didn't need to see him to know he disliked Ilahn's suggestion.

What intrigued her though was the hint of spice lacing the anger. She could understand his anger being a knee-jerk reaction to the situation or a protest to her agreeing, but why the sexual undertone?

Was it the suggestion of sharing her with another?

Did he object?

A small grin curved her lips.

Now there was an interesting thought. A possibility to explore once they were alone.

"A tempting idea but this male is enough for me to handle at the moment." Her wry reply drew a laugh from the trader. "If you could arrange for the slaves to be delivered to my camp. My Second or Commander Barrca should be there to take delivery."

"Of course." He raised his hand as she reached for her pouch. "Consider the transport and room complimentary, to mark your family's many years of generous patronage. Long may the House of Ilahn continue to serve yours, *Na* Kaal."

An astute business tactic, one she'd take advantage of.

"Much appreciated, *Na'Reishu* Ilahn," she murmured.

Another smile and a quick flick of his fingers brought two more house staff to his side. A few whispered words, and as one young woman moved off, the second asked them to accompany her, and they exited the reception area through a curtained doorway.

A short walk down a corridor lined with closed doors and the attendant stopped in front of the very last, the only one with its door ajar. The hallway was quiet, and the sounds of the celebrating group followed them.

Once inside though, Imhara knew the noise would be nonexistent. The house walls were thick, almost soundproof, offering privacy; a welcome respite from the last few hours.

Moving past the attendant, she gave the luxurious room a cursory glance. It was as extravagant and well catered as the rest of the house.

"It meets with your approval, *Na* Kaal?"

"Indeed."

"Then enjoy your evening, *Na'Reishi*." The young woman executed a bow and the door closed with a soft snick behind her, and everything went silent.

"Thank the *Lady* for small mercies," she murmured. A little of the tension roiling inside her dissipated. She turned to find Arek just standing there, watching her, his expression a combination of subdued amusement and curious confusion. "What?"

In two strides he was in front of her, his twilight gaze direct, searching. His mouth curved at the corners just a little. "I think that's the first time I've seen *Na* Kaal with her claws out."

Imhara snorted. "Miana isn't someone you'd want interested in you, Arek." Trust him to have picked up on her uncharacteristic rivalry. "I threatened her just like I do everyone else."

"Uh-huh." His smile twitched. "I'm curious, do you claim all your male slaves like that in front of her, or just me?"

Chapter 33

"CLAIM you?" A faint flush heated Imhara's skin, working its way from her neck to her cheeks even though she tried to control it.

Teasing was the last thing she'd expected from Arek.

He nodded, his small smile betraying his enjoyment at her shock. She shook her head, not at all sure whether he was ready to go where this line of questioning seemed to be headed. Not yet.

Light, she wasn't even sure!

"Arek, tonight I protected you." She chuckled, trying to keep the moment lighthearted. "If I'd claimed you, you'd have known it."

She'd been tempted. Very tempted. The tension in her belly hadn't disappeared with Miana's withdrawal, although it had morphed from the raw heat of outrage to something deeper, more combustible.

Arek's talk of her claiming him was like laying tinder to embers. It wouldn't take much to ignite either if he kept adding fuel to the flames. And this conversation was fast moving in that direction. Did he realize that?

Imhara corralled her thoughts. "If you hadn't noticed, Miana likes provoking reactions. She does it to anyone who lets her. There's every chance she saw your armband and decided to play one of her games."

She'd almost stooped to Miana's level, but annoying her further by claiming Arek publicly wasn't justifiable reason enough to push his limits. He might have committed to helping her, but their fledgling relationship remained on uncertain ground.

Witnessing the *Isha* had definitely tested him. Their confrontation in the bidding room was proof of that. And even though he'd apologized, the memory of his reaction and accusation still lingered.

"Now who's the one giving half answers?" Arek shook his head slowly. "Imhara, you were a hairsbreadth away from taking her out with a fist."

Light, why was he pursuing this?

Imhara put the width of the ornate rug between them, needing a distraction, but everything in the room, from the huge bed she had to step around to the supply of *haze* twists sitting in the burner on a table against the wall, served as reminders of what needed avoiding.

Frowning, she pivoted on her heel. "Do you really want to discuss this now, Arek?"

"I don't blame you for being reluctant to share your thoughts with me after how I acted earlier." He paused a moment, then his jaw firmed. "But I'm choosing to face what we're dealing with here head-on instead of ignoring it."

Choice.

Knowing what she did about his past, she knew how important this was to him. Imhara searched his scent for any sourness, but the odor remained pure citrus.

"I liked seeing you react that way with Miana." His admission sent a frisson of pleasure through her. "How far would you have gone to prove your point?"

His gaze glittered with curiosity as a familiar spicy scent teased her nostrils. She inhaled a deeper breath, unable to resist savoring it. It tugged at her, like the undercurrent of a deep, mountain stream, insistent and hard to resist. Her boot scuffed on the rug before she caught herself. His gaze flickered down, his slow smile confirming he'd noted her reaction.

And just that quickly, with a look that went from inquisitive to hot in a heartbeat, he ignited the flame inside her.

"All right." Resolve edged her softly spoken words.

A small tremor ran through him.

Uncertainty or anticipation?

Maybe a little of both, because each gnawed at her.

The rigid line of his shoulders tightened as she crossed the rug to him. Placing her hands on his chest, she gave him a gentle push. Holding his gaze, matching him step for step, she backed him up until he came to a stop against the wall beside the door.

She slid her hand from his chest, over his vest, to trace the edge of the gold band on his bare arm. The metal was as warm as his skin. "The emblem of the Kaal Clan."

Arek grunted. "You tapped it. Made sure Miana saw it."

"My mark of ownership. Protection for anyone wearing it." Her fingernails scratched his flesh in a light caress as they went down his arm. "I may have wanted to claim you in front of her"—dropping her hand to his thigh, she ran her fingers up the inside seam of his breeches—"but I didn't know if you'd accept this—" She cupped him, the press of her palm firm. His sharp inhalation fired her blood. "In public."

She closed her hand around him, her own breath catching as he hardened with her touch. What she wouldn't give to unbuckle his belt and feel him, flesh to flesh. He'd be smooth, velvet steel. Pulsing and hot.

"Crude but effective." She stroked the length of him, from base to tip, felt him shudder, and smiled. "You like me touching you like this."

"You already know I do." That came from between gritted teeth.

On the next stroke, he made a sound in the back of his throat, and pushed his hips toward her, thrusting into her palm. She teased him again, slowly tightening and easing her grasp, up and down, watching the skin across his cheeks tighten in pleasure, the color in them darken.

His growing hunger fed hers. Her heart pumped the heat right around her body, until she trembled like he did. She brushed her fingers over the rounded curve of his sac, squeezed it gently, then retraced his length again and felt him thicken, liking how quickly he responded.

Leaning in close, she grazed her lips against the shell of his ear and smiled at his sudden indrawn breath. His chest brushed against hers, the sensation causing her nipples to pebble.

Light, that felt good.

"You asked how far I'd have gone to prove my point to Miana." His cheek touched hers, his jaw flexing, his breathing shallow, hot against her neck. "I wouldn't have stopped with a quick feel, Arek. Given the nature of the celebration she was inviting us to, we'd have both ended up naked. There's nothing that says, *you're mine*, more than if I'd ridden you, then made you beg for release." Drawing back, she met his gaze. "And you would have. Guaranteed."

Arek stilled, his whole body stiffening. A quick caress with her thumb along his length once more, then she stepped back. The color on his cheeks matched the fiery protest swirling in his gaze. She smiled wryly and placed a finger over his lips as they opened to speak.

"Remember, you're my blood-slave. Keeping you hungry for my next feeding would make you compliant. You'd do anything to please me."

She trailed her fingertips over his bottom lip, his jaw, then moved to the center of the room. Better to remove herself from temptation.

"How comfortable would you have been doing that in front of Miana?" She cocked an eyebrow. "The other *Na'Reishi*? Or Ilahn and his staff?"

By the way his cheeks darkened with a fresh flush, probably not at all.

"Point taken," he conceded, his tone gravelly. "And what about now? Was this just a demonstration? A way to drive a message home?"

"It could be taken that way," she conceded.

Arek's spicy scent overwhelmed her and made it hard to gauge his reasoning behind the questions. Yet he stared at her, the sound of breathing harsh, the fit of his breeches over his straining erection tight, desire evident in the burn of his gaze.

He did nothing to hide any of his reactions—a warrior who hated revealing any weakness—and her pulse fluttered with the significance of the moment.

Need, hopes, desires, all too long buried, spiraled up from inside her. Her thoughts burst forth, like a dam giving under pressure, some sharp and crystal clear, the majority obscure yearnings, indistinct through denial, all raw enough to make breathing and speaking difficult.

How long had it been since she'd allowed herself the simple pleasure of looking at a man with the sole purpose of enjoying what she saw? Training with the *Na'Hord* and working around the fortress had once provided that small pleasure, yet over time she'd blocked it out, trained herself not to notice as it left her aching and unfulfilled.

The familiar dissatisfaction of unrealized dreams.

The possibilities of what Arek was asking, telegraphing, were terrifying and exciting. And there was no denying he tempted her like no one ever had before, if she was willing to take the risk.

Imhara swallowed against her dry throat. "For five years I've concentrated on nothing but my Clan, our legacy, and ensuring we all survive. I've sacrificed many things to keep that focus, including denying myself the pleasure of a lover." She retreated to sit on the edge of the bed and drew in a slow, deep breath. "So, it frightens me to admit that I want you as one, Arek. I shouldn't, but I do." She gave a shaky laugh. "And to answer your question, I hope you'd see this as an invitation, not a demonstration or a lesson." Her pulse skipped hard in her throat. "If you want this to be something more than me proving a point, then you need to tell me. You need to let me know where you want this to go."

"I decide?" Arek's voice vibrated with a deep huskiness that sent shivers over her skin. His twilight gaze glittered as he pushed away from the wall and came toward her. "And if I want to claim you?"

Imhara clenched the soft bed cover, a thrill streaking though her innards at his softly posed question. She wet her lips. "I wish you would."

His step faltered, then he chuckled, his teeth flashing white in the ambient lamplight. "*Lady's Breath*, you never cease to surprise me."

His spicy scent saturated the air, stronger than before. Imhara inhaled deeply, savoring it, swallowing thickly as her mouth filled with saliva. He came to a halt in front of her, his knees brushing hers.

"Unbuckle your sword belt."

Her hand shook as she released the catch then slid the leather free of the buckle and handed it to Arek. He placed it within easy reach, on the lid of the chest pushed up against the end of the bed.

"Lean back on your hands and don't move."

She raised an eyebrow. Did this mean he'd accepted her invitation?

Her heart beat faster. Desire and need fluttered hard in her stomach.

Was he going to claim her?

There was only one way to find out.

She did as he requested.

• • •

AREK plucked at the ties on his vest, observing Imhara as he shirked the garment.

"Five years is a long time to deny yourself."

A jerk and tug and his belt slid free from around his waist. He dropped it on top of his vest. A quick flick of a clasp eased the pressure of his breeches over his erection.

Her gaze dropped lower, drawn by his movements. The heat in her eyes, the rosy flush of color staining her cheek, the sweep of her tongue over her bottom lip impacted Arek like a blow to his gut.

Shrugging, Imhara drew in a deeper breath. Unable to resist, he watched the rise and fall of her breasts, liking the way her shirt strained over them, the material clinging to her curves, her nipples.

Just how sensitive were they? Did she like them to be played with? Stroked? Pinched? Sucked? Bitten? He suspected all, going by what he'd experienced with her so far.

"Liaisons with warriors just led to quarrels, jealousy, and competition." Her voice sounded husky. "It wasn't worth the dissention."

He nodded, having seen his fair share of fights and arguments in the Light Blade barracks. It made her admission of a moment ago, and her decision, a whole lot more meaningful.

It also reminded him of who she was.

Na Kaal.

Na'Reish, not human.

Almost as if someone had lifted a veil, the amethyst hue of her eyes registered, the markings trailing the sides of her face and neck became more prominent, her dark lips unmistakable even in the soft light.

He blinked. Since when had he stopped noticing her *Na'Reish* features?

Did it matter? The journey taken with his grandfather no longer belonged to him. This path was the one he'd chosen.

"Arek?" Imhara's soft query and frown made him wonder if his scent had changed.

He shook his head and braced one hand on the edge of the bed. With the other, he cupped the back of her head, threading his fingers through her plait, and tugged, angling her face just right, so he could place his lips on hers.

He intended a gentle kiss, one where he could explore her mouth and take his time to reacquaint himself with the softness of her lips, the scent of her skin, the textures and flavors of her mouth. But when Imhara opened her mouth and tasted him with an aggressive stroke of her tongue, the temperature of their kiss ratcheted up from passionate to raw sensuality in less than a heartbeat.

He tore his mouth free of hers and sucked in a much-needed breath, every muscle tight, tension coiling low in his abdomen.

His fingers tightened in her hair. "One kiss . . . one damn kiss and I can't think beyond how sweet and hot you taste . . . and I want more. . . ."

She palmed his erection, the pressure firmer, no longer a teasing caress, the sensation streaking through him like lightning. He widened his stance, groaning as she took immediate advantage. The pleasure of her touch hardened him in less than a heartbeat.

"*Lady's Breath!*"

Her husky laughter vibrated against his mouth. "I like hearing you curse. So hot and impassioned. Knowing I'm the cause of it makes me wet."

The memory of her cream coating his fingers sent a shudder through him. Just how wet was she?

He had to touch her and see. Going down on one knee, he reached for the clasp on her breeches, but her hands were already there. He hooked his fingers in the waistband. She lifted her hips and he peeled the material over them and down, cursing again as it caught on her boots.

Her husky chuckles made his own lips twitch as he removed the boots before stripping the breeches from her. He glanced up from where he knelt beside the bed, breath catching at the sight of her gripping the hem of her shirt and pulling it over her head.

The lamplight gave her skin a tawny hue and cast shadows that outlined every curve and hollow, from her *Na'Reish*-spotted shoulders to the lush curve of her breasts, lean ribs, and flat abdomen. His hold on her ankles tightened.

"I like the hunger in your eyes, Arek." Imhara's husky voice accompanied a sultry smile. "It excites me. A lot."

He grinned, and spread his fingers, greedy for the feel of her, but where to start? As much as he wanted to savor her breasts, the sweet scent of her arousal beckoned.

"Lay down and close your eyes." His smile turned wicked. "You get to feel, not see, what I do."

Her breath caught in her throat. He couldn't resist trailing his knuckles over each of her breasts, liking the way her skin flushed pink, her nipples budding tighter.

"Enjoying these will have to wait. I have other plans." Disappointment flickered in her gaze. "But there's nothing I like more than seeing a woman pleasure herself." Her lips parted. "Will you do that for me, Imhara? Pleasure yourself while I watch?"

Her gaze stayed fixed on him as she lay back on the bed, her hands coming to rest on her concave stomach. Something glittered in her gaze, but before he could work out what it was, she shut her eyes and began touching herself.

His jaw loosened, and he bit back a groan, impressed and elated she'd taken his suggestion to heart. He propped his chin on her knee to watch, as promised.

Although instead of playing with her breasts as he'd asked, her hands roved everywhere else—her face, her throat, her shoulders and arms, her ribs, her belly—teasing herself, and tormenting him.

"Keep going, Imhara." Unable to resist, Arek smoothed his hands up her legs. "When you finally do touch your breasts I want you to imagine it's me. That it's my hands cupping and shaping you, pinching and plucking at your nipples, giving you pleasure."

Her soft moan jolted through him. His entire body flared with volcanic heat, molten and raw, so intense he froze, unable to move until the sensation passed.

Fighting the urge to rush, he explored the contours and lean lines of her limbs, first with his fingertips, then his hands, finally with his mouth, lips, and tongue. Every openmouthed kiss on her flesh elicited a twitch, the stroke of his tongue a restless wriggle, the nip of his teeth a gratifying hitch of breath.

The telltale signs of arousal fed his own.

Hooking his arms beneath her knees, he tugged her to the edge of the bed, and used the width of his shoulders to keep her thighs spread and open, so he could finally enjoy the sweet scent and sight of her arousal. Her bare folds were plump and swollen, her inner flesh a deep pink, shiny and slick with her cream.

His mouth watered. He pressed a kiss to her inner thigh then the other, working his way closer to the treasure he couldn't wait to taste, knowing the moment he did, all his intentions of taking his time to savor her would be lost.

"Arek, please!" Imhara's breathless plea came out as a groan.

"Please what, Imhara?" he asked, his own voice none too steady. "Please taste me? Please touch me? Please stop?"

Her hands fisted in the covers beside him as her head lifted from the bed. She glared down the length of her body at him. He chuckled softly at the fire in her violet gaze.

"Don't you dare stop!" An order accompanied by a tightening of her thighs. "Do something! Anything!"

Her raw passion wrapped around him like the tail of a whip, lashing and breaking what was left of his control. With a growl, he buried his face against her, his taste buds exploding the moment he tongued her sweetness.

A lick, one swallow and he groaned, his hunger for her escalating so swiftly he couldn't stop. The craving, the heat of her against his mouth, the sound of her cries filling the room, all of it an irresistible force.

Like a *haze*-addict he kept returning to taste her, parting her with his fingers, working her with his tongue, holding her down as she undulated against him, darkly thrilled as she grew wetter and wetter. The pitch of her cries changed.

Arek wrenched his mouth away from her. He rose, the taste and scent of her on his lips, and flipped her onto her stomach. The sight of her perched on the edge of the bed, the rounded flesh of her backside just within arm's reach, made skimming his breeches off difficult. Another two clasps had to be undone before he could kick them free of his legs.

Half a dozen painful heartbeats of time spent away from her.

"Arek?" Imhara shot him an impatient look over one bare shoulder, saw what he was doing, and propped herself on her elbows so she could see him better. The heat in her gaze was like a physical touch, one that burned.

Arek drew in a slow breath, trying for calm and failing. Her mouth quirked at the corners and her tongue swept out to wet her lips.

"Let me taste you." Her demand shot straight through him like a bolt of lightning. The image she conjured with her words hardened him even more. "I've wanted that since the night you knelt at the foot of my bed naked."

The raw hunger on her face mirrored his own. She started to roll over and turn. He placed a hand on her lower back, just where the twin trails of her *Na'Reish* markings met the rise of her buttocks, and stopped her.

"Not this time." *Light*, if she came anywhere near him, the first touch of her mouth would make him lose control. He wanted to be buried deep inside her before he spent.

Kneeing her legs apart, he braced a hand beside her shoulder and leaned over, letting her feel the hard length of him against her. Her hips lifted. The slick caress, impatient, urgent, seared him.

"Arek . . ." His name a husky cry accompanied by an uncontrollable shiver that shook her whole body. A reminder she hadn't allowed herself such pleasure in five, long years.

Sliding an arm beneath her, he secured a hold around her waist. She reached between her legs to grasp him, then positioned him against her. He groaned at the wet heat kissing the tip of his erection.

"Yes . . . now." Her words came as a long, drawn-out moan, her breath hot against the skin of his wrist. Her teeth grazed his flesh then nipped. Hard. He hissed at the sting, unsurprised to see blood well from the broken skin. She licked the droplets away.

He pushed into her. One strong thrust. His cry blended with hers. Fingers digging into her hip, Arek reveled at the sensation of being so deep inside her.

"Yes! *Lady's Breath!* Arek!" Imhara's whispered words accompanied a glorious, agonizing contraction of her muscles around him. "It's been so long. . . . *Light*, you fill me."

Another silky contraction and she gasped. He banded his arm around her.

"Breathe," he ground out. "Breathe or this will be over too soon."

He sucked in his own desperate breath, felt her ribs expand. For long moments neither of them moved except to draw in lungfuls of air. Arek tried to focus on that rather than the fire licking every nerve from the waist down.

Couldn't.

His forehead thumped against the damp skin on her shoulder. "You feel so good."

So hot.

So tight.

Velvet pleasure.

The salty scent of her skin combined with the heavier, earthy scent of their arousal. His braced arm lost strength, and he dropped to rest on his forearms. Her fingers bracketed his wrists, and squeezed, as if searching for an anchor.

Imhara wriggled her hips, and he grit his teeth. "Don't move."

"Don't think I can stop." Her fingernails dug into his wrists, her nails a sweet pinch of pain. "It's too hot. Too good." Her groan vibrated through her body to him. "I need more."

He grunted, and ground against her, unable to stop the movement. Her ankles hooked around the back of his knees and tightened, sending him another inch deeper. She flexed around him. He shuddered, heart pounding so hard in his chest Imhara had to feel it against her back.

Her muscles squeezed him again, the pressure agonizing. Hot, molten fire exploded through him, wild, irrepressible. It incinerated his control.

"Imhara!" The gravelly voice didn't sound like his. He withdrew, almost to the point of leaving her, then returned, grunting with the smack and jolt of flesh against flesh. Her cry vibrated against his arm.

He tried to keep the pace steady, but with every stroke, her heat, the excruciating clasp of her muscles, the need to lose himself in the furnace burn of pleasure tormented him.

Far too quickly his rhythm deteriorated into something more frantic, every stroke hard, almost savage. Imhara locked her fingers around his wrists, her calves around his knees, pushing back against him with every thrust, her cries reduced to breathless whimpers.

A tangle of limbs, movement, sound, and sensation. Arek lost the ability to distinguish between any of it, consumed by the need to release. Imhara's escalating pleasure drove his own.

Between one heartbeat and the next, her body seized. Her face contorted. A scream ripped from her throat. The sound pierced him, sent him hurtling over the edge. Fire and heat, light and darkness, sensation and numbness—everything coalesced, imploded, and exploded in one cataclysmic rush.

His seed jetted into her, the powerful spasms so intense he roared. Imhara's incoherent cries registered, then the maelstrom swallowed her presence and swept him away on the next wave. On and on the surges came, the next more powerful than the one before, until he thought he would never be able to see or hear or breathe again.

How long it lasted he didn't know, but as the savage pleasure finally subsided, he was shaking from head to toe. All he could do was try to breathe, and regain his senses.

Light, he'd never felt so drained yet overwhelmingly satisfied.

Ragged gasps reached his ears, then the softest of whispers.

"*Merciful Mother!*" A feminine curse.

The yielding warmth beneath him shivered. His nostrils filled with a familiar scent.

Imhara.

With a breathless groan, he eased himself from her and lay on the bed beside her.

Her eyelashes fluttered then opened, the glazed look in them filling him with instant satisfaction.

"You found release." His voice was hoarse, raw, as if he'd spent the day on the training grounds instructing.

"Not sure what you'd call it." A smile curved her lips. "But I think you finally killed me."

His mouth quirked. "I claimed you."

"No need to sound so smug. . . ." Her hand inched over the coverlet and her fingers tangled with his.

Arek brushed a kiss over her knuckles. "And I intend on doing it again."

"Right now?" Her voice broke midsentence, but the flare of heat in her eyes betrayed her interest.

"I'll give you a few minutes to recover." He grinned. "I thought you *Na'Reish* were supposed to have stamina."

Her gaze skimmed south along his body, lingered a moment, then returned. "You're as spent as I am!" Her lips twitched. "Tease."

"Unashamedly."

She joined in when he chuckled.

"I do intend to claim you again, Imhara Kaal." Shifting closer, he touched his forehead to hers and cupped her breast in an easy caress. "You have my *Lady*-sworn oath on that."

She arched up into his hand. "I'll hold you—" A soft snick of sound made both freeze. The haze of pleasure on Imhara's face sharpened to awareness. "The door!"

Arek pushed up onto one elbow as she rolled toward the end of the bed, and her sword. The ornate handle on the door descended. He shoved off the mattress, adrenaline surging, just as the door flung open and black-clad *Na'Hord* warriors poured into the room.

Half a dozen.

All armed.

Silver glinted near his bare feet.

He snatched up his belt, and wrapped it around his fist, leaving the buckle end to swing free.

"Hold!" The order came from outside in the corridor.

All six warriors halted in positions around the room.

Imhara's bare shoulder brushed his arm, then she was beside him, her unsheathed sword clenched in her fist. Her fierce expression matched her stance, totally unconcerned that she stood naked in a room full of armed strangers.

Arek moved to his left, shielding her from any first strike and from view.

Two others appeared in the doorway.

Both familiar.

"Rassan!" Imhara sounded surprised.

"My apologies, *Na* Kaal, but I had little choice." The Second stepped into the room and to one side. The stoic expression on his face gave nothing away.

What was going on?

The second figure entered. The light from the nearest lamp lit his broad face. It also caught the flicker of disdain in his deep purple gaze as it passed over both them. His black lips peeled back into a disgusted sneer.

"Yur!"

The name hissed from Imhara's lips like a curse.

Chapter 34

"GET dressed, *Na* Kaal." Suppressed anger deepened Urkan Yur's displeasure.

Imhara tightened her grip on her sword, astounded that the *Na'Reishi* warrior would berate her, more concerned over her state of undress than the naked blade in her hand.

"You've disgraced yourself enough for one night." Another sweep of his gaze and Yur's expression twisted, yet the gleam in his eye proved covetous. "Conduct yourself like a *Na'Reishi* female of worth."

His gloved hand flexed close to the hilt of his sheathed sword, a move that had Arek shifting to cover her. Behind Yur, Rassan moved to his right, taking up a position in between two of the *Na'Hord*. Her Second's eyes locked with hers, his focus intense, piercing. His chin dipped slightly.

Imhara's heart thudded hard.

Light, this was it.

Her mouth dried and she struggled to lock down the surge of raw elation, numbing fear, and biting anticipation. Ruthlessly she shoved it all to the back of her mind, years of discipline helping to contain it. Inhaling a calming breath, she refocused on her goal.

Yur.

He'd come to take her to Savyr; the final gambit in their plan. Five years of scheming and maneuvering were about to end.

His appearance at the House proved unexpected. Why he hadn't waited at her pavilion and instead sought her out at the one place he despised and avoided, she'd never know. It didn't matter. But Rassan's decision to accompany him now made sense, especially with half a dozen *Na'Hord* in the room with them.

"You're lecturing me on behavior?" She laughed, the pitch harsh, mocking. "Might I remind you, you're the one who came barging into this room, showing complete disrespect for Ilahn's rules. As you'd well know. I wager you never burst in on our *Na'Rei* when he engaged the services of this House."

Yur's expression darkened and his black lips pressed into a flat line. His nostrils flared as he took a single step toward her, his boot striking the rug with a dull thud, then pulled up short.

She watched him struggle with his temper. Savyr Gannec's visits were common knowledge to those who frequented the House. Savyr liked to socialize. Accompanying the *Na'Rei* to a place where purebred demons indulged their appetites for humans had to have grated on Yur's purist sensibilities. Watching him hide his disapproval behind a neutral mask amused quite a few, herself included.

If he'd been able to get away with it, she had little doubt this place would have been burned to the ground long ago.

"Clothe yourself. Now!" Yur hissed. He snatched a garment from the floor—her shirt—and flung it in their direction. Arek caught it and handed it to her. "Your night here is over."

"Over? It's only just started, Second." She pressed up against Arek's back, slid her arm around his waist, and rested her chin on his shoulder. His scent filled her nose and she savored the wild spice and musky odor. "You interrupted what was turning out to be a very pleasant night."

Fury glittered in Yur's eyes. "Actions you shall be held accountable for."

Just how far could she push him before he broke?

"Now, for the last time, get dressed." The order spat from his mouth. "Don't think I won't command my warriors to drag you out of here naked."

Arek tensed and she pressed her fingers into his abdomen in warning.

"You're going to hold me accountable for my actions?" Imhara released him and gestured for him to collect their clothes.

He did so, then placed himself between her and Yur, not to protect but to block the Second's gaze and give her a modicum of privacy. A gesture she appreciated. He waited until she'd dressed before donning his clothes.

Imhara collected her weapon from the bed. "If you're referring to the betrothal meeting I missed tonight, I'll reschedule it for another time."

A lie but Yur would never know.

"That would be difficult considering *Na'Reishi* Greev has withdrawn his petition."

"He did?"

"As has Commander Jirri. Each expressed their dissatisfaction with your less than appropriate behavior. Something the last petitioner will seek to rectify when he becomes your mate."

"Really?" She snorted. "And who is this warrior who thinks he can control me?"

Yur bared his pointed teeth, his smile sinister. "Me."

A wave of feverish cold washed through her.

Merciful Mother, no!

The thought of him touching her, demanding her compliance, of being given the right to lead her Clan in any way he wished made her physically sick to her stomach. No murdering side-winder would share her bed or claim the title of *Na*.

Arek made a soft sound behind her, a short inhalation, and his spicy scent altered, gained some heat. She caught his forearm and squeezed.

As she turned her head to reprimand him, one of the *Na'Hord* warriors along the wall near the foot of the bed shifted, caught her eye. He'd balanced on the balls of his feet, a stance she recognized.

A dig of her nails brought Arek's gaze to her, then he glanced down and to the side. He stilled and she knew he'd spotted the *Na'Hord* warriors. Beneath her palm his arm tensed.

Twice.

"You're the third petitioner?" Imhara returned her attention to Yur. "You want to be my mate? I don't think so."

"You no longer have that choice." Dark satisfaction saturated his tone. "Your own carelessness ensured that. The *Na'Rei* has no reason to delay our mating."

The twisted logic behind Yur and Savyr's machination caused another shiver to ripple through Imhara. Both warriors had to have known she'd dismiss Jirri as a contender. His Clan's need for resources, his age, and his dismissive treatment of her all reasons to reject him.

As for *Na'Reishi* Greev, she'd probably have declined his application along similar grounds. With Yur, there was no consideration involved at all. Rejecting all three meant Savyr could then choose her mate. There was no doubt who she'd have been given to: the black-hearted *Vorc*-scat standing in front of her.

"There's always a choice, Urkan." She bared her teeth in a feral smile. "You're not assuming my title or getting Kaal territory."

Yur continued speaking as if he hadn't heard her.

"I suggest you think carefully about your actions from now on,

Imhara. Once we're mated I'll take great pleasure in disciplining you for every infraction or defiant action you or your kin commit.

"And maybe, if you behave and act like a proper *Na'Reishi* female, I might be persuaded to leniency. But knowing you, those lessons could take a long time to learn. I'm looking forward to instructing you on how to . . . behave."

Her temper ignited but she reined it in. "You dare to threaten my Clan?" She shook her head. "That won't earn you their respect."

"I don't expect it." His smile turned wicked. "But obedience and fear . . . well, they'll show me both if they care for your good health and wish to see you unharmed."

Light, he was deluded if he thought that would intimidate her.

"I won't let you use me as leverage over them. I'd die first!"

Yur's vicious smile grew. "I was hoping you'd say that."

Chapter 35

"IMHARA, behind you!"

Arek spun on his heel at Rassan's warning shout as around him the whole room erupted. Their anticipated fear was coming to pass. With Savyr's plan of mating Imhara unsuccessful, only her death would give him what he craved. And he'd given Yur free rein to accomplish it by any means possible.

The faint hiss of a blade being drawn from its sheath came from his right. He heard Rassan's battle cry, felt more than saw Imhara move to engage Yur, but then had to focus.

The two *Na'Hord* warriors moved on him, swords drawn. They outweighed and outmuscled him, their height and reach superior to his. A slave didn't stand a chance against them.

Good thing he wasn't a slave.

But both possessed swords and belt daggers. And even though he'd faced such odds in border skirmishes, he'd done it armed. His heart beat a little harder and faster.

They took their time closing in; a mistake as it gave him time to strip his belt from around his waist. Leather and metal, small defense against four weapons but better than bare hands. He'd need every year of training and battle experience to match them.

"Come, human, I offer you a swift death." The warrior on the left lowered his sword and gestured with his hand. "A knife blade to your heart before I feed on you."

A promise of mercy? From a *Na'Reish* demon?

"You think I'd willingly walk to my death?" he asked, and shook his head.

The first demon lunged at him. He sidestepped the attack, making sure to keep the warrior between him and the second. Bringing the belt up in an underhanded strike, the buckle clipped the demon's chin and scored across his cheek. The warrior bellowed and clutched at his face.

Arek dropped the belt and tackled him about the waist, driving the demon to the wall. They hit with a thump. He grabbed the wrist of the arm that held the sword, fingers searching until he found the flesh between the demon's sleeve and glove. His Gift surged, fast and hot. The rush of power seared every nerve in his hand, but he held on and pushed it into the demon.

The warrior convulsed. His mouth stretched wide in a soundless scream. Arek snatched the sword from his lifeless hand. Not waiting to see the body hit the ground, he turned.

The second *Na'Hord* warrior stared at his comrade, utter surprise on his face. "There's no wound."

His gaze lifted and locked on to him. Arek saw his confusion clear and realization cross his narrow face.

"No!" The deep rasp held a note of disbelief. He shook his head. "But I felt . . . You can't be!"

The element of surprise, so important in any battle, would be lost in less than a minute once the demon accepted what instinct already told him—that he faced an experienced Light Blade, not just some slave.

Arek didn't wait. With a cry, he engaged the *Na'Hord* warrior with a flurry of blows. No finesse, no fancy blade work, no break in his attack, just pure speed and force. The blade was heavier than he was used to but it didn't matter. He made the weight work for him with every blow.

Their clash of sword on sword resonated through the room, muscle and bone vibrating with every blow. There was little room to move between a bed and a wall, even less for a seven-foot demon wielding a five-foot sword.

Arek ducked to avoid an overhead sweep. The blade screeched against the wall. Sparks spat close to his head. Burnt metal filled his nostrils. The edge of the sword bit into the wooden frame of the window nearest the bed. It caught and held.

Grunting, Arek brought his down for an overhead strike. The blow caught the flat of his opponent's blade with enough force to tear the hilt from his grasp. The demon's sword clattered to the ground.

With a snarl Arek surged forward, wrist twisting his weapon at an upward angle. The tip of his blade speared into his abdomen, just where the edge of the armor and hips met. He drove it deep into the demon's innards and twisted it. The shock on the warrior's face was gratifying.

Black lips stretched wide but no sound came forth.

Lungs pierced.

Arek grinned. "Now I offer you a swift death!"

He sent a second bolt of power surging through his blade, as strong as the previous one, but nowhere near as painful with the metal as the conduit used to deliver the killing surge.

The *Na'Hord* warrior dropped to his knees, his shocked expression slackening. Arek yanked his sword free. The demon toppled over, his dead weight thumping hard as he hit the ground. Ominous dark stains seeped and spread into the rug around the body.

"Arek!"

Rassan's bellow whipped him around. The *Na'Chi* had his hands full holding off an opponent even though three bodies lay sprawled on the floor in front of him. The two came together in a frenzy of blows, every strike blocked or countered.

An even match, yet the *Na'Hord* warrior's shirt sleeve flapped wetly. Blood soaked it, and every strike splattered droplets through the air. At the rate he seemed to be losing blood, weakness would eventually set in, if it hadn't already. Rassan would prevail.

The *Na'Chi* delivered a nasty slice to his opponent's thigh. As the *Na'Reish* staggered and fell to one knee, Rassan stepped back.

Why had he given up the advantage?

The *Na'Chi's* gaze lifted and Arek saw the brilliant flare of yellow in the flecks in his eyes. He pointed with his bloody sword across the room.

"Help, Imhara!"

Arek's heart pounded then choked in his chest as he saw Yur backhand Imhara hard against her cheekbone. She staggered yet recovered quickly enough to deflect a vicious upward thrust from Yur's blade with her sword, but she'd lost ground.

Yur gave her no quarter, delivering several overhead blows in quick succession. Imhara blocked each, the jarring vibrations travelling the length of her blade and arm. If her muscles weren't numb yet, they soon would be. She was being driven into the corner of the room, overpowered by sheer strength.

Arek hissed a curse and started forward, already knowing the outcome. If her weapon arm lost strength, and unless she was skilled enough to wield a sword in her other hand, Yur would have her. The thought made his stomach twist and knot.

He headed around the bed then changed his mind. Rounding the end would bring him up behind Yur, an advantage he could use, but Imhara didn't have that sort of time. She needed him now.

Seizing the end poster, Arek leapt onto the bed. Imhara took another overhead blow. She grunted with the impact. The force drove her blade to the ground. Yur slammed his boot down on the flat of it, ripping the hilt out of her hand. With a sharp crack it smacked against the floor.

Yur's lips peeled back from his teeth. The warrior lunged, his dagger glinting in the lamplight.

Adrenaline surged through Arek. His breath seized in his lungs. "No!"

Time slowed.

The scene before him altered.

Imhara's face blurred, became Kalan's. The room, a shadowed clearing.

Light, not again!

He'd failed a friend before. He couldn't fail another now.

The curved dagger punched into Imhara's side, just below the ribs. She cried out. Her features contorted into a teeth-baring grimace. She grabbed Yur's wrist to stop him from driving the blade deeper.

Yur's sword rose high. He reversed his grip on the hilt, holding it like an oversized dagger. Imhara's pain-filled gaze lifted to it. It began to descend.

Arek launched himself across the distance separating them. He landed beside the demon. With an upward block he caught the strike, metal screeched on metal. Their hilts met. The angle was all wrong; he'd had no time to position himself correctly. Arek twisted anyway. With a hard pull, he deflected Yur's blade away from Imhara, unable to fling it from his grasp.

Yur's head snapped toward him, fury lashing his face. "I'll take pleasure in killing you once I finish with her!"

Arek bared his teeth. "You can try, demon!"

"I'll take my pleasure now!" Imhara ground out through her teeth with barely contained ferocity.

Light flashed on a metal blade near her waist, one bloody hand wrapped around the ornate hilt. Her own dagger. With a grunt she brought it up in a diagonal sweep, aiming high. The blade sliced deep into Yur's windpipe, from one side to the other. Blood sprayed from the heart vessel.

"That's for my family!" she rasped.

Yur staggered back, releasing both weapons to clutch his throat. The demon's gasp became a wet, gurgling sound, then a cough. His mouth opened and closed as more blood seeped between his fingers.

Arek followed through with a kick into the demon's torso. The sole of his boot hit with a dull thud. The impact sent him careening into the wall. His head struck with a sickening crack and he sank into a tangled heap against the wall.

Arek crouched and placed the point of his sword beneath Yur's chin. The iron-rich odor of blood filled his nostrils. "Nothing to say now, *Na'Reish*?"

Dazed purple eyes, bright with fear, locked with his. Every desperate breath gurgled and choked in Yur's throat. One bloodstained hand reached out and clawed Arek's leg.

Too weak to gain purchase, his fingers slipped. A silent snarl shaped his black lips.

Arek knew his smile lacked warmth. "This is for Imhara."

He drove the blade up into Yur's head.

Chapter 36

A combination of furious elation and relief flooded Imhara as Yur slid lifelessly to the floor, his eyes glazing over. The warrior responsible for the massacre of her family was dead.

Finally.

Justice was served.

Her vendetta with Savyr was in serious danger though. The moment Yur's dagger had slid into her, she'd known it.

Imhara grimaced and pressed a hand to her side, the throbbing pain excruciating and debilitating enough to steal her breath and make her head spin. Reaching out blindly, she staggered to the bed, almost not making it before her legs gave out.

"Imhara!" Rassan's voice sounded like it came from a great distance. She blinked, forcing her eyes open, never even realizing she'd closed them. Her head felt light, while all her limbs were heavy.

Across the room Rassan stepped over and around four bodies to get to her. Arek swiveled where he crouched near the still body of Yur, his fierce expression softening to concern.

"Should have seen that coming, eh?" She grimaced at the sticky warmth oozing beneath her hand and tried to press harder. "In training you always warned me—" Another wave of pain washed through her, cutting off the rest of her sentence. She groaned, unable to hold back the sound.

Rassan knelt in front of her, placing his sword down on the floor beside him. "Let me look." The flecks in his eyes were bright yellow.

Fresh blood pulsed from the wound as soon as she lifted pressure from it. Dark, not bright, which was some relief. Rassan peeled up the edge of her shirt. Strong hands caught her shoulders, and the bed dipped as someone slid onto it to support her from behind. A familiar spicy scent surrounded her.

Arek.

"How bad is it?" His terse tone sounded in her ear.

"*Lady's Breath!*" Rassan's soft curse confirmed Imhara's fear.

"That bad, huh?" She offered him a weak smile.

Her Second nodded once. "It's deep. The blood's clean. No foul odor and the blood wells rather than spurts, so the blade missed your innards. It's still flowing. That's all I can tell."

Arek's arms tightened around her. "We need to get back to camp. Get you a healer."

Rassan shook his head. "No time. She risks bleeding out before we even make it to the fortress gate."

"Then what about Ilahn? Surely he'd have access to a healer."

A laugh rasped from her throat. "Arek, we're in a room with seven bodies. Ilahn might not have liked Yur, but if Savyr finds out his Second died in his House, it'd be enough to warrant the trader's death. He'd turn us over to Savyr in a heartbeat if he knew it would save his skin."

"It's true, Arek. Yur used intimidation to find out what room you were in. For anyone else Ilahn would have had his staff forcibly escort them from the House, but he knew to resist would mean reprisal." The yellow in Rassan's eyes changed to green as he looked past her to the Light Blade. "Let her feed from you."

"What?" Every part of Arek pressed against her back went tight and the faintest odor of soured citrus tickled her nose.

"Imhara needs your blood to heal. Full healing might take a few hours, but you saw how quickly she recovered after you let her feed from you up in the mountains."

Imhara shook her head. "No, Rassan."

Arek's loathing from that time holed up in the makeshift shelter remained a vivid memory. His reaction to Rassan's suggestion now only proved how unfair it would be to put him in that position again.

Her stomach cramped and eased in the space of a heartbeat. The hollow emptiness remaining left her nauseous. The first stirrings of blood-need. She took a slow, easy breath.

"Just pack and bandage the wound. I'll take the risk." She held a hand up before he could protest. "We need to get moving. These walls are thick but not so thick Ilahn couldn't have heard the commotion. He'll be wondering what's happened. Once he gathers the nerve, he'll check."

The *Na'Chi's* brow dipped. "You can barely stand, let alone move with the speed we're going to need. And you know it." His glare heated. "You'll die without feeding. I'd offer you my vein, but the human blood in me is too weak to sustain you. Neither you nor Arek have any choice in this."

Imhara swallowed against a dry throat. Her friend had never hidden the truth from her, ugly or bad. One of the qualities she admired in him, and always had.

Arek's arms loosened from around her. One blood-smeared hand tugged at his shirtsleeve until his forearm was bared.

"Your Second is right." Terse words that made her flinch. "Feed and take all you need. No half measures this time."

Surprise and shock raced through her. "But you hate it." She managed to move a little to look at him. "Your scent—"

Twilight eyes locked with hers, level and steady. "I used to hate Annika and the other *Na'Chi* at Sacred Lake, but my attitude changed. If this journey has taught me anything, it's that I can adapt." His stubbled jaw flexed and his voice roughened. "Besides, before we were so rudely interrupted tonight, I made you a promise, and it's one I intend to keep. How can I do that if you die?"

A promise? Imhara frowned then blinked. Surely he wasn't referring to the comment he'd made about making love to her again? She inhaled deeply. He was. The spicy scent filling her lungs didn't lie.

Her throat tightened. Inside her chest, her heart beat at a rapid thrum. His words breathed life once more into long-suppressed yearnings.

To hear Arek share his journey so openly when she knew he disliked leaving himself vulnerable sparked a soul-deep warmth that rose and encircled her heart. It didn't seem that long ago when she'd wondered if he'd ever reach this point, whether she'd earn his trust and he'd consider her an ally.

He was giving her a part of himself even when he didn't want to, and the precious feeling that came with his gift was breath stealing.

Now he wanted to be her lover; something she'd never even expected or dared to hope for.

Until this moment.

She could easily love such a man. Imhara closed her eyes at the dizzying thought and tried not to let herself hope too much. But, deep down, she knew it was too late.

His words and actions claimed her heart. Absolutely.

She already loved him.

Her chest tightened. The realization was powerful and stunning.

"Imhara?" Arek's knuckles brushed the side of her face.

Did he have any idea just what she felt for him?

The scent of new-fallen rain flooded the air. Someone did.

Imhara glanced to Rassan. Surprise lightened his gaze, but then his mouth quirked and satisfaction deepened his scent.

She took a slow, deep breath and nodded. "All right."

Arek offered his arm to her again. All too aware of how badly her fingers shook, she grasped his wrist. Saliva filled her mouth as she pressed a kiss against his flesh, unable to vocalize just how precious his gesture was to her. Thanking him seemed so inadequate.

Without any further delay, she bit into him, heard his soft grunt, and then fed. The hot, sweet taste of his blood exploding in her mouth made her stomach cramp. She opened all her senses to her hunger, monitoring its intensity, allowing the warmth of Arek's blood and the energy that came with it to fill her.

Light, she could feel every cell in her body heating, absorbing his blood, repairing the damage done to her by Yur's blade in a way she'd never felt before, only ever read about in her ancestors' journals. The sharp, prickling sensation centralized around the wound.

After a few minutes, her light-headedness vanished, another couple and the agony in her side diminished to a manageable ache, like she'd overworked and pulled every muscle in her side. But with her improving health, the full-bodied, iron-rich tang of Arek's blood began to weaken. She stopped feeding.

"What's wrong?" Arek asked.

She licked her lips. "There's a point reached in any feeding where you'd begin to feel the side effects of blood loss. You've reached it. I can taste the difference. If I kept feeding and took too much, you'd lose consciousness."

Rassan lifted the edge of her shirt again and rechecked the wound site, his fingers probing in a thorough pattern as he tested the flesh. The wound no longer bled. The skin looked just healed over, red raw in the center, a deep pink at the edges.

"Any pain?" he asked.

She shook her head. “None, just a bit of tenderness and a lingering ache.”

“You still need to be careful, give it time to knit properly and for your strength to return.”

Imhara nodded. She’d seen the results of pushing a body still healing too far. Any strenuous activity could potentially tear open the wound again and they’d be back to square one. It was going to make confronting . . . She blinked and uttered a curse.

“What about Savyr?”

“Imhara . . .” Rassan grimaced and pushed to his feet.

An icy coldness prickled her skin. “No! Don’t even say it!”

His dark brows descended in a deep frown as he resheathed his sword. “You can’t go after him. That would be suicide!”

Familiar fury twisted in her gut. Savyr couldn’t be allowed to live, to continue his reign. The blood of too many lives stained his hands. His pursuit of total domination, *Na’Reish* and human territory alike, had to end now.

She pressed a hand to her side, to the tear in her shirt where Yur’s blade had penetrated, then fisted the material in her hand. Five years of prayer and oaths made at her family’s graveside to avenge their deaths, and five years of being something she wasn’t—gone, in a single thrust. One unfortunate error on her part, and she’d sacrificed years’ worth of planning.

The knowledge hit her like a fist to her stomach.

She straightened. “There’s time between now and when we get to him for me to regain my strength.”

“Don’t delude yourself.” Rassan’s hard words lashed like whip.

Her temper ignited. “We came here to kill him! You want to abandon everything and walk away? Let him *live*?”

“Of course not!” The words exploded from her friend. “I want to see him dead as much as you. We planned for every contingency we could, but we knew the odds of success coming into this venture.”

He sucked in a deep breath, and the black flecks in his gaze faded. "Making another attempt now is careless. Stupid. We took out the king's right hand. We have to settle for that small victory and move on."

Denial raced through Imhara in a hot wave that scorched every nerve, head to toe. She shot to her feet, wincing as her side protested the angry move, and snatched her sword off the floor. To come so close and turn away . . . She couldn't do it. . . . She couldn't break her oath to her family, to her people, to herself.

The weight of responsibility made her chest tighten. Why now? Just when she'd discovered a man she could love and allowed herself to hope for a future of her own? She bit her lip and pushed the pain clawing at her heart away.

"Take Arek. Leave the fortress. Get everyone home and do the best you can dealing with the Blade Council." She retrieved her dagger. "I'm going after Savyr. Alone."

Chapter 37

RASSAN'S mouth flattened. "Imhara, we gambled and we lost."

"The error was *mine*, Rassan. I'll rectify it."

"Your error? You were wounded in battle. Not something you can predict." The *Na'Chi's* gaze darkened then lit up with yellow, flickering between the two colors as his whole body shook with Imhara's announcement. "And since when did this become just *your* crusade?"

Lady of Light. It was like watching an oil lantern smash on stone and the flame ignite. Arek wasn't sure he'd ever seen Rassan so volatile, but then he wondered if Imhara had ever given such an irrational order before.

"You'll never get close to Savyr." The warrior's statement came out flat and hard. "When Yur and I left camp, Barrca and the others set the final strategy in motion. They've had almost an hour."

"What strategy?" Arek frowned, his gaze flicking between them.

Both Kaal Clan members remained silent, unwilling to unlock their gazes. Then Rassan relented, and glanced to him.

"If Savyr ever summoned Imhara to his keep, once she'd gone, everyone else would leave as well. Small groups. Abandoning our tents and supplies in camp, so none of the other Clans would suspect anything amiss. They would take only what they could carry. Oreese would use his Gift to manipulate the weather, and Atallie, her fire skills."

Atallie's name proved familiar. An image of a young woman among the cooking crew flashed through Arek's mind.

He raised an eyebrow. "Cover for their escape?"

Rassan gave a nod. "And ours should we have succeeded against Savyr."

"What would Atallie set on fire?"

"Tents, wagons, stock fodder, anything flammable, at various locations around the Clan campsites." Rassan gestured with his chin. "If we looked out that window now, there'd be a fog forming and we'd hear watchtower bells ringing."

Any fire among pavilions and tents so closely packed together would quickly burn out of control.

The soft hiss of blades sliding into sheaths drew Arek's attention to Imhara. Her lips were pressed together into a thin, determined line. Sweat beaded her brow; her face had lost color, making the markings running down either side stand out.

Arek understood Rassan's frustration. Imhara might be well on her way to recovery, but there was no way she was ready to take on Savyr alone. Convincing her of that though was going to be tough.

On one hand he understood her desire to seek vengeance, but his heart couldn't let her go to her death.

Her people needed her.

Light, he needed her. As much as he didn't want to admit it, that was the bare, selfish truth. There was something between them, and for the first time, he wanted to explore what it was, and he couldn't do that if she followed through on her plan.

There were traces of anger in her gaze, but also a wildness he recognized. A powerful combination of emotions drove Imhara Kaal, and the internal deluge submerged logic and reason. Not that long ago he'd felt the same sense of desperation and panic at realizing his carefully ordered world had been turned upside down.

"If you intend on making it through the gates before they're shut, I suggest you two get moving," she stated.

Rassan's thunderous expression returned.

Catching his eye, Arek shook his head and rose from the bed. "Imhara."

"Not you, too!" Her accusation was bitter, harsh, and she backed away from him. "You of all people should know how I feel!"

Arek followed her retreat, the scene a reversal and eerily reminiscent of the one earlier in the evening. When she hit the wall, her chin lifted.

"I do." He stopped a pace away from her.

If she didn't listen, then he would physically overpower her and carry her out of the fortress. Rassan would most probably help.

"My hatred for Savyr still exists. It won't ever go away. He took my parents from me and, in a fashion, did the same with my grandfather." He didn't hide the struggle going on inside him. "Vengeance brought me to you. Your thirst for the same made me a part of your plan to kill Savyr." His brief smile was wry. "I convinced myself it offset any differences and conflicts I thought existed between us."

Here he hesitated, uncertainty eating at his gut, then doggedly continued.

"Vengeance destroyed Davyn's life. Until I met you, I was headed down the same path." His tone gentled. "As much as I want to see Savyr dead, I now have more to live for. And so do you."

Imhara's eyelids closed and her jaw flexed. Her throat worked hard. She sucked in one uneven breath after another.

"You've always told me you'd do anything for your Clan. Make any decision, take any action, to help them." Arek wanted to smooth the frown from her brow, but he didn't think she'd welcome his touch, given he had one last thing to say to her. "If you go after Savyr now, you'll do more damage to them than he ever has. They need a leader, not a martyr."

Her eyes snapped open as her hands fisted so tight her knuckles went white. He braced himself, expecting some sort of physical response. It didn't come. She just stared at him for the longest time, her gaze haunted.

Stark.

"When you've lived with something that's been a part of your life for so long, letting go isn't easy." Her hoarsely spoken words gave him hope.

"Agreed. But it can be done. Together, if you want."

Her hands flexed and she gave a jerky nod. "I'm still not happy leaving Savyr alive."

"None of us are, Imhara," Rassan assured her.

Arek gave in to temptation and touched his fingertips to her cheek. "Disgruntled but breathing. I'm sure Rassan and I can live with that."

The wildness in her gaze seemed more controlled. She shot a look over his shoulder. "*Light*, he's too much like you."

A snort came from behind Arek. "I don't see how that's a problem."

A tentative knock sounded at the door. Rassan moved quickly for a man his size. He pressed himself up against the wall behind the door.

"*Na* Kaal, is everything all right?" Ilahn's muffled query reached them.

They all exchanged looks.

"I'll buy us some time," Imhara murmured. She joined Rassan. "Everything's fine, trader."

"Are you sure? The attendants said they heard . . . arguing."

She snorted softly. "Nice way of saying pitched battle," she murmured, then raised her voice. "Second Yur and I disagreed on a point of discussion. Apologies if we disturbed anyone. He will be leaving shortly."

A long silence, and Arek shared another look with Rassan. The *Na'Chi's* expression remained alert.

"Very well, *Na* Kaal. Please let us know if you need anything."

Arek released the breath he didn't even know he'd been holding. Bodies scattered haphazardly over the bedroom floor might have been hard to explain had the trader entered the room. At least he observed his own rules.

But for how long, that was the question.

"We need to get out of this House." Arek glanced between them. "Ilahn knows Yur came in here with his men. Isn't it going to seem strange if we walk out of here unescorted?"

Imhara shared a smile with her Second. "With so many of his clients demanding anonymity, Ilahn goes to great lengths to ensure their privacy."

Rassan sheathed his sword and headed to one of the windows. He jerked back the curtain and pushed open the shutters. The faint chiming of bells drifted into the room.

"There's a landing and stairway outside the windows in every room on this floor," Imhara explained. "They descend to the street below."

Arek scooped up one of the *Na'Reish* daggers, tucked it into his belt, and draped his shirt over the top of it. He was tempted to pick up the sword, but out on the streets, he didn't know who they'd come across. A slave carrying one would bring them only trouble they couldn't afford. A dagger, on the other hand, held the element of surprise. He motioned Imhara to the window.

Rassan stepped back and gestured for them to go first. "Time to go. We've outstayed our welcome."

RASSAN signaled them to halt in the shadowed overhang of a balcony. The reason became clear when the pounding of boot steps on cobblestones drifted through the wall of ethereal fog ahead of them. The closer they came, the more the thump of leather on stone drowned out the distant ringing of the fortress gate bells.

"Patrol," her Second whispered.

Imhara tightened her hand around Arek's and tugged him behind her into a small alcove, possibly the side entrance to whatever business inhabited the building.

The structures around them were mostly closed businesses, anonymous gray forms towering above them in the dark, with only the occasional night lamp hanging outside a doorway or a window lighting up a patch of ground on the pathway outside.

Her heart beat harder. "That's the fourth we've come across tonight." An uneasy sense of foreboding settled between her shoulder blades. "What's going on?"

A shrug accompanied Rassan's grim expression. "We need to get off the streets. There's no cover here."

This late at night, few wandered the street. Come daylight that would change as traders, slaves, and customers roamed the business district.

Her Second glanced up and down the street. "There. A stairway." He led the way.

"We're crossing the cobblestone street and heading into a small alleyway between buildings," Imhara murmured to Arek.

The closer they drew to the fortress gates, the thicker Oreese's fog became. Traversing the shrouded streets had become much more difficult, but more so for Arek, as he lacked their enhanced night-sight. Not that she minded the slower pace. The healing wound in her side ached, the stitchlike pain hurting more the faster they moved.

She counted down the distance as she guided him across. "Gutter. Step up. The stairway takes us onto the curtain wall."

"Why do you think there are so many patrols on the streets?" Arek's grip tightened as they entered the dark alleyway.

"Perhaps Ilahn's already raised the alarm."

Arek's scent thickened, and although he didn't say it out loud, Imhara knew what he was thinking. If the trader had alerted Savyr to Yur's death, then the fortress gates would be shut and patrols would be looking for them.

Regardless of the reason for the increased presence of patrols on the streets, they needed to avoid meeting anyone if it was at all possible. Her bloodstained shirt would bring questions they didn't want to answer.

"Imhara!" Rassan's urgent hiss came from the top of the stairway. A rumble of thunder accompanied his hail. "You've got to see this!"

As she and Arek ascended the last few stairs, they joined Rassan in an empty, corner guard tower. It gave a clear view of the southern and western sides of the fortress. Crossing to the southern parapet, a gust of wind carried the scent of rain and acrid odor of smoke. Wondering why the tower was empty was pushed aside as her breath caught at the panorama spread out on the other side of the river that ran beside the fortress.

To the far left, a massive fog bank blanketed the area she knew to be the Clan campsite. The pitch of tents and the odd pavilion poked through the top layer. Patches of it though glowed an eerie kaleidoscope of colors, red, orange, and gold. Shouting carried on the breeze, but the voices were indistinguishable at this distance.

"*Lady's Breath*, how much of the campsite did Atallie set alight?" Arek's soft question echoed her thoughts. "It looks like the whole camp is under attack."

Imhara grinned. It did indeed, and that could provide a possible explanation for the increased number of patrols roaming the fortress.

"If you think that's spectacular, then you'd better take a look at this." Rassan motioned them over to the other side of the watchtower.

As Imhara crossed the floor, the world lit up in a flash of light closely followed by another explosion of thunder. As her night vision returned, she had to blink several times before comprehending what she saw. The fog hadn't reached the ground on this side of the fortress, probably because Oreese had concentrated his efforts on the gates and the Clan campsite.

"*Merciful Mother!*" She gripped the cold stone wall and leaned over for a clearer view.

An Enclave gathering was impressive at the best of times. Anywhere from four to five thousand members set up tents outside the Gannec fortress every year, a massive undertaking in logistics, preparation, and execution.

Yet here, row upon row of tents, ten deep, stretched the entire length of the western wall. The sheer size of the canvas city put the Clan campsite to shame and sent chills racing down her spine.

"Savyr's army." She couldn't keep the hoarseness out of her voice as a curse ripped from Arek's mouth. "The *Na'Rei* is going to war."

Savyr would be the first king in generations to mobilize a full army and march across the border in an all-out assault against the humans since the Great War. A shiver prickled the length of Imhara's body.

"I estimate nearly fifteen thousand *Na'Hord*." Rassan's solemn tone increased her sense of foreboding. "It'd take a week, maybe two, for this number of warriors to broach the border at Whitewater Crossing. Longer if they crossed anywhere else. Time enough for the humans to rally a counterforce and confront them."

"Savyr wouldn't send his entire army into human territory through one entry point." She swallowed hard. "He'd split the army and try a multipronged attack. Skadda Pass and the slave-route would give him one approach. No wonder he was pushing so hard to see me mated before the Enclave."

And it underscored the need to cut the head of the shadow-winder from its body. Without Savyr or Yur, the Enclave and the army would be left writhing and thrashing, engulfed by an internal Clan war as the *Na's* fought for the title of *Na'Rei*.

"A couple of weeks versus months," Imhara murmured, the knot in her gut twisting tight once more. "Rassan, buying time would save so many lives . . ."

"No." He cut her off hard and turned his black-flecked gaze on her. "We're not going over this again."

"Seeing the size of Savyr's *Na'Hord* worries me, too, Imhara. Comparing the sizes of our forces, I know the odds of war truly lie in the *Na'Rei's* favor, but I still don't agree that sacrificing your life is worth the possibility of creating mayhem among the Clans." Arek's hand smoothed down her back, and the look in his eye mirrored Rassan's even though his tone was gentler. "We have to have faith that the *Lady* has a purpose for us not succeeding in this journey."

The struggle Arek felt was there in his expression; he hid nothing from her, and again she marveled at the strength he showed her. Reason over vengeance.

"We'll never get this chance again." Imhara grimaced and ran a hand through her hair. "You'd place personal desires over the common good?"

Shadows flickered through Arek's gaze, and a muscle in his jaw ticked as he considered her question. He drew in a deep breath and cupped her jaw, his thumb stroking her cheek. "This time, yes, I would."

His blunt response astonished her.

"As a warrior everything in me objects, but if I listen to my heart, then my desire is purely selfish. And my gut tells me that there has to be a reason why we're faced with this choice. I don't know the answer, so I'm going with my heart on this one. Put aside all expectations and ask yourself this. What do you really want, Imhara?"

His words tugged at her heart, and she did as he asked, looking deep within herself. Pushing aside the pressures of responsibility wasn't easy, it was part of who she was, and more times than she could count, those expectations had taken precedence over hers. But there beyond them she found the answer.

"You." The hand cupping her jaw tightened a moment. "I want you."

A lover, a mate, a future outside being *Na* Kaal—all dreams unfulfilled and things she wanted yet had never given herself permission to fully dream into being, but Arek made her want to, more than anything.

"Then just this once, listen to your heart." His hand slid down her arm until his fingers tangled with hers. "Please."

How could she resist such a soft plea?

Imhara gave a jerky nod. His and Rassan's relief saturated the air.

Almost as if he sensed she needed a moment to compose herself, Arek glanced to her Second and gestured to the army. "What are those cordoned-off sections set at intervals among the tents?"

"Slave pens." Rassan's mouth set in a grim line. "Once Savyr orders his *Na'Hord* to move, they'll become mobile. Cages on wagons."

"A portable source of food." The distaste on Arek's face matched the nausea in her stomach. "I've seen something similar while on border patrol but nothing like this."

A shout came from behind them. As one they turned. A lone *Na'Hord* warrior headed toward them from along the southern walkway.

"Looks like this might be the missing watchtower guard," Rassan murmured. "But where are his companions?"

"Do we confront him or retreat?" Arek asked, tersely.

"Retreat, for now." Imhara exited the tower via the opposite archway just as it began to rain.

Halfway across, movement ahead stopped her. She wasn't sure

who was more astonished at seeing one another, her or the three other *Na'Hord* warriors coming along the western walkway. Thunder rumbled overhead.

"Back!" Rassan called.

Imhara didn't hesitate.

"Halt!"

They ignored the warning cry.

Her Second drew his weapon and surged ahead, his speed taking the lone warrior by surprise. The demon didn't even have time to draw his sword. The fight was swift and short, and ended with Rassan heaving his fatally wounded opponent over the battlements. They all heard the body hit the water below.

"And there's the missing tower guards," Arek murmured, pointing with his chin. Two more *Na'Hord* were coming along the southern walkway. "We're going to be trapped here on the wall, Rassan."

"We can't go back to the streets." Imhara grimaced. "And the fortress gates are most likely shut by now."

Rassan sheathed his sword. "Then we jump."

Arek's head jerked around. "What?"

"It's only a thirty-foot drop to the river below."

Imhara pushed Arek toward a battlement. "We don't have time to argue."

She scrambled up onto the one next to him, wincing as her side pulled. Arek steadied her. She shot one last glance over her shoulder at Gannec Fortress.

Savyr's keep towered over the city center like a dark specter, one that would continue to haunt her thoughts with what ifs. After imagining his defeat for so long, the bitterness of seeing that dream unfulfilled twisted her insides again.

Arek's fingers squeezed hers, his twilight blue gaze reflecting her regret. "Savyr will be called to account for his actions, Imhara. Maybe not by us, but the *Lady* will see to it."

Imhara pushed resentment back and focused on the hold he had on her hand. She peered down at the river below. Fog curled over the dark water's surface.

"Ready?" Rassan joined them on the wall. She took a deep breath and nodded. "Jump!"

They leapt.

Chapter 38

A night of struggling through the storm and putting as much distance between them and Savyr's fortress left Imhara exhausted and reeling on her feet, so when they stumbled upon Barrca and several others of her Clan waiting for them with transport beasts on the trail ahead, she didn't care that they'd ignored her order to flee Gannec territory as fast as they could.

After a swift recount of events and delivering the news that Savyr still lived, Rassan insisted she feed before they resumed their escape. While feeding relieved the residing ache and soreness of her wound, it also brought the full weight of fatigue down upon her. Riding double, it wasn't long before she slept, head resting on the back of the person in front of her.

Two hard days of riding caught them up with the main group and in sight of the mountains and Skadda Pass. A trip that should have taken four days cut in half without a caravan of loaded wagons slowing the pace. Still the fast pace took its toll on everyone, and Rassan called a halt halfway up the range.

Imhara wandered a little away from the main group and found an outcrop of boulders off the trail that overlooked the mountain slopes. The afternoon sun had warmed the pitted surface, and other than the soft chattering of voices, only the distant hoot of a winged *hobaan* broke the tranquil stillness of the air.

Boot steps crunched over the ground behind her, and a moment later her Second eased his large frame down beside her. His shoulder rubbed hers as he handed her a small cloth-wrapped package.

"It's only trail rations, but by this time tomorrow evening we'll be enjoying Nenchan's cooking again," he said, with a grin.

Imhara fished out a piece of journeybread. "I'll try and imagine this is one of her oven soft rolls then instead of week-old tack." Taking a bite she glanced over her shoulder at the others. "How are the children and new humans settling in?"

Her friend peered in the same direction. "They seem to be handling it for the most part. Although the hard travelling has worn on the children," he murmured. "The healers and a few of the other humans are the only ones the ex-*Isha* humans will interact with. They're still afraid of the rest of us."

"Understandable, given what they've been through."

Imhara's gaze roved over the groups and settled on the one Arek belonged to. The Light Blade sat with one of the young men they'd bought from the *Isha*. The same one he'd shared time with during the last few meals.

Each wore solemn expressions, the younger man listening more than contributing to the conversation. Arek was probably answering questions, maybe talking to him about his new life, or at least she hoped so. Not wanting to intrude, she'd kept her distance, knowing how important it was for the youth to bond with someone.

While she didn't resent the time Arek spent with the young man, she did find herself missing his company, among other things. After the intensity and revelations of the last week, she'd looked forward to exploring their new relationship.

Granted, circumstances hadn't exactly allowed them to spend

time together. Trail duties with her *Na'Hord* then camp chores whenever they stopped had occupied them both. The one time they might have scrimped some time together was at night, but exhaustion relegated them to curling up under a blanket and sleeping as soon as their heads hit the ground.

Yet none of that stopped her wanting Arek or his company. Perhaps now she'd allowed her long-suppressed hopes to rise, squashing them to the back of her mind was no longer so easy.

Imhara shifted restlessly on the boulder and stared out over the forest-strewn hills below.

"You're not stewing over Savyr, are you?" She looked up, startled. Rassan gestured. "You're flexing and fisting your hand, and you've broken that journeybread into crumbs."

Imhara glanced down at the tiny piece left in her hand. Her cheeks flushed. "No." She gave him a wry smile. "Perhaps I should be."

"I'm glad that you're not."

She chewed her lip. "So you don't think I've failed our people?"

"Failed us?" His deep voice rumbled up from his chest. "Not at all, Imhara. Arek was right in what he said. We need you more than we need Savyr dead."

"But he'll claim a blood-feud and hunt us all down."

"And would the result be different if a new warrior claimed the throne and declared himself *Na'Rei*?" Rassan uncapped his water pouch and drank, then offered it to her.

Imhara grunted, conceding his point but also relieved to hear his reassurance. They passed the next few minutes in a companionable silence.

The heavy clattering of hoofbeats on stone broke it. Rassan's relaxed expression sharpened, and as one they rose from the boulder and turned in the direction of the trail.

Her Second grunted. "It's Barrca."

Assigned to watch their back trail, the blond-haired warrior leaned low over the shaggy neck of his mount, urging it up the last slope before the small plateau campsite. The beast labored for breath, its gasps rasping in its barrel chest. Others in camp started to rise as they heard them coming up the slope.

Imhara shared a look with Rassan. What had Barrca so concerned that he'd run an animal almost to exhaustion? The switchback trail was empty behind him.

The *Na'Hord* warrior reined in his beast and slid from the saddle, thrusting the reins at one of the younger warriors who came to take them from him. His sweat-shined face creased in a frown as his gaze searched the campsite.

"*Nu* Kaal, Second!" He started toward them. "Four patrols, moving fast in our direction."

Adrenaline surged through Imhara. "Whose?"

"The banner is black."

"Savyr." Rassan grimaced. "How far behind us are they?"

"I saw them from Pinnacle Hill just emerging from the forest." The flecks of color in Barrca's eyes were a mix of pale green and yellow. "Each patrol has spare mounts. All are *Vorc*. I watched long enough to see they're coming up the trail and not diverting to skirt the border between our territories."

Imhara glanced at their string of war-beasts. Leaving their own *Vorc* behind to allay suspicion, they'd sacrificed some speed by using the shaggy animals.

"They're either coming to stop us or to take Skadda Pass," Rassan stated.

"Either aim will give Savyr what he wants—control of Skadda Pass." Imhara took a moment to think. "If Barrca saw them near Pinnacle Hill, then they're only an hour or so behind us."

These were not regular patrols sent out to roam Clan territory but *Vorc-Masters*, those sent after escaped slaves or on raids for humans. The animals they rode were trained to respond only to their commands. She quickly calculated the time it would take their group to get through Skadda Pass.

"They're going to intercept us just before we get to the pass." She turned to the group. "Oreese! We need something to delay those patrols, but nothing to hamper us."

"That cart gets left behind. The children double with a rider. Everyone else is on foot," Rassan added. "Leave behind anything we can afford to do without. The lighter we travel, the faster we'll be."

"I'll take a few *Na'Hord* and check the screes."

At Rassan's nod, Barrca called to three others, and on two fresher mounts, headed up the trail into the pass. As if their leaving was impetus, everyone scrambled to action. In minutes those who were riding were ready to go. The handful without mounts started their ascent.

Imhara took one last glance around, making sure no one had been left behind in the rush. All that remained were small piles of supplies. The clatter of hooves on stone nearby had her turning.

A spear of pleasure surged through her at the sight of Arek astride one of the beasts, reins clasped in one hand, years of riding experience evident in his relaxed posture.

"Need a ride?"

The saddle pad behind him was empty. He kicked his foot free of his stirrup and stretched an arm down to her. The sight of his large hand, fingers extended loosely toward her, sent a surge of longing so fierce through her she fought to keep her expression neutral. She thought he'd help one of the other humans.

Instead, she smiled and reached for his hand. The warmth of his grip was nothing compared to the heat in his body as she settled herself in against him, wrapping her arms around his waist. She should have felt foolish at enjoying the simple satisfaction of him choosing her company but she didn't.

"Four patrols of warriors and trained *Vorc* will outnumber your *Na'Hord*."

Arek's statement was as foreboding as the darkening clouds gathering in the south. Three mounts ahead, Oreese sat behind one of the other *Na'Reish*, his eyes closed, his concentration on calling his Gift. This far into the mountains, manipulating the weather could be a tricky undertaking, but she had confidence in the young man.

"Barrca isn't just checking the screes for safety," she replied. "There's a large slope just as we go through the pass that can be manipulated and set off into a landslide if need be."

Arek turned his head, his profile creased in a frown. "That scree has boulders, some the size of houses. I know *Na'Reish* are strong but I've never seen them shift rocks that large before."

Imhara chuckled. "Oreese and Atallie aren't the only Gifted amongst those here in the caravan. Maag is able to shift the ground and anything that comes from it, while Ayson is a siphon. He'll feed Maag the energy she needs to bring down the scree.

"She'll seal the pass completely, cutting us off from any *Na'Reish* incursion. They'll have to head north then venture through human territory to reach us from now on."

Riders swapped places with those on foot; only the children stayed on the beasts. After about twenty minutes, the temperature dropped and clouds covered the sun. Glancing along the southern slope of the mountain, she could see a curtain of rain heading for them. Moving fast.

She was on foot for a second time when fine droplets started hitting her face, and a shout came from the rear of the group. Lungs laboring in the thin air, her shirt now damp from a combination of sweat and drizzle, Imhara turned. She shivered, not just because of the drop in temperature or her wet shirt.

The first patrol had reached their rest site. Black-clad *Na'Hord* swarmed over the flat escarpment like honey-crawlers. Mounts were exchanged in an economy of motion. The lead riders headed up the sloping trail.

Light, they were at best ten minutes from catching them.

Water teemed down the rock faces and bare hill. One *Vorc* slipped, its claws scrabbled for purchase. The patrol took up a staggered formation, and the speed of their ascent slowed.

Gathering her breath, Imhara let loose a shrill whistle. At the head of their group, Rassan turned in the saddle. She pumped her fist twice and he acknowledged her signal with a wave.

Arek drew level with her. Sweat shone on his face, and his rain-wet hair stuck flat to his head. "We pick up the pace?"

Her smile was grim. "Yes." She wiped her face with her sleeve. "From now until we get through Skadda Pass."

As the sides of the mountain converged into a narrow corridor on the rock-strewn trail, Imhara enjoyed the relief it brought from being exposed to the edge of the storm. Rain only came in gusts instead of steadily. But entering the pass meant the incline flattened out, not quite as demanding on beasts or people. The call went down the line for riders to move three abreast, pulling the group in tight rather than spreading out along the trail.

Wind howled through the passage, whipping hair and clothes in all directions, sometimes strong enough to buffet those on their feet. It was fortunate the pass possessed two sides, rather than one and a sheer cliff face.

The caravan passed the scree, and Barrca and the other three *Na'Hord* rejoined them. As they did a distant howl carried on the breeze. Imhara glanced over her shoulder. Her blood ran colder than the snow on the far peaks.

Four *Vorc* with riders had entered the narrowed passage. As she watched, another three crested. Less than five minutes behind them.

"Maag! Ayson!" Barrca's bellow echoed back from the steep slopes.

The young *Na'Chi* woman and human man dropped back on their beast. Maag pointed to the scree, and the small group moved well back from the drop area.

Imhara heard the hiss of rain on rock before she felt it stinging her face.

"That's sleet!" Arek shouted, and flipped up the collar of his shirt to protect his skin.

Imhara grimaced and copied his action, squinting against the tear-jerking wind, trying to see how far ahead the lead riders were. One rider disappeared around a bend and her heart jolted.

They were almost through the pass.

Claws scrabbling on stone carried on the wind. More howls reverberated off the walls, amplified in the enclosed space. Imhara didn't dare look.

"Ride hard!" She sucked in deep lungfuls of air. "Run!"

Those closest did, urging others on foot ahead of them as they went. Some riders picked up a third passenger. Heart pounding in her chest, Imhara ignored the growing ache in the muscles of her legs and sides.

A Kaal Clan war cry split the air. A swift glance showed Barrca and another of her *Na'Hord* engaged in battle with the lead *Vorc-Rider*. Her gait faltered.

"Keep going!" Arek grasped her arm.

"They'll be overrun!" She gasped.

Steel on steel rang out.

Thunder rumbled so hard the ground seemed to shift beneath her foot. Then, as small rocks and pebbles danced on the ground in front of her, she realized it had.

Another swift glance and a mass of rock, slate gray, almost black from the rain and sleet, rolled down the mountainside, gathering speed and debris—bushes, shrubs, other boulders—with terrifying intensity. The sound of them smashing together grew to a deafening roar.

The ground heaved. A sharp crack split the air. An entire overhang collapsed behind the battle, blocking the passageway, stopping the main *Na'Hord* force from reaching them. Debris spewed upward and outward. The vibration rattled under the ground, up through her boots, and into her body.

As if the shelf of rock mimicked the release valve in a dam, another section of the mountain broke free close to the top of the scree, this one in direct line with Barrca and the others.

"*Light*, no!" Imhara tried to shout a warning to them. The terrifying rumble swallowed her hoarse scream.

The wall of rock skimmed the slope so fast it was like watching floodwater sweep into a crevice. Hideously black, bone-shattering, sudden death. It impacted the *Vorc-Riders*, Barrca, the other *Na'Hord*, Ayson, and Maag in less than a heartbeat.

Imhara's chest squeezed tight. She could feel but not hear herself screaming. More dust and debris exploded along the narrow corridor, rolling toward them in a suffocating wave.

Arek's arm hooked around her waist. "Down!"

She barely heard him as he pulled her to the far wall. Another upheaval. The earth fell out from beneath them. They hit the ground in a tangle of arms and legs.

Arek rolled her under him. He cradled her head to his chest. The pain in her shredded her heart.

Gone! Her people were gone!

She screamed.

And the world came apart around them.

Chapter 39

"We need to keep moving." Rassan's hoarse voice rose above the sound of people coughing, groaning in pain, or quietly grieving. "We're vulnerable here."

The clatter and smashing of rock drew terrified cries from the children and momentarily cut off the crying. The rattling died down.

The wind howled, a mournful sound as it forced its way over and around the new mountain of rock blocking the passageway behind them. There was no way anyone was going to be able to shift it or climb over it. The pass was permanently sealed.

Arek released a relieved breath and eyed the unstable slope. Anything could set off a new slide. Rassan was right. They needed to traverse the rest of the trail and clear the pass.

He winced as he pushed to his feet, his boots squelching in the fine mush of sleet and dust. The ice was quickly melting now that Oreese had stopped summoning the storm. Clouds were breaking up and being scattered by the mountain winds while the sun was pushing its way through them.

Arek rubbed at the tender spot on his thigh where he'd landed on a sharp rock when he'd taken Imhara to the ground. It was the worst of many aches bruising his body but not the worst injury sustained by the group huddled along the bend in the trail.

"Up! Everyone up!" The *Na'Chi* warrior kneed his mount along the ragged line of survivors. "Jawn, get these children back on their mounts. Anyone who's injured also needs to ride. Once we reach The Overhang, we'll stop and tend ourselves. Head them out!"

Rassan drew level with him. Dust had smeared to mud on the warrior's face. The garish mask of gray and black painted every face in the group. It coated hair and clothing, and even the animals' wool had changed color to a uniform ash gray.

"You all right?"

Arek nodded. "Sore but nothing serious. We were on the very edge of the rockslide. Thank the *Lady* for the wall we ended up against. It deflected the worst of the rubble over us. Most of the blood you can scent comes from minor cuts. Ricocheting debris."

"And Imhara?"

He glanced over his shoulder at the lone figure standing with her arms wrapped around her staring back at the blocked corridor. In the minutes after the ground had stopped shaking, when he'd realized he was still alive and not crushed under half the mountain, he'd been overwhelmed with relief to feel Imhara moving beneath him.

"Battered." The sound of her hoarse, gut-deep sobbing had pierced Arek all the way to his soul. He'd been unable to do anything but hold her until it eased. "Spirit more than body."

She hadn't spoken since the landslide, just taken up silent vigil at the edge, her gaze haunted, hollow, like her heart had taken the brunt of the slide.

He sucked in a shuddering breath and scrubbed a hand over his face, grimacing at the grit that came away and the sting of cuts yet undiscovered on his skin. "There's no chance anyone will be coming through Skadda Pass now."

No way Barrca or any of the others could have survived, either.

"The pass had to be closed." The *Na'Chi's* solemn gaze was tinged with a pale gray as he surveyed the damage. "Maag and Ayson spent weeks studying the scree. They knew exactly what they had to do and how far they should have been back, but I don't think they anticipated having to do it under the pressure they did. Yet, *Lady* bless them, they still made sure the pass was sealed." His mouth pulled down at the corners and he blinked hard, his voice rough and low as he spoke. "Barrca knew that. So did the others. It doesn't make their deaths any easier to accept, but I don't think any of them would regret their actions."

Arek swallowed several times to ease the tightness in his throat. His grief might not have the same depth as those around him, but the loss of six people he'd been getting to know still impacted.

"The *Lady* will guide them on their Final Journey." He drew in a steadying breath. "And we'll remember them in our hearts."

Rassan gave a tight nod. "We'll mourn them properly once we get home." Around them people were rising, their movements subdued, chatter hushed. The *Na'Chi* tilted his head in Imhara's direction. "Shall I get her?"

"No, I'll do it. You're going to have to lead these people for a while."

The warrior hesitated a moment, then sighed. "She'll try and take responsibility for this."

"I know." Arek knew the sickening sensation of watching friends die, and the aftermath of wondering if you could have done anything differently. His smile was more a baring of teeth than anything joyous. "Leave us a mount and we'll follow shortly."

Arek waited until the last of the group disappeared around the bend in the trail before walking back to Imhara. He took his time, the loose shale and other debris crunching underfoot. The way she still hugged her arms around her waist gave her a fragile appearance.

He knew she was strong, he'd seen her fortitude so many times in the last few weeks, yet now he saw no evidence of it in her bowed shoulders and head. And as he stepped around her, the expression on her face ripped at his innards.

Tear tracks sliced through the dusty mask on her cheeks; her violet gaze stared through him, raw with grief and pain.

She looked shattered.

"Imhara." Three times he called her name before drawing a response. Her brow furrowed and she blinked. "It's time to leave."

"Leave?" Her question was flat, lifeless, unlike the spark of dull anger in her violet gaze. It gave him hope. "We can't leave. What if"—her jaw flexed and she swallowed hard—"what if one of them is alive? We have to dig them out."

Moving to one side, he waved a hand at the massive pile of boulders and rock, some as large as a crofter's hut. "No one survived this, Imhara."

She hissed a curse, expression twisting, a flurry of guilt, anguish, and fury streaking across her face. It was better than the haunted look. She shook her head. "You don't know that for sure."

"Half a mountain came down. It could take weeks to find them." Arek ground his teeth together, hating he had to do this to her. "Time. Injuries. No food or water. Exposure to the elements. Take your pick. Do you think they'd survive any or all of those things?"

A whimper escaped her mouth before she could cover it. Her violet eyes welled with tears. Arek's throat closed over and he had to clear it twice before being able to speak.

"You've a group of people heading down the trail who need you more than ever." He gestured behind her. She shook her head again. "Focus on them, not the dead."

Beneath her dusty mask, Imhara's cheeks paled. "They shouldn't have died! Not like this!"

Another curse, this one aimed at him, then she struck out, a clenched fist that he blocked with his arm. Closing his hand around her wrist, he jerked her in against him. She pummeled him, a wild bout of struggling interspersed with punches and heated words.

Wrapping his arms around her halved the power behind them. Had she wanted to, she could have jerked free but she didn't. He took the impacts silently, knowing grief drove her and not any motive to cause him harm.

Gradually, her actions lost strength, the blows stopped, and she just stood inside his embrace, her whole body shaking.

Arek pressed his forehead against hers and smoothed a hand along her back. "The day I was captured by Meelar's raiders, my best friend and I were a part of a patrol attempting to rescue the crofters the slaver had taken from their village. Despite our best efforts, that rescue failed, and I watched my friend take a dagger in the side. The wound bled like yours. I don't know if he survived." He drew in a shuddering breath. "Do you know how many times I've replayed that memory? Or asked myself if I could have done something different to avoid it ever happening? You can't change what happened, Imhara."

"The hurt doesn't stop." Imhara's whisper-thin reply squeezed the heart in his chest.

"No, it doesn't, but you can always choose to hold on to something else to ease it."

"Like what?"

"Why do you think Barrca and the others stayed where they were in the pass, fighting the *Na'Hord* patrol and using their Gifts to create the slide?" he asked, softly. Her forehead rubbed against his as she shook her head. "They did it so others would know this. . . ."

He brushed his lips against hers, putting all his concentration into creating the softest of touches, letting her feel the heat of his heart and his strength.

"A kiss?" A whisper of sound against his lips, confused yet breathless.

"Life," he murmured. "Hope. Freedom. They stayed and fought

to give us all these things, Imhara. They believed in your dream, your parents' legacy."

She hiccupped, a half gasp, a half sob. Her hands fisted in his shirt as she seized onto the strength in his words. He held her against him, pain and joy mixing with equal intensity inside him as she leaned on him, in every sense of the word. A gentle heat burned close to his heart and spread outward with every beat.

A hollow grating and crack of rock against rock tumbling down the ruined scree reminded him they couldn't linger.

"Imhara, we have to go," he murmured. "It's not safe here."

She shuddered but nodded and let him lead her to the shaggy beast tethered along the trail. He helped her mount first, then swung up behind her, feeling the absence of her during those few seconds. But once settled he pulled her back in against him and took up the reins.

In his arms, Imhara turned and cast one last look at the landslide. Her throat worked, and her eyes still welled with tears, but her chin lifted.

"*Lady* bless your Journeys!" Her hoarse call echoed back off the walls of the pass. "The Kaal Clan lives because of you all!" She met his gaze then, chin trembling. A soul-deep weariness and sadness still shadowed it, but beneath it lay a spark of the strength he'd come to admire. "Let's go, Arek. Let's go home."

Chapter 40

FIVE days saw a new Kaal caravan on its way to human territory and Sacred Lake. During the first two days, Arek helped the Clan mourn and celebrate the lives of those who'd died on the mountain. The memorial ceremony was attended by every man, woman, and child in the Clan: *Na'Reish*, *Na'Chi*, and human.

On day three, the first early winter storm struck the lower reaches of the Skadda Mountains. Scouts sent out reported snowdrifts blocking the roadway to Whitewater River. The drifts melted within a day, but the warning was clear. If they didn't go soon, they ran the risk of being trapped in the fortress all winter.

The last few days were spent outfitting and organizing supplies and transport for a small mixed-race group of Gifted and non-Gifted to accompany Imhara across the border.

The morning of the journey, again everyone in the Clan turned out to see them off. With a feast being held the night before, farewells were brief, yet as Arek nudged the woolly sides of his beast with his knees and headed out after Imhara and Rassan, he could feel the hopes and excitement of the people standing on the walls and lining the roadway.

Arek's journey by boat on Whitewater River proved significantly different to his arrival so many weeks ago. Two days' travel downstream brought them to the landing at the very eastern tip of the Skadda Ranges. After a final night in Kaal territory, sleeping at the edge of the forest that bordered their land with the Southern Province, they crossed into human territory the following morning.

As if sensing his excitement at returning to familiar territory, the beast beneath Arek's knees snorted and shifted restlessly. Chuckling, he pulled the reins in tight and slapped its thickly muscled neck.

"Easy, we'll be moving in a moment, my friend," he murmured.

Until this moment he hadn't let himself consider the possibility of returning to Sacred Lake, but now excitement and impatience mixed with a healthy dose of nerves and uncertainty. So much waited at the end of this trip. Taking a deep breath, Arek schooled himself to patience.

The sun penetrated the canopy overhead, creating dappled shadows and warm patches amongst the undergrowth. Out of the foothills of the mountains, the trees here had yet to lose their leaves, the lingering warmer weather extending their season.

"Arek!"

Rassan's hail turned him in the saddle. The *Na'Chi* stood beside his mount, gesturing for him to join him and Imhara at the edge of the forest. The half-dozen others in the party also stood by their beasts, and the way they glanced between Rassan and Imhara warned him something was amiss.

Arek clucked his tongue and turned his mount in their direction. As he drew closer, he heard Rassan's frustrated growl. The *Na'Chi* dropped the reins of his beast and strode away from Imhara, a litany of ripe curses heating the air.

"Arek, see if you can talk some sense into her!" he growled and slapped his gloves against the side of his breeches.

Arek slid from the saddle. "What's going on?"

"Simple." She threw her pack over the back of the saddle and tied it off, her movements sharp, a scowl as dark as her Second's on her face. "I've just told Rassan that it will be only you and me completing this journey."

"What? Since when did our plans change?"

Imhara turned, her expression carefully composed, outwardly calm, but the fire in her gaze scorched them both.

"Since I decided the risks involved in this venture didn't justify placing another six people in jeopardy."

Rassan folded his arms. "I'm still waiting to hear the logic behind this decision."

"The odds of the Blade Council believing the word of a *Na'Reish* demon that our Clan means them no harm are slim." She tapped one of the saddle packs on her beast. The hollow thump indicated one of the precious Kaal journals lay within. "The words on these pages won't be enough to convince them. Savyr's death might have swayed them, but since we weren't successful in that little venture, I don't know if it's wise to take so many into human territory. Two can convey our request for a truce as well as eight."

"Arek told you they found evidence in their ancestors' journals about the Old Ways." The *Na'Chi* warrior sounded like he spoke through gritted teeth. "We're giving them more proof to examine. Arek's seen the Old Ways in action. He's a Light Blade warrior prepared to stand with you when you face their Council! How could they not listen and consider our proposal for a truce?"

Arek grunted and empathized with Rassan's frustration. Imhara's sudden change of heart didn't make a lot of sense except he'd seen the flicker of shadows in her gaze when she'd mentioned the word *risks.*

It also made her behavior in the days since returning to the fortress more comprehensible. Other than attending the memorial ceremony, Imhara had spent most of her time in the library.

Her daily ritual of visiting the inner barracks to mix with the new members of the Clan had been put off with the excuse the *Isha* humans weren't ready. Her attendance at training sessions had been equally as sporadic.

Without those clues, he'd have been as frustrated as Rassan seemed to be. It was unlike the *Na'Chi* not to pick up on Imhara's behavior. Perhaps the impact of Barrca's death affected and distracted him more than he was letting on.

Whatever the reason, dismissing three-quarters of the group and ordering them to return to the fortress was illogical. The people selected to accompany them had a wide range of Gifts and skills the Guild Masters would appreciate exploring.

Both Imhara and Rassan possessed details about the demon *Na'Hord* the Blade Council would need to know. Skadda Pass might be closed to Savyr's army, but there were other, less strategic places his forces could cross into human territory. Again knowledge either of them could share with the Council.

Arek released a soft sigh and tugged off his riding gloves. His mouth twisted wryly at the situation facing him now. Two months ago he'd have fought to the death to deny Imhara Kaal and her Clan access to human territory, now he had to convince her it was in everyone's best interest to go.

And the only way he was going to do that was to neutralize every excuse she offered. A sure way to rile her temper, but he preferred to see her fighting than giving up.

"Convincing the Blade Council of your sincerity isn't going to be easy." He tucked his gloves into his belt.

Imhara gave a sharp nod. "See, Rassan, Arek agrees with me."

The warrior fisted his hands, the leather of his gloves creaking. His scowl spoke volumes as his violet gaze pierced him.

Arek held up his hand. "Imhara, I don't agree with you. Not entirely. Trusting any *Na'Reish* is a huge thing to ask. You can expect a whole host of reactions similar to mine when we first met. But"—and here he paused to marshal his thoughts—"there's always the option of claiming sanctuary. As a Light Blade warrior, I can make the claim on your behalf, and when we reach Sacred Lake, we can approach the *Temple Elect* at the *Lady's* Temple. That will protect you all until the Blade Council can meet to hear your appeal.

"Don't forget though, the Kaal journals are compelling. After reading them, I know many of the events recounted by your ancestors correlate with the time line and versions I found in our past *Chosen*-leaders' diaries. Facts cannot be ignored. The current *Chosen* won't ignore them, nor will he let the Council ignore them."

Rassan's scowl eased.

"We might not have killed Savyr. However, the significance of Yur's death can't be dismissed." Arek allowed her to see his satisfaction. "We eliminated the *Na'Rei's* Second in Command. What sort of effect will this have on Savyr's plans? At the very least, it will take some time for him to mobilize his entire army, and he can't do it without a new Second. He's going to have to find a replacement, someone as loyal and trustworthy as Yur. Not an easy task, considering the politics and strategies his Commanders will employ as they attempt to earn his favor.

"And when you add in the Kaal journals and my firsthand account of living among your Clan, I guarantee you the *Chosen*, the *Temple Elect*, Annika, and a handful of the Councilors will listen."

Imhara raised an eyebrow. She strode toward him and grasped his wrist. Shoving his sleeve up his arm, she exposed the just-healed-over teeth marks and paler scars of past bites.

"You might be a Light Blade warrior, but these brand you as a blood-slave. You told me that humans doubt the word of one so afflicted because of the addiction they believe exists between demon and slave. What makes you think they'll take your word over that?" She dropped his arm and returned to stand near her mount. "We'll encounter a patrol just inside your border, they'll see those marks, and you could claim to be the brother of the *Chosen* himself and they wouldn't believe you. We'll be lucky to even see the walls of Sacred Lake!"

Arek almost laughed at her analogy. He considered Kalan as close as a brother.

"We'll see the inside of Sacred Lake, Imhara," he assured her, and tugged his sleeve back down over his forearm.

For a moment, he hesitated, knowing in his gut that sharing his identity would matter.

To the success of the plan.

To Rassan.

But especially to her.

If he'd spoken up sooner, perhaps during the preparation phase of this journey, it might have circumvented this situation.

Pulse beating harder, he locked gazes with her so she'd see the truth in his eyes, and he steeled himself for her reaction.

"I'm not the brother of the *Chosen*, Imhara, but you're close. I'm his best friend, and his Second in Command."

IMHARA'S head pounded as she stared at Arek, her blood heating fast. Her body though turned to ice.

I'm his best friend, and his Second in Command. His soft words replayed over and over in her head.

Arek was Urkan Yur's counterpart in the human world?

She swayed where she stood and reached out to grasp the edge of her saddle. Too little sleep and a rough boat ride of conflicting emotions over the last week made her head spin.

Both warriors started toward her, their expression reflecting their concern.

She widened her stance and waved off their assistance. "I'm fine."

She dragged in a deep breath. The clean, cinnamon scent surrounding Arek assured her he spoke the truth. She held on to her temper.

Just.

Why had he kept his identity from her for so long?

Did it matter?

That he had slashed at her like the edge of a knife blade. She thought they'd reached a level of trust that superseded keeping secrets from one another.

Inside her something snapped.

Her lips twisted. "*Light*, Arek, you seemed quite happy to jump into bed with me"—her insides felt as brittle as her tone—"but you couldn't find it in you to share your name and identity?"

Beneath his tan, Arek's cheeks flushed. Anger or embarrassment?

"Imhara!" Rassan's admonishment pricked at her conscience.

"What?" She stabbed a finger in Arek's direction. "Such a significant piece of information and he hides it from us until now. Rather convenient, don't you think?"

She gulped in a breath, uncaring that she sounded like a screeching *hobaan*. It was either that or give in to the aching hollowness inside her.

Her Second's brow pulled low. "Don't pretend he's lying when his scent tells you otherwise."

"Rassan, some of her anger is justified," Arek said, the skin around his mouth creasing as he grimaced.

She snorted. "Just some?"

He came at her slowly, every line in his body as tight as his expression. He stopped an arm's length from her, his twilight eyes narrowed, his smile grim.

"I could give you a list of reasons why I didn't tell you sooner, Imhara, but you already know what some are likely to be." She did, initial trust being high on that list. His words were calm but underlaced with steel. "I hurt you. Be angry with me. I'll bear it." He bared his teeth in a semi-smile. "But don't use this as an excuse to deny the others a chance to accompany you to Sacred Lake."

Imhara blinked, her anger stalling with his words. She swallowed hard and glanced away, not wanting him to know how accurate his assumption was.

"Now, let's deal with the real reason why you don't want them on this journey." Arek's voice gentled. She almost preferred the harder tone. It didn't grate as much over the rawness inside her. "Risking lives."

Light, she couldn't deal with this right now. She turned, gathering her reins. His hand caught her arm. The heat of him behind her, the scent of him surrounding her, the warmth of his touch immobilized her.

"Just say it out loud. Once. Keep it in and the fear will grow." The words were whispered in her ear.

Hushed. Private. Intended to be just between them, although Rassan's keen hearing had probably picked them up.

Arek's thumb smoothed over her inner forearm. "The Imhara Kaal I know wouldn't hide from this."

There was just enough taunting in his tone to stroke her temper. She fisted her hand, felt him shift his stance to intercept any blow she aimed at him. Instead, she turned her head, pulse pounding in her throat.

Arek's gaze never wavered from hers, radiating such strength she could almost feel it wrapping around her, holding her upright, daring her to use it to bolster her own. His compassion humbled her, and she blinked back tears at the way she'd lashed out at him.

Particularly with such a public display of asinine behavior.

It shamed her that she'd lost control like that. Her throat closed over and she swallowed hard.

"When is the price of a dream considered too high, Arek? How many have to die to achieve it?" She drew in a shuddering breath. "You can't guarantee their safety no matter who you know or your relationship with them."

This time his smile was warm and his hold on her arm gentled. "You're assuming they're not prepared to risk as much as you in this venture. Have you even asked for their opinion?"

Rassan appeared at the corner of her eye. "What we're doing is worth risking my life for, Imhara." His green-flecked gaze remained steadfast. "We can predict, and organize, and anticipate the risks until our minds turn to mush, but you can't let the fear of losing those you care about dictate your actions. To do that means condemning ourselves to living half a life." He glanced over to where the others waited. "Are you willing to do that, Jaclan?"

"No, Second."

"What about you, Channi?"

"No, Second."

Imhara closed her eyes as Rassan asked every member of the group the same question and received the same answer. She blinked hard several times, too overwhelmed by their support to speak.

Arek seemed to know though. His fingers interlocked with hers and squeezed. "You see, your Clan aren't going to let you take that risk alone," he murmured. "They've chosen to walk this journey with us."

"I suppose you'd all ignore my orders and follow me anyway?" Her raspy question incited a few chuckles. She dragged in another unsteady breath and nodded. Their support didn't banish her fear, but it did make it easier to endure. "All right. Then let's mount up and get moving."

Twigs and debris snapped underfoot as everyone moved at once, probably just in case she changed her mind. Imhara gave a wry smile.

As Arek tugged to free his hand, she gripped it harder. His twilight gaze met hers. "Join me on the ride? After I've apologized for my atrocious behavior, I'd like you to show me your homeland."

He lifted her knuckles to his lips. "Only if you'll accept the same from me."

Chapter 41

THE half-day ride through the forest brought back a multitude of memories for Arek and left him feeling like he'd been thrown back in time to the day of the botched rescue mission.

While they didn't pass through the same clearing where they'd ambushed the *Na'Reish* patrol, he found his thoughts dwelling on the battle and how the outcome could dictate what happened over the next few days.

Had his sacrifice saved Kalan, Varian, and his friends? If Kalan had died, his absence from the Blade Council could upset Imhara's plans for a truce in so many ways. Sanctuary would be needed more than ever if that were the case. Kymora could help them in her role as *Temple Elect*.

"Riders ahead!"

Jaclan's shout drew Arek from his reverie. Pulse leaping, he straightened in his stirrups and peered ahead through the trees, adrenaline already pumping in anticipation. He counted a dozen riders, all in armor.

"It's a patrol," he called. "Imhara, pull your cloak over your head, and don't remove it until I tell you to." He began unbuckling his sword belt. "Anyone with weapons, hang them on your saddle."

"This venture is now in your hands, Arek." Imhara tugged her hood up over her dark braid and low over her forehead. Excitement and trepidation glittered in her violet gaze. "*Lady* bless this meeting."

Arek was glad to see that their rocky start to the morning hadn't soured the trust between them. He nodded and sent his own prayer to *Her*, petitioning the same. "We'll stop in the next clearing and let them come to us."

The sight of a dozen of *Her* warriors astride their war-beasts, the sun emblem etched into their armor, had Arek's breath catching in his throat. The familiar sight set his pulse pounding. The sensation of being home was almost overwhelming.

The patrol spread out and encircled them. A single rider, farther afield, weaved his way through the trees, looking for any sign of ambush. Standard tactics. A shrill whistle assured the Light Blades no such trap was pending.

As the riders converged on their position, Arek raised his hands in a nonthreatening gesture.

"*Lady's* blessing to you!" he called. "As you can see there are *Na'Chi* people among this group. Our weapons are on our saddles. Which of you is the Commander of this patrol?"

"I am." The warrior astride a brown-coated war-beast spoke up. "Commander Erron Sahn."

Arek didn't know the man or the name. With over ten thousand Light Blades scattered across six provinces, he hadn't expected to recognize him. His paler skin suggested maybe he came from somewhere in the High-Ranges Province. A winter rotation serving in Sacred Lake was probably a relief considering the icy weather in the mountains.

"Commander, my name is Arek Barial, and I'm a Light Blade warrior like yourself. I'm travelling with this group of people to Sacred Lake to meet with the Blade Council. . . ."

"Arek?" His name was uttered in a startled voice. A rider, the one who'd checked for an ambush, kneed his animal forward.

Arek grinned at the familiar voice. "Zaune?"

Beneath the leather helmet, dark spots trailed down either side of the warrior's tanned face. Light violet eyes met his, shock reflected in his lean features.

The young *Na'Chi* scout leapt from his beast, his astonished expression so unlike his usual stoic demeanor. "You're supposed to be dead!"

His accusatory tone made him chuckle.

"I'm very much alive."

"How? We searched for days and eventually found a body. It was so badly mauled. . . ." A frown marred his brow. "But he wore your amulet!"

Yenass. The farmer who'd sacrificed his life to save his. A pang of regret surged through Arek.

"You know this man, Zaune?" Sahn glanced between the two of them, his sandy brows veeing low.

"I do, Commander. He was . . . I mean . . . is Second Barial."

Light blue eyes flickered over him. "Commander Tayn's former Second in Command?"

Arek jerked at the information. He should have expected to hear that he'd been replaced, especially as everyone had assumed him dead. But it was disconcerting to realize life had moved on without him.

He shifted from one boot to the other. Who had taken on his command? And what about Kalan? Was he still alive?

Sahn flung his leg over the saddle and joined Zaune on the ground. "Apologies, we've never met, but I've heard about you."

Arek clasped his outstretched forearm, relieved to have his identity confirmed by the young *Na'Chi*. And while his unexpected appearance no doubt raised a thousand questions—he had a few of his own—they would have to wait.

"Commander, on my oath as a Light Blade warrior, I swear to you these people come in peace." Arek half turned and nodded to

Imhara. She stepped forward, pushing back the hood of her cloak. "This is *Na* Imhara Kaal, leader of the *Na'Reish* Clan Kaal, and she seeks a truce with the Blade Council. . . ."

The rest of his words were drowned out as the Light Blades reacted. Every one of them, including Zaune, drew their swords. In a heartbeat the air around them radiated with a mix of fear and outrage.

Imhara's swift intake of breath had him moving to cover her, hands raised high.

"She's unarmed." No way in *Light* was he letting them harm her. He sought out the *Na'Chi's* gaze. "Zaune, you're the best tracking scout among the *Na'Chi*. You can scent her . . . me. Do I lie?"

"Zaune?" Sahn never took his gaze off Imhara.

"It's the truth, Commander." The young scout moved among their group, scenting them, the flecks in his eyes a pale bronze. "There are other *Na'Chi*, human, and *Na'Reish* among the rest of them. None of them scent as hostile."

Sahn's light gaze pierced his. "Show me your arms, slowly."

Arek pushed up his sleeves, knowing what the Commander was looking for and would find. The warrior at least hid his disgust behind an impassive mask, unlike some of his men. Arek heard Zaune's breath catch.

"Blood-slave!" someone hissed.

"Light Blade or not, Barial, your word holds little worth with those marks on your arm," Sahn stated, mouth stretching out in a flat line. "It's a risk I can't take."

"Then I claim sanctuary for these people. That's something you can't ignore, Commander." Arek kept his voice even, calm.

"You can't give sanctuary to demons, Commander!"

The sandy-haired warrior shot a quelling glare at the man who'd voiced a protest, then his gaze took in each member of the Kaal Clan.

"Sanctuary was never intended for demons, Barial, but there are humans and *Na'Chi* among these people. I can't ignore that."

Arek released a relieved breath. At least he was a Commander who thought before he acted.

"Perhaps it's best then that the Blade Council deal with you." Sahn gave a curt nod. "Sanctuary will be temporarily honored."

"There's a lot to explain, and whether you believe me or not, these people come in peace," Arek repeated. Then because he couldn't resist asking, "Zaune, is Kalan alive?"

"Yes." The warrior's dark brows lifted. "That's right. You wouldn't know. Varian got us all back to the city. It took Annika awhile, but she healed him."

"Thank the *Lady*." His whole body tingled with the news that his friend lived. "Commander Sahn, *Na* Kaal has information about *Na'Rei* Savyr that the Blade Council and the *Chosen* need to know."

The older man's mouth curled. "A demon turning on one of their own?"

Light, once he'd sounded so hostile. How strange it was to be seeing his countrymen through new eyes.

"My Clan have never considered themselves part of the *Na'Reish* nation, Commander Sahn." Imhara's soft-spoken comment caught the Light Blade Commander by surprise. "I may be of *Na'Reish* blood, but we honor the Old Ways and the *Lady*." She held out her hands. "But if it would ease your fears, tie me. Bind us all. I just ask that you let the Blade Council deal with us."

Arek waited as Commander Sahn considered his decision. When he nodded, a half-dozen warriors dismounted and advanced with rope. Another Light Blade gathered their weapons and checked their packs for others.

Warriors escorted each of them to their mounts but none were given the reins to them. Arek met Imhara's gaze between the bodies separating them. Her lips curved in a small, nervous smile. He returned it.

Sahn swung up into his saddle. "We head for Sacred Lake, double-time!"

SACRED Lake was a large stone-walled city surrounding a lake. Mountains created a jagged line on the horizon behind it, but what struck Imhara was the open expanse of the plateau. She'd never seen anything like it before. Not only did it leave her feeling exposed and vulnerable as the group made its way toward the city, it was obvious there was no way anyone could approach the high walls from any direction without being seen.

The group passed through the gates with minimal delay, yet the scrutiny Arek had warned her about began once they were inside. The Light Blades in the towers and manning the gates were more controlled than those they passed in the streets.

When they saw her, they made no effort to conceal their unease and fear, and the stench of it assaulted her nostrils. Some even took to hurling abuse their way. No one objected.

She kept her head high and did her best to ignore the slurs, reminding herself there were justifiable reasons for them hating the *Na'Reish.* This might be bad, but instinct told her it could be much worse.

Instead Imhara tried to concentrate on her surroundings. The buildings and houses held a vague familiarity but were different enough in design and variation that she felt their alienness.

That combined with the crowd's hostility left her feeling out of place. A demon among humans. A first for her, considering her upbringing.

By the time the patrol reached a small compound, a large crowd followed them, and she was glad the Light Blade patrol accompanied them.

A warm leg brushed hers and she tore her gaze away from the crowd to find Arek riding beside her.

"I told you you'd see the inside of Sacred Lake." A smile accompanied his lighthearted tone.

"This isn't quite like I expected," she admitted.

"The Light Blades won't let them harm you. Any of you." His knee bumped hers again, a reassuring touch she welcomed. "Nor will I."

His fierce words warmed her from the inside out. They strengthened her and held back the uncertainty and doubt beginning to gnaw at her innards.

Their beasts were led through a double-gated archway into an open, hard-dirt-packed courtyard.

Arek pointed with his chin, his smile growing wider. "This is the Light Blade compound."

The pleasure and pride in his tone reminded her that this was his home, the place he'd been born and raised by his grandfather, then trained as a Light Blade. But other than that, she knew very little about him or his past.

As Arek briefly explained each building and its purpose, the noise of the main crowd was left behind outside the walls. The one gathering inside the compound was smaller and consisted mainly of Light Blades and people all dressed in monotone clothes, mostly green. Surprise and satisfaction rushed through her to see a few *Na'Chi* among the faces peering up at them.

"Arek! By the *Lady*, it's Arek!" The deep, booming voice came from a barrel-chested Light Blade warrior, a human easily in his sixth decade with a face as brown as a nut, a stark contrast to his silver gray hair. He wore practice leathers and a Light Blade amulet.

Arek twisted in his saddle, a broad grin wreathing his features. "Yevni!"

"*Lady's Breath*, everyone thinks you're dead!" People moved aside as the huge man ploughed his way through the crowd toward them.

"So I've been told."

The older man reached the barrier of patrol riders. He raised a beefy hand. "No doubt I'll hear your story soon." He gestured forward with a grin. "I believe word might have just reached the *Chosen* of your arrival. *Merciful Mother*, it's good to have you home again!"

"It's good to be home, Yevni!" The hoarse note in Arek's tone backed up his words.

Imhara peered ahead to see a wide pathway bordered with a garden on one side and formal arrangements of monoliths at even intervals on the other. Behind it and to the left stood a three-story building, and coming down the stairs at a rapid pace were a handful of people.

"Kalan!" Arek's cry was filled with a wealth of emotion.

He dismounted, boots thudding on the ground as he landed, and tried to push his way through the ring of riders. A sharp order from a tall, dark-haired man dressed in fine clothes opened a gap.

Arek shouldered through and the two men stood eye to eye, one grinning widely, the other sporting a conflicting expression of shock and emerging joy. The dark-haired man freed Arek's hands of the rope with a disgusted curse, then embraced him in a back-pounding hug.

"Arek! I didn't believe it when the messenger arrived from the city gate."

So, this was Kalan Tayn, leader of the humans and Arek's best friend.

"You look well." Green eyes travelled over every inch of Arek and he shook his head. "*Lady's Breath*, we all thought . . ."

"I was dead." Laughter rumbled up from Arek's chest. "I know. It's a long story, my friend, one I'll share with you all shortly."

A woman with long, blond hair and *Na'Chi* markings stood quietly beside Kalan, the folds of her pale blue dress clutched in one hand.

Annika Gannec.

Imhara shared a look with Rassan. His intent expression told her he also recognized Savyr's daughter. Imhara wondered if the young woman would remember them. They'd met only a handful of times, usually at one of Savyr's dinners, and those occasions hadn't been pleasant for the *Na'Chi* woman.

Arek turned to Annika, and for the longest moment, he stared at her. Imhara could see only his side profile but it was enough to monitor his expression. The creases furrowing his brow hinted at his regret, and the white lines around his mouth betrayed his pained uncertainty.

"It's good to see you, Annika." His voice was hoarse.

The startled expression on Annika's face made Imhara smile. Clearly it wasn't the greeting she'd expected.

Arek took a small step closer to her. "I'm sorry . . . for what Davyn did to you, and for my behavior as well. It's a little late, but I'm just glad for the chance to apologize to you." His throat worked. "To my sister."

He leaned forward to whisper something more to her. Whatever he said widened her eyes, then brought tears to them. Her lips pressed shut and she blinked hard to repress them. When he placed a hand on her shoulder, the tears began to tumble down her cheeks.

Arek hesitated a moment, then gathered her into an awkward hug, one hand smoothing over her back. Imhara's throat closed over, for the moment was a poignant one. He'd made the first, very important step in connecting with Annika. Imhara released a soft sigh, her heart warming at the strength he showed even in such a vulnerable moment.

A woman with long, black hair clutching a staff in one hand and the arm of another *Na'Chi* male arrived at the back of the small group. After a minute of watching her navigate the crowd of people, Imhara realized she was blind.

Her arrival gave both Arek and Annika a distraction.

"Kymora!" Arek caught the woman up in a tight hug and swung her around, laughing as hard as she was crying.

"*Merciful Mother!*" As he set her down, the woman swiped at her tears with a sleeve, then ran her hands over Arek's face, her fingertips tracing his brow, his nose, his cheeks, then his jaw. "It is you!"

Imhara stiffened at the familiarity of her actions. Who was she and what did she mean to Arek?

"Varian?" The woman reached behind her, her fingers brushing the sleeve of a tall, broad-shouldered *Na'Chi* with an ugly scar on one cheek. Dressed in practice leathers, the warrior caught her hand and tucked her in against him in a move that clearly indicated the two were close, perhaps mates. It eased Imhara's concern. "Varian, thank the *Lady*, Arek's home."

Imhara scrutinized the warrior more closely. This was Arek's *Na'Chi* friend, the one they owed for helping start the change, for helping him adjust and accept demon-blooded friends. For several heartbeats the two men eyed each other off as if neither could believe they stood facing one another again.

"Zaune tells me you saved Kalan's life. Thank you." Arek's smile grew and he thrust out his arm. "You have no idea how many nights I spent wondering if you'd all made it home safe. Thank the *Lady* you did."

More back-slapping hugs and questions bombarded Arek from all directions. The babbling of voices rose and fell as Imhara took her time dismounting, unwilling to interrupt Arek in what was a highly emotional reunion for them all.

The scents pouring off the people in front of and around him were a mixture of elation, shock, excitement, and stunned disbelief. Yet it was clear these people were his family in every sense of the word. She could see it in their faces, their gestures, their words, all reinforced by their scents.

Arek's blond head lifted and his gaze scanned the pathway. When he found her, he gripped the *Chosen's* shoulder.

"Kalan, there's some people I'd like you to meet."

His friend glanced in their direction, his features smoothing out into something more serious, even a little guarded, when he saw them. The warmth surrounding Arek seemed unlikely to include them. Not that Imhara resented the lack, but it did reinforce the fact their trust would be hard earned.

Arek's hand tightened on Kalan's shoulder and he murmured something too quiet for Imhara to hear above the noise around her.

Rassan moved closer to her, his scent heavy with wariness, as Kalan and Arek crossed the wide pathway. Kalan's green eyes noted his movement, and one eyebrow quirked. A flash of gold at his neck drew Imhara's gaze down to an amulet etched with a sun in the center.

The *Lady's* symbol.

A Light Blade amulet.

Kalan Tayn was a Light Blade warrior as well as the *Chosen*.

"*Na* Kaal." The strong odor of cloves accompanied his greeting. Curiosity generated his scent when she'd expected the sourness of hatred and fear. Perhaps he was just better able to control his emotions than his warriors. "The *Lady* welcomes those who come in peace to our city."

His odor changed slightly, deepened, the subtlest of warnings underlying his words. Curious he may be, but there was little doubt he'd take action if he thought she deceived him.

"*Her* blessings upon your House and family, *Chosen*." Imhara inclined her head. "I do come in peace. You have my *Lady*-sworn oath on that."

Whispers began around them centered on her use of their religious deity. Blasphemy. Scandalous. Shocking. All words she heard but ignored. Kalan's gaze took in the crowd. His lips thinned.

"This isn't a discussion to hold here, *Na* Kaal. Commander Sahn, if you would escort them all to Arek's apartment and the adjoining quarters, then stay with them." His gaze locked with hers. "Arek has requested sanctuary on your behalf, *Na* Kaal. Until we hear his full story and yours, this is a temporary privilege, one I'll honor, unless you or any of your people endanger mine. As you're the first *Na'Reish* in five hundred years to walk within the walls of Sacred Lake, I'm sure you appreciate the latitude you're being given."

Well aware of the significance of his gesture, Imhara nodded. "I certainly didn't expect this, *Chosen*. On behalf of my Clan, you have our thanks."

She'd been fully prepared to spend her time as their prisoner, not given the rights of a guest. Light Blade warriors might guard them, but there was respect and generosity in his gesture, something she truly appreciated.

"I'd ask that you and your people remain inside the rooms, for your own safety, until the Blade Council can be informed of your arrival. As soon as we've convened, I'll ask Commander Sahn to accompany you to the Council chamber where you can present your case." The man turned to his friend. "As much as I'd like to spend some time catching up with you, the news of Savyr's growing army holds greater importance, and I need to speak to my Commanders."

Arek clasped Kalan's arm tightly. "Try and join us later."

"Perhaps Kymora, Varian, or even Annika might visit you all while I contact the Councilors?"

Another unexpected action. Imhara couldn't hide her surprise.

Was this a show of trust? A test? Or both? Whatever the case, it wasn't an opportunity to be missed.

Arek was watching her, a relaxed smile on his face. "I think Imhara and the others would like that very much, Kalan."

"Indeed." Imhara felt the cautious stirrings of hope. "We'd welcome the chance to get to know Arek's friends and kin."

Chapter 42

"I always wondered why, of all the Clan *Nas* invited to my father's feasts, you never took part in his games." Annika appeared at Imhara's side carrying two cups, and held out one to her. "I don't think I ever heard you make a cruel comment, and I know you didn't torment me physically."

The quiet comment drew Imhara's attention away from observing those gathered in Arek's apartment. There were two separate groups, one seated at the large wooden table, the others in chairs by the great fireplace at the far end of the room.

"Now you know why." Imhara took the cup with a nod and met the *Na'Chi* woman's violet gaze. "My only regret was in not being able to help you."

"I don't know that I'd have trusted you even if you had offered it." A wry smile curved her lips. "Your reputation was . . . intimidating."

"A necessity."

"Yes. Survival is a great motivator." A sad smile curved her lips. "The Old Ways. There's so much we have to learn, isn't there? At least now we know it's possible."

Imhara shot her a sideways glance. "What you've heard and seen tonight is only a sample. We have much more to share." She was heartened they'd shown such interest, especially when she'd expected much worse. "I won't withhold this knowledge based upon a favorable Blade Council decision."

"Such an un-*Na'Reish*-like attitude." A self-depreciating laugh accompanied a shake of her head. "I shouldn't be one to judge, should I?"

"There are centuries of history and fears to overcome." Imhara tilted her head. "I didn't expect this level of acceptance in anything we had to share."

"You have an ally in Arek," Annika countered. "Do you realize how unique that is?"

During the last couple of hours, she'd learned more about Arek's past just listening to him interact with his friends than in all the time he'd spent with her Clan, but the core of who Arek was remained the same.

"He's a warrior of strong convictions. Loyalty and doing what is right is important to him." Imhara set her cup down on the nearest table. "Even if it means going against what he was brought up to believe."

"He told you about Davyn?"

Imhara nodded. Annika grunted softly and for a few moments neither of them spoke. The *Na'Chi's* pensive expression deepened, and Imhara waited, the quiet chatter of other conversations drifting around them.

When Annika finally looked up, the flecks in her eyes were a solid green, and a strong citrus odor deepened her scent.

"After Arek found that one reference to our shared history, Kalan ordered a thorough search of every history annal and journal in our library." One side of her mouth quirked upward. "We haven't found anything as rich or in depth as your ancestors' journals, just snippets and ambiguous references . . . but in order to make the alliance between the *Na'Chi* and humans work, Kalan knew we needed information."

"To convince your Council it could succeed?"

"Some of them," she conceded. "Mostly it was to counteract misinformation spread by the rebels." Here she took a deep breath. "But we also needed more information about ourselves. The *Na'Chi* have struck several problems, mostly to do with feeding or controlling our Gifts. . . ." Her gaze flickered to Varian. "There's a lot we don't know about ourselves."

"As I said, we'd be happy to share information and this includes with the *Na'Chi*."

"You have been so helpful already." Relief took the edge of Annika's tension. "Do you realize how relieved I was to hear the truth about blood-addiction?"

Arek had been the first to broach the subject of blood-slaves. Imhara had wondered at his reason for starting with such a tension-filled topic until Annika began asking questions.

"Ahh, feeding and blood-bonding." She smiled. "Rest assured, from your description about what's happened between you and Kalan, you've bonded. You may never be able to survive drinking just animal blood again, but it is not the curse you've been brought up to believe. It's one of the greatest blessings our *Lady* can bestow upon us."

Annika chuckled with more warmth this time. "And here I thought Candra's teaching accounted for the improvement in my healing Gift."

"An experienced tutor helps focus your Gift," Imhara agreed, "but the stronger the connection between mates, the more the Gift develops. Every bonding is different, but the journey can be incredibly exciting to watch and, in your case, experience."

"I am indeed blessed." She glanced to where Kalan sat.

Her eyes glittered with joy and love, and her smile, so filled with happiness, felt almost too intimate to be observing. A twinge of envy streaked through Imhara.

She sought Arek out and found him watching her. The glimmer in his gaze warmed her from the inside out, the sensation as good as, if not better than, a smile.

"*Her* plans for us all continue to surprise me." Annika hesitated a moment, then she nodded to herself. "A word of advice about the Council meeting tomorrow, Imhara. Open negotiations by announcing your intention to share all information freely, regardless of their decision concerning your petition, and you'll put a dent in any preconceptions about your Clan.

"Arek's advocacy will come as a surprise to some on the Blade Council, and it's likely to stir things up, but every Councilor knows him. There's no greater catalyst than seeing someone you know, who once opposed the *Na'Reish*, now supporting them.

"With the information about Savyr's *Na'Hord*, we're going to need your help whether some of the Councilors believe it or not." Her soft comment vibrated with a wealth of emotion. "Even though acceptance of them is a gradual process, the *Na'Chi* have made a huge difference already, and to survive a war with the *Na'Reish*, the Old Ways need to be resurrected and fast."

"Thank you. I'll take your advice."

Annika shook her head. "I should be the one thanking you."

"What for?"

"For bringing Arek home." She gestured to where he sat with Kalan, Varian, and Kymora in front of the fire. All were deep in conversation. "Losing him was a huge shock. Kymora and Kalan grew up with him. So many others grieved the loss of a friend or warrior they respected."

Annika bit her lip.

"And even though we barely knew each other, Arek and I are blood-kin. After finding out about his death, I felt cheated at having lost him so soon. We never got the chance to know one another, and

Davyn refused to speak to me about anything. So to have Arek back, and in our lives again . . . there aren't words enough to express our appreciation."

"There's nothing more important than family, Annika." Imhara reached out to grasp her arm and squeezed gently. "I think you'll find Arek feels the same as you. Shall we go join them?"

"UNFORTUNATELY I was never privy to any of Savyr's latest war plans." Imhara's gaze swept over each of the ten Councilors gathered around the wooden table in the middle of the Blade Council chamber. "I can only presume he felt there was no need to inform me as I would no longer be *Na* following the Enclave because of my enforced mating."

Ignoring the lone seat meant for her on this side of the table, she leaned over the map spread across the top of it. A quick look and she tapped five locations with her finger.

"These positions are where Savyr will most likely cross into human territory."

A silver-haired man with the broad-shouldered build of a warrior sat across from her. He grunted.

"What makes you so sure?" Brawny arms crossed over his chest. "We want to be certain before we commit patrols or any significant force to a confrontation."

"Councilor Witham raises a valid point, *Na* Kaal." Kalan rose from his chair and rounded the end of the table to stand by her shoulder. He bent to study the map. "Is there no other way through the Skadda Mountains?"

"Winter or summer, the range is a natural barrier to any incursion. It's part of the reason we've been able to keep our double life secret for so long. With only one way in and out, the inaccessibility and isolation has made any party easy to monitor and track. By sealing the pass permanently, it forces Savyr north, and if you look at the map, Whitewater Crossing is the first logical location to cross into human territory."

Councilor Witham issued a grunt. "Whitewater Crossing lies within Kaal territory."

"It does." More than aware of his unspoken question, Imhara met his gaze head-on. "Savyr could use that point to launch attacks against either of us, so it makes sense that we defend it."

The woman dressed in Healer green leaned forward in her chair. "But it would be easier to do so if Light Blade patrols worked with you rather than against you?"

Imhara inclined her head. "Of course it would, Councilor Candra."

A Light Blade entering through the large, wooden doors interrupted their discussion. The young woman paused a respectful distance from the table.

"Your pardon for this intrusion, Councilors, *Temple Elect*." In her hand she held a wax-sealed parchment. "*Chosen*, I have a message for you from Commander Onson."

"Thank you." Kalan took the missive.

With a bow the Light Blade took her leave.

"Go on, *Na* Kaal," Kalan prompted, tucking the message into his belt. "You mentioned several other locations?"

"The next two are places where Whitewater River widens. It becomes shallow enough for an army to cross. The remaining locations, while far north, give Savyr access to villages within a couple of days' ride of the border. Blood-slaves will be easier to procure from these remote places than those closer and more easily defended."

Imhara hesitated before voicing her final insight. She straightened, and inhaled deeply, testing the air. There was little to no sourness tainting the air. Instead a a citrusy anticipation exuded from Kalan.

She pointed to the final place on the map and ran her fingernail east. "If Savyr chooses to go north, then he also has a clear run at Sacred Lake if he comes via the Western Isle and across the plains."

From the startled looks on several Councilors' faces, Imhara knew they hadn't anticipated that strategy. Kalan, Witham, and Benth had, if their somber expressions were anything to go by.

"Savyr has an army fifteen thousand strong the last time I saw it," she stated. "Even replacing Yur, it would take twelve days for this army to reach the nearest crossing point and invade human territory."

"Twelve days!" The lean-faced Councilor to Imhara's left was visibly shaken. His pale gray gaze widened. "But it's been just a week since you fled the Enclave! He could be halfway to our border by now!"

"We have to send out messengers and recall every Light Blade." The only other woman on the Council clasped her hands so tightly her gnarled knuckles turned white. "We have to be prepared!"

Several others voiced their agreement and began listing off tasks needing to be completed.

"Twelve days minimum, Councilors." Imhara broke in over the top of the chatter. "I quote that as an estimate only so you understand one possible time frame. However, I doubt the *Na'Rei* will move that quickly. Finding a successor for Yur will take time. Savyr will not want just anyone as his Second."

"How much time?" Candra asked, her dark eyes solemn.

"Yur's death is a blessing in disguise." Annika shifted in her seat, a grim smile lifting the corners of her mouth.

"The *Na'Rei* needs to find a loyal supporter." Imhara met Annika's gaze and nodded. "Not an easy task with a den full of ambitious Clan Commanders vying for the position."

"Cutthroat politics," Annika muttered.

Imhara's grin held little warmth. "That's an accurate description."

"So this should buy us some time," Kalan mused. His statement lightened the bitter odor of fear in the room. "Let's take a break. We've covered a lot of ground so far. When we return, I'd like to talk to your Gifted Clan members, *Na* Kaal."

Heavy satisfaction saturated Kalan's scent, as if he were pleased with the reaction her information had provoked. Imhara wondered at the timing of the recess break. She glanced once more at the map, then the Blade Councilors.

Some were already talking amongst themselves, mostly about the threat of Savyr's imminent invasion. Was Kalan giving them time to deliberate about the actions that needed to be taken?

Shooting him a sideways look, she discovered him watching her. One dark eyebrow arched. She blinked.

Outnumbered by the *Na'Hord*, his Light Blades would need all the help they could get. With the variety of skills the Gifted members of her Clan could provide, his request to speak to some of them became clear.

Imhara almost smiled.

"I'll let the others know you'll be needing them shortly." Stepping back from the table, she gave a half bow. "They'll be ready to answer any of your questions, *Chosen*."

Chapter 43

AREK paced the length of the rug in the center of the main room in his apartment, his mood as somber and anxious as the Kaal Clan members gathered there with him. Taking her ancestors' journals with her and accompanied by several Light Blades, Imhara had left the apartment over an hour ago to meet with the Blade Council.

Needing fresh air, he headed out onto the balcony and leaned on the low wall looking out over the compound, taking in but not really seeing the training session going on over at the parade grounds.

His request to attend the meeting with Imhara had been denied. Considering the importance of the information, Arek wanted to be there so the Council could understand the significance of what Imhara had sacrificed to get it. His deepest fear was that they wouldn't see past her *Na'Reish* heritage.

The irony of what he felt wasn't lost on him. Kalan had to have experienced the same fears and range of emotions for Annika as he did for Imhara.

"You're worried." Rassan's deep-voiced comment came from the doorway behind him. "Should I be concerned for the safety of my *Na*, Light Blade?"

"Concerned?" Arek straightened and turned to face the *Na'Chi* warrior. "No. Sanctuary has been granted. Imhara is safe."

"Then why does your scent reek of apprehension?"

"I hoped to sit in on the Council meeting with each of you, but I've been denied permission."

"Why?"

"My friendship with three of the Councilors is no secret." He shrugged. "I'm guessing Kalan is trying to give the impression of impartiality."

"Your *Chosen* seems like a fair man." Rassan strode over to join him at the wall. "I was impressed with the way he questioned and listened during our conversations yesterday when your friends visited. They all seemed open to what we had to say."

Arek nodded. "Annika and the *Na'Chi's* arrival at Sacred Lake helped open a lot of people's minds. The simple fact is we need to change if we're to survive in this war against the *Na'Reish*. But more than that, we need people who are willing to initiate it, not just be led along. Kalan made changes on the Council to try and do that, but it's still a long journey."

In the short time he'd been absent from the city, a lot had changed. Kymora stepping down as *Temple Elect* had shocked him, and to hear she'd suffered at the hands of rebels left him furious. Yet her ordeal and the *Na'Chi's* role in her rescue had created a greater acceptance of the half-bloods. That and the decline in the rebel movement gave him hope for the outcome of the Blade Council.

"What do you plan to do now that you're home?"

Arek shot a sideways glance at the warrior, more for the neutral tone he used than the question he'd asked. It wasn't like him to be indirect. "Speak plainly, Rassan."

Violet eyes flecked with green met his. "Will you stay and resume your life as a Light Blade?"

Arek stared down at his boots, brow creased as he considered the question. Honestly, he hadn't thought past surviving the Enclave, then getting the Kaal to Sacred Lake.

He could imagine settling back into the ranks of the Light Blades; it was what he knew. His passion for serving the *Lady* remained, and *She* would always play a central role in his life, but the motivation driving him had changed.

In some ways he was like Kymora. His focus had altered. For the better.

While some of his transformation could be attributed to Annika and the other *Na'Chi*, much of it could be accredited to Imhara. She'd unveiled the last of the lies controlling his life, then cared enough to lend him her strength to piece it back together.

"I don't know." And that was the *Lady*-spoken truth. It felt odd admitting that. "Being a Light Blade is my calling, but I suppose it depends on the outcome of the meeting. If the Council agree to the truce, I think I'd like to return with you to Kaal Fortress, to help ensure the transition."

For the first time, he wanted more than a life of fighting and serving others. He wanted Imhara involved in it.

"So you would return out of duty to your people? Not because of Imhara?"

Arek grunted at his directness and scuffed a boot on the flagstone. He didn't know if he was ready to have this conversation.

"I haven't really thought about this, Rassan."

A deflection at best, and a sidelong glance assured him he hadn't fooled or deterred Rassan.

"You've thought about it enough to bed her. A huge leap from wanting her dead." The *Na'Chi* tilted his head, arms folding. "And I haven't seen her with a lover in five years, so she cares for you, Light Blade."

The words pricked at Arek. His stomach clenched. Well, he had asked for directness.

Neither he nor Imhara had discussed their relationship. Not the longevity of it, or any commitment beyond the moment. It was probably a backward way to go about conducting themselves, but then nothing in their relationship had been normal.

At least, not for him.

And despite the warrior's assurances Imhara cared for him, discussing their relationship without talking to her first didn't seem right, yet Rassan deserved some sort of an answer.

"If you want to know if I have feelings for her, yes, I do. But if you want me to explain them, I can't."

It was the best he could do.

"Matters of the heart aren't easy to define." Rassan's dark lips curved at the edges. "Yet judging by your scent, your heart already knows what it wants."

His *scent*.

Arek's head snapped up. "What's that supposed to mean?"

"You'll figure it out." The warrior's smile widened. "Eventually."

Arek was about to demand he explain when footsteps sounded from inside the room.

Jaclan appeared in the doorway. "Arek, there's a Light Blade at your door asking for you on behalf of someone called Davyn."

"My grandfather?" Arek glanced to Rassan. Their conversation wasn't finished. He wanted to know what the *Na'Chi* meant by his last comment, but he also wanted to see Davyn. There were questions he wanted to ask. "I need to see him."

The warrior nodded. "Then go see your kin, Arek. I'll let Imhara know where you've gone when she returns."

"SO, you've risen from the dead."

The raspy growl came from somewhere to Arek's left and held a familiar sharpness that never failed to grate against his nerves. He stood in the doorway, waiting for his eyes to adjust from stepping into a darkened building from direct sunlight.

"Word travels fast in this compound," he replied, his tone as dry as Davyn's. The Light Blade who'd accompanied him to the prison beneath the barracks remained outside with those on guard. "Especially to places you least expect."

Cool air brushed against his face as the darkness receded. Several lanterns hanging on hooks around the room illuminated it enough to see his grandfather seated on a bench pushed against the stone wall in his cell.

Davyn's prison lay belowground, and besides the iron bars that divided the room in two, a visiting area with a simple table and chair, the other his cell, the place could have been mistaken for a storage facility.

In the small cell, he had a bed, a low table stacked with books, paper and ink, and a pot privy—a far cry from his luxurious apartment. No doubt his grandfather resented living there. Would his opinion have changed if he'd experienced any of the *Na'Reish* dungeons and cages he'd seen in his time in demon territory?

"I still have friends in the ranks, Grandson. Those who haven't forgotten the meaning of friendship and loyalty."

Months of incarceration hadn't curbed the bite in his tongue.

"You asked me here to berate my behavior?" Arek grimaced, regretting his retort even as he said it.

Even after months of not seeing him, taunting his grandfather was such an ingrained response. Such had been the state of their relationship for so many years.

He ran a hand through his hair and pulled the chair out from under the table, the hollow wood scraping on the stone floor loud in the confined area, and sat down on it. He hadn't come to argue.

Davyn grunted. "So, are you going to sit there and stare at me or explain how you're still alive?"

Arek told him about Yenass's sacrifice, his recounting terse and to the point.

Davyn shifted his bulky frame to the edge of the bench and into the light cast by the single lantern within his cell. Pale blue eyes stared intently at Arek from beneath silvered brows, his age-worn face no longer darkened by a tan.

Silver gray hair brushed the collar of his shirt, a longer style than he'd seen his grandfather wear in the past, but then the warrior no longer needed a close-cropped style to fit under a helmet. He'd been stripped of his Light Blade title.

Disgraced and shamed.

A life ruined by hatred. One he'd almost copied.

"So you ended up on a demon auction block?" The older man's mouth twisted, his cheeks flushed a ruddy color. "A *Na'Reish* slave?" He pushed to his feet and came to the bars of his cell.

"Not exactly." Arek wondered just how much he should reveal of his time spent in *Na'Reish* territory. He could already anticipate Davyn's criticism. "It's a complicated story."

"Come here." The request was gruff and Davyn's eyes glistened in the ambient light. He reached his arms through the bars, large hands gesturing him forward, almost as if he were asking for a hug.

Surely the old man hadn't mellowed with age, or perhaps his premature death and resurrection had made him rethink his attitude? Whatever the case, Arek joined him at the bars.

Hoping.

Once he was within grasping distance, his wrist was seized and the sleeve of his shirt tugged up.

"*Mother of Light!*" Davyn hissed and released him as if he'd been burned. "The rumors are true! You *are* a blood-slave."

Loathing coated every word like the spittle gathered at the corners of his mouth. Several other curses blistered the air.

Harsh, hate filled, bitter.

All aimed at him, then Savyr.

The same tirade and mantra he'd heard all his life.

Arek clenched his fists. "I'm not going to waste my breath telling you why I have these marks on my arm. You won't accept what I have to say anyway." He didn't bother to try to hide his disappointment or anger. "You've clung to your hatred for so long that it's twisted you. And you tried to do the same with me!"

"I kept the memory of your parents alive. I made sure you knew who was to blame for ruining our lives."

"You perpetuated lies." Arek grasped the bars to Davyn's cell. "Savyr hasn't ruined your life. You have. Can't you see that?" An ache started in his chest. There would be no point confronting him with his questions. "I came here hoping you might have changed. It hurts to see that you haven't." He shook his head. "There's no reason for me to stay any longer. *Lady* bless you."

He headed for the door.

"No blood-kin of mine would suffer the shame and humiliation of being a blood-slave. You betray everything we fight for!"

Arek flinched at the accusation. His jaw flexed. He should have expected it.

"The betrayal and shame is yours, Davyn." He squeezed the latch. "It always has been. You know being a blood-slave is one of *Her* Gifts to us. Yet you continue to deny the truth." He lifted the latch and sunlight streamed into the room. "Good-bye, Grandfather."

"I'm not your grandfather. I don't recognize you." The pitch of the tirade rose. "You're not my grandson! He died months ago. With honor. Fighting those he hated with every breath. That's the way I'll remember him."

Arek stepped through the door. The two Light Blades outside turned, their expressions a mixture of astonishment and sympathy.

Inhaling a deep breath, he pulled the door shut with a firm snick.

The door muffled Davyn's shouting. The vibration of the latch catching eased the ache inside his chest.

"I'm ready to return to the apartment now."

Back to Imhara.

His journey with Davyn was finished.

Chapter 44

LACING her fingers together in her lap to hide their shaking, Imhara schooled her face into an attentive expression, one she'd used frequently when attending an Enclave. The scrape of wooden chairs on stone was loud within the Blade Council chamber as Rassan took the seat next to her, his large frame almost dwarfing the one he sat in.

Arek was the last to sit. He acknowledged all the Councilors with a half bow before pulling out the chair to her left. Behind them the double doors thudded shut as the Light Blade guards sealed them within the windowless room.

Imhara bowed her head as *Temple Elect* Sartor gave the opening prayer. After countless meetings over the last few days, the Council had made its decision. They were ready to announce whether they would agree to a truce with her Clan.

Finally.

Kalan slowly rose from his seat. His expression was as inscrutable as those seated alongside him. A prickling began between Imhara's shoulder blades as his silence drew out.

She inhaled a steady breath, but there were too many scents mingling in the air to decipher which was his. They overlapped one another, a ripe combination, with no clue as to the outcome of the decision pending.

"This has been a long few days of discussions and deliberations," he began, voice carrying clearly through the room so that everyone could hear him. "The lost knowledge you've shared with us and the discoveries made, *Na* Kaal, have been enlightening, exciting, and confronting, on many levels.

"As you've learned, several months ago we faced a similar situation when Annika and the *Na'Chi* arrived here. Their existence revealed the shared history of our three races, and a conspiracy that almost brought us to civil war. The results were several hard lessons learned, not the least of which is that change takes time."

Kalan smoothed a hand over the cover of one of her ancestors' journals, and his gaze glazed over as if he were seeing something in his mind.

"For us, the Old Ways are a step forward, a future to aim for, and it's reassuring to see the progress we've made over the last few months with the *Na'Chi* has set us on this path.

"That your ancestors were able to maintain this tradition over hundreds of years, and to see you continue it, despite the culture you were forced to endure, is a prime example that we can only aspire to. Your people honor the tenets of the *Lady* in the truest sense of *Her* teachings."

Here *Temple Elect* Sartor nodded, his dark gaze meeting hers, and his smile was full of warmth. Imhara inclined her head, pulse beating rapidly. Kalan slid the journal across the wooden table toward her, his smile brief.

"Our Guild-masters have expressed great interest and have spoken favorably of a sharing of skills, with particular reference to your Gifts and healing abilities."

Here the *Chosen* glanced at Councilor Candra. The older woman gave a succinct nod of agreement.

"And the information you've shared with us concerning *Na'Rei* Savyr will prove valuable in the coming days. I tell you this so that you'll understand the Council does acknowledge a truce may be possible with the Kaal Clan. We can see the benefits of everything you've shared with us."

Imhara's heart rate lifted, and she swallowed against a dry throat, wishing she dared take a sip of water from the cup in front of her.

Kalan's gaze swept over the room, and for the first time, a shadow flickered through his gaze. "The Council though has decided that a truce is inadvisable at this time."

Every muscle in her went tight as the meaning of his words sank in. She clenched her hands beneath the table, unable to think for several heartbeats after the announcement.

The majority had voted against the truce?

Her request had been denied?

"What?" Arek's startled outburst echoed the shock beginning to settle into her body.

What sort of future did that mean for her Clan? Where did that leave her? Her parents' legacy?

"I see." Barely a thread of sound came from her throat.

"Well, I don't!" Arek rose from his chair, shaking his head. He leaned across the table, blue eyes glittering. "What do you mean you've voted against the request? What are the last few minutes of that speech supposed to mean?" Every word cut through the air like a knife. "You build up the Kaal Clan's hope and now dash it with an unfavorable result? That's coldhearted and cruel, Kalan!"

Arek's impassioned words made Imhara's throat close over.

"Arek." She reached for his hand, her smile brittle. "Let him finish speaking."

His fingers twined with hers, his grip hard. The skin over his cheekbones pulled tight as his jaw flexed.

Yet the tension in the air didn't just radiate from him. It came from across the table as well, but again with so many odors fighting for dominance in the air, Imhara had trouble distinguishing whom the tension belonged to.

"We received a message two days ago from the Commander of the border patrol post in Tianda. The *Na'Reish* have started their assault on our territory." Here Kalan glanced to Imhara. "An advanced force of nearly a thousand *Na'Hord* have been spotted crossing Whitewater River at one of the locations you identified, *Na* Kaal. They've set up an encampment on our side of the border. Tianda was attacked night before last. The war has begun."

Imhara's heart pounded and an icy shiver ran through her as she shared a look with Rassan. Arek sank into his seat, cursing under his breath.

Shadows flickered in the green depth of Kalan's gaze. "This decision to delay the truce between our peoples has not been made lightly, *Na* Kaal." His tone turned bleak. "With war now upon us, the Council feels our efforts must first be to protect our border."

"The Kaal have resources that can help you." Arek's voice was gruff. "Surely you all can see that!"

"They do but you're forgetting what happened when we tried to move too fast with an alliance before, Commander. The conflict brought about by such a change almost tore us apart. The Council are concerned that this could happen again at a time when our focus needs to be on the border." Kalan grimaced and his voice softened. "I'm sorry, Imhara. Please understand our position.

"Personally, and I know several here share my view, I would agree to the truce in a heartbeat. Yet I serve . . . we all serve others outside this chamber who won't or can't accept such swift changes, and now more than ever, the people need stability." He drew in a deep breath. "When you're ready to leave, you'll be given safe passage to return across the border."

Imhara pushed to her feet, every limb feeling heavy. The strident scraping of the chair on the floor raked across raw nerves. For half a heartbeat, she thought about appealing their decision. Glancing at each Councilor, she took in each expression, gauging her chances.

Some were stoic, others resolute. Some like Annika, Kalan, Sartor, and Candra were unhappy. That was some consolation, given she'd enjoyed the brief time she'd spent getting to know them.

The truth though sent a cold shiver down her spine. Her heart thudded painfully in her chest.

There would be no truce.

Despite Kalan's encouraging words of possible future negotiations, conflict had a way of pushing other priorities aside. A war with the *Na'Reish* would last months, perhaps years.

As for what it meant for her personally . . .

Light, the pain in her heart was enough to steal her breath.

Any future she imagined sharing with Arek was gone, stolen by a duty that bound him to Sacred Lake. His oath to protect his people would send him to war with the *Na'Reish*.

Without a truce, there would be no visits. No chance for her to see him. And no point in pursuing a relationship that couldn't be sustained. Her throat closed over.

Like a candle in a windstorm, the last of her hope spluttered and died.

Reaching out, Imhara smoothed her fingers over the leather-bound journal Kalan had pushed toward her. Her hands shook as she lifted it.

Instead of hope she'd return home with nothing but bad news.

Merciful Mother, she'd condemned them all to total isolation.

And, in time, death.

Everything she'd fought for, every sacrifice made, every life lost to get to this point now seemed such a waste. She'd failed her people again.

She should feel angry, disappointed, sad.

Something.

Instead she just felt tired. Drained.

And . . . empty.

"Then we'll leave first thing tomorrow morning." Imhara swallowed hard and forced more strength into her voice. "For what it's worth, *Chosen*, the Kaal Clan will defend against any *Na'Reish* incursion, and we will assist any Light Blade patrol at our border. Kaal territory will be a safe haven for any human or *Na'Chi*, regardless of the Blade Council's decision." She met his gaze. "Even if you don't see it, the *Na'Reish* are as much our enemy as yours."

"I understand." Kalan inclined his head. "Thank you, *Na* Kaal."

"Perhaps, in time, the Council might reconsider its decision." The words were as hollow as she felt. The ghost of a smile curved her lips. "Until then, may the *Lady* protect and bless us all."

For the first time, she found no comfort in the familiar salutation. Turning on her heel, she nodded to Rassan and headed for the exit. She left Arek sitting at the table, unable to look at him and keep control of herself. She didn't want to see his outrage or empathy. The scent of both was strong enough to make her step falter as it was.

Outside the chamber their Light Blade sentries rose from the benches. The walk back to their quarters was in silence. Every step closer to the room grew harder and harder. As one of the Light Blade warriors pushed open the wooden door, those who had come with her across the border, spurred on by their shared dream, turned where they sat or stood, their expressions expectant.

Hopeful.

Imhara paused on the threshold, her fingers numb as they gripped the journal tighter. Rassan's hand came to rest on her shoulder.

"Remember, *She* walks with us, Imhara," he murmured. "This path might end here, but our journey continues, just in a different direction."

But which direction?

For so long she'd moved them all along one path, their destination clear; now they stood at a cliff edge with no discernible or alternate route.

They couldn't go forward. The Blade Council ensured that.

They couldn't go back. The *Na'Reish* would never welcome them. Every member of their Clan now had a price on their head.

No alternate answer was forthcoming. Perhaps in time the *Lady* would reveal *Her* path for them. Meanwhile, endurance seemed to be the lesson of the day.

"We've faced difficult times before." Her Second squeezed her shoulder. "We can do it again. Just have faith that *She* will show us the way rather than trying to guess it now."

Imhara gave a half laugh, half grunt. "You're scary when you do that, you know?"

"Do what?"

"Know what I'm thinking."

His soft chuckle warmed her. "Come on, let's tell everyone together."

Together.

The word gave Imhara the strength she needed, at least for now.

Taking a deep breath, and with Rassan at her side, she stepped into the room to deliver the less than satisfactory news.

Chapter 45

THE silence in the Council Chamber was absolute as Imhara and Rassan walked out. The huge carved doors closed behind them, and Arek forced himself to wait another ten minutes as the Councilors filed out, leaving only Kalan, Annika, and Candra in the room with him, before he rose once more from his chair.

The heat inside him reminded him of a furnace used to melt steel. All consuming and powerful yet also destructive. His skin burned with it from the inside out.

"What a farce of a decision, *Chosen*." Harsh criticism leveled at his friend, knowing the vote had been a joint one, yet he didn't care. His gaze strafed the three of them. "Imhara's given her life to seeing this truce succeed. You all know that, yet you allow others' fears to dictate your journey, your future."

He made a rude sound of disgust and jabbed a finger at them.

"Dangling the possibility of a truce in front of her without a time line is despicable. She may have thanked you for your consideration, but she doesn't believe it'll ever happen. Neither do I."

He sucked in a hard breath. Right now his temper, just like impure metal placed in the furnace, threatened to explode. He held on to it, but only just.

"If I had my Light Blade amulet around my neck, I'd break the chain and lay it down here."

Kalan's dark brow arched. "You'd resign from your role as a Light Blade warrior?"

He gave a sharp nod. "Yes." The moment he uttered the word, the burning inside him eased, almost like someone had placed a barrier between it and him. "I've walked my last journey within these walls."

"What path do you take now?"

Candra's quiet question should have caused his gut to twist with uncertainty and doubt, but the answer crystallizing in his mind allayed it all.

"My own."

And he wanted Imhara there beside him, to finish the journey they'd begun together the day he'd woken chained in her bed. For one aching moment, the thought of never seeing her again tore at him. If he stayed that's exactly the path his future would take.

Rassan's earlier warning echoed in his mind. *Your heart already knows what it wants.* The *Na'Chi* had been right.

The truth had been there all along.

His heart missed a beat, then swelled until it pressed hard against his chest. He couldn't let Imhara leave without him.

He loved her.

It'd just taken him until now to realize it.

"My allegiance lies with the Old Ways. With *Na* Kaal."

And he was impatient to find her and tell her.

Their path certainly hadn't been smooth or even, and Arek doubted it ever would be for long, but that was half the adventure. Yet doubt speared through him at declaring his intentions before discussing his decision with her. He just hoped Imhara agreed to have him.

Kalan smiled and shared a look with Candra and Annika. "If that's your decision, then I have a favor to ask of you."

Arek gave a short nod.

Kalan's deep green gaze locked with his. "As *Chosen*, as a Light Blade, and as your friend, you have my oath that I'll fight hard for this truce between your new people and us. We won't survive this war very long without their help.

"I want you to remind Imhara that our paths are interwoven, that she can't give up on her dream or the legacy her parents left her. We need each other. We need the Old Ways." He gestured to the three of them. "Tell her she has our support. It's just going to take time."

"A couple of razed towns and this Council will regret its decision," Candra muttered, dissatisfaction coloring her tone. "Arek, you can also tell Imhara she can expect a few of my healers to accompany her back to Kaal territory. Her people have knowledge we need now more than ever."

Arek frowned. "You'd defy the Council's decision?"

Candra snorted. "What part of Kalan's speech mentioned restricting the Guilds, or anyone for that matter, from wandering back and forth across our common border?" The older woman gave him a sly grin. "There's more than one way to achieve our goal, young Light Blade."

Arek stared at the Master Healer in astonishment, then grunted. He looked to Kalan and found his friend with a similar smirk shaping his mouth.

"You planned this?" A half question, half accusation.

"When the Council vote went against the truce," Kalan admitted.

Annika smiled. "Your decision saves us the trouble of finding someone to go with Imhara and her people."

Candra's soft chuckling jerked his head in her direction.

"Ah, the *Lady* works in miraculous ways, doesn't *She*?" She slapped her wrinkled hand on the edge of the table, her smile stretching wide. "After years avoiding the arena, welcome to the world of politics, my boy."

Arek shared a confused frown with his friends. "What are you talking about?"

Her chuckling turned to outright laughter. "You're now our first *Na'Reish* diplomat."

"I hope you haven't packed my armband."

Imhara spun around, a hand to her chest, cursing as her sudden movement knocked her pack off the bed and to the floor, spilling its contents across the rug.

Arek hovered in the doorway to his bedroom. So preoccupied with her thoughts, she'd never even heard him enter the apartment or approach the room. The way he leaned against the frame, arms folded, one long leg crossed over the other, his breeches molding tight to his thighs set her pulse tripping.

Gone was the anger she'd felt in him in the Council chamber. He seemed remarkably relaxed, considering how volatile his temper could be. Even his scent lacked the residual heat of a person calming down. Instead a soft smile curved his lips and something deep and warm flickered in his twilight gaze.

"The armband?" She frowned.

He stepped into the room and knelt to help her pick up her strewn belongings. As he handed them to her, she repacked the bag.

"Is it here?" he asked.

Imhara flipped open one of the side pouches and handed him the gold band. "Why would you want it?"

Arek's visage became contemplative as his long fingers smoothed over the Kaal emblem etched into metal. "That first day in the library, when I delivered *k'sa* to you and Yur, I remember Rassan handing me this band to wear. At the time I saw it as a mark of your ownership, of submitting. A negative experience. How wrong I was.

"I hope you don't mind, but I'm coming with you tomorrow when you leave for home." His announcement made her gasp. He gave her a small smile. "After the Blade Council's decision I realized my future was with you, not them. I renounced my service as a Light Blade warrior. My blade and allegiance are yours if you want them."

Imhara felt her jaw loosen. He'd chosen her over service to the *Lady*?

"Arek, no!" She shook her head. "You can't break your oath to *Her*. Why would you do that? I have nothing to offer you." She choked back a strangled half laugh. "Nothing except isolation and persecution from an enemy who will hunt us until we're dead."

"You offer me much more than that, Imhara Kaal." The skin around his eyes tightened. "I have a life because of you, and a future, two things I'd like to share with you."

He flicked the edge with his nail, and the metal rang out with a pure sound. The corners of his mouth turned upward just a fraction.

"This armband. I'd like to have a second one made, and two smaller, thinner ones." His fingers curved to demonstrate the circumference he wanted, then they closed on her upper arms. "That seems about the right size. I'd like you to have the smaller ones. Do you think that could be arranged?"

Imhara's skin heated where his fingers touched her. "Arek, wearing two bands holds a special meaning in our Clan."

"Yes, only mated couples wear them." His twilight gaze lifted and locked with hers. "I'm aware of the traditional significance. Wearing two bands, placed on my arms by the woman I love seems much more fitting than being chained to her bed, don't you think?"

Her heart lurched in her chest, and a rush of heat suffused her entire body. The pack slipped from her nerveless fingers and the items scattered once more across the floor.

"You love me?"

Jaw flexing, Arek gave a single nod. "I do."

He wet his lips, the action definitely a nervous one. His scent confirmed it.

"Sere Jirri and all those other *Na'Reishi* were fools for wanting to change you and make you something you're not." He placed the armband in her hand and wrapped her fingers around them. "I'd be honored if you'd consider my petition to be your mate. And I'd be blessed by the *Lady* if you loved me in return."

Imhara replayed his words in her head, and her heart swelled with an indescribable warmth and joy. With every hard beat, she let it fill her.

"Arek, without a truce, my Clan stands alone." She closed her eyes, feeling the sting of tears in her throat. "You can't want a future like that."

"You don't stand alone." Arek's hand cupped the back of her head, and she felt his lips brush her forehead in a fleeting caress. "The Blade Council may have declined your petition, but Kalan won't give up. He gave me his oath to fight for us. You've made friends here, Imhara, and they'll be joining us when we leave here tomorrow."

His face was blurred as she stared at him through stinging eyes. "Who?"

"Some of Candra's healers. It's a start. War might be inevitable but, *Lady* willing, the Old Ways will survive." Yet again Arek brought her strength and hope. The calloused pad of a finger brushed across her cheek. "You're crying tears of happiness, right? I mightn't be able to read your scent, but I know that's a smile on your face. So is it my proposal or the news that Kalan supports us that has you so overjoyed?"

His fingers threaded through her hair. Uncertainty tightened the lines on his face as he waited for her to answer him.

"Both." She placed her palms on his stubbled cheeks; her thumbs stroked the lines of worry away from under his eyes. "Although I have to admit, your proposal took me by surprise."

"Well, I was working on a limited time frame—you're leaving tomorrow."

"Yes." Imhara placed the armband in his hands. "I accept your petition, Arek Barial."

"Thank the *Lady* for that." The light that flared in his gaze matched the heat in her heart. His lips slanted over hers, and the low sound of need welling in his throat filled her with pleasure.

"I never thought I'd say these words to anyone." Her soul sang at being finally able to share her heart with him. "I love you, Arek."

His long, drawn-out sigh of relief belied the gleam of heat in his eyes.

"I'll never tire of hearing them," he assured her. "Practice on me all you like." He grinned. "Now I made you a promise that night at the House of Ilahn." His leg stretched out and he nudged the door closed with his boot. "It's a good thing we have all night, as I intend to keep it."

Imhara laughed softly as Arek's head dipped and he kissed her again. She wrapped her arms around him and sent a prayer heavenward.

Lady *bless this union forevermore.*

Words she'd repeat during their mating ceremony as they exchanged armbands.

Their next journey—of making a life together as mates—would begin on that day.

And she looked forward to it with all of her heart.